THE RED FOX

To Kathy with my love

We have here in America an all too obvious and objectionable prejudice against Russia. And this, you will agree, is born of fear. In Russia, something strange and foreboding has occurred, it threatens to undo our present civilization and instinctively we fear change. . . . There are those among us who whisper that this change will mean darkness and chaos, there are those who claim it is but a golden light which, starting from a little flame, shall circle the earth and make it glow with happiness. All that is not for me to say. I am but a messenger who lays his notes before you.

—Louise Bryant, *Six Red Months in Russia,* 1918

PART ONE

MAY BRIGHTMAN

The Russian Revolution, when it comes, will be all the more terrible because it will be proclaimed in the name of religion. Russian policy has melted the Church into the State and confounded heaven and earth: a man who sees a god in his master scarcely hopes for paradise, except through the favours of the Emperor.

—Marquis de Custine, *La Russie en 1839*

I

I was to learn that all the real secrets are buried and that only ghosts speak the truth. So it was fitting: even for me, all this began in a graveyard, among mysteries, memories, and lies.

That year, the twenty-eighth of October was cold and threatened rain, and as I walked away from the little frame church with Father Delaney, our breath misted in front of us. It was autumn; but autumn already cringed before winter. The three tall oaks that screened off the graveyard were stripped bare as old bones and the summer's grass had died down between the headstones, falling into the brown, tangled surf of a fossilized sea. We walked slowly, in silence. I came here only one day a year, but it was as if I'd never been away. Every step brought a rush of memory: the *flick-flick* of the old priest's heavy trousers as he walked beside me; the smell of wet leaves under our feet; a rusted iron cross glimpsed in the undergrowth: JENNIFER, AGE THREE WEEKS, 1917. Year after year, none of this changed, and when we finally stopped before my father's stone, it could have been five years ago, or ten, or fifteen. All the old emotions welled up—the shock, the grief, the fundamental disbelief—but they were now so expected, so customary, that even their melancholy was comforting. Gently, I looked down at the slab of polished red granite, and the old priest murmured a prayer under his breath, saying the words in Latin as he knew my mother always liked. I bent forward. Half kneeling, I placed the usual bouquet of cornflowers against the smooth stone, then drew myself up and raised my eyes. My father's grave was right on the crest of the hill; from where I was standing, you could see for miles across a spur of the Tuscarora Mountains, northwest of Harrisburg, Pennsylvania. Low, gray clouds trailed tendrils of showers over the opposite ridge and now a few drops touched my face. The wind, suddenly gusting, bit at my cheek. I turned my head to one side.

Father Delaney ducked his head too. He must have been cold; he was wearing only his priest's black suit with a tartan scarf looped round his neck, as if wishing to cover his collar on this dubious ground. I had always liked him. He was in his sixties or early seventies: heavily built but stooped, with the sad, drooping face of an Irishman and the thick hands of a miner, which his father had been. After a moment, the decent interval, he said, "I'm glad you came, Robert. To tell the truth, I wasn't sure you would."

I looked at him, a little surprised. "Why is that, Father?"

"Oh, I always understood why your mother came, but I was never sure about you. What you thought about it. What your feelings were."

My mother had died the previous winter; for the first time I was making the annual trek by myself. Every year, for so many years, she had come out of love, devotion, and loyalty—and the desire, above everything else, to disprove the doubts I'd seen flicker in so many eyes. *A hunting accident. Leastwise, that's what they're calling it. . . . I don't care what anyone says, it's not right, letting them bury him here. . . .* I'd always assumed that the priest had simply transferred these reasons to me, though he was right, they didn't apply. I had my own. I knew, after all, that everything my mother had refused to believe was perfectly true. My father had killed himself. For me, the only mystery was why.

Finally I said, "She loved him very deeply, Father. It's a shame we couldn't have buried her here."

"I'll miss her. Every fall, I looked forward to her visit."

I glanced away, back toward the headstone. As a boy, it had frightened me, as though it was the single jaw of some great, terrible trap. Later it had seemed merely frustrating, a door that was locked, bolted, and barred—no matter how hard I knocked, it never swung open. Now it was only a monument, but it occurred to me that its letters, so deeply carved in the granite, were gradually growing obscure, turning into a kind of hieroglyphics. My own mother was gone; now I was the only one left to decipher them.

MITCHELL SVEN THORNE
FEB 17 1902 — OCT 28 1956
London Paris Capetown Mexico Rome

Mitchell: never Mitch. *Sven:* after a great-grandfather, from Stockholm. *Thorne:* originally it had been Torne, the name of a river that runs down the border between Sweden and Finland. Soon enough, no one would know even these elementary facts. As though to confirm this, Father Delaney now asked, "Those cities . . . I was trying to remember why they were there."

"You remember, Father. He worked for the State Department. Those were the places he served."

"Ah, yes . . . and you were born in South Africa, weren't you?"

I nodded. I'd only lived there a year, though the fact had dogged me for the rest of my life: it's an inconvenient birthplace for a journalist to have in his passport.

Father Delaney shifted his weight on his feet. "You were fourteen, weren't you, when your father died?"

"Yes. Almost fifteen."

His lips compressed and he shook his head. "That was too young, Robert. I still remember how you looked at the funeral, and then those first years when you came with your mother. You were always so stiff and silent. Sometimes I thought you must be terribly angry, and then I wondered if you weren't afraid, like someone who has a secret they're too frightened to tell."

I looked at him, startled. Did he know? Had he guessed that I knew for certain what everyone else only suspected? I turned away quickly, staring out at the valley. The rain had moved closer, wrapping itself around the hills and obscuring the landscape beyond. Below us, a hawk was quartering over a field. I watched him for a moment, but all at once—the familiar shape of this day jarred by the old priest's hints—I found myself looking straight into the past. *Sunday, October 28, 1956.* A cabin, not ten miles from where I stood now. My bedroom, cold and bare, the mattress stripped of its sheets. Myself, stretched out on the bed, staring up at the ceiling. Beside me, strangely miniaturized voices emerge from the earphone of my transistor radio. I'm listening to the "Post-Game Show." The Giants have beaten the Eagles 20–3.

Alex Webster gained so many yards; Frank Gifford caught so many passes. . . . The voices drone on. I cease listening. This is the weekend when we're closing the cabin for the season and my mother has been moving around in the other room, cleaning, but now the screen door snaps shut as she steps outside. A moment later, I swing my legs over the edge of the bed and sit up, an action which brings my eyes level with the window. It is now that I see my father. He is hurrying away from the cabin—for one instant, I can believe he's walking up to the car—but just as he enters the woods, I see the gun, his shotgun, the Remington Wingmaster 870 pump. And I know. In that instant, the tension I've felt both in him and in my mother all the previous week suddenly crystallizes. I *know.* My heart pounds. *No one, under any circumstances, should take a gun into the woods without warning everyone else about what he's doing.* It's his golden rule; he'd never break it himself. . . .

"Robert?"

Gently, Father Delaney gripped my arm and brought me back to myself. I tried to smile. "I was just thinking, Father. Trying to remember what I'd felt then . . . I suppose you're right. I was angry. But I'm not sure I was afraid. If I was, perhaps it was because my mother felt it all so intensely."

"Yes, she did. But I'm thinking of you—If you don't mind, I'd like to ask something personal."

"Of course, Father."

"I could never say this when your mother was alive, for I know she wouldn't have wanted me to. And I hope she'll forgive me now, for presuming . . ." He hesitated, then looked up at my face. "When your father died, you knew there were all kinds of rumors?"

"Yes."

"You knew at the time? As a boy?"

"Yes, I knew."

He shook his head. "I should have said this years ago, but I'll say it now. Those rumors weren't true, Robert. I never knew your father well, but I knew him well enough. Believe me—they weren't true."

For a second, the briefest instant, we looked each other in the eye. Then I glanced away. But finally, in gratitude for everything this old man had given us over so many years, I managed the lie: "Thank you, Father. I know . . . I believe you."

———

For five minutes, as Father Delaney made his way back to the church, I stared into the valley.

Advancing like a heavy mist, the curtain of rain drew closer, until finally its outline was lost. Then I felt the first drops, cold and prickling, on my face. I looked down at the tombstone; in a second, as the rain grew heavier, it began to shine with a slick, velvety sheen. I wondered whether I'd kept its secret, wondered whether the old priest had believed his own words. It was hard to say. He was an old-fashioned Irishman who probably attached little importance to the literal truth and would let God take care of the dead while he concerned himself with the living. Long ago, I realized, he'd seen how troubled I'd been: now, he merely wanted to lay that trouble to rest. I only wished that he could: but what other people only suspected, I knew for certain and their dark imaginings were my clearest memories. Now, as the rain fell upon the cold stone of my father's grave, my mind again slid back to that day. Again, in horror, I watched my father disappear into the woods. Again, in terror, my heart began pounding. Again and again— I'd seen it all a thousand times, but nothing changed. There was still nothing to do but run. Running, running: but never quite fast enough. Finally, at the edge of the woods, I slumped to the ground. Before me lay a clearing, a patch of dried-up swamp filled with dead marsh grass and fern. Beyond this I could see a dirt road, and at the top of a hill, to the left, a blue Chevrolet sedan pulled onto the shoulder—innocent images of fatality that would haunt me for years to come. Tears burned my eyes. My breath trembled in my chest. I look around desperately, but in this dead landscape nothing moved. Knowing my father had to be near, I tried to shout, but my strength—no doubt like his—was exhausted and not even the birds were disturbed by my cry. And then, with the great roar of the shot, the question exploded within me: *Why? Why did you do it?*

More than twenty years later, as I wrenched myself back to the present, I knew it was still the only question to ask.

Why?

I stared down at his headstone—a door, locked and bolted, a tablet engraved with words in a language nobody spoke. Would I ever discover the answer? Did even he know what it was?

Just then the rain began falling in earnest, cold and driving; with a shiver, I turned up my collar. Still, even as it drenched me, I welcomed that storm. *Let the dead bury the dead.* The rain and the wind were alive, telling me that I had my own life to live. Once a year, I took a day off from that life to remind myself that somewhere inside I was still that boy in the woods, but now that day was over.

I took a step back, turned away. Head down, shoulders hunched, I made my way up the path toward the church.

2

As I said, everything began in that graveyard, but at the time I had no way of knowing this. October 28, that year, seemed no different from any other: an end, not the beginning of anything. Why had my father killed himself? As I got into my old green Volvo and lurched down the side road away from the church, the question seemed no nearer an answer than it had before. I told myself what I always did: let it lie, forget it, what else can you do?

But I could never forget, of course; not quite. And perhaps my mother's absence this year made it even more difficult. As the road twisted and turned through the tattered, autumn hills of Perry County, I could sense her beside me and hear her voice, low and murmuring, as she remembered him—for, paradoxically, that was always her way of forgetting. She'd close her eyes and lean back on the seat, and slowly the stories would come out, but stories so carefully and formally elaborated that they only served to distance him from us, gradually turning him into a character in an old movie that flickers on and on through the late-show dawn. Long since, I'd learned all the scripts by heart; now, making my way back to the Interstate, I wondered which ones she might have selected this time around. My mother, *une vraie française,* had first met my father when he'd been posted to Paris in 1938. So perhaps she might have recalled the crazy comedy about a bright young diplomat, speaking ludicrous Iowa French, who'd helped a manufacturer with some permits, received a dinner invitation in return, and then walked off with his daughter. Or she might have selected a melodrama —Bergman and Bogart—for she and my father had been falling in love just as Europe staggered toward war: drinking in the Café Flore as the

Germans marched into Austria, huddling in my father's frigid apartment on Montparnasse as Chamberlain flew back from Munich, and joining the "phony war" crowds at the hit of the 1940 season, Maurice Chevalier's *Paris Reste Paris*. Decades later, *that* particular detail could still provoke my mother's bitterest laugh. "But we didn't see the joke any better than other people," she'd quickly add. "After the Communists made their deal with Hitler, it seemed there was nothing to believe in, not even war. . . ." But of course the war came. They hurriedly married at the end of May, as the Germans raced toward the city. After that— another favorite tale—there was a classic chase sequence, for my father suddenly panicked. Fearing that his diplomatic status might not guarantee my mother's safety, he'd rushed her out of Paris when the British Embassy was evacuated in the first week of June. "Your father had his little English car and he steered it like a bicycle through all those refugees. I remember that we reached Bordeaux the day before Paris fell and listened to the broadcast on a portable radio. In those days, radios had very big batteries which gave off a peculiar smell when they grew warm—for years afterwards, that smell haunted my dreams. . . ."

The war, however, merely provided the most dramatic of her stories; there were plenty of others. My father's classic gaffe with Christian Herter . . . the incredible saga of their sea voyage to Capetown . . . a bizarre servant in Mexico City . . . Now, as the miles slipped by, I ran through them all; and, a little to my surprise, the process worked once again. I skirted Harrisburg, dawdled through Hagerstown, and finally, as Interstate 81 swung west, I could feel the mystery of my father's death begin to recede for another twelve months.

I arrived home shortly past noon.

For me, "home" is now Charlottesville, Virginia, a small Piedmont town about a hundred miles southwest of Washington: birthplace of Lewis and Clark, seat of the University of Virginia, discreetly Southern. As always, when I arrived, I couldn't quite believe that I'd actually settled there. Its population is only thirty-five thousand (swelled a trifle by the students), whereas I was brought up in a succession of world capitals, went to school in New York (Columbia), and spent most of my journalistic career in Berlin, Warsaw, and Moscow—all large cities, whatever your ideological persuasion. Nonetheless, when I tired of the Betacam rat race and came home again, I found New York and L.A. unendurable in turn and decided to try someplace smaller. Charlottesville won out for two reasons: the University, with its excellent research facilities, and the town's proximity to Washington, where I have most of my contacts. Now, after three years, I fitted right in—dreary proof that I was growing middle-aged, I suppose. But it's a town that lets you alone, and I was able to live the kind of life I wanted: work, small pleasures, quiet routines. Up at dawn, I usually wrote till noon, then strolled along to Murchie's—a local landmark—for the papers and cigarettes. For lunch, I normally indulged myself at the Mousetrap or one of the other student hangouts—beer, sandwiches, an eyeful of coeds—and finally, protected by an alcoholic haze, I'd dutifully continue on to the Alderman Library for last week's *Izvestia* and the penance of some academic prose. That afternoon, turning off Emmet Street, I picked all this up in the middle and dropped in at the Mousetrap, but then decided to skip the University—there was no sense pretending I was going to get any work done today. Instead, I bought some food at the supermarket and headed straight home.

I live on Walsh Street, near the old black section of town, in a white frame house decorated with Victorian gingerbread. I left the Volvo in the lane, then staggered up the walk with the groceries, maneuvered through the front door, and went straight through to the kitchen. The house felt cold, so I laid a fire in the old wood stove (the size of a locomotive and almost as complicated), then made coffee and carried it into the living room.

Usually, the visit to my father's grave was just a day's excursion, but this time I'd worked it in as the last leg of a two-week trip to New York and Boston, so the room had a forlorn, abandoned air. Taking possession of the place again, I went around plumping cushions and opening curtains, put some Haydn on the stereo, and then slumped down on the sofa. Now the coffee table was directly in front of me, a large pile of mail strewn across it. And perhaps I was simply tired, or perhaps it was the peculiar quality of this day, but I saw nothing unusual in this and, almost absently, began sorting through the envelopes. Texaco wanted $58.93 . . . Jimmy Swaggart devoutly prayed that I'd purchase a Bible, bound in Genuine Olive Wood, for a minimum donation of $25 . . . There was a letter from my agent about the French rights to my second book, but we'd already covered that in New York, and then junk, oddments, more bills, and a whole slew of magazines: *The Economist, The Spectator, Foreign Affairs, Slavic Review, The Journal of Soviet Studies,*

BBC Monitors Soviet Broadcasts, The Red Army Journal: Extracts and Commentaries . . . I finished my coffee and carried the whole mess into my workroom.

Like the workrooms of most men, I suppose, mine gives a fair portrait of its owner—all the more so in my case, since I designed and built it myself. It's converted from an old screened porch running the full length of the house. Floor-to-ceiling bookshelves cover the inside wall (two thousand volumes, mostly about the Soviet Union), and on the outside, under the windows, there's a maple counter that constitutes my principal workspace. The tools of my trade were scattered there in their usual disarray—papers, drafts, offprints from journals, notes to myself (illegible), a couple of Uher tape recorders (one of which worked), an IBM Selectric, an old Underwood I'd been dragging around for years as a sort of lucky charm, and my latest toy, an IBM PC: 640K, Corona hard disk, C-Itoh printer . . . but perhaps you don't share the new electronic enthusiasms. In any case, as I say, these bits and pieces provide the surest clues to my character. They should tell you I'm something of a solitary: growing up as an "embassy brat," I learned to get by on my own, and then my father's death seemed to set me apart from everyone else. But I also like my comfort—in my workroom, I'm never far from a comfortable chair—and one of the reasons I left journalism was the sheer misery of it, the borrowed apartments, pool offices, endless fast food. And lastly, you should be able to guess that I love my work. In a sense, that's also connected to my father. He died in 1956, a year before Sputnik, and in the great panic that followed, my high school in Washington began offering courses in Russian. It was just what I needed—something to lose myself in—and soon I was totally enthralled by the language, the country, the people. It's a fascination I've never lost, and for most of my adult life I've earned my living, in one way or another, as a "Russian expert": as a journalist in Eastern Europe and Moscow, briefly (miserably) as a teacher, and now as a freelance writer. Even on that afternoon I couldn't resist, and flipped on my machine. It greeted me with the IBM beep, and then a page from my third book flickered into green, ghostly life. I read it through, even felt my brain stir a little, but I knew I was too tired to do anything useful, so I went back to the living room and read myself to sleep. When I awoke, it was after three and the phone was ringing.

Groggily, I staggered into my workroom to answer it—and felt the usual chest-tightening sensation when the girl said, "Western Union."

"Yes?"

"We have a telegram for you, Mr. Thorne. The text reads: DEAR ROBERT. TRIED TO REACH YOU ALL WEEK. URGENT. PLEASE CALL 416 922-0250. LOVE. MAY."

May. May Brightman . . . even after all these years, hearing her name was like a blow to the pit of my stomach.

"Mr. Thorne, sir?"

It took me a moment to recover. I cleared my throat. "I'm here, operator. Could you tell me where that was sent from?"

"Yes, sir. The point of origin is Toronto, Canada."

She was Canadian, though I'd never known her to live there.

"And could you read back that number again?"

She did so, and I hung up.

May Brightman. I stood there, my hand on the phone. May . . . It had been a long time since I'd heard from her. Three years? Five? But of course she always did keep in touch—maybe a woman who rejects you can never quite leave you alone . . . Except that sounds bitter and that's not what I felt. Enough time had passed, God knows—I was over her now—so there wasn't that pain. But there was still something else—a species of regret, a strange lack of completion. What had happened between us? Standing there, almost twenty years after the fact, I still didn't know. She'd loved me, she'd never denied it. But when I'd asked her to marry me (I was very young and sufficiently romantic to do the deed on a bench in Central Park, a cinematic mist in the air), she'd said yes right away, only to change her mind the next week with no clue as to why. Did she know herself? Maybe not. Maybe no woman, in her place, ever does. In any event, May Brightman had become another question I couldn't answer. Indeed, as I pulled myself together and went back into the living room, I thought how uncanny it was that she had called today, for there was another link to my father. I'd lived my life within the shadow cast by his death, and May had been my great attempt to step outside it. When she'd turned me down, I'd retreated again. If, to admit the truth, I was a lonely man today—albeit as comfortable with my loneliness as a fish is with the sea—she was part of the reason. Not the first cause, but the second . . .

What could she want?

In the living room, whiskey in hand, I pondered the question. Working it out, I realized it had been five years since we'd last met. That had been in France, just around the time I'd left television. I'd been fairly hard up—somehow she'd known—and she'd offered me the use of her place near Sancerre while I finished my first book. This was typical of our contacts over the years. You couldn't say that we were now "just friends," for the original relationship had been too complicated and intense, and its ending too mysterious, to permit anything so neutral. Yet she did keep in touch, almost protectively—perhaps she felt a shade guilty. I wondered, in fact, if that wasn't all she now wanted, just a word to know how I was keeping.

Except the telegram had said "urgent" . . . not a word you'd normally associate with her. When I'd first met her, in New York, she was studying the cello at Juilliard and one of her instructors had complained that she had a "lazy bow": which, in certain moods, was just what she was like, a soft note lazily drifting through a summer's afternoon. Since her father had money, she'd never worked, and so far as I knew she still lived alone—if she'd turned me down, I at least had the comfort of knowing she'd never accepted another. Maybe, because of that, she'd grown a trifle eccentric over the years, but she'd always had the calm, cool confidence of the rich and wasn't easily flustered. There was nothing "urgent" in her life whatsoever—in fact, the only time I'd seen her truly afraid was the one night when she'd tried to tell me why she'd decided not to go through with our engagement—but, almost twenty years later, that could hardly be the cause of her anxiety. What the hell. I put down the bourbon and picked up the phone.

She answered on the first ring—as though she'd been sitting there waiting. And she was obviously very upset.

"Robert . . . Robert, thank God it's you."

"I'm sorry. I only got back this minute. Western Union just called."

"I've been phoning you. . . . I phoned every day last week. I sent another telegram Wednesday—"

"I was in New York. What's the matter?"

She took a breath. "I'm sorry—I'm all right. It's my father. He's disappeared. . . . I know it sounds insane, but he's vanished. He just went off—no one's seen him."

I'd never met her father, but I knew he was important to her. In fact, I'd sometimes suspected that her refusing me had some connection with him, for her change of mind had taken place after she'd flown up to Toronto to see him—to tell him the happy news, as I'd thought at the time.

"When did this happen?"

"Ten days ago. A week ago Saturday."

"You've told the police?"

"Yes. They . . . they were worried he might have been kidnapped, but there hasn't been a ransom note and now they say he's just gone off on his own and will turn up when he feels like it."

"Well . . . they're probably right. It's upsetting—"

"*No.* They're not right. He'd never go off without telling me."

Her voice had exploded with anger—the intensity of it was startling—but then she caught herself and added, "Robert, I'm sorry to trouble you with this—"

"No, no. Of course not."

"Maybe I shouldn't have called."

"Of course you should have called. I'm just trying to think. What can I do?"

She hesitated. "There's one thing. I'm afraid—I'm afraid he's killed himself. I know all the reasons why you'll say he hasn't—the police have already given them to me—but I'm still afraid. . . ."

Suicide. On this day, of all days, it wasn't a question I could easily dismiss. "Why do you think that?"

"I'd rather not say. Not on the phone."

"But you do have a reason? Something specific?"

"Yes."

"Have you told the police about it?"

"They don't think it means anything. That's why I called you. I need someone who can find things out for me. Someone who knows how to ask questions . . ."

"May, I'm not a policeman. I want—"

"But you're a journalist, Robert. You can get things out of bureaucrats."

I paused. Once upon a time I had been a journalist, but I'm not any longer. And I hate getting things out of bureaucrats. "What sort of things?"

"It's personal. I'd rather not say. Not till you get here."

"So you want me to come to Toronto?"

"Yes. I know you must be busy . . . but it won't take very long.
I'm sure it won't take very long."

She was right; I was busy. The past two weeks had been a holiday,
more or less, and I was anxious to get back to work. She said, "And of
course I'll pay your way—you—"

"Don't be silly." I thought for a moment longer, but there really
wasn't much choice. She was clearly upset, and even if I couldn't help
her—and I was certain I couldn't—I could at least hold her hand till
her father showed up. "You're sure you can't tell me anything more?"

I heard her sigh. "You know I'm adopted?"

"Yes. I remember."

Remember: I could sense her falter as I said the word, as if she was
uncertain about how much she could rely on the past we hadn't quite
shared. But then she went on, "It has something to do with that. That's
what I'd want you to find out about."

"All right."

"You'll come?"

"Of course. I can probably be there tomorrow."

A breath, all relief, fluttered down the line. "Thank you, Robert.
Bless you. I'll meet you at the airport."

"No, no. That'll only get complicated. Just give me your address
and I'll try to make it by early afternoon. And you try to relax."

So she told me where she lived, we said goodbye and hung up
. . . and right away I knew that something was wrong.

It was an odd sensation. Strong. Definite. And yet unaccountable.
For a moment, I thought it was just the call itself—a strange summons,
under strange circumstances: fears about the suicide of a father on precisely *this* day. And given our past connection, any conversation was
bound to be awkward.

But such feelings could hardly be the cause of the intense unease
that now swept across me. May's request, by any standards, had been
unusual, and if I'd had the faintest idea of where it was going to take
me, I would have felt foreboding. But in fact that wasn't at all what I
felt. It was a more particular sensation—as if I was being watched, as
if someone else was with me in the house . . . and then—thinking this—I
knew what it was.

On the phone, May had said she'd sent me *two* telegrams: the one

I'd received today, but another last Wednesday when I'd been in New York. It hadn't been in my mail, I was certain, and now I checked again to be sure. It wasn't. Carefully, I played my arrival back through my mind. As I'd come in, I'd had a bag of groceries in each hand. To work the lock, I'd balanced one on my knee. And then I'd kicked the door shut behind me and gone straight through to the kitchen. From there—the sequence was perfectly clear—I'd carried my coffee into the living room, tidied up for a moment, and slumped down on the sofa. *And that's when I'd discovered my mail:* a great pile, two weeks' worth, scattered all over the coffee table . . . instead of lying in the hall, under the mail slot, where it ought to have been.

3

My father's grave . . . May's call . . . the little mystery of my mail
. . . By the next morning, these seemed merely a coincidence, hardly
worth troubling about. Besides, I was fully occupied with the mechanics
of my departure, for Charlottesville isn't the easiest town to get out of.
There's a local airport, but in the end it was simpler to drive to Washington, leave my car with a friend, and fly out of Dulles. This made me
much later than I'd intended: it was after three as the 727 slid down
from the bright fall sky and deposited me at Toronto International.

Like most Americans, I don't know Canada at all—it's where the
winter comes from—and I hadn't been there in years, so the city struck
me as a great deal bigger, richer, and noisier than I remembered. But
I was still in North America; it was built out of concrete and neon, hype
and nerve. On the radio, the helicopter "traffic eye" described the traffic
jam we were caught in, from the front seat the cabbie explained why
he preferred Orlando to St. Petersburg for his winter vacation, and beside me—discarded and already starting to fade—the Toronto *Sun*'s
"sunshine girl" burst innocently forth from her bikini. Looking out the
window, I watched the cars, people, and money roll by.

May lived downtown, in an area the cabbie called Kensington Market. I had him drop me at the edge of it and walked a little, passing
through crowded streets jammed with stalls selling everything from lob-
sters to African beads. This was obviously an old immigrant district. The
Jews had gone decades ago, leaving behind a couple of restaurants and
a boarded-up synagogue. Most of the shouting around me was in Portuguese and Italian, and even the Italians and the Portuguese, I suspected,
were on their way out. On Spadina Avenue the faces were mostly yellow,

and behind them, in turn, were fresh hordes, the most surprising of all: refugees from the suburbs, rich kids all stuffed with health food and pot. On May's street, the signs were everywhere: exotic plants dangling in windows, workmen off-loading drywall, young matrons pushing wicker prams down the street. Today, this was a slum-in-transition; five years from now, it would be a chic address for young marrieds—which, it occurred to me, was just the sort of investment a rich man might make for his daughter.

I went up to the door and rang the bell.

No answer.

I waited a moment; then, setting down my bag, I walked around to the side of the house. There was a lane here, with an orange Volkswagen Beetle parked halfway up it—the only car May ever drove—and a board fence down one side. Peering over this, I could look into her garden. It was very long and narrow. A brick path ran down the middle of it and on either side of this, completely filling the space, grew shrub roses, a tangle of gray thorny canes, dabbed here and there with clusters of blood-red rose hips. It was now after four and the day was fading fast, but a patch of wan sunlight had found its way between the surrounding houses and sheds. Peering into this halo, I could see May halfway along the path, squatting with her back to me. Her long, reddish-blond hair cascaded over a blue wool poncho which, in turn, was worn over an ankle-length burgundy dress. Squatting as she was, she'd pushed the dress between her legs, making a basket of her lap, and was filling it with dead canes as she worked. Her secateurs snapped, then she duck-walked ahead. I was about to call out to her, but something held me back and I watched her in silence. May had always possessed a mysterious quality—it had been part of her attraction—and now, as I felt it touch me again, I thought I understood what it was. The garden, in this strange autumn light, was like an old photograph, faded, cracked, creased, all bent at the corners—a long-ago photograph of girls in large bonnets whose eyes are forever lost in shadow as they squint into the sun. That was May's quality, I thought; she didn't quite belong to this time. . . . But now she stood up. Holding her dress in front of her, she walked back down the path toward a weather-beaten shed at the back where she spilled the cuttings onto a compost heap. When she turned around, she saw me. A shadow, quizzical and anxious, fell across her face. But then she smiled. "Robert . . . Robert!"

"I just arrived. Should I go around to the front or can I get in here?"

Bustling forward, she showed me where two boards had been hinged to make a gate and I stepped into the garden; then she took both my hands in hers and we kissed . . . just a sociable brush of her lips on my cheek. But then, with a sigh that was almost a groan, she fell against me and I held her. "Thank God you've come," she whispered. "You're sure you don't mind? I was afraid—"

"Of course I don't mind."

With a shudder, she started to cry, pressing her face into my shoulder. I squeezed her against me, but it was odd—holding her, I felt completely alone, as if there was something false in her tears. Then I understood: she was crying out of fear, not sorrow, and you can't comfort fear. I held her more tightly. "Don't worry," I whispered. "He'll be back. It'll come out all right."

Getting her breath, she eased away and tried to smile. "This is awful."

"No."

"Yes, it is. I think I brought you all the way up here just to be able to do that."

"A trip worth making, then."

She smiled again. "Thank you . . . for coming. For saying that."

I smiled. "I'll always come. You know that."

Did I mean this? In truth, I wasn't quite sure—though I *had* come, after all. Maybe she had her doubts too, for she looked away almost shyly, then took my hand and led me up to the house. At the rear, looking onto the garden, was a breakfast room; beyond this lay a large, comfortable kitchen with a quarry-tile floor and old pine furniture. Sitting on the edge of a table, I watched her make coffee—Colombian beans, Braun grinder, Melitta filter—and was again struck by the sense of dislocation I'd felt in the garden. There, because the garden itself seemed out of time, she'd fitted right in; here, where everything was right up to date—even the antique furniture—she seemed out of place. But each small gesture helped her get a grip on herself and finally she started to talk, small talk about getting the garden ready for winter, questions about my trip, Charlottesville, my writing. As best I could, I brought her up to date on my life and got the impression that her own hadn't much changed. She'd taken up the flute, was studying composition at the Toronto Conservatory of Music; she had her house, loved the garden, saw just a few friends. She'd moved to Toronto three years before, but still traveled a lot. . . . As she went on, she became more composed, though nothing could hide the terrible anxiety she was feeling. More than was justified? Probably not—her father had disappeared, after all. Yet something about her anxiety brought the question into my mind. Her face was haggard and etched with worry, and while the coffee dripped through, she excused herself and went off to the bathroom, looking a bit better when she came back . . . except in her eyes. For when the rest of her was calmer, you could see even better the quick, darting fear that lurked in them. But perhaps this wasn't really surprising—I reminded myself that it had been going on for ten days. In any case, when we were sitting, and quiet, with second cups of coffee in front of us, I said, "Do you think you can tell me what happened?"

She lifted her cup, then set it down. "There's not much to tell. It was the police who found out, actually. On Saturday, around three in the morning, a squad car drove past my father's place and saw that the door was open . . . standing open. It almost looked deliberate, they said. One of the patrolmen rang the bell, but there was no answer, so he went inside. No one was there. They waited around, but after twenty minutes or so they sent in a report on their radio and locked the door. An hour later they came back but there was still no answer, so they sent another car in the morning. A neighbor gave them my name."

"This was Saturday . . . the eighteenth?"

She nodded. "But I suppose he left during the day, on Friday. I don't think it was Thursday because I spoke to him then."

"And nothing seemed wrong?"

"No, not really. It's hard to say . . . when you look back—"

"Yes. But once you knew, what happened then?"

"The police made their checks—they were serious to begin with because they knew he was wealthy—and I started calling his friends. But no one had seen him or heard from him. He wasn't in hospital, he wasn't dead in the morgue, he . . . ."

Her voice trailed away. She'd been in control of herself, but all at once she was right on the edge. I tried to keep my tone neutral: "Were there no signs that he'd gone on a trip? Clothes missing? Luggage?"

"The police made me check but I couldn't be sure. The basement is full of old luggage—he could have taken a couple of suitcases and I wouldn't know. I'm not really sure what clothes he owns."

"Does he drive a car?"

She nodded. "He doesn't use it much anymore, but it was in the garage—the police said it probably hadn't been driven for weeks." She closed her eyes for a second. "I've been all through this, Robert. It's useless. There've been no strange withdrawals from his bank, American Express say he hasn't used his card. . . . There's just no sign of him at all."

I leaned back, then pushed my chair away from the table; I suppose, knowing she wasn't going to like what I had to say next, I wanted to put a little distance between us. Then I went on, "All right, I accept that he's missing. At the very least, he's been damned inconsiderate—but then old men sometimes are, you know. What I don't see is suicide. He was wealthy. His health—it was still good?"

"Yes."

"No one's found his body?"

"That doesn't mean anything."

"There's been no note?"

"But that doesn't mean anything either."

"Not definitely, I suppose—but it's hard to disprove a negative. Until he comes back, you have to say that suicide is a possibility, but it doesn't seem very likely."

She hesitated, glancing down, then looked up again. "I told you I had a reason."

"Yes. Something to do with your being adopted."

She began to speak—but then stopped herself and reached out for her cigarettes. As she lit one, I watched her face. It was broad, girlishly freckled, with a slightly snub nose. In a way, she did look her age, but something was missing—she was like a young girl who'd suddenly woken up to find she was forty; it was hard to account for the intervening years . . . or was that simply because I hadn't been part of them? Maybe; but then I thought it went further than that, for as she brought the cigarette up to her lips, I noticed that her hands displayed a similar sort of displacement. The wrists were thin, delicate, very long, like the wrists of some wistful Pre-Raphaelite maiden. But the fingers themselves belonged to a real country girl; they were practical and strong, bony, the nails now bitten down to the quick. Bloomsbury girl . . . hippie lady . . . princess . . . peasant . . . she was a little of each.

Now, guardedly, she said, "You knew I was adopted?"

"Yes."

"All right. I was adopted as an infant, in 1940. I was just a few months old. I only remember Harry . . . my father. I don't even remember his wife—my legal mother—because they separated just a year or so later. I stayed with him. He's the only family I've ever had. Or wanted." She looked up at me. "I didn't even know I was adopted till I was fourteen."

Harry Brightman. I remembered now—that's what she always called him. Harry or Father. I looked at her. "Wasn't fourteen a little late to tell you?"

"It hadn't made any difference before. It didn't then. It didn't later. . . . I think he might never have told me at all, but I asked him if I could meet my mother and he had to explain. We were in France for a holiday. I remember we were in Cannes, sitting in a café. You could see the ocean. I said that when we got home I'd like to meet my mother. I'd never asked before, and I suppose I only asked then because of my age, but that's when he told me. He said that he didn't even know where my mother was and that she wasn't my real mother anyway—I was adopted."

"And what did you feel?"

"I was dizzy for a second. That's all. Then everything settled back down. Nothing had changed. And once I knew my mother wasn't my mother, I had no desire to meet her." She hesitated, then continued. "But I don't want you to miss the point in all this. It didn't make any difference. It never has. On that day in Cannes, he told me everything I know about my adoption—I was a baby, it happened in 1940, it took place in Halifax. But that's it. The subject had never been raised before, and hasn't been since. . . . That is, until a few weeks ago."

"Then what happened?"

"Nothing really. But he started to talk about it. At first he was vague. Hints. Then he began asking if I didn't want to know where I came from. . . ."

"And what did you say?"

"That I didn't. I'm not a child anymore—it doesn't mean anything to me. Then he started to press—didn't I want to know who my real father was . . . ?"

"And?"

"*He's* my real father. I don't want another one." She looked up at me. "But you see what I'm saying? Something about the whole subject was bothering him."

"Is that surprising, though? He's an elderly man. He probably won't live much longer. Perhaps he only wanted to give you one final chance—"

"It was more than that."

"All right. But why does any of this make you think he's killed himself?"

She flinched at the words, but held steady. "I'm not sure. But it could, couldn't it? What if my biological parents came back? Or . . ."

"Or what? What difference would it make? If you were a child—if you'd just been adopted . . . yes, I could see it. But now? You'd all go out to lunch, shake hands, and that would be the end of it."

"Not necessarily. Say there'd been something wrong about the adoption, something illegal."

"Do you think there was?"

"No. But . . . people buy babies. Maybe . . ."

I waited, but she didn't say anything more. I thought over what she'd said. It sounded farfetched; but even if Harry had bought her, I didn't see who would care, forty years after the fact. I said, "Did you tell the police all this?"

She nodded. "They didn't think it was important. They're sure he wasn't being blackmailed, because of his bank records. They told me they'd look into it but I don't think they have."

"And you want me to?"

She looked me square in the eye. "Yes."

"So far as you know, this was the only strange element in your father's recent behavior."

"Yes. It's the only thing I can think of."

"All right, then, I'll do it. I don't promise much—even if I do find out something, it probably won't be connected to your father's disappearance. But I'll try."

She smiled. "Bless you, Robert. I knew you would."

I squeezed her hand. "Remember: no promises."

She smiled and nodded. And then, after the strain of all this, I sensed a certain embarrassment come over her, so I said, "I just thought of something. I left my bag on your front porch."

She laughed. "Don't worry, the neighbors are honest. Go and get it, then I'll show you your room."

She led me up to a bedroom on the second floor, and after taking a shower, I stretched out on the bed and began to think . . . though more about May than her father. So far as he was concerned, I had few worries: Harry Brightman, I was willing to bet, was pursuing an old man's folly, chasing a woman whose existence he'd been too embarrassed to admit, especially to his daughter. May's adoption, the possibility of sui- cide, buying babies—all that had nothing to do with it. The police, I suspected, had also reached this conclusion, and in fact I could see only one point contradicting it—May's fear itself. She *was* genuinely upset, there was no doubt about that. And she wasn't the sort to cry wolf. On the contrary, self-sufficiency had always been one of her hallmarks, so that her call for help now was ample testimony to the devotion she felt toward her father. Should I be surprised at such feelings? Did I have a right to be? Hardly. If May was dominated by her father, in life, I had lived far more completely under the influence of my own father's death.

I lay still, listening. Beyond the window, the day was already darken- ing and sounds from the street were hushed and remote. The house was silent. I listened to it: like all silence, it had its own timbre, and this was gray, cold—strained in some fashion—and as I tried to define what this quality was, my mind slipped back to the afternoon and the rose garden, all enclosed, with May's kneeling figure trapped in that high, wan halo of light. The silence of a nunnery . . . that's what now came into my mind, and I wondered whether that might be true, that some devotion I'd never known about had locked her away from me, that she'd used me to try to break its grip and failed, making her the victim in a tragedy that dwarfed my own. Or, on the other hand—my mind now began racing—maybe such thoughts were just pure projection; God knows I've been called a monk often enough, and more than one woman has complained that she felt, with me, that she was competing against some ghostly presence, all the more powerful for being invisible. Perhaps that was the answer, for now a memory came back. It was a memory of our last night, the last time we'd made love: May had returned from seeing her father but she still hadn't told me that she'd changed her mind. Her passion had been fierce that night, almost desperate. Later, I'd assumed that she was trying to console me, offering one final gift. Now I wondered. Might she not have been giving me a last chance to woo her away? Perhaps I'd been struggling that night with an invisible protagonist of my own—May's father, and her love for him—and when I'd lost, I'd lost for both of us. . . .

But I stopped myself there—this *must* be projection. Besides, it didn't make any difference. All of us—ancient combatants or not—were long dead. Today, I was merely a stand-in for that long-ago actor, and my role was a mere formality. Hold hands, murmur soothing words, wait for Harry to return with his tail between his legs. On which note I drifted off into sleep.

I didn't sleep long, but when I awoke it was completely dark outside my window. I pulled myself together and dressed. May was downstairs and smiled as I came into the room—though I think we both felt a little awkward now. "I was wondering if you'd fallen asleep," she said.

"I did for a while. And I've woken up starving. Why don't we get something to eat?"

"I'll make something."

"Let's go out. On the way over here I thought I saw a Jewish restaurant. If they make a good borscht . . ."

We put on our coats. The night was cool, with a wind, but the restaurant was just around the corner. It was one of those old-fashioned Jewish restaurants with a counter at the front where ancient men drink tea with lemon, read *The Jewish Forward,* and pick their teeth. In back, there were cheap tables, chunky waitresses, and excellent food. I had decided I wasn't going to raise the one obvious subject, but then May herself brought it up. As I dunked a piece of potato into my soup, she said, "This is like Russian food, isn't it?"

"Some Jewish cooking is, but this is more Polish. Which has always struck me as funny—the Russians and Poles are the most anti-Semitic people on earth, but they're all raised on good *yiddisher* food. Even the Germans are, a little."

"I remember Harry once saying something like that. He's German, you know. Brightman . . . Hellman. Heinrich Hellman . . . He was born in Berlin. Both his parents died in the First World War and an uncle in Winnipeg adopted him—the uncle changed the name."

"So your father was adopted himself, and then he adopted you?"

"I never thought of that. As I said, we never talked about it at all." For a second, her voice seemed to falter, but when she went on, her tone was normal again—normal, but self-consciously so, as if she was deliberately trying to erase the desperation she'd shown me before. "I know that his uncle was married, but there were no other children. When he died, he left his fur business to my father. He moved it to Montreal and then expanded to Toronto."

"It seems a strange business to be in. But I suppose not in Canada."

May smiled. "I'm not much of a Canadian. When I was a little girl, he took me to Banff and I saw a bear through binoculars, but that's the closest I've ever been to the wilderness. Actually, you know, you'd enjoy talking to him. He always says that he made his real money out of Russia, not Canada—he claims that Stalin made him a millionaire."

I swallowed cabbage roll. "I don't get it."

"Well, I'm not sure how true it is. But as well as manufacturing furs—turning them into coats—he had an import-export business. In the thirties, he brought in a lot of fur from the Soviet Union."

Once, in Leningrad, I'd gone to one of the fur auctions. It was enormous, with buyers from all over the world. I said, "Did he ever go there? To Russia?"

"Oh yes, several times. You really should talk to him. I know he got to meet one of the important Bolsheviks . . . not Lenin but . . . Zinoviev?"

"Yes." It made sense. Zinoviev, a close friend of Lenin's and the first head of the Comintern, had been relatively cosmopolitan and well-traveled—qualities that would have made him interested in a foreign businessman intrepid enough to visit post-Revolutionary Russia. Of course, those same qualities had made him the first of the major Bolsheviks whom Stalin had purged. That had been in 1934, so presumably Brightman had gone before then. "I'd love to talk to him," I said. "There aren't many witnesses from those days still around . . . and most of those who are don't like talking about it—the subject only reveals their own ideological follies."

"Not Harry. He was only interested in money and made no bones about it . . . which he always claimed the Russians appreciated."

For the first time, I was feeling a glimmer of interest about this man, and suddenly an image of him flashed before my eyes. It had to be pure invention, since I'd never seen him, but it was very vivid just the same. A street market. Stalls. A big, bulky figure wrapped up in a long beaver coat and a large fur hat, his face turning away from me. I said, "I take it that his business was really his life."

She hesitated. "I'm not sure. But no, it wasn't. He sold out about fifteen years ago and he's been happy since. He travels a lot—I get that from him. He loves art and collects it—linocuts, woodcuts, that sort of thing. And there's me. He's very devoted to me, he always has been. That's why I know . . ."

Up to this point, talking about her father objectively, she'd been under control; now her features started to crumple and she worked to get a grip on herself. As deftly as possible, I steered the conversation away. We finished eating, but when we were done it was still only ten. I didn't want to go back to the house, where we'd have to talk some more, so I suggested we walk; after my sleep, I wasn't tired anyway. May explained the city to me: the streets ran north-south, east-west on a grid. We headed up Spadina—a broad, barren, windy street—then turned east along Bloor. This was obviously a main drag; even in the cold, there were lots of people about, hurrying east toward the bright lights in the distance. That was Yonge Street, May said. Across the road, she pointed out some of the University of Toronto buildings, including the Conservatory of Music, all built in magnificent Victorian-Gothic granite. We continued along in silence, but as we came up to a corner, May pointed down a side street. "He lives just up there . . . Harry, I mean."

"Can we look?"

"All right. It's not far."

Almost at once, only a few blocks from the center of the city, we were in a solid old residential neighborhood. This was definitely not poverty row: the houses were large Edwardian structures, reposing on generous lawns in the shelter of huge maples and elms, while the curb was lined with BMWs, Mercedes, and good sensible Volvos. A man passed us, a tense smile on his face—he was being tugged along by a pint-sized dachshund. After five minutes I wasn't sure where I was, but then May stopped under a streetlight and pointed across the road. "That's the house. Behind the fence."

The fence was low, wrought-iron, with a gate. A tall hedge grew behind it—a black mass of shadow—and an immense elm dominated the lawn. The house was dark, almost lost behind the tree, but was plainly very large: three stories plus a garret, with a jagged range of peaks, gables, and turrets running across its roof. It might have had an ominous, haunted-house look except for its substance; it was too solid for ghosts. May said, "It's too big for him. He's always saying so, but he can't bring himself to move."

"Can we go in?"

She looked nervous. "I'd rather not . . . I spent one night there, the first night, hoping he'd come back. But then I couldn't stand it. I was too frightened."

"Are you collecting his mail?"

"No . . . I suppose it still comes."

"Let me get it, then. Do you have a key?"

She didn't want me to; I could see that. But I just stood there, and after a moment she fished a key out of her purse and I crossed the road. The gate opened with a squeak and I went up a stone walk to the door. This was large, glossy black, and bore a knocker appropriate to a fur dealer—a brass snowshoe rapped a fox on the nose. I fitted the key. It worked a dead-bolt lock; that is, you had to use the key to lock the door as well as open it. Conceivably this explained why the door had been found standing open on the night Brightman had disappeared: if he'd been in a hurry and slammed the door behind him, the bolt would have struck the doorframe, forcing the door to bounce back. Now I pushed it inward, plowing a fair heap of mail ahead of me into the entranceway. Then I stood a moment, inhaling that special smell of rich house: waxed wood, polish, wool carpet, cleanliness. I couldn't find a light switch, but after a moment my eyes adjusted to the gloom and I picked up his mail and stepped into a foyer. The hall ran straight on, with stairs to one side of it; two rooms, with sliding doors, led off to my immediate left and right. The doors on my left were partly open, so I stuck my head in, peering across a shadowy vista of furniture toward the dark glitter of glass-fronted cabinets. I stepped back. The kitchen, I guessed, was straight ahead, down the hall. It was very dark. The eerie stillness that settles in abandoned rooms had fallen over the place—and all at once something became real to me: Brightman was missing. I felt ahead to the stairs. There was a lamp on the newel post and I pulled it on, then started up, the banister guiding my hand, ankle-deep carpet cushioning each step. The landing was dark, the second-floor landing pitch black. But I groped ahead and almost immediately felt a doorframe. The door was open. I stepped into the room and punched on a light.

I had found my way to Brightman's library.

Or I suppose that's what he called it. It was very large, with a peculiar quality; heavy, old-fashioned, not quite North American. Dark oak paneling came up to your waist, the walls and ceiling were joined by elaborate moldings, and in the center was a large plaster medallion from which a chandelier hung. Despite its size, the room felt cramped, for it was jammed with books, cabinets, display cases, and the furniture was heavy: an elaborate desk stood just inside the door; oak chairs, covered in brocade, were grouped round the fireplace; and then a sofa and more chairs were ranged near the display cases at the back of the room. It was like a museum—a room belonging to one of those nineteenth-century gentleman collectors with an interest in "natural history." The display cases, in fact, were filled with stuffed animals, each caught in a natural pose (a beaver, up on its hind legs, was chewing a twig gripped in its paws; a lynx padded furtively over a log), and this made the glassy glitter of their eyes all the more gruesome—though I suppose such a collection was reasonable given Brightman's business. And yet this collection, I realized, was only an afterthought compared with the framed prints and engravings that occupied one whole side of the room. There were five rows of them, running from the wainscoting almost to the ceiling—they were filed on that wall, not displayed, and didn't invite you to look at them so much as count them . . . which I did: the total was 228 woodcuts, wood engravings, linocuts, lithographs, and monotypes. I don't know much about art, and I know virtually nothing about graphic art, but as I went down that wall I managed to recognize a few of the names: Käthe Kollwitz, Gaudier-Brzeska (three linocuts), Gertrude Hermes, Robert Gibbings, Rockwell Kent . . . All of them were modern, or at least of this century; all were black-and-white; and many had that heavy, dramatic quality you find in the propaganda art of the thirties: crude social symbolism, poverty, subjects taken from industry—pitheads, gasworks, the complex of lines and shapes formed by cranes at a dockside. One, I saw, was by the Russian artist Vladimir Favorsky: cossacks, workers, soldiers, Lenin and Trotsky, their figures all pulled and stretched into a map of Russia during the Civil War of the twenties. Presumably, Brightman had picked it up while he was over there, but when I took it off the wall, I saw that it was from the 18th Venice Internationale in 1930. I replaced it and stepped back. And wondered.

In the restaurant, I'd had a first glimmer of interest in Brightman himself; now he seemed as fascinating a father as any orphan could wish for.

I stared about me. In the hall, I'd felt his absence; here, his presence pressed in from every direction. Almost in a trance, I made a second circuit of the room, ending by his desk, just inside the door. Though ornately carved, its top was scarred and it was clear that Brightman had actually worked here—there was a mug of pencils and pens, a stapler, a roll of tape, envelopes, bills. And there was also a photograph. It was small, four by six, in a plain wooden frame. Brightman. And my imaginings hadn't been so far wrong. He was a big man, heavyset, with a broad chest sloping into a heavy belly. His face was broad and genial, his hair thick, though receding slightly from a high forehead. The photo had been taken outdoors: he was wearing a lumberjack shirt and his hands were thrust into tweed trousers. It struck me as a little peculiar, having a photograph of yourself on your desk, but when I picked it up, I saw its real value. On the back, penciled in a clumsy hand, were the words: *Harry Brightman, taken by May Brightman with her own Brownie, Georgian Bay, Aug. 1, 1949.*

I set the photograph back in its place. Harry Brightman, as May had seen him. But who was he? What sort of man had lived and breathed in this room? And why had he left it? For the first time, it occurred to me that the answer to this question might be more interesting than I'd assumed. But I wasn't going to answer it now, and May, I suspected, had started to worry. Taking a last glance over my shoulder, I pressed the wall switch, stepped into the doorway . . . and froze.

I stood utterly still. Before me, the hall was pitch black. But I knew I wasn't alone.

Steps, soft as breaths, were coming along the corridor. Toward me. Right past me. And then, for an instant, I saw a face—a face, a glint of red hair—and with a wild glance that face looked right into my eyes: a face as thin as a weasel's and very pale.

And then it was gone.

My heart thumped—thumped so hard it was all I could hear. I could scarcely breathe. I strained to listen. The carpet on the stairs was very thick, but I made out quick, padding steps. . . . I waited for the sound of the door. But heard only silence. . . .

A minute passed. He must have been on the third floor all the time. Not Brightman. Definitely not. But *someone* . . .

Cautiously, I edged into the hall. The stairway was black as a well, but then I reached the landing and the newel-post light glimmered up from below.

A step at a time, I went down. Then, three from the bottom, I stopped and listened again. Nothing. He must have gone . . . but if he hadn't, if he was waiting along the hall leading to the back of the house, I would be completely visible the moment I stepped off the staircase.

Gripping the banister, leaning forward, I pulled the chain switch on the newel post.

Red spots danced in front of my eyes. I waited, letting them fade, then stepped silently down the last couple of stairs, into the hall. Nothing moved. It took all my nerve, but I felt my way along, toward the back. There was a little light here, gray and filmy as fog, and after a moment a door loomed up in front of me. Beyond it lay the chill gloom of the kitchen. I waited, listening. The fridge coming on nearly made me jump out of my skin, but there was no one here, and when I checked the back door it seemed firmly locked. Quickly, I made my way back to the front. He'd either gone out this way or through the basement. I opened the door, stepped into the night . . .

But then stopped.

I looked over my shoulder, realizing I'd forgotten the dead bolt. Striking the doorframe, it had bounced the door open, and now it swung in the wind, creaking a little, just as it must have done on the night Harry Brightman had gone.

4

I didn't tell May.

She was already frightened—and now that I suspected she had reason to be, there was no point in alarming her further. In fact, the more I thought about it, the more it seemed that the real importance of what had happened concerned me, not her. Up to this point, I'd been a rather reluctant good Samaritan. And of course that still might be my position—Brightman, after all, was a rich man, he lived in a rich neighborhood, and perhaps I'd only interrupted a burglar. On the other hand . . . It was this "other hand" that now gave me a twinge of guilt. If Brightman's disappearance was more than inconsiderate—if it had a darker side—then conceivably his concern about May's adoption *might* be linked to it. I still didn't see how, but the next morning, really for the first time, I began taking the whole business seriously.

I worked fast. Once upon a time I'd been a fair reporter, and information had been my bread and butter. When you're just starting out, you obtain it by the exercise of certain skills—later on, you simply use contacts. That's what I needed now, and I began searching for them at the main branch of the Toronto Public Library, first with *The New York Times Index,* then in a microfilm reader. There I learned that adoption, if not exactly front-page news, had become something of a social issue in the late seventies. Procedures were being questioned; adopted children were demanding the right to know their "birth" parents; various organizations were agitating. I read through a dozen stories, mainly concerned with the United States, but one compared American practices with those in other countries, including Canada. I'd never heard of the writer, but of course I know a dozen people on the *Times.* Phoning from May's place, I quickly discovered that my man was now staffing at CBS and tracked him down there. As expected, he was happy to help—now I was one of *his* contacts. To get his paragraph on Canada, he told me, he'd spoken with a woman at the Toronto *Globe & Mail* named Eileen Rogers. I called the *Globe,* and it was my lucky day: Miss Rogers knew my name, or pretended to, she'd done a three-part feature on "Adoption in Canada," and she didn't have a date for lunch.

We went to a restaurant in a small hotel off Bloor Street, not far from where May and I had been walking the previous night. It was quiet, pleasant, elegant; a courtyard had been glassed in, and ad men and TV types padded their paunches and expense accounts as the pale October sun filtered down through the roof. Eileen Rogers fitted the place well enough. She was a real type—the young, tough, ambitious lady reporter who'd worked her way up from the women's page to the political columns and was now scanning the wider horizon beyond. That horizon, I expected, extended south of the border, for she was curious about all those Canadians who've made it big in the American media—Peter Jennings, Morley Safer, Robin MacNeil, a dozen others. I gave her some hints and names, but mostly, of course, she was earning the right to drop *my* name, which was fine, because in return she gave me a top-class briefing on Canadian adoption law and procedures. In Canada, she said, adoption was under provincial jurisdiction, just as, in the United States, the field belonged to the individual states. Most of the provinces (again, like most of the states) had established official or semi-official bodies to handle the whole business: they were usually styled Children's Aid Societies here, but differed little from the "adoption agencies" in the United States. She didn't think much of them on either side of the border.

"It's disgusting, actually. They have a sort of monopoly on infant misery and all they care about is maintaining their power. They've built up huge empires—bureaucracies, programs, funding from here, funding from there. Doing that series, I learned to *loathe* social workers."

I sipped white wine, forked salad. "How does all this affect me . . . if I'm trying to track down someone's parents?"

"Oh, you run right up against the basis of the whole system."

"Which is?"

"Secrecy. Absolute, sacrosanct, legalized secrecy. Once a mother signs over her baby she loses all rights to it—and the kid loses all its rights as well. Neither of them can ever find out about the other. That's the

basis of the Societies' power: they get complete control. It's all rational-
ized—adoptive parents mustn't be haunted by the specter of the birth
mother returning—but it's all bullshit. They threw it out the window
in the U.K. with no ill effects, and in some countries it's never been true.
Finland, for instance."

According to her, if May had been adopted through a Children's
Aid Society—in her case, it would be the Society in the province of Nova
Scotia—there was only one way to find out who the birth mother was:
an inside contact. She hinted that under the right circumstances she
might be forthcoming, but I held off on that. Just possibly, there was
another way. Most adoptions were handled by the Children's Aid Societies, but private adoptions, arranged through lawyers and doctors, still
existed.

"The agencies hate them, of course, but lawyers make money from
them—also sacrosanct—and in some cases they're just more convenient
all round. It makes it easier for the rich to hide their kids' indiscretions,
and then there's the sort of case where the parents are wiped out in a
car crash and a relative picks up the children."

"So the lawyer would be the key, then?"

"Yeah. If you could get him to talk."

It was around three by the time I got back to May's house and told
her the gist of what I'd found out.

"So it's going to be very hard," she said, "if I was adopted through
one of these Societies?"

"Yes, but I think this girl knows some people inside the system,
at least in Ontario. That would be a big help."

"You won't get in trouble?"

"Don't worry. It would be easier, though, if we knew whether or
not you were adopted privately."

"All I know is what I told you. I was adopted in 1940, in Halifax."

"But your father must have a lawyer?"

"Of course. His name is Stewart Cadogan—I don't much like
him."

"Do they go back that far, to 1940?"

"Probably. He's old enough."

"He'd probably know anyway. Phone him and find out. If he says
you *were* adopted privately, make an appointment and we'll go see him."

We were in the kitchen again, drinking coffee. Now May glanced quickly down at the table. "If you don't mind—if you need to see him—I'd rather you went by yourself. As I say, I don't like him. We never get along."

Her fear—I felt it flicker again. "May . . . you're sure that's everything you know—you realize there's no point holding anything back?"

She reached up with both hands, combing her fingers back through her hair, but then she smiled and her voice was calm. "You have to understand, I don't care if *you* know. If there's something to know—if he has something to tell you—I don't mind your finding out. But *I* don't want to . . . not unless I absolutely have to."

"All right. But you may have to, whether you like it or not. You realize that?"

"I know. But I've lived all my life with one story and I'd prefer not to change it. Even if my adoption is connected to Harry's going away, I'd rather you take that connection to the police and let them find him. If it's possible . . . if you could do it like that."

I nodded, though I wasn't exactly happy about it. "I'll try . . . but you know, this lawyer may not be prepared to see me alone. Your adoption is confidential, privileged—"

"Don't worry. I'll fix it."

I waited in the kitchen while May used the phone in the hall. In ten minutes, she was back. "Good news. My adoption was private."

"But he won't talk about it?"

"Well, he didn't want to, but I persuaded him. My God he's officious—I have to write a letter giving him formal instructions."

Stewart Cadogan, Q.C.; I was looking forward to meeting him. He'd agreed to see me that day, but not till six-thirty, and so I set off at dusk in May's Volkswagen, braving the city's traffic for the first time. It wasn't difficult. Toronto is a commercial town. At that hour, no one was making money in the great skyscrapers, but the crowds hadn't begun to spend it yet in the restaurants and bars, so the streets were gray, empty, forlorn. Cadogan's offices were on Victoria Street, just beyond Yonge. I parked, then walked a block to an old, red-brick house with stone steps, a columned porch, and a heavy oak door festooned with the appropriate plaque. Inside was a dim foyer and a desk for a porter; this gentleman, black-suited and very ancient, led me upstairs. Old, rich law firms can be very impressive, and Cadogan's fell into that category; padding along in the porter's dignified wake, I could almost hear the money rustling in their escrow accounts. I passed through a door into an outer office; a secretary, kept late for my benefit—and a trifle peevish—took me over.

"You're Mr. Thorne?"

"That's right."

I would have put her age at sixty. She wore a navy suit with a white blouse, and the eyeglasses dangling round her neck bobbed with her goiter. She pressed an intercom. "A Mr. Thorne to see you, sir."

The indefinite article, somehow, made me feel less than reputable, but at least they hadn't kept me waiting, and as the secretary held the door, I stepped straight through into Cadogan's sanctum. It was large and gloomy. The rugs on the floor were probably Kashans, though a trifle threadbare, and the fire in the marble fireplace was blue, flickering coal—the overall effect was one of wealth, but wealth that was practical, parsimonious, Scotch. Greeting me, Cadogan lifted himself out of a chair behind an old wood desk. He was very tall, somewhat stooped, with a large, bald head. His hands were also large, the knuckles bumpy and twisted. He could have been a school principal, a retired parson, or, indeed, just what he was. Accepting May's letter, he indicated a leather club chair by the corner of his desk. I sat, and watched him fish spectacles from the pocket of his suit coat. Fitting these to his nose, he began to read, frowning and suspicious. When he was finished, he laid the sheet of paper on his desk and pressed it flat with one of his huge bony hands. Then he glanced up at me.

"You'll not take this personally, Mr. Thorne, but you'll understand that I was reluctant to see you?"

"I gathered that, yes."

"You'll even admit, perhaps, that your situation is somewhat equivocal?"

"Yes, I suppose I would."

A smile flickered. "Then you'll be aware that mine must be too."

I said nothing. After a moment, he grunted—which I took as a sign that he'd come to some provisionally favorable conclusion about me. He got to his feet. "It's after six. You'll take something to drink, Mr. Thorne?"

"Thank you, sir. That would be very pleasant."

He stepped around his desk to a lacquered cabinet near the fire-place. His suit was brown; for him, no doubt, an example of sartorial daring. It was several years out of date and, as with many old men, seemed to hang a little loosely on his large frame.

He took bottles and glasses out of the cabinet. "You're a young man and will prefer whiskey. I am old and must make do with sherry." This was a joke, so I smiled. But in fact he didn't look around to see what effect his remark might have had. I watched him pour. Naturally, there was no offer of water or ice. He brought me my glass, and I noticed that his hand, extending it, trembled slightly. I sipped. To my surprise, it was Canadian whiskey; I would have guessed Scotch. This must have shown on my face, for Cadogan smiled. "In this country, Mr. Thorne, we call it rye."

"It's very good, wherever you're from."

Perhaps he thought me incapable of normal civility, for he nodded a little, as if surprised. Then he settled himself behind his desk, his glass of sherry lost inside his vast hand. "As I understand it," he said, "you're trying to find Miss Brightman's father."

"Not quite that. May thinks her adoption might have some connection to her father's disappearance and has asked me to look into it."

His eyes didn't leave mine, but his hand edged over his desk to a file that was lying there. "Adoption. A very private concern."

"Yes."

"Intimate business. *Family* business."

"I understand."

"You realize, I suppose, that I offered to tell Miss Brightman everything I know about the matter, but she asked me to tell only you?"

"Yes."

"She must trust you."

"Yes, I think she does."

"Without wishing to give offense, Mr. Thorne, may I ask if you're absolutely certain that you understand what trust means in a matter like this?"

He had, mildly, given offense, and I didn't mind showing it. "I don't think you have to worry about that, Mr. Cadogan."

"Good. I shall cease doing so. But you also understand that I am under no obligation to tell you anything at all. May Brightman is my client, as well as her father, and she has an obvious interest in this. But these papers come from Harry Brightman's file, not hers. Only he, strictly speaking, can give you permission to read them."

"I'm sure that's true—strictly speaking."

He shot me a glance. "As a lawyer, Mr. Thorne, I find nothing wrong with strict speaking."

I hesitated. I didn't want to argue with him. Besides, I knew that eventually he'd do as May's letter had instructed. I said, "Can I ask if *you* think there's some connection—that is, between Brightman's disappearance and his daughter's adoption."

He frowned, irritated at this change of direction. But then he grunted again. "I don't say yes, Mr. Thorne . . . but I don't say no, either. In any case, I'd let you see these because I know that Harry Brightman would wish me to do as his daughter has asked . . . and because, as you will see, they contain very few secrets." Abruptly, before I could question this, he shoved the file across his desk. "You will know nothing about adoption law, but that is hardly necessary. May Brightman wasn't adopted under any statute that is in force today—indeed, in 1940, the relevant law dated back to the twenties. It is a quirk in that law which gives her case a peculiar interest. You'll understand as you read."

Without saying anything, I opened the file. The first item was a carbon, on flimsy paper, of an old memo from "T. Tugwell" to "G.C." It summarized the Nova Scotia Adoption Act—Chapter 139 of the Revised Statutes, 1923—and concentrated especially on the "consents" that had to be obtained before an adoption decree would be granted. Theoretically, these might include the consent of everyone from the child itself, if it was over fourteen, to the husband, if the person being adopted was a married woman, but they could also be waived under a variety of circumstances: if the person whose consent would normally be required was insane, was in a penitentiary, had neglected the child, or allowed it to be "charitably supported." Furthermore, the memo went on, if a person whose consent was normally required couldn't be found, the court could advertise for that person and then declare, if he or she still hadn't come forward, that consent was taken as given. Finally the memo concluded: "NO, the child's physical presence would not normally be required in court; and YES, our client would have to be married. *This is not stated as an explicit provision of the law but in practice is almost always required.*"

Thanking God that I'd never been tempted by a legal career, I looked up at Cadogan. "I assume this was drafted after a request by Brightman?"

"Yes. It's not in the file. Probably he came into the office and spoke with my father personally."

I looked back to the top of the page. " 'G.C.' is your father?"

"Yes."

I turned back to the file. The next items were letters to Brightman, at a hotel in Halifax, more or less restating the memo, and a letter to a law firm in Halifax saying that he would approach them. Brightman had acknowledged this with a note, so for the first time I saw his signature—broad, open, easy, in keeping with the face in the photograph.

Cadogan said, "You'll have noted that the important point is the requirement to advertise—Section 4, Chapter 139. The paper used for such notices is normally the provincial government's journal of record, *The Royal Gazette,* and the next items in that file are tear sheets from it."

They were old and yellowed; as I took them up, the brittle paper flaked under my fingers. On this page were estate notices, appointments of Crown Attorneys, regulations concerning the blackout—for this was 1940 and the Second World War was underway. In the middle of all this was the heading: *Adoption Act; re Florence Esther Raines.* Beneath it was printed:

TO: Florence Esther Raines, whose present address is unknown and who is the mother of Elizabeth Ann Raines:

TAKE NOTICE that pursuant to the provisions of the Order, a copy of which is given hereunder, you are advised that a petition has been presented for the adoption of the child Elizabeth Ann Raines, a copy of which petition is hereunder given; and that said petition will be heard and considered at County Court Chambers at the Law Courts, Spring Garden Road, Halifax, N.S., on Friday, the 28th day of June, A.D. 1940, at the hour of ten o'clock in the forenoon.

R. A. Powell,
Duke Street,
Halifax, N.S.,
Solicitor for Petitioners.

Skipping down the page, I came to the petition itself: the complete, comprehensive, and legally certified story of May Brightman's adoption:

1940 C.C. No. 1289
In the County Court for District
Number One
In the Matter of
Chapter 139, R.S.N.S., 1923
"Of the Adoption of Children"; and
In the Matter of
ELIZABETH ANN RAINES
PETITION

— —

To his honor A. F. Best, Judge of the County Court for District Number One:

The petition of Harold Charles Brightman of the City of Toronto, in the County of York, in the Province of Ontario, merchant, and Ellen Sarah Brightman, his wife, humbly sheweth:

1. Your petitioner, Harold Charles Brightman, has resided at Toronto, in the County of York, for some years, and is a merchant dealing in furs; your petitioner, Ellen Sarah Brightman, is the wife of the said Harold Charles Brightman.

2. Your petitioners are desirous of adopting a female child, Elizabeth Ann Raines, who is the illegitimate child of Florence Esther Raines of Halifax, in the County of Halifax.

3. Said child is of the age of 10 months, having been born on the 12th day of June, A.D. 1939. Said child was abandoned into the care of Charles Grainger, M.D., within a few weeks of her birth, and has been charitably maintained by him since that time.

4. Your petitioners believe that the mother of the said child was of the Protestant faith. Your petitioners are members of the Church of England, and would give the said child instructions in the doctrines of that Church.

5. Your petitioners are both over the age of 21 years, and are of sufficient means and ability to bring up the said child and are able to furnish nurture and education.

6. Your petitioners request that the name of the said child Elizabeth Ann Raines be changed to Sarah May Brightman.

7. Your petitioners therefore pray that an order be made by this Honorable Court pursuant to the provisions of Chapter 139, R.S.N.S., 1923, whereby the said child may be adopted as their child by your petitioners.

And your petitioners will ever pray, etc.,

HAROLD CHARLES BRIGHTMAN

ELLEN SARAH BRIGHTMAN

I turned the page over; the last item in the file was the adoption order itself. I wasn't stunned by all this, but I was more than a little surprised, especially in light of what I'd been told about "secrecy" by my lady reporter that morning. I looked up at Cadogan. "So this means that May Brightman's adoption has always been public knowledge?"

"It was an exceptional case, of course. But the various suggestions she made on the phone—blackmail and so forth—are out of the question. There have never been any secrets about her adoption and, as you see, it was all entirely legal."

"But not," I thought aloud, "entirely regular."

"How is that, Mr. Thorne?"

"I'm thinking of Brightman's marriage . . ." I flipped back through the file. "In this first memo, there's the clear implication that he wasn't married when the proceedings began. Your clerk stressed that he'd have to be. So it must have been a marriage of convenience, especially remembering that he divorced so soon afterwards."

Cadogan gave me a frosty smile. "Surely, Mr. Thorne, all marriages should be convenient. There's nothing illegal—or even irregular—about that."

But I wasn't going to be put off. "Still, it must normally work the other way round. That is, the desire to adopt a baby arises out of the marriage rather than preceding it."

"Perhaps that's so," he conceded. "But I suspect that Harry Brightman wasn't the first man to desire a child without having to put up with a wife. He was a wealthy man, even then. Like many wealthy men, he simply arranged matters to suit him."

Somehow, this rang a bell, and I had it . . . but not quite. Brightman, a wealthy man, wants a child. But not any child—*this* child. Instead of adopting in his own town, he travels all the way to Nova Scotia because . . . but then the thought slipped away. And I tried a different tack altogether. "I gather that you weren't a member of the firm when all this was happening?"

"Technically speaking, I was, but I had been seconded—if you like—to the Royal Canadian Air Force. This was 1940, remember. There was a war on. You people weren't in it, but we were."

There was a slight hint of disapproval in this, and I wondered what he would have said if he'd known that my father, at precisely that point, had been carrying on business as usual with the Germans in Paris.

I said, "So your personal knowledge of the matter is limited? It's all secondhand?"

"If you like. If that's material."

"I was just wondering if you ever talked to Brightman about it."

"Very little, and only much later. I handled the divorce—he had to tell me a little about it then."

"And when was that?"

"I think 1951 or '52. By that time, he had been living apart from his wife for many years."

"Could his wife have anything to do with this?"

"No."

"But you don't entirely rule out a connection between Brightman's disappearance and the adoption?"

Now, for the first time, Cadogan seemed uneasy. His eyes dropped. Then, with a fussy movement, he removed his spectacles and slipped them into his pocket. He said, "Mr. Thorne, when men say they wish to speak frankly, they usually intend to tell you a lie, but in fact I want you to know what's in my mind. That is difficult, however. I have been Harry Brightman's lawyer for a very long time. He has less legal business today than formerly, but what there is I handle myself. And when he sold his business—a complex matter—I handled that. Even going back further, he frequently called on my services. He manufactured and sold furs, but he also imported and exported them. Ocelots come from Argentina, jaguars from Brazil, there are problems selling mink in America . . . he was always having difficulties with permits and regulations of one sort or another. You understand?"

"Go on."

"All right. On the last occasion I saw him, our regular lunch, I sensed that something was different. I mean, I had the feeling that something was troubling him, something that lay beyond the normal bounds of our relationship. He mentioned a woman. It was clear that he meant a liaison, an infatuation in his past . . . but it was all very fleeting. It wasn't the sort of thing he'd normally have spoken about—and you realize that it's not the sort of thing I'd normally speak of to you."

I nodded. Indeed, the difficulty he'd had in speaking at all made me sense that his feeling for Brightman was more "personal" than he'd let on. "I understand, sir. Did he mention a name?"

"Anna. He said, 'When I look back, Anna is my deepest regret.' We'd been talking about the past, the war. He'd had something to drink, perhaps more than he'd usually take. He spoke as if I knew what he was talking about."

"But you didn't?"

"No."

"And you didn't like to ask who this woman was?"

"It would have embarrassed us both."

"I see. . . . But there are no Annas involved in any of this. The baby was called Elizabeth Ann—"

He lifted his hand from his desk in a dismissive gesture. "Does that make any difference? A nickname, a pet name . . ."

And now, at last, I had it. I could hear May's voice in my ear: *He said he wanted to tell me who my real father was.* But surely the usual focus of interest was the mother's identity. . . . All of which must have shown on my face, for now Cadogan said, "I take it you've drawn the obvious conclusion, Mr. Thorne?"

"Yes, sir."

I had. May Brightman was Harry Brightman's natural child. In adopting her, he'd merely been adopting his own illegitimate daughter. I said, "Did you just reach this conclusion then, during that conversation?"

"No, it was a suspicion I'd held for a good many years."

"Had you ever tried to confirm it?"

"No. It was none of my business. Conceivably, I realized, it might have had some effect on his will, but I drafted it to take that into account." He hesitated a moment. "In that conversation, you see, I thought he was depressed, not quite himself, but there was nothing dramatic about it. I have no reason to suppose that it had anything to do with his going away. If he hadn't, I doubt that it would have stuck in my mind."

I nodded. The old man leaned back in his chair. Then, rather deliberately, he looked at his watch. "If you don't mind . . . I think I've told you all that I know."

"Yes, sir. And I thank you for doing so."

I rose. Cadogan didn't hold out his hand. I considered, then decided not to offer him mine. But as I turned to leave, he stopped me.

"Mr. Thorne . . . Earlier, I asked if you knew the meaning of trust. I hope you now understand why."

Would I tell her? That's what he was asking; but, right then, I couldn't have answered, so I merely nodded, turned, and went out the door. Outside, the porter was waiting and I followed him down the stairs and through the big oak doors to the street. The sidewalk was dark and deserted; a drizzle was falling. Standing there, I let it prickle, cold and sharp, on my face. I took a deep breath. Would I tell her? I really had no idea what to do. And all at once—it must have been the rain—I was back in that graveyard where my father was buried and an uncanny sensation passed through me: an obscure, distressing feeling that I was not here by accident, that somehow Brightman's fate was intimately connected to my own. In a strange way, the story of May's origins was becoming *my* secret, and so, by a natural progression, was becoming allied to that other secret I held—the truth about my father's suicide. No wonder I found it disturbing. But there was an assumption in this—that I'd definitely keep back what I'd discovered. Should I? May's instructions had been clear enough: she didn't want to know unless it became absolutely necessary. Perhaps, given that, I had no right to tell her, for there was still no certainty that the adoption and Brightman's disappearance were connected. Why, given the facts, should he have fled? No doubt they would have upset May to some extent, but hardly as much as his abrupt departure had done; in the end, after all, the truth could only have served to draw them closer together.

What should I do?

As I walked along, a soft voice began whispering the answer: Let it alone, let it alone. But I suppose, even then, I knew that I wouldn't.

Whether I liked it or not, this *was* my secret now—I'd found out something that no one had ever been intended to know, and there had to be more.

What was it?

As I reached the car, I remembered what the King of Hearts had told Alice: "Begin at the beginning, and go on till you come to the end: then stop."

For May Brightman, and perhaps for her father, the beginning lay in Halifax, Nova Scotia, during the blitzkrieg spring of 1940.

5

When I was living in Moscow, the first "ordinary" Russian friend that I had was a man named Nikolai Morozov. He was an engineer who'd become a bureaucrat, but like many scientifically trained Russians, he fancied himself as a frustrated literary man. He loved poetry; above all, he loved Kipling. I'm not sure why. Kipling is frowned on in the Soviet Union ("an imperialist reactionary," etc., etc.), so perhaps he thought he was being daring. Or possibly—though Nikolai spoke English well—he found Kipling's straightforward rhythms and rhymes easy to enjoy. In any event, I once drove with him to Leningrad. We arrived early in the morning of a cool March day and a terrible fog had come up from the Neva, the Gulf of Finland, and the various other swamps and lagoons around which the city is built. Immediately, Nikolai began to declaim:

> *"Into the mist my guardian prows put forth,*
> *Behind the mist my virgin ramparts lie,*
> *The Warden of the Honour of the North,*
> *Sleepless and veiled am I!"*

"Kipling," I mumbled, a little sleepless myself. "His famous poem about Petersburg."

"It is Kipling, yes, and it *should* have been his poem about Petersburg. But in truth it is about a place in Canada called Halifax, Nova Scotia."

This, until I arrived that morning at the end of October, was the sum total of my knowledge about Canada's famous eastern port, and though I wouldn't have sworn to the town's virginity, Kipling was dead right about the fog. Blindly, we descended through it, flaps down, wheels down, the whole plane feeling tentatively ahead for the first touch of the ground beneath the thick, ashen coils that swirled under us. Then, frighteningly close, it was there . . . and we glided onto a rain-slick runway with the gentleness that only cockpit computers and fervent prayer can bring.

I took a cab into the city. It was a small, Victorian garrison town mellowed by time and now softened by the fog and the rain: gray, narrow streets; weather-beaten clapboard houses; and that odor of salt, fish, and diesel oil that is common to ports the world over. My hotel, the Nova Scotian, was right downtown, and my room overlooked the harbor. Eating breakfast, I peered out the window while the persistent, mournful note of a foghorn shivered the glass. Though the fog was bad, it wasn't bad enough to close the port down. An Esso oil tender puttered back and forth several times, then a grain carrier, flying the Hammer and Sickle, inched its way up the channel, and finally, as I sipped my coffee, a warship nosed into view, gray as the fog, sullen and menacing as a shark. I guessed it was a destroyer, and the sight of it brought my mind back to business. May Brightman had been adopted in June 1940, the same month that France had fallen. The United States was still eighteen months away from war, but down in this harbor the first of the Atlantic convoys had been preparing to run the U-boats' gauntlet—as Edward R. Murrow would have put it. I wondered if Harry Brightman had watched them. It was possible, though presumably he would have had other things on his mind. The woman he'd made pregnant, for example, Florence Raines. Or perhaps Charles Grainger, the doctor who'd taken possession of the child. Or possibly the child herself, the little girl he'd later called May. What should he do? How should he handle it? Forty years later, I began backtracking over his problem.

At this point, I still had no clear idea what I would find. I'd be disappointed if I found nothing at all, but then I wouldn't be completely surprised—a negative expectation that had been another reason why I'd finally decided to tell May nothing. Yet I was, I knew, playing a little game with myself. I was going to set aside all doubts and suspicions and play boy reporter. Forgetting what all this might mean, there was a technical problem and I was now going to solve it—*che sarà, sarà*.

I began by trying to find Florence Raines, a search that took me first to the telephone book—several listings for Raines, but no "F"—and then to the Provincial Building on Hollis Street, an old stone edifice that housed the registry of vital statistics. The clerks were patient and efficient; within an hour, I established three facts. First, Florence Esther Raines had been born in Springhill, a small mining town in the northwestern section of the province. Second, she had married one James Luton Murdoch, in Halifax, on March 22, 1943. And third, she had died, also in Halifax, on June 12, 1971.

It was around noon when I came up with this final fact, and of course it set me back on my heels. Florence had been the obvious candidate to relate the inside story of the adoption; if, in fact, there was anything connnected with the adoption to cause Brightman to panic forty years later, she might well know what it was. But then I told myself that Florence Raines's death wasn't the end of the world and went back to the hotel and checked the phone book for Murdoch, her husband. But when I dialed, a female, youngish, told me he wasn't at home.

"Could you tell me when he'll be back?"

"Not till the end of the month. He's in Montreal, with his sister."

I was, I suspected, speaking with one of Florence's legitimate daughters—who probably knew nothing about her mother's youthful indiscretion, and wouldn't want to talk about it even if she did. "It's important that I get in touch with him. Could you give me this sister's address?"

She gave it to me, but for the moment I filed it under "last resort." I had one better hope: the doctor. He wasn't listed under "Physicians and Surgeons" but was still alive in the White Pages: Grainger, Charles F., M.D. I dialed the number and a woman—I would have guessed housekeeper—picked up the phone.

"Oh no, the doctor's not in, I'm afraid."

"Do you know when he'll return?"

"That's hard to say, sir. He says five but that's maybe six and more likely seven. It's Friday, you see. His day at the clinic."

So he still practiced. She gave me the clinic address and I went straight downstairs and into a cab. The rain was now falling more heavily. Veiled in Kipling's mist, the city slipped by, gray, old-fashioned, oddly appealing. Even out of sight of the water, you knew it was there by the steep tilt of the cross streets that led down to the harbor—an incline against which both pedestrians and buildings braced themselves. We crossed through the shopping district, which wasn't much, and gradually the streets grew scruffy. Shabby houses. Cheap shops. New York Cafés and Rainbow Grilles with narrow, dingy doors leading to the narrow, dingy rooms above. People scurried along the sidewalks with their heads down. White-bread faces. Draft-beer faces. Black faces . . . In fact, I suddenly realized that there were quite a few black faces, which surprised me enough to mention it to the driver.

"You American?" he replied.

"Uh-huh."

"Well, slaves used to come here, eh? To escape. The Underground Railway, they called it. This whole section of town was called Africville." After a moment, having imparted this lesson in local history, he added, "You know where this place is exactly?"

"Just that address."

He found it anyway, a small frame house on one of the meaner of these streets. There was a crudely lettered sign: *Daly Street Community Clinic,* but I would have recognized the place immediately without it, for versions of it exist all over the world: half-forgotten outposts of the sixties where a few hippies and radicals—like Japanese soldiers marooned on Pacific atolls—have rallied to make their last stand. I went up the walk and tried the door. It was open, its hinges loose—closing it behind me, I had to lift it back into place. I was in a shabby hall. There was a scent of poverty, masked by carbolic. Once, I suspected, the walls had been adorned with posters of Che, Stokely, and Ho; now there was a bulletin board with a mimeographed flyer advertising a lesbian dance and another promoting a meeting to protest cuts in welfare spending. I stuck my head through the doorway. A bespectacled girl with lanky brown hair was sitting behind a desk talking into the phone. "I know . . . I know . . . exactly . . . You just can't treat people like that . . . exactly. Just a sec." Resentfully, she looked up at me. "Yes?"

"I'd like to see Dr. Grainger."

"He's pretty busy right now."

"It isn't a medical problem. I just want to talk to him. Could you say it's about Harry Brightman?"

She looked dubious. "Harry Brightman?"

"That's right. I think he'll know the name if you mention it."

"Well . . . you'll still have to wait. Go down the hall, to your right."

Unenthusiastically, I followed her instructions and passed through an arch into a large, square room, no doubt the front parlor when the house had been lived in. The light was dim, but I told myself I was breathing the pure air of good works. Around the walls, perched on straight chairs, sat a variety of people, some young, some old, some white, some black, but all poor: street kids, an elderly woman with a shopping bag, a pregnant black lady. . . . I took a chair beside the pregnant woman and asked, "Do you know Dr. Grainger?"

She looked at me suspiciously. "Sure, I know him."

"I've never been here before. Will we have to wait long?"

She paused before answering, perhaps listening to the girl in the office, who was still on the phone: "Exactly . . . exactly . . . You have to have that perspective. . . ." At last, the black lady said, "It all depends. If you want to see him, you will. But there's another doctor here who'd be a bit quicker."

"But you think Dr. Grainger is better? You'd recommend him?"

Softening a little, she placed her hand on her belly. "Well, Dr. Charlie brought me into the world, he brought my mother into the world, so he might as well do the same for this one."

I smiled. "I guess he's been here a long time."

She nodded, tugging her raincoat more tightly about her. "As long as I can remember. My mother was born in 1933, so as far back as that." Then she frowned and looked about disapprovingly. "Of course, it wasn't always like this. I remember how it was when I was a little girl. He lived here then, you see. You went in a side door and then down to the basement. His surgery, he always called it, like they do in England."

"Dr. Charlie" . . . doctor to the poor, medical man with a social conscience. A strange friend for Brightman? This was an interesting question, and I pondered it, but it wasn't so interesting that I failed to notice the passage of time. That girl never seemed to get off the phone. One of the kids, a black with beads of sweat gleaming in his hair, began to shiver, and I wondered what he was on. I closed my eyes. I did Russian verb tenses. I tried to think of the book I should have been working on. But at long last the girl from the office appeared in the doorway and looked toward me. "Could you come with me, please?"

I could, and did: along the hall, through a doorway, into the staff room—cheap chrome chair, dinette table, mugs turned upside down on a paper towel to dry. I was now at the rear of the house. The girl held a door open at the back of the room. "This is his study. Could you just wait here? He'll be down in a sec."

I stepped past her. Oddly, the room I entered immediately reminded me of Brightman's though it was almost exactly the opposite—very small, very dim, with a low, cramped feeling. In a way, it was more like my own workroom in Charlottesville, for it too was a winterized sun porch: the ceiling and walls were tongue-and-groove boards, and a pair of battered French doors gave onto a weedy, tangled garden. I listened as rain rushed off the roof and slapped at the leaves. Still, despite this, it was Brightman's room that I thought of. It was a retreat, in the same way, and overstuffed in the same way—though with books rather than pictures. Bookshelves were everywhere; brick-and-board shelves teetering against a wall, shelves made from old orange crates piled one on top of the other, even an old glass-fronted bookcase shoved into a corner. I've always snooped at other people's reading, and here you could hardly avoid it. There were some medical texts, as you might expect, a sagging shelf of journals and an old encyclopedia, but mostly there were paperbacks, rows of them, thousands. Many, I saw, were very old, with that peeling cellophane stuff they used to coat them with, and a lot were ancient Penguins from the days when they had uniform covers. Orange for novels. Blue for biographies. I pulled one out. The pages felt sugary under my fingers, like the pages of *The Royal Gazette* I'd handled in Cadogan's office. But then, I realized, many of these books were from precisely that era. *You and the Refugee*, a Penguin "Special" . . . *What Hitler Wants* by E. O. Lorimer . . . *Germany Puts the Clock Back:* "A New Edition with Additional Material Added April and August 1938." That had been precisely one year before the outbreak of war, two before May's adoption—so it was possible that Brightman might have stood here and seen this very book, newly purchased, on Grainger's desk. I poked along the shelf, my eye caught by a row of uniform red hardbacks. Pulling one down, I saw they were all Left Book Club editions from the thirties: *The Coming Struggle for Power* by John Strachey. *Soviet Communism: A New Civilization* by Sidney and Beatrice Webb. *A Handbook of Marxism* by Emile Burns. . . . Once upon a time, it seemed, Dr. Charlie's do-gooding had possessed an edge: he'd had at least an intellectual interest in the Left.

But just then—I still had Strachey's book in my hand—he came into the room.

I smiled. It was hard to imagine this old gentleman as a rebel or protester of any kind. Dr. Charlie was very short, with a kindly, lined face and a shock of fine white hair that sprayed up from his head. Dressed in a white doctor's gown, he was the sort of elderly medical man who might have given sage advice to a young Dr. Kildare. He eyed me. "Now, then," he said, "you're not Harry Brightman."

"I'm sorry, Doctor. The young lady misheard me. I want to talk with you about Brightman but my name's Robert Thorne."

"Charlie Grainger." He stuck out his hand—small, firm, warm. Then he grinned. "To tell you the truth, I'm relieved. If you had been Brightman, I would have been seeing a real ghost from the past." He pointed. "Have a seat. You should find a chair under those books."

He went around behind a desk in front of the French windows, where he too had to clear a space for himself. I said, "You like to read, Doctor."

"Well, what I really like is understanding . . . not that I claim to." He looked around the room. "In fact, all these books merely add up to three questions. Number one: 'Who benefits? Who profits?' "

"Lenin's question?"

"If you like. But lots of other people have asked it. Then comes 'Who rules the rulers?' which is the wise man's question, and finally 'What the hell will they do to us next?' which is *my* question."

I smiled. I wondered how old he was. Well over seventy, certainly. Now, settled behind his desk, he folded his hands in front of him and eyed me with a bright, questioning concern. I almost expected him to ask: What ails?

I said, "I assume you haven't seen Brightman lately?"

"I haven't heard his name in thirty years, Mr. Thorne. Maybe more. I'm surprised I recognized it. . . . Funny, though. I did, right away."

"Well, he's missing. That's what I wanted to ask you about. Two weeks ago, he left his home, and no one's seen him since."

"That's too bad. I hope nothing's wrong. So . . . you're from the police?"

"No. I'm a friend of his daughter's. She asked me to help look for him."

He shrugged. "I don't know what to say. I certainly haven't laid eyes on him. You don't think he'd come here? You realize, I only knew him very briefly, and that was a long time ago."

"I understand. But part of the mystery around Brightman's disappearance is the motive. His health was good, he had money. In fact, in the weeks before he vanished, the only thing troubling him was his daughter's adoption. He seemed to want to tell her about it."

For a moment he looked uncomfortable, which was more or less what you'd expect. But then, recovering himself, he smiled. "It was all such a long time ago, Mr. Thorne."

"Yes."

"*Did* he tell her about it?"

"No."

"But you want to ask *me* about it?"

"Yes. But I don't want to put you on the spot. Let's say that I've read the petition, talked to Harry Brightman's lawyer about it, and have therefore drawn the obvious conclusion."

"Which is?"

"The child Brightman was adopting was his own illegitimate daughter."

There was a moment's silence, but finally Grainger gave a shrug and a little wave of his hand. "I probably shouldn't comment on that . . . but maybe it's a little late in the day to get sticky over ethics. Let's proceed as though your conclusion were true. What difference does it make? So far as I'm aware, there was nothing about the adoption to disturb anyone."

I said, "I'm not sure what difference it makes . . . or that it makes any at all. I suppose that's why I'm here. His daughter—her name is May—doesn't know the true story, but I'm sure—as you say—that it wouldn't disturb her. If anything, I think she'd be pleased. . . ."

"Is she close to her father?"

"Very."

"Then you'd think she'd *definitely* be pleased. And why not tell her? As I remember him, Brightman wasn't the squeamish type—

perhaps some people would feel a certain embarrassment about that sort of confession, but not enough to make them disappear. After all, his daughter is a grown woman now." He leaned back, hooking his arms behind the chair. "It sounds to me, Mr. Thorne, as if you're barking up the wrong tree."

"Well, probably I am . . . but there are still a couple of things that make me curious."

"Such as?"

"Think about what you just said, Doctor. Why not tell her? I'm sure that most adopted children are sometimes anxious about their status, their relationship with their adoptive parents. Brightman could have allayed all those anxieties. Yet he never did. Perhaps you wouldn't have told a young girl the full story, but, as you say, May is now a grown woman. But he never told her the truth. How come?"

He shrugged. "I don't know. I suppose there might be many reasons . . . perfectly innocent ones."

"Maybe. But you can take it a little further. May, you see, not only doesn't know the truth, she claims she doesn't *want* to—she's very clear about that. Even now—even though she's asked me to look into this for her—she'd rather I take what I find to the police without telling her about it. Don't you think that's a bit odd?"

He shook his head and smiled. "Nope. I'm really not following you, Mr. Thorne."

Actually, I was thinking aloud, and the more I did so, the clearer things seemed to become. "Brightman," I went on, "never told his daughter the truth even though the true story—on the face of it—would only bring them closer together. What's more—though I admit I'm guessing here—he somehow communicated to her the idea that she'd be better off not knowing what the true story was. You see? It implies that the 'true' story either may not be true or is incomplete. There has to be more."

His head tilted back as he thought, but then, with a shrug, he looked down. "If there is anything more, Mr. Thorne, I don't think I know it."

His gaze met mine. Held it. In the end, it was my eyes that shifted away. It seemed pretty clear that he was telling the truth. Finally I said, "Can you tell me what Brightman was like at the time it all happened? Did he seem upset? How did you first meet him, for instance?"

"Oh, that was long before, in the late twenties or early thirties. He imported and exported furs, you know, and after Montreal closed down for the winter, he'd ship them through here. One of those times he fell ill and consulted me in the usual way. Did you know him at all?"

Did . . . but that was natural; he hadn't seen him in years.

I shook my head. "We've never met."

"He was a fascinating fellow, least he was then. He'd been to Russia early on and even claimed to know some of the big Russian leaders. In those days, I was a bit of a socialist, so that interested me. He played chess as well—one of my hobbies. When he came to town, I'd sometimes go to his hotel and have a few games. Beat him, mostly."

"You became friends, in fact?"

"I wouldn't say that. We knew each other. But I never saw him outside of Halifax."

"And what about the adoption itself? How did that come about?"

A moment's hesitation; then a shrug. "I suppose there's no harm telling you. . . . In fact, there really isn't much to tell. He just appeared in my office one day and said he'd made a girl pregnant—a waitress, a girl in the hotel, something like that. He didn't want to marry her, but he wanted to see that the child was looked after. The question was, would I see the woman through her pregnancy and then arrange for the adoption? I agreed."

"Wasn't this a little unusual?"

"Of course. Let's say, Mr. Thorne, that I talked to Brightman for a long time about it, then talked to the woman—also at length—and *then* I agreed."

"I'm sorry. I didn't mean anything. But you did get to know the woman, Florence Raines?"

"Not really. She was a pretty blond thing, I remember. Healthy. Once the agreement was reached, I saw her in the usual way, then took the child after it was born. Beyond the medical necessities, I didn't get to know her at all." He leaned forward. "You understand, there was nothing improper about this. Even today, some girls prefer to give their babies up privately and have their doctors arrange it. Legally, it's perfectly normal . . . the only difficulty I can remember was that this woman disappeared without signing some papers, so some extra legal steps were necessary. I forget the details. In the end, it didn't make any difference."

"And you're sure that was the *only* difficulty? I'm trying to think of some problem *then* that might be coming back *now.*"

Again, Grainger leaned back in his chair; then, leaning back even further, he reached into the side pocket of his medical gown, drawing out a package of cigarettes and a blue Bic lighter. He worked the lighter, then he rocked forward, his face turned down, in concentration, toward the orange flame. All of which was perfectly ordinary; yet, to my eyes, these gestures completely transformed him. For a second I wasn't sure why, but then it occurred to me that age is the greatest disguise of them all. Now, though he didn't look any younger than he had a moment ago, I realized that he hadn't always been old. I don't mean that the persona he'd presented up to this point had been false, but it *had* been a persona: a mask called "Dr. Charlie" which time, circumstance, and convenience had made him put on. The "real" person behind this mask was much more substantial; not merely a kindly old doctor, or a cracker-barrel philosopher, but a person—among other things—who'd once had a passionate relationship to all the books in this room.

Conceivably, he wasn't entirely unaware of the effect he'd created. As he exhaled, his eyes leveled with mine and he said, "Let's not mince words, Mr. Thorne. We both know that money changed hands. Naturally I had nothing to do with it, but Brightman was a wealthy man and I'm sure he made it worth her while. Why would Florence Raines have made difficulties? Remember, the world was very different then. Most girls in her position would have felt lucky to have a Harry Brightman looking after them."

I sat back. Dr. Charlie, indeed, was nobody's fool. And of course he was right. Besides, Florence Raines couldn't be making trouble today, since she was dead. Yet, more than ever, I sensed that trouble—of some sort, somewhere—existed. Brightman had never told May about the adoption. Why not—assuming the story was as straightforward as it seemed to be? And, also assuming that it was really that simple, why should Brightman have become so concerned about it today, and why would it make him panic and flee? Yet he *had* fled. And someone had been poking around in his house . . . even in mine—at the very moment when May had been trying to reach me. Outside, the rain kept driving down, and behind us, back in the clinic, a phone started ringing. I knew I should go: but I sat there in frustrated silence. And the frustration must have shown on my face, for the old doctor said, "I'm sorry, Mr. Thorne. I wish I could be more helpful but I don't really see how." Then, with a smile—the Dr. Charlie mask was back on—he added, "Of course, when you're as old as me, you sometimes don't know how much you've got in your head, so if you want to keep asking questions . . ."

The hint was perfectly reasonable. I smiled. "You've been very patient, Doctor. I shouldn't take any more of your time . . . and despite what you say, you've been very helpful."

He nodded, and then, as I began to get up, he asked, "How do you go on from here?"

I shrugged. "Florence Raines married. She's dead herself but apparently her husband is still alive. And she had children. I can speak to them."

"You can hardly expect her children to know about this."

"No. But presumably the husband might."

His eyebrows lifted. "Even there you may be presuming too much. Most wives have a few secrets to keep from their husbands. Why would Florence Raines tell anyone what she had done? And you know—this is just something to think about—you might end up causing a great deal of pain for no reason."

I nodded; it was a valid point. "On the other hand," I said, "May Brightman is going through a great deal of pain for a very good reason—her father has vanished. And she's afraid he might have killed himself. At least Florence Raines is dead. No one can hurt her anymore."

"Perhaps. But why don't you think a bit, Mr. Thorne? I told you I didn't know Brightman well, and that's true. But I clearly knew him better than you do. If Harry Brightman didn't tell his daughter about the adoption, he probably had reasons, and good ones. And if Harry Brightman has chosen to disappear for a time, I suspect he knows what he's doing. I wouldn't tell you to mind your own business, Mr. Thorne . . . but you might give Harry a chance to mind his."

A nice speech, nicely delivered. I extended my hand. "Thank you, Doctor. I'll bear that in mind."

He came around his desk, and I followed him out through the staff room. We said goodbye in the hall. As he disappeared up some stairs, I hurried past the waiting room and the little room with the girl and the phone—the girl was still talking—and levered open the door. Outside, the rain was now falling in dense, slanting sheets. Not encouraging . . .

but then I couldn't see much encouragement anywhere. Trudging unhappily up to Gottingen Street, where I found a cab back to the
hotel—one small piece of luck—I began to consider my options. It
wasn't a very long list. Florence's children were out; even if you dis-
counted the ethical problem Grainger had raised, and even if she had
told them her secret, it was unlikely that they knew the story in the kind
of detail I needed. The lawyer Brightman had used for the petition—
R. A. Powell—might know one or two things, but it would be impossible,
coming straight in off the street, to get him to talk; I'd have to persuade
Cadogan to lay the ground for me. Which left only one other choice:
James Murdoch . . . and he was in Montreal. Should I go there? In the
hotel room, toweling myself dry, I thought about what Grainger had said
just as I was leaving. It made a lot of sense: and yet its effect on me
was probably just the opposite of what he'd intended. More than ever,
I was convinced that something was very, very wrong. Grainger had
given me a much clearer picture of Brightman, at least as he'd been in
the past; indeed, I could just imagine the young, progressive doctor—bookish, full of ideals—and the young businessman—well-traveled,
with artistic interests—getting together for their chess games. But this
was a far different image of Brightman from the one I'd been carrying
around in my head. I'd begun with the assumption that Brightman, an
old man, had fallen prey to an old man's folly: that his disappearance
would have, if you like, some conventionally comic explanation. That
assumption had been modified by my visit to his house, and now I discarded it altogether. Grainger, if only by that odd transformation I'd
witnessed, had reminded me not to be fooled by appearances; and in
his last little speech he'd done it again. *If Harry Brightman has chosen
to disappear for a time, I suspect he knows what he's doing. I wouldn't
tell you to mind your own business, but you might give Harry a chance
to mind his.* But what was Brightman's business? And if it wasn't the
business of an old man in his dotage, but that of a substantial, wealthy
man who must possess some kind of courage and imagination—witness
those early trips to Russia—why would he have botched it so badly? Because that's what must have happened. He would never, intentionally,
have upset his daughter so seriously or created a situation in which the
police—however unenthusiastically—were searching for him. Something must have gone wrong. But what? It was impossible to say . . .
but the only clue, so far, was May's original one: the adoption. Which

meant seeing James Murdoch. Which meant, in turn, my reserving a seat on the next morning's plane to Montreal.

It was about two-thirty now. Frustrated, feeling at loose ends, I phoned May: no answer. I had a coffee in the restaurant and read the history of the Sambro Light on the place mat. The rain was still teeming down. As I looked out the window, it was easy to decide not to go for a walk.

But then I had an idea; not exactly an inspiration, but it would keep me busy till tomorrow. As a little girl in Cannes, May had been briefly curious about the woman her mother had been; if I decided to tell her who her true father was—and I still hadn't made up my mind—that feeling would likely revive, and at least I could tell her where her mother was buried. Borrowing an umbrella from the doorman, I walked up to the main branch of the Public Library, where I obtained the Halifax *Chronicle-Herald* on microfilm. Florence Murdoch had died on June 12, 1971. It was a year much as I remembered, full of strikes, hijackings, Palestinians, and plummeting currencies. Among these events, her passing seemed decent, domestic, eminently respectable:

> Murdoch, Florence Esther. On Monday, at home, in Halifax. Dearly beloved wife of James Murdoch, and dear mother to John, Devon, June, William and Susan. Service and interment from West Baptist United Church, Old Guysburough Road, Wednesday, June 16. In lieu of flowers, please send donations to the church pastoral fund.

I read this through, noted the details; even noted that Florence had been involved in church affairs—the donations—and added the pastor to my list of people to speak with. But that was a long shot, and I had no intention of pursuing it then. Still, as I handed the microfilm back, it occurred to me that I might as well drive out there. I couldn't think of anything better to do, and I'd enjoy seeing more of Kipling's foggy city. Or country, as it turned out. Back at the hotel, the desk clerk showed me Old Guysburough Road on a map, and it was deep in the boondocks. This meant renting a car, but since you could do it from the hotel lobby, I decided to go on, and by four o'clock I'd set off. It was almost dark. Tacking against a modest rush hour, I made my way across town, my eyes shifting along the glistening path of the headlights.

Suburbs, as uniform as exit signs, flickered by, and then scrub farms, and then scrub bush. On Old Guysburough Road, the landscape grew even more desolate—rocks, brush, little streams. Blind tracks led off to nowhere; I caught a glimpse of tar-paper shacks in the trees. And finally, coming over a rise, I spotted the church, propped against the side of a shallow valley. Along both sides of the road, fields had been cleared and there were several small houses set up on blocks, each with a stove-pipe chimney for its space heater. A line of telephone poles wobbled into the distance, and by the ditch two children played in the rusted shell of a car. Over the entrance drive, a rickety trellis proudly pro-claimed: *West Baptist United Church.*

I turned in, parking on a dirt lawn all churned up and rutted by the parishioners' pickups. No one seemed to be around; indeed, the church looked nearly abandoned. The cement steps leading up to the main doors were cracked and crumbling; rusted metal swings, on one side of the lawn, were tied back with a rusted chain; and a picnic table, missing one leg, had fallen onto its side.

The rain was pelting down, but I still had the doorman's umbrella; getting out, I hurriedly popped it open, then slammed the door shut be-hind me. I waited a second. No one appeared. I stepped forward, my feet squelching in the mud. A path led around the side of the church. It was very dark in the shadow of the building. Overhead, the rain drummed on the tin roof and water gushed from a drainpipe as I stepped around the corner. The path was graveled here, leading to a side door, but there was no sign of a light: apparently I'd have to give up on the pastor. I stayed on the path, however, for it now swung sharp right, cut-ting through an open field and then passing among stunted trees which seemed to be the remains of an orchard. The night and the rain pressed down; despite the umbrella, I began getting wet. Head down, I hurried on along through the trees. Beyond them was a fence, with a gate; be-yond this, the graveyard and a long stretch of dark fields. Pushing the gate open, I stepped ahead. Now the path branched in a dozen direc-tions, for the cemetery was informal, almost homey, the graves laid out haphazardly. There weren't very many, and most of the stones were modest: many were plain wooden crosses, some were cast from cement. Bending forward a little—the rain deftly trickling under my collar and down my neck—I passed among them. Florence Murdoch, née Raines, was at the back. And though you could hardly call it pretentious, her stone was more substantial than most of the others—a piece of low, gray granite with a beveled edge and simple lettering:

FLORENCE ESTHER MURDOCH
1919 — 1971
"Home at Last"

In the rain and the gloom I stared down at it, just as I'd done in front of my father's grave only a few days before. Was that why I was here? It was hardly the time or place for self-analysis, though you had to wonder. . . .

But then I peered harder.

For my father's grave, year after year, was mute, ignoring the questions I put to it—while Florence's, to my surprise, eloquently answered them all.

It was a fluke, of course, my being there. But then I would have found out eventually, either from James Murdoch when I'd spoken with him—the moment I laid eyes on him—or even from the preacher. But that wasn't necessary. For now, on one side of the stone, completely spoiling its dignity, I saw an oval, silvery protrusion about six inches long. To be charitable, it looked like a large locket; to be accurate, the hood ornament of a '55 Dodge. It had a hinged lid, like the metal flaps that cover outdoor electrical outlets, and I bent forward, half kneeling, to lift this up. Underneath was a smooth plastic, or porcelain, oval—again, vaguely reminiscent of a brooch—and on this, transferred by some new miracle of mortuary science, was a color photograph of the deceased.

I stared at it, and swore under my breath.

She was a pretty blond thing, I remember. . . .

Well, not exactly.

Just possibly, Harry Brightman had been May's father—but Florence Raines, this very black woman, had never given birth to such a lily-white child.

6

I drew myself up and stepped back from the grave.

Lifting my eyes, I watched the rain glitter against the gloom. Beyond the low, crouched shadows of the headstones lay a sagging wire fence and then a muddy field, jagged with the broken stalks of last summer's corn. The fence grated and squeaked in the wind. From the field, alarmed at my presence, two old crows lurched into the air and clumsily lumbered into the dusk. They cawed twice, then disappeared.

I didn't move. For a moment I was too stunned to feel anything, even the rain. But as the numbness began to wear off, what I felt was so strong that I shuddered. I felt fear—but not my own fear, someone else's. A long-buried odor was finding its way up from this grave. Now it was loose: the smell of fear that springs from mortal danger. I looked down at the headstone. Men hide many things, from treasure to shame, but their motive is always the same—fear of loss, fear of discovery, fear of treachery, but *fear* of some kind. And what I'd discovered today was proof that someone had once been terribly afraid.

Just then I turned around. A light had come on at the side of the church. The side door swung open, a figure emerged. And in the spill of light from the door, I could see he was black. Of course. This was a black Baptist church, these mean concessions comprised some sort of black enclave, and here black Florence Raines had been brought to her grave. Bent over and clutching a plastic raincoat closed at the neck, this figure pulled the door shut behind him, then turned. At which point he saw me. All things considered—the gloom, the rain, my umbrella hoisted above the headstones—I suppose I made an arresting sight. And, indeed, he froze in his tracks. For a moment we stared at each other.

Then, just as I expected him to shout, I shook my umbrella in acknowledgment and began walking toward him. He watched me every step of
the way—through the gate, through the trees, up the path—but as I
drew closer, and my respectability became a little more evident, I could
see him relax. Gradually, his broad, chubby features assumed an expression, both solemn and welcoming, that would have told me he was a
pastor even if I hadn't caught the white flash of a collar inside his coat.

"Good evening," I said.

He nodded. "May I be of assistance? Were you looking for a particular stone? It's quite dark. . . ." He was a rotund little man, almost bald
except for a few stiff curls of white hair over his ears. His expression,
fixed and determined, both noted our difference in color and refused,
resolutely, to raise it. His suspicions of me—so his expression seemed
to say—had a completely different cause.

"Thank you, Reverend. I apologize. I'd intended to call, but there
didn't seem to be a light."

"Oh no. That's perfectly all right. This is a public place, and you're
entirely welcome. I only wondered . . . because of the hour, you see."

I nodded. He wasn't wearing a hat, and he had no umbrella, but
I could sense that he would have refused any offer to shelter under my
own.

I said, "I'm interested in a woman who's buried here, I believe a
former parishioner. Her name was Florence Murdoch."

"Yes. She did attend here. A very fine woman. I only knew her in
the last years of her life, but she was very devoted . . . to the church,
to her family. Her husband still comes to us, as do two of her daughters. . . . I take it you were a friend?"

"No. I never met her."

"Then I'm afraid I don't understand."

"It's confidential, Reverend. I'd like to tell you, but I shouldn't."

He stiffened, then frowned; and then this frown became more quizzical than angry. "Tell me," he said, "is it important—to this confidential matter—that Florence Murdoch be black?"

I hesitated. "She was, of course?"

"Of course."

"And why should that be important, Reverend?"

"I've no idea—but it was important to that other man."

"What other man?"

"He came to see me, about a week ago. And that's what he asked me—was Florence Murdoch black? He was . . . unpleasant about it. 'Black, like you,' he said. I told him, 'No; black like a Negro.' Which is the word I prefer . . . however old-fashioned it makes me."

His face turned up to me, almost challenging, while the ceaseless drum, splash, and drip of the rain filled up the silence. Another man, asking after Florence Raines. Brightman? "Was this was an older man . . . still vigorous, a big fellow, but—"

"No. He wasn't like that at all. This man was short, with red hair. I remember what he looked like."

I shook my head. "Then I don't know him."

Except I did . . . it was the red-haired ghost who'd flitted through Brightman's house while I was looking through his study.

"Well," the Reverend said, "let me tell you what I told him. Leave her alone. Let her rest in peace. If she sinned, her sins were paid for long ago."

"Reverend—"

But now he smiled and held up his smooth, pink palm. "Really, that is all I have to say. The church is closed, but if you wish . . . ? No . . . Well then, I'll say good night." And he turned, his plastic raincoat stiffly rustling, and headed down the path.

Standing there, soaked despite my umbrella, I watched him go; and as he disappeared around the corner, that odor of ancient fear came back more strongly. Another man who knew Florence Murdoch's secret . . . or was it hers at all? Poor Florence: she'd presumably been a patient of eager, idealistic Dr. Charlie. Still standing there, getting soaked, I swore softly under my breath. How shrewdly the old man had lied. In journalism, you meet more than your share of professional liars, but I suppose nothing beats the inspired amateur. His cool had been breathtaking and I'd been taken in all the way. *Let's not mince words, Mr. Thorne. We both know that money changed hands. . . .*

With another curse, I drew the umbrella tight against my head and slogged back to my car. It was full dark now; as I started the engine, the black night glimmered in the headlights and the rain flashed in the beams. There was no one about: the Reverend was gone, the road empty. Turning onto the highway, I put my foot down, impelled now by a sense of urgency that seemed fully justified by that odor of danger I couldn't dispel. I thought of May: *she'd* been afraid. Had she lied, like Grainger?

And who was this other man burrowing into Florence Raines's past? Whatever I'd thought before, everything was different now; everything had changed before that black woman's grave.

It was five-thirty when I left the church, almost six-fifteen when I reached Grainger's place. He lived on a side street, in what seemed to be a university district. His own place was modest: two stories, clapboard siding, a porch with a lot of Victorian gingerbread. No lights. I parked on the other side of the street, then hauled out my trusty brolly and crossed over. If anything, the rain was coming down harder, scratching the night with the grain of a very old photograph and spreading down the glistening street like fat in a pan. I ran up to the porch, my steps clumping. There was a fine bay window, its curtains drawn, but I could peer through a crack into a dark interior, lit only by the yellowish glow of a light on a side table. I felt sure he wasn't there, but knocked anyway, then rang the bell. Pressing my ear up to the glass, I listened to its buzz rattle in the emptiness within.

I went back to the car, dried my hands, lit up a cigarette.

Grainger wasn't here; so where could he be?

I worked it out. Despite his skill, he must have known, at the end, that I'd find out he was lying—because I'd told him I intended speaking to Murdoch, and once I'd laid eyes on *him,* the truth would be obvious. Another small point: I hadn't mentioned the fact that Murdoch was in Montreal, so Grainger would have assumed I'd be seeing him almost at once; if he wanted to do something about it, he'd have to act fast. But what could he do? If he tried to run and hide, he couldn't expect to get very far; he was an old man, with a social position, and he would have made no preparations. He might try a friend's, a hotel, maybe a cottage, or even someplace more inaccessible; but it didn't make that much difference. I could go looking for him—but I could also just wait; eventually he'd have to come back. And I thought of that. Go back to the hotel. Run a hot bath. Tomorrow, begin with the housekeeper. . . . But I didn't like it. I could still taste that odor of fear in the back of my throat, and I didn't like the dark look of the house. So, though I didn't have much hope, I put the car into gear and headed back to the clinic: it was the only other place I could check right away. Slowly, I found my way through the maze of a strange city at night: one-way streets, illegal left turns, signs that were legible only once you were past them. Eventually, almost by accident, I found the right street. In the dark, and under two inches of water, it looked no better than it had this afternoon. Dirt lawns, fenced round with old pipe, were turning to mud, and the blue glow of TV sets seeped through dingy curtains. Pulling up in front of the clinic, I saw it was dark. I splashed up to the door. A sign, printed with Magic Marker, was pinned to it: CLOSED TONITE *j penny.* I knocked anyway—there was no buzzer of course. I rattled the knob . . . nothing. I didn't like it. Places like this stayed open till all hours, and even after it officially closed, there'd be endless meetings to plot the revolution's next phase and usually someone who'd bed down on the couch. I looked again at the sign: its very presence indicated that such an early closing was out of the ordinary.

Frustrated, I stood there for a moment. But then, remembering the pregnant black woman in the waiting room, I stepped off the porch and walked around to the lane. Halfway along it, under a little peaked roof, was a side entrance: Dr. Charlie's old "surgery." It didn't seem very likely, but I told myself it was possible—a cot, a hot plate, a tin of baked beans—and so I put my head down and ran up the drive. Sheltered as I was by the clinic and the building next door, the rain wasn't so bad. I came up to the entrance. It was dark as a well. Cement steps led down. Feeling forward, I went down them, plunging from the last into ankle-deep water. It was very dark, especially under the umbrella—but I was damned if I'd put it down—and I groped ahead to the door. Which was shut. Locked. Padlocked . . . and when I pulled at the hasp, I knew it hadn't been opened in years. I waded back toward the steps . . . but that's when I heard someone come down the drive.

I stood still.

Grainger? Sharp and grinding, the steps came on quicker. And though Grainger was a spry old party, such steps couldn't be his. I pressed against the wall, and eased the umbrella shut. Coming closer, the steps paused . . . and then came forward again. And then stopped—at the top of the stairs. I held my breath. A toe, pivoting, scraped along asphalt. A second later, I heard a little *snick* and a flashlight came on. A narrow beam darted down, into my well. Found the door. Steadied against the lock . . . then winked out. It had missed me because of the angle. And then, as a yellow blotch pulsed in front of my eyes, the steps went away.

I waited a second, not quite sure which way they'd gone.

Cautiously, I edged up the stairs.

Staying in a crouch as I drew level with the drive, I looked back toward the street, but both the drive and the sidewalk were empty.

I stepped up, turning round and looking toward the back of the house.

Behind me, a car passed in the street; overhead, beyond the rain and the sound of the city, I heard the drone of an airplane. I stared into the darkness. Shadow folded in upon shadow, the rain swirling the night into tunnels and gyres; but there was no sign of anyone. I listened. Tires hissed. The plane grumbled away. I stepped forward. Rain sounds filled my ears: the metallic drumming of the drops on the flashing of the roof, a plopping drip from the eaves, the staccato splashing on asphalt . . . I stopped. I'd now reached the back of the house, where I'd sat this afternoon, talking with Grainger. I waited and listened. A downpipe emptied here with a gush and there was the softer sound of the rain on the grass of the garden. I took a single step forward. Now I could see the yard, overgrown with bushes and weeds. At the back was a high wooden wall, the back wall of a neighbor's shed or garage. A spade leaned against this, and a tipped-up wheelbarrow and a bicycle with only one wheel . . . all these objects being clearly visible in the long, distorted oblong of yellowish light spilling out from the back of the house.

I took two quick steps into the yard.

The grass came up to my knees; at once, my pants were soaked through. But now I could see the French doors at the back of Grainger's study. One of them was ajar, and a man, in a tan raincoat, was bending over the desk where Grainger had sat. . . . It took me about five seconds to decide that this figure wasn't Brightman himself, but that was four seconds too long, for now he turned and saw me. He hesitated; I didn't move. And then, quite calmly, he stepped through the doors. As he did so, his body turned to one side and the light fell on his face. I recognized him at once: it was the man I'd seen in Harry Brightman's hall, the other man who wanted to know if Florence Raines had been black. He had a thin face, his teeth were pushed forward in his mouth, and his brush-cut hair had a reddish tint. In Brightman's hall, I'd seen him for no more than a second or two, but I had absolutely no doubt—it was the same man.

Did he know me?

I wasn't sure. He had a good look at me as he came through those doors, but nothing moved in his eyes. Perhaps, to him, it didn't make any difference: for he had a gun in his hand, and guns don't encourage distinctions. I froze at the sight of it. For a second, that's all I could see, and all I could hear was the beat of my heart, now drumming so hard it drowned out the rain.

He stepped slowly toward me . . . he had to, because I was between him and the drive. And now, for an instant, his eyes met mine and I was sure he had no idea who I might be. Slowly, his shoulder brushing the back wall of the house, he edged past me. Then stopped. He was at the corner of the house; to go up the lane, he'd have to turn his back to me or walk backwards along it. He chose the former—I think he was going to run—but as he began turning, he slipped: with one foot in the muddy yard and the other on the asphalt, he did the splits between them.

He swore under his breath.

And I went for him then, two steps and a dive: a dive that took him down so easily that my momentum carried me right over the top of him. On my back, in the wet and the dark, I frantically clawed for his arm, his right hand, the one with the gun, desperately jerking it into the air before I realized the gun was long gone. Still hanging on to him, I scrambled up. He grunted, kicked . . . and then swung with his other hand, which now held a knife. Jerking his right arm, I whipped him away from me. He staggered, lunged; I whipped him round once again, and again—he was stumbling, trying to keep his feet under him—until finally, with a ripping sound, his raincoat came away in my hand. The sudden release of his weight sent me staggering backwards, the raincoat fluttering off in the dark. I fell to one knee. My breath burned in my throat, the cold rain trickled over my lips—and when I looked up, I saw he still had the knife in his hand.

Slowly, I got to my feet. Took a step back.

Useless. Because he'd only trap me in the yard . . .

But in fact he took a step sideways, to his right. Which I countered with an identical movement of my own. Then another. Two more—we were circling each other. He stopped. I stopped. I peered at his face through the darkness. His eyes darted about, looking away from me; and now, as he moved again, I realized he was edging toward his raincoat, which was spread, like Sir Walter Raleigh's cloak, across a puddle at the back of the drive. He was welcome to it—given his knife, I couldn't have stopped him in any case—and my only concern was to stay out of his way. So I took a step straight back . . . and my foot grated down on the gun.

I think he must have guessed, from the sound: for he stopped dead in his tracks and for a frozen instant we stared at each other; but then I bent over, scooped the gun up, and leveled it at him.

Flee a knife, charge a gun. . . . It sounds good, but when the barrel's pointed at you, *discretion is the better part of valor* sounds better. He took one last look toward the raincoat—I thought he still might lunge for it—and then jumped back into the darkness. Before I got my wits back, he'd ducked down the drive.

I lowered the gun. The rain fell, I could still hear that plane . . . and now it was over, the shock finally hit me: my heart started pounding as if I'd just run a mile. I waited a second, gathering myself together. Then, with my breath back, I stepped into the lane, picked up the raincoat, and stared out toward the street. With the wind, the rain, and the gleam of the streetlamps along the slick pavement, it was easy to imagine figures lying in ambush on either side of the drive. But after three soaking minutes, I was sure it was safe, and eased the hammer back on the pistol. I own a Smith & Wesson, but this was a Colt. The two makes are quite different, and I was very careful to make sure it didn't blow off my foot. Finally, when I was certain the safety was properly set, I slipped it into my pocket and then walked out to the street.

In both directions, as far as I could see in the blackness, it was empty.

I got into my car. Driving slowly up to the corner, I turned right, then cut back and forth for the next dozen blocks, but I saw nothing. Which was probably what I wanted to see. When I finally parked, and lit up a cigarette, my hand was still shaking.

Now, sitting in the dark, with the windshield wipers frantically beating at the rain, I took a look at the raincoat—apparently the prize we'd been struggling over.

It was ripped at the shoulder, but otherwise intact. An Aquascutum, though manufactured in Canada. It had an inside pocket, like a suit coat, and this contained a Parker ballpoint pen and an empty Air Canada ticket folder. In the left side pocket I discovered $12.87 in Canadian notes and coins, a crumpled Kleenex, and a brown leather key case with three keys, one with a Hertz tag. This was fun, though not very informative, but as soon as I turned the coat over and searched the right pocket,

I found something a great deal more interesting: a brown manila envelope which had obviously been taken from Grainger's desk. "Jenny" was scrawled across it, and it had already been torn open to reveal a regular letter-sized envelope inside. Clipped to this second envelope was a note: *JENNY. You'll remember my visitor this afternoon, the man I spoke to in my study. I expect he'll be back. Tell him you don't know where I am and try to get rid of him, but if he starts making a fuss, give him this envelope. I'll be gone for a week, so cancel my appointments next Friday. Don't worry about this—just do as I ask. Dr. Charlie.*

I'd been right, then. Grainger had realized I was going to discover the truth and was trying to avoid me. But at the same time, it seemed, he was prepared to give me some sort of explanation, for when I tore the second envelope open, I found half a dozen foolscap sheets, handwritten, that were addressed to me. Looking about, making sure that the black, wet street was empty, I turned on the dome light and started to read:

Mr. Thorne—

If you have this in your hands I can assume that you've now discovered that what I told you this afternoon wasn't the truth. Probably I should apologize for that, but I'm not sure that I want to. I only told those lies to fulfill a solemn pledge made many years ago and which I found, as I talked to you, I couldn't abandon. As you will have guessed, that promise was made to Harry Brightman, and perhaps he wouldn't want me to break it now. But I don't see the point of going on. Having spoken with James Murdoch, you will know our story is false, and your attempts to discover what I can easily tell you may only distress many innocent people. Besides, it was all so long ago that I hardly think it can matter.

Having said this, however, I must now disappoint you: what I'm going to tell you here isn't the truth, only the truth as I know it—and I'm certain I was told a good many lies.

Again, of course, the source of those lies was Harry Brightman, and he told them to me right in this office, where we talked this afternoon and where I'm writing this now. That was in 1939, just after the outbreak of the war. By then I'd known Brightman for a number of years, and though I'd first met him much as I told you, we were a good deal closer than I implied. I liked him, almost to the point of fascination, and I think he liked me. A number of circumstances drew us together. We were both young men pursuing conventional careers but in an unconventional way. Brightman, a businessman, was making his fortune out of the Soviet Union, and I was attempting the difficult feat of being a practicing doctor and a practicing socialist at the same time. Brightman was a great storyteller; I, an excellent listener—and the tales of his trips to the U.S.S.R. enthralled me. I wouldn't have described him as sympathetic (to the Left, I mean), but he was genuinely curious and observed what was happening in Russia with an unprejudiced eye. Thinking back, I would guess that my youthful idealism amused him, but I believe he also respected me for it. When I opened up my first clinic, he made—unasked—a large contribution.

In any case, by the autumn of 1939 we were close friends, and I suppose the story he told me, even if it was false, was the sort of story you can only tell to a friend. It all began (he said) shortly before he'd first met me, at the time of his first visits to the Soviet Union. (I can't remember the precise date, but it would have been in the mid to late twenties.) As you may know, he went there originally to purchase furs at the invitation of the state agency concerned with fur exports (Sojuzpushnina). He'd described that trip many times: his own excitement, the slow passage up the Kiel Canal to the Baltic, his arrival at the Finland Station with its ghost of Lenin. That first time, he said, there weren't many buyers, only two or three dozen from a handful of countries. Nonetheless, the whole business was of great importance to the Soviet authorities: fur was one of their only exports to the West, and was therefore one of their few sources of hard currency. Consequently, Brightman and his companions were wined and dined in great style: there were official receptions, private droshkies to take them around, side trips to Moscow, visits backstage at the Bolshoi. (Brightman always joked to me that every official he met began their meeting with a vodka toast and the presentation of a special kind of chocolate with a picture of Pushkin on the box.) This courtship apparently went on for weeks, and in the course of it Brightman met a man named Grigori Zinoviev. I assume you know a little about Soviet history, but Zinoviev was a major figure, an Old Bolshevik, a close friend of Lenin's and the first head of the Comintern. Brightman had often told me about his meetings with this man—I was a little in awe of a person who'd met such a man—but now he told me that he'd had an affair with a woman on Zinoviev's staff named Anna Kostina. This was (in 1939) the first time he'd mentioned her, but as he spoke it was clear to me that he loved her. (I still believe that he did—and I suppose that belief made it easier to believe everything else.) Their affair, he claimed, had begun on his first trip and continued on subsequent ones. The last of these had been made in 1933 or '34, and on the eve of his departure Anna Kostina had told Brightman that he had made her pregnant and that she intended to bear his child.

At this point, it's important to keep all these dates straight. Brightman was telling me all this in 1939. If his story was true, Anna Kostina would have given birth five or six years before. But during that time the Great Purge had begun—and in the first of the trials, in late 1934, Zinoviev had fallen. The details won't concern you, but he was actually tried and sentenced twice, the second time to death, and a number of his friends and associates fell with him, *including Anna Kostina.* Apparently she hadn't been executed, but had received a long sentence in what we'd now call the Gulag.

But what about Brightman's child?

This, of course, was the reason he'd come to see me. He'd long since assumed (so he said) that the child was lost, or at least that he'd never see her, but now he claimed to have received word from inside the U.S.S.R. that it might be possible to get her out. But to do so, he said, would require my help: specifically, he wanted me to provide him with the papers necessary to get the child into the country. He'd already worked out how I could do this. As it happened, I had two children of my own, one six years old, the other newborn. If I applied for a passport, submitting Brightman's photograph instead of my own, and had my two daughters included on it, Brightman could travel overseas as me and return with the child.

I agreed to do this.

It makes no difference why; I understood what I was doing, and wanted to do it.

Shortly afterwards, having received "my" passport, Brightman departed for Europe, and a few months later—early in 1940—I had the unique experience of meeting "myself" at the dockside. But I was now given quite a surprise. The child Brightman *should* have brought back was a six- or seven-year-old. In fact, the child in his arms was an infant. It was all very cunning. He had no difficulty bringing her into the country, for she merely took the part of my younger daughter rather than my older one. But was this, in fact, the child he'd originally intended to get? He said not; he claimed that it had proved impossible to bring his own child out, so instead he'd rescued the child of another Russian friend who was in some sort of political danger. Who was this friend? He wouldn't say. He merely insisted that the danger was real, and that he therefore wished to adopt the child as quickly as possible. Again, he asked for my help. I was more reluctant to give it to him—I was now convinced I'd been lied to—but I was involved so deeply that it was hard to object. I looked around for a way to do what he wanted. It seemed difficult, perhaps impossible—until we had a stroke of luck: Florence Raines. You will have guessed, in a general way, her involvement, but I will tell you the details if only to ensure that you leave her family alone. In 1939 she was a young black woman who'd been my patient for several years. In the usual way, she came to me and I discovered that she was pregnant. This calamity, though common enough, was especially hard on her because she had a job with the Board of Education (a job other people might have despised but which seemed an excellent one to her) and she would lose it automatically on "morals" grounds. Desperate, she came to me a few days later and asked for an abortion. I agreed—until a further examination convinced me that it would have been dangerous, for medical reasons. I helped her, though, as best I could, providing a letter to her supervisor requiring her to take an extended medical leave. This was accepted. Accordingly, she went to stay with her mother, who lived a little outside of town, and there I brought her child into the world. Since the grandmother was prepared to keep the child with her, this seemed to cope with the problem and I forgot about it. Then, a few weeks after Brightman's return from Europe, Florence called me. Her child was very sick, perhaps dying. I immediately went to her house, where I discovered that the grandmother had been very ill with the flu and the child had contracted it. A day later, despite my best efforts, it succumbed. I saw my opportunity at once and without even consulting Brightman I took it. Of course, I had to break the law to do so. Normally, when someone dies, the doctor prepares a death certificate, which is submitted to the local authorities, who then issue a burial order. But I didn't want Elizabeth Raines to die; not officially. I explained to Florence that the normal burial of her child would probably lead to her own exposure, and that if she "looked after" the burial on her own, I would ignore the requirement of the death certificate. Florence agreed immediately, though it took her longer to square the grandmother. She accomplished this, however, and so I acquired, as it were, a bona fide infant identity. I presented it to Brightman. He was leery at first, but soon saw the virtue of the solution chance had now offered us. He insisted (sensibly) that Florence be kept in the dark, thereby necessitating a "public" adoption procedure, but even this was a help—it removed any mystery about his new daughter's identity. She would be provided, so to speak, with a genealogy that would lead everyone away from her real one (whatever it was). The only problem seemed to be the mother's color. But that was really no problem at all. Race was not a part of a child's birth records in Nova Scotia, and so as long as no one met Florence or any other member of her family (a sheriff, say, serving a paper), we'd be all right. Now Brightman's money came into play. He handled this part himself, so I don't know the details, but both Florence Raines and her mother disappeared. (I'd assumed forever; until you told me, I had no idea that either had come back to Halifax.) And so, some little time afterwards, the adoption went through.

The above, Mr. Thorne, is everything I know about this matter. Once the adoption was complete, my contacts with Brightman became infrequent, and I haven't seen him at all since 1945.

I have no idea why he has now disappeared.

Let me also say that I'll answer no more questions about this. I have written this in my own hand, so it constitutes a "confession"—you should believe it for this reason alone—and if you present it to the police or a Crown Attorney I might be obliged to answer to them, but I won't answer to you. For me, having stated everything that I know about it, the matter is closed.

Still, I have thought about this for a very long time, and as a last word I suppose I might as well give you my theory as to who the child was. I assume that some of what Brightman told me was true; it was a good lie, and the best lies always contain some of the truth. He did go to Russia, after all; I'm still certain he had an affair with Anna Kostina (though the child couldn't be hers); and I'm sure he did get to know many men, like Zinoviev, in the senior Communist leadership. So I suspect that Brightman's daughter was (is) the child of one of those men—someone who believed he would soon fall victim to Stalin's Terror. Of course, that doesn't much narrow the field, but as a theory it fits most of the facts. I hope it's true. If it is, you may agree that neither Brightman nor myself has cause to feel any shame.

Charles Grainger, M.D.

The rain drummed on the roof of the car, the smoke from my cigarette curled back from the window, and with a soft, sibilant hiss, a car drifted by down the street. . . . I lifted my eyes from Grainger's letter, and then, looking through my own ghostly reflection into the glittering night, I felt something like awe—an astonishment so complete that it left me dumbfounded. I'd never known anything like it. His story was extraordinary in itself, but the circumstances by which it had come into my hands—on this cold, rainy night; in this dark little city—seemed to lift it into the message-in-a-bottle category. Revolutionary Russia . . . Zinoviev, chief of the Comintern . . . a child snatched from the jaws of the Red Terror . . . even if it wasn't true, you couldn't ask for anything more melodramatic. Question: who was May Brightman? Answer: a fascinating political mystery.

I stubbed out my cigarette. Lit another. Put the car into gear. And then for ten minutes I simply drove around the dark streets. Did I believe it? Was this the truth, as Grainger knew it? And how much of this "truth" was a lie? Above all: who was the man in the alley?

Like waves on a beach, the questions began piling up and they were no easier to catch hold of than the surf. But as I made my way back to the hotel, I began to grasp a few things. I had a clearer picture of Grainger, to begin with. As he himself had said, the best lies contain some of the truth, and that went for the lies he'd told about his own past. He'd been "idealistic," all right, and definitely "a bit of a socialist":

so idealistic, and so much a socialist—I was prepared to bet—that he'd been a member of the Communist Party with connections that went straight back to their embassy. Was that too big a leap? I didn't think so. Lots of Communists become kindly old men. And some coincidences are too great to ignore. Brightman, doing business with Russia . . . Grainger, the accidental "socialist" friend. No, it was too good to be true. The Russians, inevitably, would have been curious about Brightman—and they would have taken steps to satisfy their curiosity. Grainger was that step, and I had no doubts at all that the original meeting between the two men had been at his initiative. Indeed, it was even possible that Grainger stood at the center of all I'd discovered. *He* could have had the friend in Russia; Brightman could simply have been doing his bidding. Yet, at this point, I drew back: I wasn't prepared to cast Brightman in so minor a role—*he'd* adopted May, after all; *he'd* disappeared; these ghosts had come back to haunt *him.* As well, tilting the balance, there was one other thing. . . .

Or perhaps it was two; or even three.

That evening, as I changed out of my soaking clothes, sipped a long whiskey, and watched the lights crawl back and forth over Halifax harbor, I kept coming back to them. *May.* She was number one. How much had she known? If she'd known nothing at all, then the last few days had been a proof of woman's intuition, par excellence. And I wasn't sure I believed it. Perhaps she hadn't known what I'd find, but she'd known I'd find something. She'd run me up the flagpole, then waited to see who'd salute. Why? Why not tell me the truth? But this led to problem number two: me. That incident with my mail was still working away at the back of my mind; I'd been involved, somehow, even before I'd known there was something to be involved *with.* But why was I involved? Why had May turned to me in the first place? Blessed as I am with a reasonable ego, it's probably not a question I would have troubled to ask except for another coincidence—but that was a big one: Russia. At first, Brightman's connection with the country had seemed a peripheral question, adding a dash of color to his character. But now it seemed central. *And Russia was central to my life as well.* I didn't need Grainger's little lectures about Zinoviev or the Purge Trials—those subjects were my bread and butter. Wasn't it passing strange that someone like myself should have stumbled into this peculiar eddy of Soviet history? But that raised point number three . . . because maybe this history wasn't so ancient. Sitting there, my feet up on the heater and the whiskey warming me inside, I played through that scene in the alley, and there were no doubts left. When the red-haired man had taken his tumble, he'd uttered a curse—a curse I'd recognized at once, but only because I'm fluent in Russian, *moy tvoyou mat!* being more or less their equivalent of "motherfucker." A Russian: a real, live Soviet Russian . . .

What was he doing?

What could he want?

Why would he care about Florence Raines, or what Harry Brightman had been up to in 1940?

Twice more, I read through Grainger's letter. Over and over, I kept asking the questions. By eleven-fifteen I hadn't found any answers. After that, it didn't seem to make any difference.

The phone rang.

It was May, about to go into hysterics.

They'd found her father, dead, in Detroit.

PART TWO

GEORGI DIMITROV

Sitting in Moscow, the controllers of the Third International—which is only an instrument of the Soviet government and is entirely dependent on Soviet financial support—consider themselves, by reason of the money they distribute, the absolute lords and masters of the Communist parties they sustain.

—Karl Kautsky, *Die Internationale und Sowjetrussland,* 1925

7

He spoke deliberately, with the patient condescension of a professional coping with a layman. "Mr. Thorne," he said, "have you ever seen someone who's killed himself with a shotgun?"

I am moving in a dream. I float, suspended in the fiery sunlight. Sweat burns on my skin, my eyes sting, and when I emerge from the forest onto a road, dust cakes against my lips. Beyond, the woods open up, and now I start running again. He must have come here, I think, he must have come here. The trees are larger, the sunlight falling in long shafts between them. Finally I see a tumbled-down shack. That's where he is. He must be inside. And so I run faster. And then, glistening—

"Yes," I said. "I have."

Katadotis, a lieutenant of detectives in the Detroit police force, raised his eyebrows. Avoiding embarrassing questions, I quickly added, "It was a hunting accident, Lieutenant. Not very pleasant. So I know what you're talking about, and I appreciate your concern for Miss Brightman. I just want you to understand that I never met Brightman and it's stretching things to describe me as a friend. Accepting that, I'd be happy to identify his body."

He hesitated, convenience and duty struggling together in his mind, and I glanced at my watch. It was now twenty past two. Early that morning, I'd flown from Halifax to Toronto, and then May and I had come on to Windsor, the small Canadian city across the border from Detroit. For two hours now, we'd been shuffled from office to office in the Beaubien Street headquarters of the Detroit police, waiting, answering questions, filling in forms, waiting again. To begin with, May had stood up to it well, but finally she'd broken down. No tears, no hysterics: she simply couldn't take any more and had lapsed into a sort of blank listlessness. A policewoman had now taken her off and a doctor was supposed to see her. As for myself, I was naturally distressed for her, but I was also feeling considerable frustration and resentment—mainly at my own impotence. When May had first called me in Charlottesville, I hadn't thought there'd be anything to do; then, in Halifax, I thought I really *was* doing something. And now, no matter what I did, it didn't make any difference.

Wearily, I watched Katadotis' face. He was about fifty, somewhat old for his rank: a patrolman who'd made it onto the detective squad at the very last moment. His fingers, short and stubby, seemed uncomfortable among the papers on his desk, and his three-piece suit was a shade too tight. As he shrugged, finally making up his mind, his shirt collar pressed into the flesh of his neck.

"I don't think it makes much difference, Mr. Thorne. I wouldn't want to sound crude, but he took both barrels of a twelve-gauge shotgun right in the face, so there's not much left to identify. I don't see that we need trouble Miss Brightman. All I need is someone to go through the motions and sign my form."

"All right. I can do that."

"There's no doubt, you see. It's him . . . and it's suicide."

Yes. He was right on both scores. There weren't any doubts—none in their minds at least, and by this time I was even ready to set mine aside. What I'd discovered in Halifax was moot, relevant only to the motivation of an act whose details themselves were indisputable. The Savage-Stevens shotgun that had killed Harry Brightman had been purchased at a Grosse Pointe sporting-goods store with his Visa card. There was no doubt about his signature on the form, and no doubt too about the note he had left. Written in his own hand, it had been addressed to May. *You know how much I love you, but I can't go on. For me, this really is easier. Your loving father, Harry.* He had left this, neatly folded, on the dashboard of the car, and must then have maneuvered himself and the long gun into a practical posture of self-annihilation—the gun braced against the door on the driver's side, his body half reclining on the passenger seat. Finally, overcoming the difficulty faced by all shotgun suicides (Hemingway used his toes, I believe; my father, a stick), he had jabbed a tightly rolled copy of the De-

troit *News* against the gun's trigger. Death—obliteration—must have
been instantaneous.

Taking a breath, I asked, "Will there be an inquest?"

"That'd be routine, Mr. Thorne."

"What about May? Would she have to attend?"

"You understand, that wouldn't be for me to decide. I'd guess
they'd want her to, but probably they'd be satisfied with a deposition."
He shrugged. "She's Canadian, remember. The M.E. can issue a sub-
poena, but we can't enforce it."

I nodded.

He cleared his throat. "Of course, there'll be one or two other for-
malities as well."

"Such as?"

"Well, there's the matter of Mr. Brightman's remains, to begin
with. Pending the inquest, we hang on to them, but once he's done we
release them."

"How long would that be?"

"That'd be hard to say. I just wouldn't want her making arrangements—setting a date—till she's all clear with us."

Arrangements. For a second, I didn't understand what he was talking about. But of course he meant the funeral; and of course I'd have
to support May through it.

"Another point, Mr. Thorne, just so there's no misunderstanding.
We only release Mr. Brightman's remains here in Detroit, so she'll have
to get them over the line on her own. I know there's a certain procedure
to go through, but you'd want to talk to Canadian customs."

I closed my eyes: I could just imagine the bureaucratic niceties involved in transporting a corpse across an international boundary. But
I nodded. "I'll look after it, Lieutenant." This promise was a penance:
an apology to May, and Brightman's shade, for my uncharitable
thoughts—and for not having found him before he died. "Is there anything else?"

Katadotis shuffled papers on his desk, his eyes screwing into a frown
and his lips making small, compressive movements as if he was trying
to determine some taste. At length, he selected a form and peered at
it, holding it a little away from himself: he needed glasses but was
too proud to wear them. He said, "That's about everything, except for
the car."

"What about the car?"

"According to this, they're done with it. We could release it right now and you could take it straight back with you."

"Lieutenant, I sincerely doubt that Miss Brightman wants to return to Toronto in that particular vehicle."

His frown was full of understanding. "I guess not. I was just thinking that it'd save you a trip."

Brightman, it had turned out, had killed himself in the front seat of his Mark VII Jaguar saloon—a model, if I remembered correctly, that was about as large and conspicuous as the *Queen Mary*. In a way, the car was now a mystery all on its own. How could May have forgotten about it? The police had found one car, a Buick, in the garage of Brightman's house, but May had never mentioned the Jaguar. She claimed he never drove it and garaged it miles from his home—it had just slipped her mind. Now I cursed the thing under my breath. "Couldn't one of your men drive it back?"

"We wouldn't want to take that responsibility, Mr. Thorne. It would go against policy." Then he brightened. "But supposing you did want to take it back, I'd probably be able to detail a policewoman to go with Miss Brightman. That is, if a doctor would sign she couldn't travel alone."

Or she could hire someone in Toronto to come and fetch it . . . except I knew I wouldn't let her; in the end, I'd get it myself. I sighed. "Perhaps I should discuss it with her."

He drew the telephone toward him, his huge hand almost swallowing up the receiver. He dialed very deliberately, his stubby fingers carrying each numeral through to the stop, then releasing it with great care. He made three calls: the last of these—a source of satisfaction rather than embarrassment—determined that May was sitting right outside his door. We rose. His office was merely a cubicle within a larger partition, its walls formed from varnished wood and frosted glass like the principal's office in an old-fashioned high school. Six desks took up most of the space. At one of them, feet up, arms spread wide, a detective was reading a newspaper, while a uniformed patrolman scribbled away at another. I crossed the room. There was a wooden bench in a corner for visitors and May was waiting there. Her face was terribly drawn. She was wearing an ancient navy blue suit, and this, combined with her long hair—like a pretense of youth that has failed—made her look all the more haggard and old. I sat down beside her. On the far side of the wall, someone laughed heartily. In the distance, a phone began ringing. Then stopped. I took her hand and whispered, "How are you doing?"

She managed a smile. "Better. I let him give me something. I'm sorry. All of a sudden . . ."

"That's okay. Just take it easy. We're almost finished, but there are still one or two details. I'm going to have to identify your father's body."

She looked at me, then glanced at Katadotis, who was pretending to be busy on the far side of the room. "You can't," she whispered. "You never met him."

"Don't worry, they understand. We've worked it all out."

Her look faltered, and she turned away. "I don't know, Robert. Dear God, I should at least—"

"It will be better like this, believe me." I hesitated. "But we have to decide what to do about the car."

She closed her eyes now: I was afraid she might begin crying again. "I feel so sick about that. If only I'd told them . . ." I held her hand. There wasn't much I could say. If she'd remembered the car, the police might have found him. And if only I'd called out to my father—just once—he might have stopped. Yes. That was true. But it's also true that if people want to kill themselves, they'll find a way. . . . I was suddenly very tired. I leaned back until my head rested against the partition. It trembled slightly as someone came in. This was another detective, black, carrying a Styrofoam cup of coffee. A phone began ringing in another room. Out in the hall, someone was whistling. I caught Katadotis giving me a look, but then he glanced away. For him, I thought, this scene was routine, and all our terrible emotions were as familiar as the highway signs on the road he took home every night. A feeling of unreality passed over me. I thought about May. *Why hadn't she remembered the car?* And the question I'd asked last night in Halifax came back again. *How much of this had she known from the very beginning?* But none of that made any difference now—because this was the end. Besides, we were all liars here. We were all acting parts. May was the Grieving Daughter, I was the Concerned Friend, Katadotis was the Dutiful Bureaucrat. But what we actually felt probably had little to do with Harry Brightman. I wondered if May wasn't feeling relief; at least the suspense was finally over. Maybe she even felt vindicated: everyone had doubted her, but now all her fears had proved true. As for myself, Brightman had almost passed out of my mind in the past twelve hours—if he had any emotional reality at all, it was only because of the peculiar correspondence his death had with my father's. And Katadotis, behind his concern, only wanted to be rid of us as fast as possible.

Beside me, May cleared her throat, but her voice was still rough. "What about the car?" she whispered.

"We have to get it back to Toronto. They'll release it now if we'll take it away. I could drive it back to your place and they'd send a police-woman with you on the plane."

She thought for a moment, then nodded. "All right . . . but I don't want anyone with me. You drive the car, but I'll go by myself."

"You shouldn't. Not alone."

"I'm all right now. I'll go over to Windsor and take the train. I'd like that, I think. I'd have time to pull myself together." She touched my hand. "But you're sure you don't mind, Robert? You've done so much already, I feel badly. . . ."

This appeal—given what I'd been thinking—only sharpened my pangs of conscience. In fact, I wasn't at all sure that she should be travel-ing alone, and I now imagined catastrophe piling upon catastrophe, with May wandering around empty train stations overcome by hysterics. On the other hand, it was clear to me that I was going to end up dealing with the car one way or the other and I preferred doing so now. The whole business was over, I told myself, I might as well get it over *with*.

I levered myself up and crossed the room to Katadotis. "I'll take the car," I told him, "but she wants to go back alone."

His eyes flickered over my shoulder, then turned glassy. "She proba-bly knows best, Mr. Thorne."

"Yes. But get a car to take her across the border."

"No problem there."

He went into his office. I helped May on with her coat, and when Katadotis returned we all went outside. November was here; there was a wintry chill in the air and the sunshine was brittle as glass. In silence, feeling a little awkward, we stood together inside the carved stone en-trance of the headquarters building and stared out at the street. Then a scout car—that's what they call them in Detroit—pulled up at the curb and Katadotis motioned us into the wind. May took my arm as we went down the steps, leaning on me so hard that I had to stiffen myself.

She was no mystery now . . . she was an exhausted, middle-aged woman whose father was dying over and over and over again—but she still couldn't believe it. I said, "Listen, are you sure you're going to be all right?"

She kissed me lightly on the cheek. "Bless you, Robert. Please don't worry."

"I'll probably be back tonight, but late."

She nodded, then smiled almost sheepishly. "I don't know what to say, Robert. If you hadn't been here I don't know how I would have got through this."

"Forget it. I'll see you tonight."

She gave me another quick kiss, then nodded at Katadotis and got into the car. Almost solemnly, Katadotis and I watched the car disappear, but as soon as it did I could feel his mood shift. Now, man to man, we could get down to business.

And what a business it was.

"If you'll just follow me, Mr. Thorne, we can walk to the morgue."

We headed down Beaubien. I hadn't been in Detroit for years, but the place seemed even more desolate than I remembered. The streets were deserted. The buildings around us were like the ruins of some earlier, greater civilization, long since overwhelmed. Only by lifting your eyes above the cheap aluminum storefronts and street-level squalor could you see the remains of past glories: skyscrapers from the twenties and thirties, many of them stone, their façades elegantly carved, their proportions supremely confident. Now most of their windows were boarded up and behind the grimy glass of others I read faded, despairing signs advertising bargain-basement rents. I felt depression creep over me—from this town; from this errand. We turned a corner, onto Lafayette. The morgue was across from the Water Board, behind Sam's Cut Rate Drugs. Katadotis signed me in and I followed him down a hall and through some doors to a long, half-lit, white-tiled room where the temperature was always 38 degrees Fahrenheit—just as it is in morgues all over the world. The banks of stainless-steel crypts, behind meat-locker doors, lined the walls. Waiting for Katadotis to scrounge up some official, I started to count them, remembering that night in Brightman's study when I'd counted his pictures. Yes—there was the true reason for my depression: I'd never discovered their secret, and Brightman, occupying one of the 186 slabs before me, had rendered all my questions irrelevant. Except, it turned out, he wasn't there at all. Katadotis came bustling back with a frown on his face. "There's been a screw-up, Mr. Thorne. They've still got him downstairs."

He led me outside, to an elevator. Descending a floor, we stepped into a large, low basement room. Fluorescent lights gave off a wan blue haze and the tiles were a dirty-brown color. Every sound seemed to echo in the chill air. Four steel tables, like a line of perspective, were spaced through the room, with three men grouped around the one farthest away. I could hear a low murmur: "Kidney, 156 grams . . . spleen, 333 . . ."

Katadotis turned grim. "Sorry, Mr. Thorne. No reason you should have to go through any of this."

I could have told him I'd done the obligatory stint as a police reporter, but that would have been bravado. He marched off. I grew conscious of a wet, washed smell in the air and realized I wasn't trying too hard to breathe. I licked my lips: but you could taste that smell too. I watched Katadotis consult with the men around the table and after a moment he beckoned. Unhappily, legs stiff, I crossed the room. Coming up to the table I told myself not to look, but of course you do: a corpse, half covered in a baby-blue plastic sheet. But at least it wasn't Brightman—I wouldn't have to look at his guts—for now Katadotis stepped around the table and gestured me beyond it. Here, pushed casually into a corner, was a wheeled stretcher. Katadotis murmured, "I don't know how this happened, Mr. Thorne. They should have sent him up hours ago."

I stared down. Brightman was encased in a body bag, a heavy green vinyl bag like a suit bag. As Katadotis began to work back the zipper, I felt slightly sick. I looked away. The zipper stuck. With a grunt, Katadotis gave it a yank. I forced my eyes back. But he must have worked the zipper the wrong way, or possibly the body had been put in upside down; in any case, my first view of Harry Brightman in person consisted of his ankles and feet: stiff, splayed out, the toes separated and curved like claws.

"Jesus Christ," Katadotis muttered, and zipped him back up. But somehow the absurdity of all this relieved my feelings and I relaxed. Struggling with the zipper, Katadotis tried again, but there seemed to be no choice: he had to reveal the whole body to show me the head.

Skinny: ribs like blue shadows under the skin.

Shriveled: an intricate patina of wrinkles where the neck merged with the chest.

A smaller man than I'd expected . . .

Harry Brightman, taken by May Brightman with her own Brownie, Georgian Bay, Aug. 1, 1949.

I tried to summon up that photograph, like a ghost, to see how it fitted this late corporeal home, but in thirty years Brightman had changed. The hair, though, was more or less right, still thick, an indeterminate brownish-gray color. As for the rest of his face . . . there was scarcely anything there. For one ghastly instant, I was back in that woods, looking down at my father. But then that passed. No, this mess had nothing to do with me. It had nothing to do with anyone now.

Steadying my voice, I said, "He must have held the gun away from his face."

Katadotis, surprised at this professional observation, gave me a look. "That's it. We figure five, six inches at least. They do it like that if they want to wipe themselves right off the face of the earth."

Was that what my father had wanted? Another moot question: as unanswerable here as it was in front of his grave. I nodded. "All right, Lieutenant."

Katadotis took up his clipboard. Holding it a little away from himself, he intoned, "Do you, Robert Thorne, to the best of your knowledge and belief, identify the human remains you now see before you as those of Harold Charles Brightman?"

"I do." My voice sounded ridiculously solemn, but Katadotis nodded happily and filled in his form. "If you could just sign here, Mr. Thorne . . ."

I scrawled.

"Great. That's it."

Eyes front, we made our way out. We rode the elevator in silence, though Katadotis gave me one shifty look, as if mildly embarrassed—perhaps he was wondering if I'd noticed that he'd neglected to zip Brightman back up. But my own performance, I decided, didn't give me the right to criticize others, and when the elevator jerked to a stop, I made straight for the open air. Fussing with his coat, Katadotis said, "Better she didn't have to go through that, Mr. Thorne."

"Yes."

"Anyway, you wait here a minute and I'll get a car. Then we'll head out to the pound."

He walked away. Turning my back to the wind, I got a cigarette going. So that was the end of Harry Brightman. There was nothing anyone could do to him—or that I could do for him. And perhaps it was all for the best. I looked at my watch. Getting on toward three. I probably wouldn't get away until four, and I guessed that Toronto was a good three hours away. So say seven-thirty. Not that it made any difference—I'd have to spend the night at May's anyway—but if she was feeling all right, I'd go home tomorrow. Yes. Go home, then come back for the funeral—expensive, but I'd prefer it. Get this out of my mind, get back to work. . . . But then I swore under my breath. The trouble was, I didn't want to get back to work, I wanted to find out what had happened to Harry Brightman. Fact: someone had broken into my house and gone through my mail. Fact: someone had broken into Brightman's the night I'd been there. Fact: that same person, a *Russian,* had pointed a gun at me last night in Halifax. All of this had to mean something. But that meaning, whatever it was, kept running up against the last fact: Brightman had killed himself. I'd pushed Katadotis and an earlier detective—the one who'd actually conducted the investigation—about as hard as I could and there appeared to be no chance of foul play. Conceivably, someone might have forced Brightman to write that note, but he'd bought the gun of his own free will: the clerk remembered him and claimed that the purchase was entirely normal. What I'd discovered was probably connected with Brightman's killing himself, but, now that he'd done so, it didn't make much difference. Nothing could bring him back now. And even if he'd been blackmailed or otherwise hounded to death, discovering the reason, even the person who'd done it, wouldn't do him any good and might only hurt May.

Tossing my cigarette into the gutter as Katadotis pulled up, I got in beside him. No, I thought, there was nothing to do but resign myself, sit back, and watch this miserable city slip by. The place matched my mood and as we turned down toward the river, something of this must have shown on my face, for Katadotis grunted, "Quite a town, Mr. Thorne."

I kept my voice neutral: it was his home, after all. "Everyone says it's a lot better than it used to be."

A smile flickered. "Mr. Thorne, my father came here fifty years ago to work on Henry Ford's line, and he thought it was paradise. Now it's like something you pick up on your shoe."

I wasn't going to give him an argument. We turned onto Jefferson, broad, empty, and desolate. We passed blocks of low, anonymous buildings: cheap furniture stores; liquor stores; warehouses, abandoned and filthy. Further on, set well back from the road, I saw a large apartment block, a sign in front of it advertising "Elegant and *Secure* Living." All the faces on these streets were black, though beyond lay Grosse Pointe with its lily-white Park, Farms, Woods, and Shores. But long before this we turned onto St. Jean, part of a veritable war zone. Down the right-hand side of the street stood the empty, burned-out shells of small frame houses. A whole neighborhood had been razed—the fire next time had been *this* time, and I asked, "That's not still left from the riot?"

"Sure. And collecting a little insurance."

Porches leaned; window frames dangled; tongues of soot licked up walls. The sidewalks had been abandoned and thistles and weeds were invading the street. Bouncing and heaving, the car lurched over ruts in the ruined road. On the left, a chain link fence appeared, with the auto pound beyond. Signs flashed by. KEEP OUT! *Premises TV Monitored* VIOLATORS WILL BE PROSECUTED   TOW TRUCKS ONLY ALLOWED IN YARD PARK CAR ON STREET   WALK IN! I began to understand why they'd wanted to release the car today—in this neighborhood, no one wanted responsibility for an antique Jaguar any longer than necessary.

Ignoring the signs, Katadotis turned in at the gate and drew up beside a small shack. I waited while he went inside. A smell of exhaust and burned rubber tainted the air; a winch whined in the distance. Like fossilized bones of the creatures for whom they were named—cougars, mustangs, bobcats, ramchargers—the remains of thousands of cars were scattered everywhere and whole body shells, flattened, were stacked up like hides. It was a Pop Art masterpiece, a landscape of the surreal; and since the cars impounded for traffic offenses were arranged in rows and segregated by make, the place even had the peculiar order of certain dreams. *Motown U.S.A.* The perfect expression of the place, I decided, was indeed a museum of road junk.

Katadotis reappeared, accompanied by a mechanic dressed in overalls.

"This is Jerry, Mr. Thorne."

I nodded, and Jerry said, "That's some kind of car you got, Mr. Thorne, but I'll be glad when you take it. Nothing left but the drive train, you leave it here a couple more nights."

I gave him another nod and he turned, leading us confidently into the landscape of this strange world: mountains of tires, valleys of broken glass, defiles of stacked-up batteries and radiators. Brightman's Jaguar was way at the back, and had already been assimilated to the Pop-Dali style of the place. To its left was an enormous pile of old wheel rims; behind it, arranged in an arc, were a dozen black motorcycles. Only a naked lady, reclining on the car's vast hood, was required to complete the ad for some elegant whiskey.

Katadotis shook his head mournfully. "It's a real shame, Mr. Thorne. If she'd told us he was driving that car, we'd have picked him up the minute he came over the border."

I stared at the car. As a boy, I'd been crazy about cars, knew them all, and seeing this model again—not uncommon on the embassy circuit—I recognized it at once. A Mark VII, circa 1955. A stripped-down version, with an aluminum body, had won at Le Mans. It was painted white and truly enormous, its lines rounded and flowing—a rich man's horseless carriage from an era when liners still plied the Atlantic.

"It seems to be missing some hubcaps."

Jerry grinned. "Yeah. And one of the guys must have cut the Jaguar out of the hood. The radiator'd go next."

Fishing keys from his pocket, he opened the door and slid behind the wheel. There was a choke, of course. And a starter button. But these antiques were still working and the engine caught first time, idling with true British discretion. Jerry got out and patted the roof. "Runs like the lady she is. Should look under the hood. He kept her real nice."

Yet May had forgotten the car's very existence . . . you couldn't help thinking this. But she had no use for cars; all the time I'd known her, she'd only driven Volkswagen Beetles. This great boat just hadn't registered.

Katadotis stepped forward, holding a large manila envelope toward me. "The contents of the glove compartment, Mr. Thorne. You have to sign for them, and of course for the car itself." As I took it from him, he handed me a form and I read it through—finding no mention of compensation for hubcaps or hood ornaments. But I signed it anyway—"received in good order." Katadotis went on, "That just leaves us one problem, Mr. Thorne. The registration was in his wallet and we have to keep that . . . personal effects of the deceased. What I did, I had them make a photostat and then I wrote you this note. If anyone still doesn't like it, have them call me."

"I'll do that, Lieutenant."

I stepped forward warily and slid onto the seat, halfway intimidated at the prospect of driving this monster. When I took a breath, my nose filled with the smells of leather, polish, wax—the fat, fruity smell of rich car. I looked around. The carpet on the passenger side was stained, and there was another stain—you could see that someone had tried to towel it off—on the roof above the window. Other than that, however, it was clean enough: real nice, as Jerry would say. In fact, as I sat there, I realized how beautifully the car had been cared for. The huge dashboard, probably walnut, was lovingly polished, and there wasn't even dust on the gauges. Brightman had loved this machine: it made sense that he'd chosen to end his life here.

Katadotis leaned through the window. "You okay, Mr. Thorne?"

"Yes. Thank you, Lieutenant."

"Well, I'm sorry that we had to meet under these circumstances, but you've been a great help, believe me, Mr. Thorne. You've been a real good friend to Miss Brightman."

We shook hands. Jerry shouted directions. I eased off the clutch. . . . As the transmission took hold, it was as if a great locomotive was delicately nosing me forward. I held my breath; hung on to the wheel. Turned right at the tires. Right again at the door panels. Left at the fence. I reached the gate, still in first gear, then daringly shifted to second as I started down St. Jean. How bizarre this all was. I was Churchill, touring the lines after D-Day. Or James Bond: all around me were black townships in South Africa where diamond smugglers were working. . . . I turned left onto Jefferson. For the first time, I put my foot down a little, and switched up into third. The Jag moved as if in a dream, with no sense of effort or strain. I decided to count my blessings. Tomorrow, I'd be home in Charlottesville. In a month, this would all be forgotten. All those unanswered questions were frustrating, but I told myself to be philosophical. As a journalist, you learn that 90 percent of your questions never get answered, and your best stories are never turned out of the typewriter—which may be the greatest blessing of all. So I relaxed. Checked my watch. Three forty-five. . . . I hadn't eaten since this morning, on the plane, and I was more than a little hungry. As between Detroit and Windsor, I know where I'd rather live, but when it came to restaurants, I wondered if I wasn't better off here. Besides, looming up on my left were the towers of the Renaissance Center, the massive hotel and office complex that's supposed to "revitalize" downtown Detroit. I knew I'd find something in there, and so I ponderously turned the great car and rolled sedately down an access ramp to a parking lot. I found a spot . . . and then, despite my philosophizing, I delayed. Lighting a cigarette, I tore open the envelope Katadotis had given me, searching for one last hope, some clue the police might have missed. But there was very little inside, and certainly no revelations; nothing to prevent me kissing Harry Brightman goodbye: just a government map of Ontario, an old Rand McNally map of the New England states, and a membership in the Canadian Automobile Association that had expired in 1968. . . . I tossed them back where they'd come from, a glove compartment that was the size of most trunks.

And then a face leaned down toward the window.

I rolled it down.

"Mister?"

It was a young black man—the attendant, I realized, who'd let me in at the gate.

"Yes?"

"I got an urgent call for you, up in the booth."

"I don't understand. A telephone call?"

"Yessir. The man said, the man in the big white car that just came through."

"What's his name?"

The black kid looked impatient. "Your name's Brightman, isn't it? He just said to go fetch you."

"Hang on," I said, "I'll be there in a second."

8

"Mr. Brightman?"

"Yes. I'm Brightman."

"But I know it is you, Mr. Thorne. I only wished to get your attention."

The voice was male, and the accent was Russian.

"Who are you?"

"Never mind, Mr. Thorne. We've never met—but now I think that we should."

"I'm not so sure. Perhaps we already have."

A pause. Then: "It is interesting that you say that, Mr. Thorne. But I assure you we've never so much as laid eyes on each other."

And I believed him—it wasn't the Russian from Halifax. But he must have been following me, whoever he was; it was the only way he could have known I was here. I looked around. The booth was only four feet by eight, but was nonetheless fairly substantial: baseboard heaters; built-in coat locker; a shelf with a portable television—Monty Hall was dealing away in full color. There were tinted-glass windows on all four sides, and I knew he had to be close by, but there wasn't much I could see: the booth was on the downslope of a hill, so I could just make out the tops of the cars passing along Jefferson while the far side of the road was completely hidden from view.

"Mr. Thorne?"

"Yes. I'm here."

"I am surprised you are not more interested. I can tell you everything, Mr. Thorne. How it was done. What has happened to Brightman. Everything."

"I'm listening."

"No. It is better to meet face to face."

Russia. Brightman had been there, I had lived there, that man in Halifax, and now . . . I said, "There might be other things besides Brightman to talk about."

"Oh yes. Many things."

"Such as?"

"Whatever you wish."

"You're Russian. Maybe we should talk about that."

"If you like. We can talk about anything. . . . We can talk about the *byliny* or the *beguny* or the Black Hundreds—anything. I am a regular Peter Kirillov, Mr. Thorne. Just ask me, and I'll point you where you want to go."

A car, leaving the lot, came up to the window. The kid stuck the ticket into an electric timer, which came down with a clunk, then passed it outside.

"Mr. Thorne?"

"All right."

"Good. It is four o'clock now. In one hour and a half, at five-thirty, come to 362 Grayson Street. It is just an old garage, but from there we can go somewhere else."

"All right. I'll be there."

"Very good. And of course you will come by yourself. No police. This is not for them. It has nothing to do with them. You must realize that. I am serious. I will tell you about Brightman, but I will tell you something else. That will be personal, Mr. Thorne. You understand? Something you wouldn't want a policeman to hear."

Silence.

"What do you mean?"

"What I say."

His breath, rustling into the mouthpiece . . . and then the line went dead and I was standing there, the phone squeezed in my hand.

Something personal. Something you wouldn't want a policeman to hear . . .

I put the phone down. I had no idea what he was talking about—but for some reason my palms had started to sweat. From the very beginning, I'd had the feeling that all this would double back on me. And here it was. Yet none of it was tied to me personally—there was nothing I wouldn't want a policeman to hear. . . . May. She was my connection. And it could not be more innocent. Russia? It linked us all—me, Brightman, the man on the phone—but I had no guilt there. . . . That made no difference, however. My skin had gone clammy, and I'd begun to feel very queasy, as if . . . as if what? *As if, somewhere inside, I already knew—*

"Sir?"

I turned around.

"That's okay, sir. Just wondered if you was finished using the phone."

I dug up a couple of dollars and got out of his booth. The wind, gusting off the Detroit River, pressed my raincoat tight to my body, and grit, blown across the huge lot, stung my cheeks. For a moment, I wandered among the long aisles of cars. Turning my back to the wind, I got a cigarette going and tried to calm myself down. There was no time for soul-searching—I had some decisions to make. First, what should I do? Call Katadotis? But even as I thought this, I knew that I wouldn't. Even ignoring the warnings my mysterious caller had issued, he would obviously be very cautious and at the first hint of the cops he'd take off. But that raised the next question. If I kept our appointment, what would happen? One Russian yesterday, a second today—and the first had a gun. It made you think. Certain initials even began blinking at the edge of my brain. But it was too incredible and it just didn't feel right. *Komitet Gosudarstvennoy Bezopasnosti* may be hard to pronounce, but after eight years in the U.S.S.R. I could smell a KGB officer a mile away and certainly sniff one at the end of the phone. This smell was different; not official at all.

I flipped my cigarette away. In truth, I didn't have the faintest idea what it all meant, or could possibly mean. But I knew I'd go anyway: I'd never forgive myself if I didn't. And there was, I realized, no time to debate about it. My hour and a half had already shrunk fifteen minutes. Grayson Street, an old garage—I had to find out where they were, then get myself there. Not in a cab; I'd want my own transportation. And not in Brightman's car, which had already been recognized. Therefore . . .

My mind began steadying itself on these practical details. I looked around. By now, I'd wandered into the middle of this vast parking lot. To my left, behind a high wire fence, was the muddy trench of the De-

troit River, with Canada huddling glumly on the opposite bank. In front
of me, rising up like some urban mirage, were the towers of the Renaissance Center. I made for them, thinking I could rent a car there, but
in the end caught a taxi out front. I was curious: the man on the other
end of that phone must have been following me all morning—unless
he'd been following May and had picked me up later—and I wondered
if he was still on my tail. After ten minutes, I decided he wasn't. By
then we were on Michigan Avenue. The cabbie turned around, headed
back downtown, and dropped me at a Hertz office on Washington Boulevard. After the usual routine, they put me into the driver's seat of a
Pontiac and the clerk showed me Grayson Street on a map.

Heading north, I nosed up Woodward, resolutely keeping my mind
on my driving: it was the easiest way of forgetting how nervous I felt.
Five o'clock. A gloomy dusk hung over the city as the rush-hour crowds
fled toward Ann Arbor and Flint, Ypsilanti and Lansing. I joined the
escape. Caught up in the edgy panic, I let the traffic suck me up Gratiot,
then down the Chrysler Freeway. Like most Detroit expressways, it's
built below grade, a canal full of carbon monoxide and noise. Overhead,
an electric sign gave the temperature (49 degrees) and flashed the fact
that 5,467 Fords had been built that day, while on WXYZ the disk
jockey intoned, "Like Mr. Ford used to say, 'I don't believe in caging
birds or animals or any living thing.'"

I fought clear of all this at the Plymouth Plant exit. I was now in
Hamtramck and began hunting for Grayson. Trapped between the ex-
pressway approaches and an old railway spur, it turned out to be almost
impossible to get to: blocked off by high fences or separated from ordinary roads by immense vacant lots. But I made it on my third pass, bumping across an abandoned siding and then turning down a stretch of gravel
until the street signs started.

It was getting dark now. Only a few kids were out on the sidewalks,
and a pair of black men in boots and overalls plodded slowly home.
Though not as bad as St. Jean and the area near the auto pound, this
was still a melancholy place. The houses were identical cinder-block bungalows. Most were shabby and the lawns were minuscule, though a
few—somehow even more pathetic—boasted a spindly hedge of suburban shrub by the door. I slowed down, trying to spot house numbers,
but just then the garage itself loomed up. It appeared abandoned, and
was built in an old-fashioned style that made me think of gas stations

you sometimes find in country towns. The pumps had rounded tops and the building itself was peeling stucco. Accelerating a little—why give myself away?—I continued past it and turned down a side street.

I parked and looked at my watch. Ten minutes early. I stared down the street. Lights were on in the houses; a door banged somewhere and a woman's voice harshly called out a name. About four blocks along, the road petered out at a railway embankment protected by a sagging metal fence and lit by a single curved light. I cranked down my window. Behind me, in the side-view mirror, the lights of a car drifted down Grayson, and a moment later a black kid on a bicycle came riding up, his shining eyes quietly marking my ofay face. Then he disappeared in the gloom.

I lit a cigarette, smoked it slowly. I thought about a time in Moscow when I'd waited like this. I'd been doing an article on the Soviet Army and had made contact with a *Mladshii Lietenant* in a Guard's Division. He was only going to tell me about the food, his leave, his pay—the ordinary miseries of day-to-day life in any army—but we both knew that this was technically espionage, and that only the most technical definitions would interest a Soviet court. Now, by comparison . . . but maybe it was a comparison I'd better not make. I flipped my cigarette out the window, got out myself. The street was empty except for the beat-up old heaps drawn up at the curb, one of which was resting right on its wheel rims. I locked the car door and walked back toward the corner, my steps grittily crunching on the cement of the sidewalk. At Grayson, I paused a moment, looking around. To the left, a block away, a few indistinct figures were grouped around a car. Somebody laughed. Then the car door opened and in the glow of the interior light I caught the shine of legs and shoes and the flash of a smile. Kids, I thought, horsing around. . . . I looked right, toward the garage. I couldn't see it from this angle, but a dark, empty space marked where it was. On the far sidewalk, a single man was walking toward me, hands thrust deeply into the pocket of his windbreaker; on this side, further on—beyond the garage—two men were walking away from me. Streetlights spread shadows into the gloom. As the two men passed into one of these areas of light, I saw that they had green garbage bags over their shoulders: heading for the coin wash, doing their laundry before the crowds came after supper.

I started ahead. Each step made a precise, distinct sound. Behind me I heard those kids laughing and then one of them hooted, "Jesus,

man, whose side you on?" and they all laughed some more. The man
in the windbreaker passed by me on the far side of the street; up ahead,
the two men with the laundry bags disappeared in the dark. And then
I could see the garage. Quiet. Recessive. Like some forlorn crossroads
gas station on a lonely stretch of road in the bush. There was a sign
on top of it, braced by a wooden scaffold—COMMERCIAL LOT FOR SALE
MURPHY REALTY   543-6454—and beside it was an overgrown yard and
a boarded-up house.

I slowed my pace: but no one showed himself. Coming even with
the station, I angled across the asphalt apron toward the two skinny
pumps. I stopped there and looked around. The dark building, the black
asphalt, merged with the gloom. The whole street seemed to recede. And
still no one appeared—indeed, the street was now completely deserted,
for, looking back, I could see that even the man in the windbreaker had
gone on his way. Stepping closer to the pumps, I realized that their hoses
were cut and the glass over their gauges was broken. Inside, you could
see the faded seals from the Michigan Department of Commerce. The
dial was set at 39.9 cents a gallon and the last sale had netted $12.94.

Dark. Cold. And I had that sense of being out in the open. . . .
But he had to be able to see me. I began to fidget, tugging my gloves
over my fingers, putting my hands in my pocket, taking them out again.
Then—what the hell—I lit up a cigarette and let the Bic's flame show
off my face. Still no one came. I smoked slowly, standing still but looking
around in every direction. Shadows. The wind . . . Not too bad, I
thought; or it wouldn't be if Grayson Street was a film set, I was Hum-
phrey Bogart, and Lauren Bacall was back home fixing dinner. As it
was . . . A couple of minutes slipped by. I smoked the butt down, then
ground it out. Where in hell was he? I walked across to the gas station's
office, thinking that he might be inside and still hadn't seen me. I
stopped in front of the window. On it, one letter for each pane of glass,
the words b-a-r-g-a-i-n g-a-s were spelled out in white paint. Close up,
you could see the mark of the brush, and when I shaded my eyes and
looked through the "r," the old, dusty glass filled my nose with a dirty,
coppery smell. It was dark inside, hard to see, but I could tell no one
was there. The place was a shambles. A plywood counter had been
turned over and there was rubbish everywhere—bottles, flattened cartons, old cans, plastic jugs. No one had been here in weeks. I stepped
back. But then I tried the office door and the knob turned easily. I hesi-

tated, then stepped inside. It was darker. Colder. I stood in the doorway, feeling the darkness and emptiness of the street out behind me. I stared ahead. In the corner of the room was an old Coke machine, that kind with the white enamel lettering, and a wire rack for empties beside it. Feeling an urge to call out, I repressed it, then changed my mind. "Hello? Hello? Anyone there?"

Whistling in the dark . . . Now the silence left me feeling more than a little foolish. There wasn't even an echo, just grit grinding under my heel as I shifted my weight. To the left was the gray patch of the doorway in to the service bays. Now that I'd come this far, there was nowhere else left to go, so I stepped through; but just inside, wanting a clear line of retreat, I waited again. Open space stretched before me. It was very dark, but enough light leaked in from the street to make the darkness swirl and eddy like fog. *It is just an old garage, but from there we can go somewhere else.* I looked around. I could see two greasy pits where they'd taken out the lifts, a length of rubber hose dangling from a hook on the back wall, and right by my head there was a pasted-up picture of Miss Rheingold, 1955. But nothing more. Slowly, I edged into the gloom. The floor was cement, but huge chunks of it had chipped or crumbled away, so that patches of damp earth showed through. Smells: oil, that smell that cold concrete gets, the sour smell of wet earth. My toe nudged a can. I flicked it into the darkness, where it rattled away. Pivoting slowly, I looked back toward the street. Most of the panes in the service doors had been broken; on the others, scrawled in the dust, were the usual obscenities, and at ticktacktoe, "x" had won three times out of five. . . . Deciding that no one was there, I flicked on my lighter and looked at my watch. Five thirty-eight. Was I being stood up?

Irritation. But I felt myself relax a little as well. I was certain now that no one was about to step out of the darkness and that made it easier to pretend I was being ever so brave. The trouble was, the obverse of fear isn't courage but boredom. I stamped my feet. Lit a cigarette. Began checking my watch every two minutes. Maybe he was lost, I thought, though that didn't seem right for a real Peter Kirillov. Peter was a mythical figure from the days of the Old Believers, holy Russian pilgrims who dreamed of a mythical Kingdom of the White Waters where righteousness reigned. The road there was hard and long, but in a certain village, if you could only reach it, Peter Kirillov would show you the right way. . . . A car came up Grayson, casting a huge net of shadow around me—very melodramatic, but then it passed silently by. Five forty-six. . . . He wouldn't come; I was sure of it. Or perhaps he was being subtle. Perhaps he was already here, watching, waiting for me to leave; then he'd follow me and present himself when I least expected it. Actually, that was not inconceivable—and it made an excellent excuse for leaving right now. But I told myself to wait. Till six. Give him that long and then go.

Five forty-nine. I began moving around, just to keep warm. My eyes were getting used to the dark. I realized that the place had been abandoned for years; half the floor had crumbled away. There were a few plastic jugs and quart oil cans littered around a squashed cardboard carton or two, but the interior had been stripped to the bone by a generation of kids. Everything useful was gone. At some point vagrants had built a fire in the corner; tossing my cigarette onto a gray pile of ash, I continued along the back wall . . . and that's when I heard a slight sound. It wasn't much, barely a rustling . . . though more metallic than that. Yet not exactly a scrape. It came again. I stepped further along till I reached another doorway. The door itself was gone, but it was hard to see out because something was blocking the way. I went closer. It was just one of those big metal dumpers for picking up trash. I stepped outside, into a dark, cold zone that smelled of wet cinder and ash. I listened again, but didn't hear anything—it was probably nothing more than a rat—and then, deciding to walk around to the front of the building, I began to edge sideways between the dumper and the back wall of the garage. Old burdock. Gutter, dangling from brackets. An electric meter, all smashed to hell . . . Finally I squeezed around the edge of the dumper—and then the sound came again, from inside. A settling sound, a weight shifting. I hesitated—I don't much like rats or dark holes. But then I reached up, grabbed the top edge of the dumper, and pulled myself up. I looked in. Dropped back. I wasn't sure what I'd seen. I took out my lighter. Clumsy with my gloves, I adjusted the flame as high as I could, then hoisted myself back up. The damn thing was so rusty that the metal felt like sand under my fingers. With a grunt, I stretched forward, leaning my chest across the top rail, and stuck out my right arm. The orange flame of the Bic hissed and bent in the darkness. I looked down. The bottom of the dumper had rusted out years ago; now weeds poked through the filmy metal and a black puddle glistened in the mud. There wasn't much to see: a pile of old Quaker State oil cans, bits of muffler and pipe, half a door panel, and a painter's plastic drop sheet that was wrapped around something. All twisted and folded, the clear plastic sheet was shot through with wrinkles and fissures, like an ice cube. But the wrinkles were wet and red. And frozen at the center was the body of a fat, hairy man with no head, hands, or feet.

I fell back, my knees banging the dumper, the red afterimage of the lighter's flame pulsing before my eyes. I froze in a crouch. *Dear Jesus.* Then I blundered away, charging back down the gap between the wall and the dumper. Weeds grabbed my legs. The wall grazed my cheek. The dumper pressed in and something sticking out from the wall jabbed at my thigh. With a gasp of relief, I squeezed through. I staggered ahead, then stepped on something—the top of a trash can—and my ankle turned under me. Falling to one knee, I reached down and touched the cold ground and steadied myself. And then I remembered those men with the laundry bags and understood what they'd contained; and with all the ease of a child, I was sick.

For a moment, I closed my eyes against the horror.

I opened them slowly. Vomit steamed around my feet.

It didn't happen to you. It's all right.

Catching my breath, I found an old end of Kleenex and wiped my mouth. Pulled myself upright. My ankle was throbbing, my knee ached, there was a stinging scrape along the side of my face. I swore under my breath. *It's all right. Take it easy.* I peered around the corner of the garage. Night uncoiled down the street. Windows glowed like cats' eyes and I could hear the buzz of a streetlamp. But I couldn't see anyone, so I forced my legs to move. Across the asphalt apron of the garage. Then the sidewalk. Left. *It's all right.* Don't run. The corner. Left one more time . . .

I made it to the car and got in; and then I couldn't stop myself, and locked all the doors, as if that headless corpse might follow me here. As I stared into the darkness, my reflection mistily drifted over the window. Lights were on in the houses but no one was out in the street. In the distance, I could hear the low-gear grunt of a truck. The wind, coming up stronger, bumped at the car. . . . I took a deep breath, let it out slowly. Five minutes, I thought, maybe less: I'd come that close to seeing a murder, maybe being murdered myself. In delayed response, my heart began to race in my chest and I felt faint. With shaking hands, I fumbled a cigarette up to my mouth. I tried to start thinking. Who was he? Who had killed him? Why? Who, except you, knew he was going to be there? But then I got hold of myself and shut down my mind—there was no point asking questions no one could answer. There was no time for theory, no time for abstractions. Are you in danger? It was the only question that counted. And the answer was no, not now, not here. Proof: whoever had killed him hadn't waited, which must mean that they hadn't known I'd be coming. Or maybe they didn't care. *Something personal, something you wouldn't want a policeman to hear* . . . Maybe that had all been a lie; maybe it had nothing to do with me at all. So what do I do? Should I—? *No. No big decisions. Just get the hell out of here. Right now you couldn't think your way out of a wet paper bag.*

With relief, and a vicious twist of the key, I started the car. Truth: I didn't want to think, or question, or know. I only wanted to get away from this spot. But, like a careful drunk, I made myself do it slowly. I turned away from the curb. Straightened out. Lightly put my foot down . . . and maybe that's why I saw it. As I came up to the next corner, I stopped the car dead.

I twisted back in my seat.

Behind me, stretching along the curb, were the half dozen cars that had been parked in front of me. They were all rusted, dented heaps, held together by body compound and inertia. Except for one, that is: a late-model Pontiac as bright and shiny as the one I was driving. I thought for a second, then clunked the car into reverse, the engine whining shrilly as I backed down the street. I stopped. Quickly opening the door, I walked back to the other car. I leaned forward, cupping my hands, and peered in the driver's-side window. It was a standard-issue two-door sedan: autotransmission, plush velour seats, the dash neatly wiped—I didn't have to see the Hertz litter bag to know it was rented. I tried the doors, but they were locked. It was obvious, though. He'd done just as I had: Parked here, then approached the garage circumspectly . . . though not circumspectly enough.

For some reason, this little discovery steadied me, and by the time I was back in my own car, I felt more under control. Doubling back to the Chrysler Freeway, I followed the rush-hour traffic north but got off before Flint. Then I just drove around for a while. Bit by bit, my nerve came back. And as I drove along a cluttered neon boulevard of car lots and muffler shops, I realized I was hungry. I pulled into a McDonald's and used their washroom to clean up a little; but restoring myself to respectability killed my appetite for their kind of food, and I drove further down the street to a shopping center. What I found there wasn't much better—something called The Chances R, a bar with a Western motif: saloon doors, waitresses in cowboy hats, wagon wheels hanging from the ceiling with lights in the hub. I took a stool and ordered a bourbon—cheap and disgusting enough to jolt you out of anything. But the steak sandwich wasn't too bad. By then, my mind was more or less back on the rails, and with coffee and cigarettes I tried to work out where I stood. Point one: there was no reason to panic. The man who had called me, assuming he was the man in the dumper, had known I was involved in all this, but whoever had killed him probably didn't; or didn't care if I was. Otherwise, they would have hung around and killed me as well. Point two: I didn't want to go to the police, at least for the moment. *Something personal, something you wouldn't want a policeman to hear . . .* That was part of it. And maybe—after my panicky flight from the garage—I wanted to recoup self-esteem, at least in my own eyes. I'd come this far on my own; I could go a bit further. Which was why, when I'd finished eating, I walked through the plaza until I found a hardware store that was still open and bought a five-pound sledge.

It was after seven now. Back on the freeway, heading south, traffic was thin. I was only ten minutes getting down to Hamtramck, though it took another twenty to find Grayson Street again. Nothing had changed. Passing the garage, I saw it was as dark and calm as I had left it. But there was no reason why it shouldn't be. They might not find that body for months—they might never find it.

I turned down a side street and parked about three cars ahead of the Pontiac.

Headlights off, motor running. I leaned back to switch off the interior light, then eased open the door. The cold wind struck my eyes. That acrid, chemical smell burned in my nose. I shut the door carefully, leaving it open a crack, then walked back down the street. I was heading toward Grayson and now a car passed there, its lights sweeping the corner. I stopped, undecided; almost went back; but as it passed further on, I went forward again. Standing by the Pontiac, I swiveled around. It was parked right in front of a house where the lights were on, but the place next door was dark. I drew back the sledge and swung as hard as I could. At the first blow, the window only gave slightly in its frame and didn't even crack, but the second starred it like a piece of old ice and the third pushed a big chunk inside the car. With my hand, I pushed more bits and pieces away, then reached in and opened the glove compartment. And found what I wanted: the rental form. I pulled it out and walked smartly back to my car. No one had seen me. Two minutes later, I was back on the freeway.

I headed south and this time went right downtown before pulling off. Then I parked and read through the form in the glow of the dashlight. His name had been Michael Travin. He had a Maine driver's license that gave a home address in Lewiston. The car had been rented from the Hertz counter in the Renaissance Center and the local address was room 909 in the Detroit Plaza Hotel—the hotel that's part of the complex. Hertz had imprinted his Visa card. He'd paid three dollars for extra insurance. . . .

Decision time. But not really. I found Michigan Avenue, followed it straight down to Randolph, and that took me right into the Center. I parked in the same lot where I'd left Brightman's Jaguar. The cold, dusty wind was fierce off the river. As I walked up, the towers glowed like copper against the night sky. I went in by the main entrance and found the hotel desk right in front of me, but I walked around for a moment, getting my bearings. The place was like something left over from a sci-fi spectacular: the main lobby was a brightly lit, five-story atrium where trees breathed the man-made air, fountains splashed into artificial lakes, and concrete "seating pods" projected out into space. Impressive enough, and security was probably better than normal: but the place was very big, very busy, and despite everything I still looked very respectable.

Smile.

"Hi. I'm Mr. Travin in 909. I can't find my key, so I must have left it with you. I hope."

Smile.

"Just a—yes, Mr. Travin, you did. Here you are."

"Thanks."

I strode firmly away from the desk, but then blundered about, not sure which way to go, for a network of circular stairs and escalators wound you round to various levels inside the lobby—it was that kind of place. Eventually, however, I followed a bellhop into an elevator, which then shot me up to the guest rooms. Emerging, I found myself in an empty, curved hall. I followed this around. The door to 909 was like any other door in any other hotel. I hesitated a moment and almost knocked; then just inserted the key and went in.

At once, instinctively, I knew that the room was empty.

I flipped on a light. I was in a little hall, the bathroom on my right. I stuck my head in. Neat. Tidy. The towels weren't fresh but they were neatly hung up. The shower was one of those molded plastic units—not up to the standards of the lobby—and there were a few drops of water around the drain; but nothing more. I backed out, then stepped into the main part of the room. This too was nothing more than a standard first-class American hotel room. There was a desk-bureau, with a mirror and a wicker chair; a TV set on a plastic pedestal; a tub chair, covered in vinyl; and then the bed, a single, with a night table and a lamp. Even the room's only picture was standard—an abstract that could have been taken from any doctor's office, New York to Los Angeles.

Standard. Empty. Barren.

And no sign of Michael Travin at all.

I looked everywhere . . . not that there were many places to look. There were no bags, no clothes in the bureau or closet, and the room was so neat you would have thought the maid had just finished. The bed was made. Ashtrays were clean. The wastebasket was empty. I turned on the television. It was tuned to one of the Canadian stations in Windsor. I pulled back the drapes. There were no messages scrawled on the windows, and the lights of the city winked up at me dumbly. . . .

I lit a cigarette, took a drag. The room was so neat and tidy that you'd think he'd checked out. But he hadn't—otherwise I wouldn't have been able to get the key in his name. And a maid, I realized, hadn't done this: the towels were hung up, but they hadn't been changed, and though the ashtrays were clean, there were no fresh matchbooks. What had happened?

But now a peculiar feeling came over me. I don't know how to describe it—a creepy, paranoid prickling at the back of my neck. I hadn't felt it in years, not since I'd lived in the U.S.S.R. . . . and then I knew what it was and I spun right around and began searching again, searching now for the signs of a search, a search that would have been made so carefully that even if you did find traces of it you wouldn't be sure. Not quite. Not ever . . . On my hands and knees, I felt along the edge of

the carpet, and yes, it was loose; if I pulled it back here, I could take
up the whole room. Had the contractor been sloppy or had somebody
lifted it? Then I traced out the seams in the wallpaper, feeling along
with my fingernail. Loose again. Natural wear, or had someone been
using a razor? I turned the chairs upside down, pulled out the bureau
and the bed, checked the TV—and found three screws that might have
been freshly scratched. They'd been looking for something small, I
thought, some sort of paper or document. Or maybe not: when I turned
over the mattress, I found a six-inch cut where they'd slipped in their
probe. But, whatever they'd been looking for, I was now certain of one
thing. CIA, SIS, SDECE, STASI, BND . . . "Security," everywhere,
leaves the same mark, but there was only one source for the peculiar,
lingering scent I sniffed all through this room: KGB.

Which didn't especially excite me. I was more accustomed to the
Komitet than I was to dead bodies. But I began to think fast. They, after
all, must have moved *very* fast. At four o'clock Travin calls me in the
parking lot. Looking down, I could make out the booth—was it even
possible that he'd called from right here? No. He might have recognized
Brightman's car from this height, but not me—and he'd known my
name. We'd then set up our meeting. Five-thirty, that was. So, sometime in the hour between four and five, they'd picked him up and started
following him. That had probably happened right here, for they would
have had this room under surveillance, but in any event they'd followed
him to Grayson Street. What had they thought he was doing there? Hiding something? Not likely. Surely there was only one thing they could
have thought—that he was meeting someone. But that hadn't concerned them, I'd already worked that much out. What did interest them,
then? When you thought about it, all they'd really taken trouble about
was his identity. They'd cut off his head, hands, and feet, so that establishing the identity of the corpse would now be a forensic miracle. But
then they'd been very sloppy, for they'd forgotten the car. Or had
they known about it at all? If they'd followed him there, they must
have. . . . But they'd ignored it, and come here and searched the room
instead. Which might mean something: maybe they already knew that
the Travin identity was false and that, by itself, it wouldn't help establish who the man actually was.

Possible.

But maybe not.

For their differing reasons, both the Kremlin and the Pentagon find the notion of an all-powerful, super-efficient Soviet state very convenient and promote it like hell. But for anyone who's ever lived in Russia the idea is laughable—and the KGB's screwed up before.

Using a Kleenex, I picked up the phone.

"This is room 909, operator. I'd like to speak to information in Lewiston, Maine."

"Yes, sir. That's a toll-free call, sir . . . just one moment."

She got off the line as the long-distance operator came on: "Information for what city, please?"

"Lewiston, Maine."

"Yes. Go ahead."

I pulled out the Hertz form, spelled Travin's name, and gave his address. After a moment, she said, "We have no Travin listed there, sir."

"Could it be a new listing, operator?"

"No, sir. We have no listing at all."

I hung up . . . but then had another idea. I called down to the desk.

"I'd like to check out, if I could. Mr. Travin in 909. I'm in quite a hurry. Could you have someone bring up the bill."

"One moment, sir. . . . Yes, will that be on your Visa card?"

"Please. I think you already have it."

"Yes, Mr. Travin. I'll just check it through and then someone will bring it up to your room."

Ten minutes later, careful to hide my face, I stuck a dollar around the door and received Travin's bill in return. But it wasn't very informative: same address, same phone number, same Visa number as on the Hertz form. He'd had breakfast in his room every morning, two other meals in one of the hotel restaurants, and drinks in the bar. All in all, he'd been staying here for six days; unfortunately, he'd made no long-distance phone calls. So . . . the men who'd searched this room hadn't slipped up, after all. The name Travin, his driver's license, the credit card, his hotel bill—they added up to a dead end. In a few days, Hertz would sound the alarm. The police would come up with the car but then go no further. Even if they found the body and concluded it was Travin, it wouldn't do them much good. Michael Travin, whoever he was, had effectively vanished from the face of the earth.

I took a long breath, walked over to the window, and looked out at the night. The lights of an ore carrier twinkled out on the river and made me think of Halifax. I'd been there yesterday: it seemed centuries ago. Brightman's death was a chasm, a great void . . . and what did it have to do with all this? *I can tell you everything, Mr. Thorne. How it was done. What has happened to Brightman. Everything.* Had Travin been killed because he knew? And was that why they hadn't worried about me—because as long as I didn't get to talk to him, I *wouldn't* know? But questions like that were beyond me, and I had more immediate problems. Where was I in this? What should I do now? I sensed that I'd reached a turning point—emotionally, in terms of my own commitment, but in other ways as well. There were some practical questions. I am not a professional adventurer. As a writer, my time is my own, but there was the small matter of money and the more subtle one of energy. Did I really want to make the investment? Then there were legal considerations. Right now, my legal position was fine, not even iffy. I hadn't actually seen a crime committed, and you're under no obligation to report the dead bodies you find lying around. The car was nothing. As long as I paid Hertz for the window, no cop on earth would think of pressing a charge. Theft? I hadn't taken anything of value. Obstruction of justice? No one knew the rental form had been in the glove compartment except me; besides, the police could get the original from the Hertz office. No doubt I'd violated some local Hotel- and Innkeepers Act by getting into this room, but even that might be hard to prove since I hadn't had a criminal purpose. What had I taken? Destroyed? No, if I picked up the phone right now and called the police, I'd get nothing more than a lecture on good citizenship. *If* . . .

But just then there was a knock at the door.

I froze.

The knock, a little heavier, came again.

I took a deep breath. "Yes?"

"Mr. Travin, sir? Valet service, sir. They called up from the desk, sir, and said you was checking out. Don't want to be forgetting your suit."

"Just a minute."

I was even more careful than I'd been with the bellhop and made absolutely certain that the woman didn't get a look at my face: Travin was dead—I didn't want to become him. Yet now, in an odd way, I was being visited by his shade. Pulling off the plastic wrapping, I spread the suit out on the bed, and it lay there in grisly imitation of its owner: *sans* head, hands, and feet. Other than this, however, it was perfectly ordinary: gray, one pair of trousers, no vest. *Sears, The Men's Store,* said the label. But then I saw there was a little brown envelope twist-tied to the hanger. *We Found This in Your Pockets* . . . I tore it open, spilled it out on the pillow.

One book of matches, from something called the Mikado Room. Seventy-seven cents in change, including one Canadian quarter. And a claim check from a photo store. . . .

I picked up this last item. It was the usual thing: the strip of envelope they give back to you when you take in a film. It was gray, over-printed with the number 2009 and the store's name and address: *Jack's Photo Supplies, Berlin, N.H.*

Well, well. Maybe they'd screwed up after all.

And right then, I made up my mind. I wasn't entirely sure why. I'd been joining the dots in one of those puzzles they used to put in the paper, and here was another. That was part of it; and so was Russia, and all I felt about that country, and May Brightman was still in it too. But there was something else; and it was "something personal," just as Travin had said—a feeling, present from the very beginning, that all these events, however impossible it seemed, led back to me.

But maybe the reasons don't make any difference. A rose is a rose: you do what you do. With Travin's suit bundled under my arm, I took the elevator down to the lobby, and forty minutes later, behind the wheel of Brightman's enormous white boat, I entered the Detroit-Windsor Tunnel and crossed back over the Canadian border.

9

Windsor to Toronto, Toronto to Montreal, then south to the border again: Route 26 through New Hampshire, back roads to Interstate 91, then west on 84 through Pennsylvania. . . . Twenty-four hours after leaving Detroit, I was sitting in a restaurant in Washington, D.C., but on that trip you'd have to say I took the long way around. I was exhausted by the end of it, though I made plenty of stops—mainly for gas, which Brightman's mammoth machine guzzled insatiably. But I also detoured to pick up my bags at Toronto International Airport, where I'd left them when I came in from Halifax, and for a few hours I flaked out in a motel near Kingston, Ontario. And most important of all, I jogged through Berlin, New Hampshire, to pick up Travin's photographs.

As the miles rolled by, I thought and drove, and drove and thought, until my mind was humming along with the tires. On the highway, I made pretty good time, but mentally my progress wasn't so even: I kept swinging back and forth between confidence and doubt. What if I found nothing? What if the whole thing was meaningless? My conscience prickled, I felt halfway a fugitive, and the further Detroit receded behind me, the more unbelievable my speculations seemed to become. Brightman had killed himself: I had no reason to suspect, let alone contradict, that conclusion. And I had no certain knowledge that anyone, let alone the KGB, had searched the hotel room. But then, just as I grew convinced that I was making a fool of myself, my mind headed off in another direction. Travin was dead. Someone had killed him. And even if Brightman hadn't been murdered, you can hardly call suicide normal. No: something very peculiar was happening. . . . I suppose, even before I picked up those photographs, that I was convinced: my mind just needed time to get used to it.

Berlin, when I got there, turned out to be a pulp and paper town whose smokestacks trailed a livid, sulphurous haze across the New England hills. I would have put its population at something like fifteen thousand, big enough to boast a Woolworth's, a newspaper (the Berlin *Reporter*), and a municipal building with a fine old clock tower. Pleasant; a little ramshackle; even pretty if you looked away from the smokestacks, for the Androscoggin River flowed through it. It was the sort of place that perfectly expressed small-town America before the Midwest was discovered. Despite the name, I didn't see much sign of a German influence and was more aware of a French-Canadian element—Canucks, as they say in New England. There was a grocer called Mercier, a Club des Raquettes, and a red-brick Ste. Anne's on your way in. Of course, that first trip, I noticed this only in passing: my mind was entirely concentrated on the photo shop, where I laid down $65.48 and received two oversized gray envelopes in return.

I had no idea what to expect when I opened them, and for the past fifty miles had been bracing myself for something completely banal. Travin's girl in the buff . . . his last fishing trip . . . sunsets . . . Still, even as I took them from the woman in the store, I knew that I hadn't entirely wasted my time. The two envelopes were stapled together, and scrawled across the first was: *M. Travin, RFD 2, Berlin, tel. 236-6454.* This, I thought, was more likely to be his real address than the one on the driver's license. But that piece of information was only the consolation prize. When I opened the first envelope itself I hit the bonanza. Twenty-four five-by-seven enlargements spilled onto my lap. Each shot was different, but they all had one subject: May Brightman.

Which was about the only thing I *hadn't* expected.

Detroit had canceled out Halifax. The past twelve hours, and my discovery of Travin's body, had carved a great gulf between the present and everything that had gone before: May's adoption, Dr. Charlie, Florence Raines, that lawyer in Toronto. . . . They were figures from a vanished age—but now they were alive again.

Almost in bewilderment, I began sorting through the photographs. By checking the negatives—they were all 35mm—I was able to arrange them in the order in which they'd been taken, and judging by the backgrounds, this must have been during the summer. All of the photos were "candid": May, clearly, had no idea what was happening. Three had been shot from a car as she came out her front door, another strip caught her in a crowd, probably shopping in that market near her house, and a third consisted of three frames showing her sitting on a bench in a park. One of these was very overexposed, but the other two were perfect, very crisp and clear. Her expression was calm and composed as she enjoyed the sun; and though you could see her age in the wrinkles around her eyes, there was still something girlish about her—a patter of freckles high on her cheeks, the way her loose blond hair spread across her rough-knit sweater. The next set, almost by design, was a direct contrast to this. Two frames: in both she was wearing a white business suit and looking rather awkward, somewhat as she had yesterday morning inside the police station. Her hair was pulled into a bun; she might have been wearing a shade too much lipstick. Altogether, she reminded me of a proper suburban matron—an English matron—dressed up for her monthly visit to town. In fact, there was something English about her, or at least European. But then the next four shots reminded me that her special quality wasn't national at all, for Travin had crept down her lane, just as I'd done the day I arrived in Toronto, and photographed her working in the garden. I could guess just where he was standing—it was hard to imagine that she hadn't heard the click of the shutter. But the results had been worth the risk, for one of these shots was actually a very fine photograph, and all three caught precisely the quality I'd seen that first day: there was something essentially anachronistic or other-worldly about her. Bloomsbury girl and hippie, princess and peasant—she contained contradictions that removed her from this time and place. In Travin's photos, she was wearing a large straw hat that partly shaded her face and a long, high-necked dress worked with lace, and draped around her neck and over her shoulders was a long, tasseled shawl. The effect of all this was attractive, but undeniably odd: it was like looking into the past and watching a highborn Edwardian lady at play. What an enigma she was. And Travin, I finally concluded, would have agreed. As I flipped back through the prints, it was obvious that his principal interest had been her face, as if he'd wanted to compare this face, *her* face, with another. Travin had also been asking the question: who was May Brightman?

Naturally, when I opened the second envelope, I was hoping to find the answer inside. And maybe it was there, if I'd only been able to see it.

This envelope held only three prints: six-by-eight enlargements that were all identical except for slight differences in the developing. I saw at once that they'd been made from a copy negative; that is, they were photographs of a photograph. Travin had done this reasonably well—the lighting was good, and he'd used a tripod or maybe even a copy stand. But they were undoubtedly copies; even the best of the prints was subject to a sort of translucent blurring, as if a very thin coating of egg white had been painted over the image. In addition, the original must have been very small and also a trifle underexposed, which the developing had tried to compensate for, though not very successfully. Nonetheless, there was no problem making out what the photographs showed. Fourteen men were standing in the backyard of a house, with a large wooden shed or garage in the background. Their attention had clearly been called to the camera, but they were very informally posed: they'd just stood still, looked up, smiled, and one had crossed his arms over his chest. The yard looked very bare and unkempt. The shed in the background was weathered and a border of grass and weeds was growing in front of it. The sun, shining into the yard from the upper left, cast the shadow of the house across some of the group, obscuring their faces. On the far right stood a picnic table covered with bottles and dishes; one corner of the tablecloth flapped in the breeze. A few canvas deck chairs had been placed around the table, and two of the men were sitting in them, one with a plate on his knee. Nine of the men wore suits, or at least jackets and white shirts, while the remainder were more casually dressed: sweaters, a checked lumberjack shirt, a white shirt but no tie (the man with his arms crossed). It was evident from these clothes (baggy trousers, fat little ties) that the photograph must have been taken in the late thirties or forties. But then this would have been obvious anyway. Two of the men had been circled with white marking pencil and, in the same way, a single line had been written across the bottom of the photograph. *Halifax, 1940,* it read—or, more exactly: ГАЛИФАКС, 1940.

Tilting the photograph to catch the light better, I stared hard at the smaller of the two circled figures. It was Brightman. It had been impossible to connect the bloody stump in the Wayne County morgue with the face in the photo May had taken "with her own Brownie," but there was no doubt about this. He was standing at the back, his shadow stretching up the wall of the shed. A big, barrel-chested man. Thick hair, receding a little and pulled straight back from his forehead as if he'd just run his fingers through it. He was dressed in a dark suit; his hands were thrust down into his pants pockets and his jacket was open; his tie had been flopped up by the wind. . . . Harry Brightman, as he'd looked when he'd adopted his daughter. Had he been thinking about her at that very moment? It was almost possible to imagine this, for his face showed an abstracted, impatient expression as though he wished to be elsewhere. Why? Who were these people around him? Friends? Colleagues? Could one of them be May's real father?

Fascinated, I moved my eyes over the photograph, examining all the other figures but especially the second man who was circled. Even without this mark of special importance, something singled him out. Well away from Brightman, he was standing in the foreground, near the picnic table: a short but powerful man, with a broad, fleshy face and heavy lips turned down in a sulky scowl. Perhaps he too wished to be elsewhere. I let my glance wander a moment, then looked back, hoping such a heavy, determined face might ring some bell; but it didn't. Nor did the others. And yet . . .

Russia.

Brightman.

Halifax, 1940.

Dr. Charlie. . . .

As I sipped a coffee in Macauley's Inner Circle Restaurant, with the photographs spread out before me, I felt that I was closer to some real answers than I'd been before. The men who'd searched Travin's room had been looking for these photographs; I was almost certain of that. Therefore, I *wasn't* making a fool of myself—and that alone was reassuring. In addition, the photographs brought Brightman's disappearance and May's adoption irrevocably together, for Travin had been interested in *both* father and daughter. Yet everything that had happened in Detroit also proved that the connection wasn't "personal" in any obvious way: it wasn't a case of May's "real" mother, or anyone else, trying a quiet spot of blackmail. May's adoption gave a particular focus to her father's past—a focus that had burned its way right into the present—but it was his past itself that was the problem. Who was May Brightman? This question, the question Travin had been asking, now seemed only one aspect of another: who was Harry? I had no clear idea of the answer. But that afternoon, as I drove away from Berlin, I had some real clues to play with, and I began putting them together. May and Harry, together, made up the mystery, and Russia was the key to its solution. Brightman had been there, I had been there, and a number of real, live Russians—and one dead Russian—apparently had an interest in this. And when you think of Russia, you think of Communism, a word that connected up nicely with the year 1940, and even better with Dr. Charlie, the doctor who was "a bit of a socialist," the doctor with all those left-wing books in his den. Finally, there was the photograph itself, with its Cyrillic lettering, and that odd group of men. I'm not sure why, but something in their stance—an aggressiveness, a tension—struck me as familiar. Funny associations played through my mind: old Jimmy Cagney movies about gangsters holed up in the hills . . . old pictures of railway executives posed around the Last Spike . . . and, since I was thinking of Russia and Communism, I also thought of those formal, frozen portraits of Engels and Marx, Lenin and Stalin, that are the iconography of Soviet sainthood. This sounds very vague; and it was. But it was more than a hunch. I suspected that I knew more than I yet understood. I needed one final hint, a last nudge, one more prompt. . . . I'd joined up the dots, but couldn't make out the picture they formed; I'd filled in the blanks, but couldn't pronounce the word the letters spelled out. Or, more precisely, I now had the photograph, but I still needed the caption.

I began looking for it in Washington—and found it three days later in New York.

As searches go, this one was not that hard, and indeed it was a pleasure for me: something like work, even a return to civilization. I faced nothing more threatening than a recalcitrant microfiche reader, and the greatest challenge to my intestinal fortitude was the Washington *Post* cafeteria. Nonetheless, I didn't forget Travin's fate, or Brightman's. Retrieving my own car, I ditched the Jaguar in a parking garage, and though I stayed at my mother's house in Georgetown, I was very discreet. I kept away from my friends, eschewed certain obvious contacts and haunts, and otherwise kept my head low. With May, I was vague. Though she'd returned to Toronto without mishap, she was still upset—naturally enough—and tried to make me promise that I'd give up what I was doing. But I brushed that off, and once I was satisfied that she was really all right, I told her a story about having trouble with the car and said I'd call her again in a couple of days.

A week, in fact, was the deadline I gave myself. This was less arbitrary than it sounds. I knew the sort of job I had to do, and experience told me that I'd either wrap it up quickly or not at all. Who were the people in the photograph? What had they been doing in Halifax in 1940? Above all, who was the other man whom Travin had circled? Assuming it was possible, then answering these questions should be a task of only middling difficulty.

I had three clues: Brightman, Halifax, and 1940. The first I dispensed with quickly. If I'd run Brightman's name through the files of the Toronto papers, I likely would have come up with one or two references, but there was nothing in Washington. My second clue, Halifax, was more productive—a huge explosion in 1917, innumerable royal visits, naval activity all through the war. And 1940 was a bonanza: all those stories my mother had told me scrolled through the scratchy, glaring field of the microfilm lens:

February 11: The U.S.S.R. launches a new, massive invasion of Finland.

April 9: Germany attacks Denmark and Norway.

May 10: Germany overruns Belgium.

May 13: Germany invades France.

May 26: The Allied evacuation at Dunkirk begins.

June 14: Paris falls.

June 21: France surrenders. . . .

It was all there in black and white, and there were plenty of pictures: Molotov, Chamberlain, Weygand, Churchill, Reynaud, Guderian, Roosevelt, Lindbergh. . . . My man, obviously, was a much smaller fish than any of these; he would be a minor figure, a face in the background, some assistant or aide. But I was sure he was a public man. If the photo had no wider reference, why tear Travin's room apart trying to find it? Pushing on, I checked all the papers, the Library of Congress, then made copies of the photo—blocking out Brightman—and showed them around. Two guesses took half a day to track down, I wasted an evening with an old UPI man in a bar, but finally, widening the search, I got lucky. This was in New York, in the Bettmann Archive, which—being the last place I looked—is undoubtedly where I should have gone to begin with. The Archive houses one of the largest collections of historical photographs in the world, and they are superbly organized. Instead of making you paw through trays of prints, or file folders that end up spilling all over the place, they have a nice, neat system of index cards: a small print of the photo is reproduced on one side of the card, there's a brief paragraph of commentary, and then half a dozen index headings. My first break came under "War, Spanish Civil": a picture of a stocky man hoisted on the shoulders of some grinning members of the International Brigade. I couldn't make up my mind; this man was like Travin's man—he had the same sort of presence—but the photos were too dissimilar to let me be certain. Now, though, I knew what I wanted, and I quickly found three other shots, the best of them in the "Date File" for 1933. It had been taken from above, and showed the head and upper body of a man in his mid-forties. He had dark, thick hair and dark eyes, and his powerful shoulders bunched the cloth of his suit. His expression was determined, but also slightly distracted, as if he'd looked away for a moment after a period of concentration. Even in this casual portrait, the force of the man's personality was evident, especially in contrast to the figures behind him. One of these was a man slumped forward in utter dejection; the second was a guard with a vacant expression who was wearing the uniform of the German police. Under "Description" the index card said:

> Georgi Dimitrov (1882–1949), Bulgarian-born Communist leader, was accused by the Nazis of conspiring to set fire to the German Parliament buildings (the Reichstag) on Feb. 27, 1933. His trial at Leipzig was an international sensation and made Dimitrov a hero of anti-Nazi and left-wing groups around the world. Dimitrov brilliantly defended himself, ridiculing both Göring and Goebbels in court, and was finally released. Marinus van der Lubbe (the slumped figure behind Dimitrov) was ultimately convicted and executed for the crime. Dimitrov subsequently became head of the Comintern and was later Premier of Bulgaria.

Setting the two photographs side by side, I went back and forth between them, but there was absolutely no doubt. The second man whom Travin had circled was *Georgi Dimitrov,* the man the Nazis had tried to frame for the Reichstag fire; *Georgi Dimitrov,* undisputed leader of the Popular Front against Fascism; *Georgi Dimitrov,* last head of the Comintern.

As I leaned back in my chair, there were no fanfares, no ringing bells. Just that hush that surrounds any true secret. For that's what it was. From the middle thirties, Georgi Dimitrov had been one of the most important of all the Communist leaders. And Brightman had known him. What's more, they'd both been together in the spring of 1940—just after Brightman had returned from Europe with May and started Dr. Charlie along the devious course of the adoption.

The centrality of all this was obvious. Yet, as I stared down at Travin's photograph, I realized that many of the details of what had happened were less so. What had the two men been doing? Who were the other men with them? And what was the relationship between Dimitrov's presence in Halifax in 1940 and Brightman's disappearance today? Those aren't the sorts of questions you can answer by searching the library shelves. That afternoon, as I boarded the shuttle back to Washington, I knew I had to pick someone's brains, and by the time I landed, I had a short list of three. At the top of it was a man named Leonard Forbes. When it comes to the Comintern—the organization the Russians used to control the Communist parties outside the Soviet Union—there are maybe a dozen men in the world who know as much as he does—but no one knows more. A tall, rumpled, genial professor who teaches at Georgetown, I'd met him first during my own miserable spell in academia, and we'd been friends ever since. Now in his sixties, and recently a widower, he lived by himself. At six-thirty he was still in his office, but readily accepted my invitation to dinner. "I have an ulterior motive, so it's on me. How about Chez Odette's in half an hour?"

"Terrific."

When he arrived at the restaurant, Leonard was his usual self, his understated wit slyly poking away at the universe. We talked friends, doings at the university, politics. But when our coffee arrived, Leonard lit up a cigar, folded his hands on his paunch, and grunted, "So what's it all about?"

"Take a look at this," I said, and handed him the best of Travin's "Halifax, 1940" prints.

He peered at it a moment. Then his face tightened in concentration and he irritably pushed his glasses up on his forehead and brought the picture close to his face.

Then he put it down and looked at me. "A fake," he said.

"A copy, certainly."

"I mean the writing's fake. Even if the picture is genuine, it wasn't taken in Halifax in 1940."

"Because," I said, "Georgi Dimitrov wasn't in Halifax then?"

"So you recognized him?"

I smiled. "Not in thirty seconds, I didn't. But eventually." Then I added, "Leonard, you realize this is all under your hat?"

"Oh yes. I can see your article now, splashed across *The New York Times Magazine.* But be careful. I still say it's a fake."

"Could you swear he *wasn't* in Halifax?"

"No. I suppose not. But it's unlikely."

"Where was he, then?"

"Moscow, at a guess. Where else? He didn't travel around incognito. He was one of the best-known Communist leaders in the world then—in the Party, they called him *Deda*—Grandpa—and that wasn't for nothing. Besides, the Comintern, especially the foreign sections, had just been hit by the Purges. I expect he was spending a lot of his time on Gorki Street holding hands with the survivors."

Leonard, on his home ground, can be hard to keep up with, so you don't want him to get too far ahead. "Gorki Street . . . you mean the Hotel Lux, where all the foreign Communists stayed?"

He nodded. "Ulbricht, Béla Kun, Thorez, Togliatti. They say that Tito literally ran into Earl Browder under the shower . . . a grisly experience, I should imagine." But then he stopped himself and frowned. "Let me see that again." He stared at the photograph. "What the hell, that *is* Browder." I leaned across the table to look. I would never have recognized him straight off, but with the name in my mind I saw it at once: Earl Russell Browder, general secretary of the Communist Party of the U.S.A. Slowly, still staring down at the picture, Leonard murmured, "You know, I wouldn't swear to it, but this guy, the one with his arms crossed—I forget his name, but I think he was the head of the Canadian CP . . . Buck. Tim Buck." He looked up at me. "If this is one of your stunts, I'll admit it's very ingenious. How did you do it?"

I held up my palm. "It's not a stunt, I promise. Just go back to Browder. I thought he was in jail around this time."

"Well, the trial was 1940—passport fraud—but I don't think he actually went in until later."

"So what this might show is a meeting, in Halifax, between the head of the Comintern and a bunch of top North American Communists?"

"If it's real."

"Don't worry, it is." I picked up the photograph and looked at it again. Dimitrov, Browder, this Canadian Communist . . . and now I recognized the yard they were standing in. I'd been there myself: it was the yard behind Dr. Charlie's clinic in Halifax. I lit a cigarette and made an executive decision. It wasn't hard—I'd trust Leonard Forbes a long way.

"Len, this is absolutely confidential."

"Sure."

"Okay. I don't understand most of this, but my way into it was the man at the back, the other one who's been circled."

"Don't know him."

"You wouldn't. He's dead now, but he was a Canadian, a wealthy businessman. Not at all the sort you'd expect to see running around with these revolutionary types. But he was in the fur business, and made several trips to Russia in the twenties. Apparently he got to know Zinoviev pretty well, and even had an affair with some woman on his staff. Her name was Anna Kostina—I don't suppose you've heard of her?"

He pursed his lips around his cigar and shook his head. "No. I don't think so."

"She was tried in 1934, along with Zinoviev, but I don't think they killed her."

Leonard shrugged, then shook his head again. "It doesn't ring a bell. She probably went through one of the *osoboe soveshchanie,* and in those years—'36, '37, '38, '39—you're talking some pretty big numbers: over a million Party members arrested, six hundred thousand shot outright, ninety percent of the rest dying in the camps. A single face doesn't stand out from the crowd, if you see what I mean."

"What I'm driving at is this: could this businessman, through people like Zinoviev and this woman, have become close—personally close—to Dimitrov?"

"I suppose it's not unreasonable—though I'm not sure I follow you. But Zinoviev was the first head of the Comintern, and already in the twenties Dimitrov was head of the Comintern's Balkan Section. So if this Canadian fellow knew Zinoviev well enough to have an affair with a woman on his staff, I guess he might have run into Dimitrov."

"But Dimitrov, back then, wasn't very important?"

"No. Revolutionaries like him were a dime a dozen. His break didn't come till 1933, when the Nazis tried to frame him for the Reichstag fire . . . if you can call that a break. But I suppose it was—his trial turned him into a newsreel celebrity. He made Göring and Goebbels look like fools and they finally cut their losses and simply deported him. The next year—or the year after, I guess—he was elected head of the Comintern. In a sense, he owed his career to Hitler."

"But come back to 1940. What was his position then? You said the Purges—"

"Actually, they hit the Comintern a bit earlier, say in the summer of '37."

"But they didn't touch Dimitrov?"

"Not directly, though a lot of other Bulgarians got it. All the foreign sections did. There was literally only one person left alive in each of the Polish and Hungarian units."

"But Dimitrov survived?"

"Yes."

"Why?"

Leonard shrugged. "Come on. You know better than that. In general, Stalin used the Purges to consolidate his personal power, but why any particular *individual* died—or escaped—is almost impossible to say. Actually, in Medvedev's book, I think he says that the NKVD began some sort of investigation against Dimitrov but it was never carried through. You could never say why."

"But—again going back to 1940—he might have been *afraid* he was going to be purged?"

"Oh, I'm sure he was. In fact, 1939, 1940, would have been an especially bad time. Dimitrov, remember, was the originator of the Popular Front: Communists were to unite with liberals and socialists to take on the Fascists. CPs all over the world became very popular."

"You mean, until Russia and the Nazis signed the Molotov-Ribbentrop Pact."

"Exactly. August 23, 1939: Stalin and Hitler embrace in the interests of peace-loving peoples everywhere—and the next week invade Poland together. Overnight, the whole Comintern policy switched right around. Now the Nazis were the good guys. But of course this was an incredible disaster for the Western CPs, and Dimitrov—to coin a phrase—was their embarrassment made flesh. Now I think of it, it's a miracle that he survived."

"But he *did* survive. He remained alive, both personally and politically—he remained head of the Comintern. And in that capacity—if you accept the photograph—he made a secret trip to North America in the spring or summer of 1940. Why? How come?"

Leonard pushed his lips out, let his chin settle back into the folds of his bow tie, and shook his head in his most professorial manner. "You can't expect me to answer that. No one could say, not on the basis of this."

"Guess."

"Scholars don't guess."

"But dinner guests do. Have some more brandy . . . and I promise that nothing you say will ever be used against you."

He hesitated for another half minute—though I knew he couldn't resist. Unlike most academics, Leonard possesses a brain and relishes using it. Leaning forward, he took a sip of his brandy and then propped the photograph against his coffee cup. "I'd say—since you've put a gun to my head—that your best bet is to work back from the *time* and *place* of this thing as much as from the people in it. Now, 1940 was a very interesting year. From the looks of this—as you say—it was probably taken in the spring. By that time, the Nazis have already invaded Poland and divided up Eastern Europe with Stalin. Now they're just turning west, into France—the 'phony war' is over and the real thing is well under way. . . ."

"I know. Remember, my mother and father were there."

"All right, then. Put that together with the place—Halifax, Canada. Also interesting. Why not the U.S.?"

"Convenience. Logistics. Dimitrov would have had an easier time getting in up there than down here."

Leonard grinned. "I now see why you were such a failure in academia—never accept the simplest explanation for any question. Besides, maybe you're wrong—maybe it had something to do with the fact that the Canadians were already into the war while we were still talking about it. In a way, that probably didn't mean very much; that early on, I don't suppose they had much of a military. What they did have, though, was industrial production. I know they built an awful lot of guns and ships and Merlin engines for the Spitfires. And you can see how that might tie up with Dimitrov and the Communists. In the thirties and forties, the CP still had clout in the trade unions, which meant they could have had a real effect on the industrial war effort. Strikes, slow-downs, refusing to work overtime, even sabotage . . . You can see how important all that would have been. And of course the *official* Party line said the war was of no consequence to real proletarians. All the same, we do know that sensible people in the Soviet Union understood that they'd end up fighting Hitler eventually. Therefore, the real inter-ests of the Russians required CP unions over here to *back* the war ef-fort, not obstruct it, and maybe Dimitrov was sent here to tell them so." He took a sip of his brandy. "You can even tie in this other man, the businessman—"

"His name was Brightman."

"Was he a Red?"

"I wouldn't think so."

"No, he sounds like a junior Cyrus Eaton—a capitalist who did enough business with the Russians to develop a certain rapport with them. Which would have made him perfect . . . Say the Canadian gov-ernment was worried about the effect the CP unions might have, and wanted someone from 'above' to give them a good talking to? Dimitrov, with all his prestige in the West, was a perfect man to deliver such a lecture, and this Brightman character was the perfect man to arrange all the details. It would have been done on the quiet, of course. Given that Browder was present, maybe Roosevelt was in on it too." He ground out his cigar. "What you'd want to do," he added, "is track down the rest of the people in that photograph. If they turned out to be CP trade union leaders, I might say that this is more than pure speculation, embar-rassing nonsense . . . which you've skillfully suckered me into."

I smiled, though I doubted if it was nonsense at all. On the con-trary, it sounded like an exceedingly reasonable theory—it just didn't do me very much good. If Dimitrov was connected with the child—if, not to beat around the bush, he was May's biological father—why had he needed Brightman at all? If he'd come to Halifax on legitimate politi-cal business, why the complicated scenario with Dr. Charlie, the pass-port, and so forth? I said, "So your explanation is entirely political . . . I mean, you can't see Dimitrov having any personal reasons for being there? You said he was under suspicion—that the NKVD was already investigating. . . . Could he have been defecting? At least thinking about it . . . ?"

Leonard made a face. "You're asking a hell of a lot from one photograph. Who knows what he was thinking? He *didn't* defect, we know that. Almost none of them tried to escape that way, even when they had the chance. They were Communists, remember, absolutely loyal—even as the gun was pressed into the back of their necks. And if Dimitrov was thinking about it, how come he ended up next to a Stalinist like Browder?"

"What about his family?" I asked. "Do you know if they were in danger?"

"If *he* was, they were . . . that goes without saying. But I don't think they were in any particular danger."

I took a sip of Drambuie, considering this. My mind had been following the obvious track, the dotted line that wound through all this history; if I dug down, would I discover the treasure? It was remarkably close to Grainger's outline. Dimitrov: a major Communist with connections that led back to Zinoviev and other people Brightman had known. Dimitrov: he hadn't been purged, but in 1940 he would have been *worried*. It all fitted. But something was missing . . . until, as it were, I pushed in my shovel at random.

"He did have a family, however. A wife . . . children?"

"He was married twice. His first wife died early on, I think before the Reichstag fire. I'm not sure whether they had children or not, but he adopted a couple with the second woman, after the war. Fanya . . . Boyko . . . there may have been another. The Bulgarians always made a fuss about it—kindly Uncle Georgi and so forth."

Somehow, I managed not to give myself away. But there it was, surely. Dimitrov, in mortal danger, had been unable or unwilling to save himself, but had wanted to rescue his child. Later, having survived, he redeemed himself with Fate by rescuing two others. Of course, that still left plenty of questions. Had Dimitrov brought May with him to Halifax, or had Brightman? Was it possible, in fact, that Brightman's efforts had been a form of insurance, a second option if Dimitrov hadn't been able to make the journey himself? Above all, why should any of this concern people so desperately now—why wasn't it merely a curiosity, an anecdote I could tell Leonard and which we might turn into a footnote? Finishing my Drambuie, I could feel all these questions well up in my mind, but for now, at least, I held back. The waiter hovered with coffee; I waved him away. Leonard looked tired, and he'd given me so many answers it seemed ungrateful to ask him for more.

I drove him home—he lived just across the Fairfax County line from Arlington—and by the time I headed back it was past eleven. Staying off the turnpikes, I took my time along Wilson Boulevard to the Key Bridge, then headed back into Georgetown, coasting sedately down Q Street just before midnight. These blocks, making a village, are where Washington's rulers live: on quiet, narrow streets behind black wrought-iron fences and neatly trimmed hedges; in tastefully restored terrace houses with bow fronts and carved lintels over the windows. My father had bought a house here when his own father had died, and my parents had always kept it, giving them a place to call home as the State Department shunted them all over the world. It was small, the end door in a row of three: white-painted brick; wrought-iron railings for the tiny three-step stoop and wrought-iron grilles over the first-story windows; a graceful dormer roof for the attic. I had always loved the house, but with my mother's passing it had turned into a problem. I couldn't bear to sell it but I didn't want to live in it, and so I used it now as a pied-à-terre on my trips into Washington. Given the taxes, it was a luxury I really couldn't afford, but tonight I was grateful for it. There was only one disadvantage: as with most of these houses, there was no garage, not even a lane, and the curb was so jammed with cars that I had to park around the corner, halfway up the next block.

The street was quiet; slamming the car door seemed an uncivil disturbance. Over on Wisconsin, the traffic made a soft, cozy hum and the wind rustled gently through the trees: old oaks whose shade was so thick that you were cool even in summer. I walked along in their shadow. On my right hand, the parked cars lent a soft sheen to the night, and as I walked on, memories swelled in the darkness. No wonder. My whole childhood had been spent just like this, *coming back* to this house: my return rendered all the more poignant by the certainty that I'd soon be leaving again. I could never walk down this street without getting the same old feelings: anxious expectancy, then glad recognition, and finally a fresh flowering of excitement because the place was never quite as you remembered. I'd loved it here. So had my mother—probably more than I had. After my father had gotten her out of France, she'd lived here for almost eight months by herself and she always claimed that it made her feel completely at home: it was so old, she said, and almost inconvenient enough to be French. Indeed, the house was really *her* house; my father had liked it, of course, but I associated him more with our summer place in Pennsylvania or our cars (one old Packard especially) or trips to New York on the train. . . .

But now I'd reached the door: three stone steps, then you're inside. Now I stood in the hall, its shadowy perspective stretching before me, the maple floor and oak paneling softly gleaming. To my left, a little light filtered into the dining room and glittered against the glass doors of a cabinet. Flipping on the light switch, I hung up my coat and went straight upstairs, but instead of going into my room, I ascended the narrow, switchback staircase that takes you up to the attic. I'm not sure why. I must have been thinking of my father, still caught up in the train of memories I'd brought into the house, for the attic had always been his retreat. There were two low rooms. The smaller of these had always been a storeroom, the larger my father's study, where, after his death, my mother had kept those of his possessions she couldn't bear to part with. I opened the door. Nothing here had been changed for years. Thus, since I knew precisely what to expect, there was an instant when that's what I saw, the past forming itself from the soft highlights within the shadowy gloom. There were the Art Nouveau curves of his Horta armchair; the neat rows of *Foreign Relations* lined up in the bookcase; the framed Foreign Service map (with its washed-out colors) that would always be the world to me; and beneath this sat his desk, with its serried ranks of framed photographs: my father's graduating class at Foreign Service school; my father, pinched in a high collar, helping the embassy staff bid farewell to some ambassador; my father at meetings and conferences; my father playing center field on the consulate softball team; and my father, fixed smile on his face, shaking hands with all those names you can barely remember: Acheson, Dulles, Christian Herter . . . For a second, as I say, that's what I saw. But then I realized what was actually in front of my eyes.

It would be wrong to call that room a shambles, or say it had been dismembered—that would imply a degree of violence that just wasn't there. But someone had taken it apart, just the same. The spine of every book had been sliced open with a razor: but so neatly that a piece of tape would mend them again. The old map had been pulled completely apart: but then neatly propped against the side of the desk. And although every one of those photographs had been removed from its frame, all the pictures, and all their little cardboard mattes, were arranged in separate, neat piles.

Brightman's house . . . Travin's room . . . and now this. I was almost too tired for shock, and the question—*What were they looking for?*— barely registered. But then I felt very afraid. Quickly, I crossed the room to the window. Peering cautiously into the street, I could see two men get out of a parked car, about thirty yards down the block, and silently close the doors behind them.

Later, I was to realize how lucky I'd been. Since I'd parked so far from the house, my car had given them no warning; in all likelihood, they hadn't even seen me come down the street—only my turning on the light in the hall had alerted them. But, as I say, I only worked that out later: then, I just moved, and without hesitation. I think that saved my life. Striding out of the room, I ran down the stairs to the second floor, then raced down the hall to the back stairs. These took me to the kitchen. I felt my way through the darkness to the back door; as I reached it, I could hear scratchings around at the front. I stepped into the night. The backyard was small—six feet of patchy lawn, two feet of border, a chest-high fence. I vaulted this, landing among my neighbor's fall bulbs. I scrambled ahead, through some shrubs, leaves shaking like tambourines and shadows poking into my eyes. Groping along the wall of the house, I came to a gate and stepped onto the sidewalk. I decided against my own car. Walking quickly, but normally, I turned down 31st, reached Q, then ran all the way across to Wisconsin. There were still a few people about; keeping close to them, I hurried south till I finally flagged down a cab. Half frozen, I slumped down on the seat and told the cabbie to take me to the Hay-Adams. It's expensive, but that night it seemed far safer than home.

10

It was three days before I got back to Berlin. Once again, it was a question of taking the long way around—and even before I left I had to make several detours.

The most important, of course, involved May.

Up to this point, I'd faced no direct threat to myself, nor had she; but now both of us were in danger. My encounter in Grainger's lane and the grisly events in Detroit could be written off as chance or coincidence, but not the search of my mother's house; that changed everything. I was now a target, even if I didn't understand why. But this meant that May was in danger as well—she had to be, since she was the only reason I was involved in the first place. That night, pulling myself together in the Hay-Adams, this conclusion seemed at first inescapable and then horrifying: for as soon as I'd thought everything through, I called her number in Toronto . . . and there was no answer. I called at midnight, at one, at one-thirty, then every ten minutes till three in the morning, and she still wasn't there. Falling asleep in a fever of guilt, I awoke at seven. Still no response. Then, as I began phoning the airport, something occurred to me. I had one other name in Toronto—Stewart Cadogan, Brightman's lawyer. So I dialed his number instead. At seven twenty-five there was no one in his office, but at seven thirty-one, by God, the old man picked up the phone himself.

There was a moment's pause as he took in my name. Then he grunted, "I'm surprised you'd start doing business this early, Mr. Thorne. But gratified. I've—"

I was in no mood for his crustiness and cut him off. "This is urgent, Mr. Cadogan. I'm very worried about May."

"For what reason?"

"Never mind. I just want you to send—"

"But I think I do mind, Mr. Thorne. You almost make it sound as if she was in danger."

"She is."

That made him pause for a second. "Why do you say so?"

"Because I've been calling her home since yesterday evening, almost continuously. There's nobody there."

"That would hardly indicate—"

"Listen, I don't want to argue. Just send somebody around there and make sure she's all right."

The anger in my voice finally got through to him. "I apologize, Mr. Thorne. I'd not understood that you were so upset. And of course, if you wish, I'll send someone to her house—I'll go myself—but I really don't see the need. She's not there—because yesterday afternoon she left for France."

"France?"

"Yes."

"You're sure?"

"Yes . . . or reasonably so. Yesterday afternoon she came by my office and said she was on the way to the airport. She had her bags with her."

I thought a moment, digesting this. It seemed incredible. She could only just have arrived back from Detroit. But she did have a house in France, so it was possible.

"How did she seem?"

"Calm. Subdued . . . but calm."

"You weren't surprised by her leaving at such a time?"

"I'm not sure it was my place to be surprised, Mr. Thorne. She said she was exhausted, that she wished to get away. I know she loves France and spends considerable time there—it seemed not unreasonable. And she left me various instructions concerning her property, the will, her father's remains . . . indeed yourself, Mr. Thorne."

"What do you mean?"

"What I say. Miss Brightman gave me your number in Virginia

and I tried to call you yesterday. She wished me to thank you on her behalf and since—she said—your efforts would have left you considerably out of pocket, she instructed me to give you a check for ten thousand dollars."

I was stunned—by everything, but the money especially. And the fact that I had spared a few thoughts for what this was costing me didn't make me feel less offended. After a moment I said, "Of course I won't accept her money, Mr. Cadogan—money has nothing to do with this and in any case that's a ludicrous sum."

"Mr. Thorne, she asked me—on her behalf—to insist."

"All right, you've insisted. But I still won't accept it."

"Very well. There was one other point. She wanted me to thank you for what you've done, but also to say that now you should stop. She was very determined about that. She said she would write you later and explain, but for now she wanted me to make you promise, unconditionally, to give up all the inquiries that you've been making into her past. They'd only cause harm; they'd only hurt her. That's what she said."

I made no reply. I was trying to understand what she was doing, and I suppose, from one point of view, it might have made sense—get away, wipe the slate clean.

"Mr. Thorne?"

"Yes."

"I ask you for that promise."

"I'm not sure I can give it."

"Mr. Thorne, please consider this carefully . . ." But then he stopped himself. And when he went on, he surprised me. "I'm sorry, Mr. Thorne. It was presumptuous of me to say that, for I know you will consider it as carefully as anyone could. But I am worried about her . . . despite what I've said. Perhaps it would be best for all of us to do just as she asks."

I hesitated. Had she told him something she hadn't told me? Perhaps she had, for now the old man went on, "You understand that I am discreet, Mr. Thorne—by my own nature and by the nature of my profession. But perhaps you don't know how often I curse that discretion. I do so now, for there is a great deal I would like to say which I can't. So I only say this. I have known the Brightmans for a good many years, and I know that May Brightman was always her father's protector—that was her life—and he was hers—that was *his* life. Now, you see, all she has left are those memories. If you were to alter them, or reveal that they had a false basis, you would be doing her a harm greater than you could possibly know."

"I think I'm aware of that, Mr. Cadogan."

"Very well. Do as you think best, and if you need me—for any reason—I can always be reached through this number. Please don't hesitate to use it."

"Thank you, sir. I'll remember."

We hung up. And for a moment, as I stood by the phone, I felt a funny mixture of feelings. Relief, consternation, something else . . . God only knows what it was. Mistrust? Suspicion? Her flight, the offer of money—so much money—and then her demand that I not go on—what did it mean? Then, as I asked myself this question, I was able to answer another. I knew what May had told Cadogan: she'd told him about our broken engagement. Yes, I was certain; that had shifted my status with the old man, lending me a legitimacy—as an old friend of the family—that was not far removed from his own. But there seemed, under the circumstances, only one reason why she would have confided this to him: to give him an extra call on my loyalty. After all, he'd been clear enough; to go on would be a betrayal of May.

Should I?

For me, this was a very real question, and I spent much of that day, and another sleepless night, thinking about it. In fact, I did not want to betray her; more importantly, I did not want to put her in danger. But the more I thought about what had happened, the queasier I felt. Her flight to France, in the final analysis, didn't seem natural and certain old questions would not go away. In Halifax, I'd wondered for the first time how much she'd actually known, how much of the truth she had told me; and, try as I might, her forgetfulness about Brightman's Jaguar still seemed peculiar. Then there was the money—and though I was probably being a little self-righteous, I still felt offended. It looked like a bribe.

But—of course—this argument had another side as well. She'd run off, but so what? It was her way of handling grief. And her grief, after all, would have a peculiar cast simply because it was the confirmation of her own worst fears: those fears would now seem a self-fulfilling prophecy, making her responsible for her father's death. Insane, but people are like that. . . . Then there were my own motives to consider. If I truly mistrusted her, perhaps the reasons were to be found in myself and the old wounds my ego had suffered. She'd betrayed *me*, after all: perhaps my psyche was now taking belated revenge. And this explanation seemed distressingly reasonable because the alternatives, when you thought about them—and I spent a lot of time thinking, that afternoon, in the Hay-Adams bar—bordered on the ludicrous. If I was going to suspect her, what could I suspect her *of?* Did I really imagine that she'd been involved, malevolently, in her father's disappearance and death? The idea was crazy.

Yes, it was crazy; but, rightly or wrongly, I suppose it was questions like these, which she herself had sowed in my mind, that ultimately decided me to disregard her wishes and go on. But I had other reasons too, and no doubt these showed how much this whole business had become my own. I'd started out as a spectator, become an unwitting catalyst, but now I'd seized the initiative. Because I'd broken into Travin's car, I—alone?—knew about Dimitrov. More: I had a way of tracking back over Travin's footsteps. Where would they lead? Could I live with myself if I refused to find out? And there was one final matter which I could not disregard. I was a target, that was clear, and I had been from the very beginning—that's why they'd taken May's telegram that very first day in Charlottesville. Or was that the real explanation? Might there not be another? *Something personal, something you wouldn't want a policeman to hear* . . . Sipping bourbon in the Hay-Adams bar, I began to work out a theory. Brightman had gone to Europe in late 1939 or early 1940, and had probably made his return journey just as Hitler launched his attack in the West. Therefore it was conceivable, even likely, that he'd been in Paris at the time the French had surrendered. A tricky moment. What if something had gone wrong? He was, after all, traveling with false papers. A couple of calls to the Canadian Embassy established that the Canadians had evacuated Paris with the British (and my mother) on the tenth of June 1940, *so after that date he couldn't have turned to his own people for help.* No. But the U.S. Embassy was carrying on business as usual *and my father was working there.* Had they met? Had my father rendered Brightman assistance—perhaps in an irregular way? Was I more directly involved—and hence more directly a threat—than I'd ever imagined? Speculation, that's all you could call this. But it did fit some of the facts, and even the possibility that it might be true made it impossible for me to turn back.

So I went on.

But cautiously.

Taking the most roundabout route I could think of, I flew to New York, took the train to Hartford, a bus to Boston, a commuter flight to Portland, and finally—the next morning—I rented an old Ford and headed off to New Hampshire. That afternoon, as I headed into the White Mountain area west of Berlin, I was reasonably confident I was alone. Even so, I was careful. Berlin's a small town, and there aren't that many motels. Giving them all a miss, I went on to Lancaster, about twenty-five miles to the west. By then, it was early evening, too late to do anything. I took a stroll through the town, bought a Boston *Globe*, then watched TV and went to bed early.

The next morning, I put my "plan" straight into action. This was simple enough. There was no listing for Travin in the local directories, and the number he'd left with the store didn't answer. But that didn't discourage me. He would have used a different name with the phone company, and you could hardly expect him to answer his phone, given his present condition. I had to hope, however, that the basic information he'd left with the store was genuine. If it was, I should be able to cross-reference the phone number and address and discover where he was living.

When I arrived in Berlin around ten, my first stop was the post office. No one there remembered Travin's name, but a clerk penciled in RFD 2—the rural delivery number he'd left with the store—onto my map. Following these directions, I stuck with the highway for three miles, then turned left onto an unmarked secondary road. Running straight for a time, it eventually began climbing steeply, then twisted its way through a thick stand of spruce.

The first mailbox—the next step in my plan—appeared shortly afterward.

It was a square one, at the end of a short drive leading to an aluminum "universal" home. The letters on the box were black and silver stick-ons, the sort farmers use on their pickups. I slowed to read them, pressing the microphone switch on the cassette recorder I'd picked up in Boston. I knew this couldn't be Travin, but you have to start somewhere—so W. F. Grafton became first on my list. Around the bend, in quick succession, there were three more places, just like his. Then came a gap—a mile of cedar and spruce—and then a large New

England–style house, all turrets and porches and dormers. Before each, I slowed slightly and murmured the owner's name into the mike. The miles rolled on. I learned that orange reflective letters are easier to read than black ones, I wondered about the etiquette of rural styles of address—the formality of "H. Edward Wilmott"; the terseness of "Carson's"—and I tried, unsuccessfully, to discern the patterns of land development here: a few suburban bungalows would be pressed tight together at the side of the road, then you'd have two miles of wilderness, a patch of rural slum, a fine old farmhouse overlooking a valley, and then bungalows and TV antennas again. After a time, however, even these signs of relative civilization petered out, and the forest pressed in. Logging roads led into nowhere. A big sign, in the shape of an Indian, pointed down a lane to a kids' camp. Then nothing. More trees. Miles of them. Until, with a hollow rumble, my wheels kicked up the logs on a bridge and I flashed by a hunting camp. Then nothing again. . . . By noon, I'd looped back to the main road, and finding Route 3 again, I turned toward Lancaster.

In my motel room, I ate a Big Mac, then played back my tape, giving myself a list of all the people living on RFD 2. Now, tediously, I looked up all their names in the phone book—hoping to match the number Travin had left with the photo store. In twenty-five minutes, I had it. Michael Travin had been staying at something called Gerry's White Mountain Camp.

This was the opposite of what I'd been hoping for—hotel, lodge, campground: these were the sorts of places where he might have stayed for a couple of days before moving on. I tried to recall what it looked like, but all I got was an image of bush, so I drove out there. Even knowing where it was, this took almost an hour, for it was at the "wilderness" end of my run: the road cut across a narrow notch in the hills, passed over a stream, then climbed steeply up a higher hill beyond. The mailbox, drooping on its post, was at the bottom of this upgrade, at the junction of a narrow dirt road that ran back into the bush. Drawing up beside it, I got out of the Ford and looked around, but memory had served me regrettably well; there was really nothing to look at but trees—no buildings, the nearest house was five or eight minutes back, and there wasn't much further on till you curled down the far side of the hill toward the highway. I walked up to the gate. It was new and padlocked shut, but it was just a regular metal farm gate. The road to the camp itself, disappearing into the trees behind it, might have run on for miles.

I drove back to Lancaster.

By then, it was after three in the afternoon. I called the camp number a couple of times, but there was no answer, and then, before it got too late, I decided to check a point. Lancaster, though smaller than Berlin, is the seat of Coos County, New Hampshire; as such, it boasts a fine old courthouse—with as much varnished brightwork inside as a millionaire's yacht—which contains the local deed registry. A clerk gave me a hand with the books, and I traced out the history of Gerry's Camp. The original Gerry had been one Gerard Ledoux, who'd put the land together in 1947. In 1962, it had passed by probate to his wife, who'd hung on to it for another three years. Since then, it had changed hands fairly regularly about every two years, the last purchaser, a man named Evans, having bought it ten months previously. I wasn't much disappointed by this; I hadn't really expected to find Travin listed as owner. Going back to the motel, I tried the camp number again—but still got no answer.

No answer.

That evening, again watching television—Lancaster had few other diversions to offer a stranger—I wondered about this. It did seem a bit funny. This was November. I hadn't hunted in a long time, and I'd never hunted in this state, but I guessed we were close to the deer season: hardly the time when a hunting camp would close down. Of course, everyone might be off in the bush, or the camp might have gone bankrupt—or conceivably Mr. Evans had purchased the land for different reasons altogether. Still, as I went on trying the number and getting no response, I decided I wasn't going to let up on the caution.

The next morning, around nine, I drove into Berlin and paid a visit to the Pinkham Notch Shop, a sporting-goods store on the main street. Here, a friendly, knowledgeable Canuck sold me a bush shirt, a heavy wool sweater, a camouflage poncho, a rubberized groundsheet, two canteens, one hatchet, a Russell belt knife, a flashlight, a Silva compass, Bushnell 10-power binoculars, and a nylon pack to put everything in. He had no maps, but I assumed I wouldn't have to go far. I went on to a grocery: ham, cheese, bread, a liter of cheap Valpolicella. Back in the car, I filled up the canteens with the wine, then drove out of town.

The day was no better than yesterday, cold and drear, but inside the old Ford's comfortable fug (oil, ancient dust, cigarette smoke), the cold world turned remote, like a movie, or the miniaturized landscape toy trains pass through: the Androscoggin River was a twist of gray modeling clay, toothpicks made birches that rattled their branches against the slate sky, and the thick stands of spruce were bits of pipe cleaner dipped into ink.

Slowly, I climbed through the hills of RFD 2. Out of habit, I kept one eye on the mailboxes, and noted that a few red flags were up, signaling the mailman to stop for a letter. I recognized landmarks now: a twist in the road that revealed a long, forested valley, a hill topped with an enormous, gnarled spruce. And I even had my favorite sights: an old frame farmhouse with a white paddock and three Shetland ponies and the burned-out shell of a barn beside the white splash of a stream.

After a time, a pickup truck passed me—the first vehicle I'd seen on this road—and then, getting closer, I slowed. Once again, loose logs bounced under my wheels as I crossed over a bridge, and a hundred yards on, the road bent slightly left. As it straightened out, it passed the camp gate—still locked—and began climbing steeply again. At this point I checked the odometer. One and two-tenths miles further on, a logging road ran off to the left. It was further than I would have liked, but there was really no other place to pull over, and the ground, though bumpy, was firm. I nosed the car in. Ten yards on, the track widened a little and pulled a bit right, then became so overgrown as to be completely impassable. But this was perfect for me: the jog meant the Ford wouldn't be seen from the highway.

To keep dry, I went through the contortions of changing inside the car. The flannel bush shirt—an ugly green and black plaid—went over my regular shirt. Then came the hiking boots and the sweater, which was loose enough to be comfortable. Next I packed up the knapsack, making sure the binoculars and groundsheet went in last, and slung it over my shoulder, paper-boy style, so that it rested on my left hip. Finally, on top of everything else, came the poncho. Drawing up its hood, I stepped into misery.

Coniferous forest, especially if it's been cut over recently, makes about the worst bush in the world. After five minutes, I knew this stuff was pure hell: a northern equivalent to the Amazon jungle.

The trees, mainly spruce, grew so tightly together that you could barely move, and their thick, heavy boughs made it impossible to see where you were going. Dead branches jabbed like spikes. Underfoot, branches left from past cutting had turned slick as ice. And everything was wet—after ten feet, my pant legs were soaked. There was nothing to do but grit my teeth and bull forward—though I was ass backwards about fifty percent of the time. I blundered through huge, sticky cobwebs; branches slashed a dozen stinging cuts on my face; and the rain sifted down as an acrid, resinous haze—it was like taking a bath in retsina. To make matters worse, I'd started high up on the slope and kept sliding downhill, though I was trying to make a straight course, a little east of north, that would keep me parallel to the camp road. After ten minutes, though, I gave up on all that fancy stuff and just tried to make sure I didn't circle back on myself. Eventually, things got a little easier. I stumbled onto a deer path—running northwest, downhill, but I was in no mood to be finicky—and for ten minutes I enjoyed quick, easy going. Then the ground opened up, spruce and pine giving way to maple and oak—their leaves gleaming russet and gold in the gloom—and I was even able to glimpse the miserable sky overhead.

I took a breather then and tried to fix my position. I'd been walking for forty-five minutes but probably hadn't traveled a mile from my entry point. I'd been well up the mountain to begin with, but had definitely been angling downhill, which meant, by my calculations, that I'd eventually intersect the camp road. But I didn't want to do this; or at least not too soon, or in an uncontrolled way. My idea was to reconnoiter the camp, making absolutely certain that I saw the occupants—if any—long before they spotted me. I looked around. I was standing in a clearing full of small oaks, but there was one tall larch nearby and I decided to climb it. Not easy: there were no low branches, so I had to cut notches with my hatchet and shinny the first ten feet, and by the time I reached the first big branch my fingers were glued together with resin and bark. But I got what I wanted—a view—and at twenty feet I hung on and peered out. Across the valley there was nothing to see, just a long gray sweep of trees. But looking backwards, up the hill I'd been coming down, I saw just what I wanted: a rocky outcrop, near the summit. I took a compass bearing on it, clambered down, and allowed myself two gulps of wine before starting out.

It was twelve-twenty when I left for the knoll; I reached it exactly two hours later.

By then, I'd begun to get the hang of these woods. For reasons of soil or climate, the evergreens—like some drab forest infantry—commanded the heights while the hardwoods marched in their bright dress uniforms along the lower slopes. And on the lower ground, as the hillside flattened out into the valley, the trees were much older, or at least larger, and grew further apart. Since all of this made the going much easier, that's where I stayed, keeping parallel to the hill, which, of course, I'd eventually have to climb. But here I could walk rather than scramble; find my way rather than blunder on blindly. My steps and my breathing fell into a rhythm, while my mind found a nice quiet spot at the back of my skull and happily dozed. Still, this comfort was only relative. I was still cold, and very wet—the rain came down hard for ten minutes, and these open woods gave me little protection. But I made steady progress, and when the rain slacked off, I even caught a whiff of that lovely forest fragrance—damp earth, fresh water, pine needles, the soft rot under logs. After I rested awhile on a rock, my breath finally stilled and I listened quietly to the soft forest drip all around me. Memories came back. Pennsylvania. Hunting trips with my father. The perfect silence that forms just before your finger squeezes the trigger; the ache you always get at the back of your legs. . . . Five minutes later, coming into the open, I was able to look up the hillside and see my knoll, almost directly above.

From now, it was all uphill—and it was a high hill—but this was easier than I expected. The ground was much rockier, the footing easier; and though the hardwoods petered out, this stonier soil supported fewer trees altogether—some spruce and pine, but more birch and cedar. Up the steepest slopes, I had to crawl on all fours, but most of the time I could find a spot to wedge my foot in, and frequently small runs of boulders formed traverses that let me work my way up at an angle. Even better, about halfway up I hit a rocky ledge, a sort of shelf, that made an easy path. I worked along this quite comfortably, now and then catching glimpses—huge sweeps of space—of the valley below me. And then the path opened up, a big blast of wind hit me, and I stepped onto the knoll.

But it really wasn't a knoll. As I rested a moment, leaning back on a rock, I realized it was a flat ledge—an expansion of the ledge I'd been walking along—that projected from the hillside like a fungus jutting out from a tree. It was completely open, the wind blustered in my ears, and up this high even the dark, overcast sky was dazzling. Shading my eyes, I stared over the valley. A dizzying expanse of space opened out: a curve of high gray sky above, a curve of dark khaki below. I guessed that the valley was about two miles wide, though I've never been a great judge of distances. The opposite hill was a little lower than the one I was on, but higher hills rose beyond it. Though the floor of the valley was rough and wooded, I also caught a glint of water through the trees—a substantial stream, if not quite a river. On the far side of this, a little way up the hill, Gerry's Camp was clearly visible: one large building, two smaller ones, a trickle of smoke.

Reassured that it was there, I turned away for a moment. In behind a big boulder I stretched out my groundsheet, holding down the corners with stones, and set out a rather soggy picnic. But I was starving—even my pasty sandwiches tasted terrific, and I refused to complain about the plastic aftertaste the canteen lent the wine. Finally, stretching my legs out, I relaxed with a cigarette. I even thought of a fire, but then decided against it. I could build one all right—I could sense various old skills coming back—but in this rain it was bound to smoke, and if I could see smoke from Gerry's, presumably they would see mine. Taking no chance, I let a second cigarette warm me instead.

By three o'clock I was ready to get down to business.

At the extreme edge of the knoll, a couple of boulders made a kind of chair, and I wedged myself in and examined the valley with my binoculars. I could see the road I'd driven up, but the camp road, the one with the gate, wasn't visible at all. Indeed, the most conspicuous feature of this landscape was the stream, a snaking gleam through the trees. At one point, the bank opened into a meadow—presumably a spot where it flooded in the spring—and just beneath the camp itself, the bank was very rocky, a scree of small boulders about twenty yards wide. On the far side of the stream, this rocky beach ended at the base of a hill, almost a cliff, which sheered up to a wide, flat terrace that was quite open except for a few cedar trees. It was here that the camp had been built.

There were three separate buildings. The largest, its front facing me directly, was the type of New England farmhouse I was learning to admire. It was built on two levels: two full stories and an attic with dormers. At the eastern end rose a high, hexagonal tower and a roofed veranda wrapped around the ground floor. The roof of the house was shingled with cedar shakes, very weathered; judging by them, and the sag in the roof of the veranda, I guessed that the place had been allowed to run down, though somebody was clearly taking care of it now: even in this dull light, it gleamed with fresh paint—white for the walls, dark green for the shutters and trim. Parallel to this main building (no doubt the "lodge") stood a smaller one, about the same vintage: a kind of coach house. And off to the right, and closer to me, there was a long shed with a metal roof.

Amidst all this real estate, I detected a few signs of humanity.

Smoke still trickled from the chimney, a white wisp against the gray sky; and just as I lifted the binoculars, I was fairly certain that I'd heard the faint, faraway *whap* of a door slamming shut—a back door, perhaps, for no one appeared at the front. In addition, three vehicles were parked on a patch of gravel in front of the metal-roofed shed: a small brown pickup truck, a yellow Volkswagen Scirocco, and a rusted sedan whose boxy shape took a moment to recognize . . . an ancient Datsun 510. So, I thought, someone was home—why didn't they answer their phone?

But as I stared down at the place—keeping those flat, hard binocular images steady in front of my eyes—I wondered if there wasn't a more relevant question. What had Travin's status been here? If this was really a hunting camp, had he been a guest? An employee?

Thinking this over, I crouched in my eyrie and tried to keep warm with my wine and my cigarettes. Half an hour slipped by. I kept telling myself that this wasn't too bad; indeed, the rain stopped completely, and after a while the wind switched around, putting me comfortably in the lee of the hill. I watched a hawk drift over the valley and studied a doe taking a drink from the stream—each sip paid for with a frightened, quivering look. Ten more minutes, one more cigarette . . . And then, without warning, a figure stepped off the veranda. I grabbed up the binoculars, pushed hair out of my eyes, thumbed the focusing wheel.

The figure was a man, walking briskly across to the cars.

I only had him perfectly clear for a second, just as he stepped into the pickup. Blue jeans. Windbreaker, unzipped. A hint of reddish-brown hair. . . . A glimpse, that's all it was, but in a way that made him almost easier to identify.

Surprise?

Elation?

Fear?

A little of each. As the truck backed around and turned into the trees, I set down the glasses and let go of my breath.

A short, red-haired, weasel-faced man.

The man in Halifax, behind Grainger's place.

The man who'd floated in the darkness beyond Brightman's study, then disappeared down the hall like a ghost.

II

—

I watched the camp for six days.

To begin with, I used the knoll as my base, and by the time I was through, I'd even made the place halfway comfortable. An extra ground-sheet, rigged between two cedars, kept off the rain; and wrapped inside a sleeping bag, with a couple of butane camp stoves angled to reflect their heat off a big rock, I stayed reasonably warm. My meals were sandwiches and Dare cookies, I replaced my canteens of wine with a thermos of coffee and brandy, and I improved things on the optical side with a 20-power Zeiss telescope. So conditions were passable, if not exactly cozy. I soon developed a routine. I left my motel around five every morning, and was normally blundering through the bush as dawn dribbled over the horizon. On the knoll by seven, I'd bundle myself in my sleeping bag and watch the mist uncoil over the stream or a few straggling ducks, their necks stretched out before them, beat a hasty retreat down the valley from Canada. My first sighting usually came around eight: one of them would step onto the veranda with green plastic bowls for their dogs. Sometimes hours then passed before I saw them again—boredom was as much a problem as anything. My first coffee break, a great event, was at ten, I munched my sandwiches at noon, then there was more coffee at two. I always left by four-fifteen—I didn't want to get caught in that bush after dark.

What did I gain by all this?

Not much.

Travin had "known everything"; Travin had known *why* Brightman had died. Thus, having traced Travin this far, I assumed that I would know too—that I'd make the final connection between Brightman,

Dimitrov, the adoption of May, and the eruption of all these events into the present.

In fact, what I now discovered seemed to lead in a completely different direction. Sitting up on that knoll, half frozen, I knew that the people I watched through my telescope were connected to Brightman, but the hows and whys now seemed to evaporate.

Still, I did gather some data. There were five men, no women, staying at the camp, and with the help of the telescope I soon learned to distinguish them. The red-haired man, the one I'd seen in Brightman's house, was obviously the leader. Twice I saw him ordering the others about—gesturing, pointing—and they obeyed him without hesitation. But it was equally clear that he wasn't running a hunting camp. Their one visitor came on the third day I watched them, but he was wearing a suit and left after an hour.

By that time, the third day, I was frustrated. My expectation in Washington—that I was on the brink of a solution—had now retreated into the distance. Yet I wasn't sure what to do. Getting closer to the camp wasn't the answer. With the telescope I could see well enough; the trouble was, what I wanted to see wasn't the sort of thing you ever *do* see: plans, relationships, motives. I thought of breaking into the house and searching it, but on top of all the other risks—and I wasn't sure I had the nerve—there was the problem of the dogs. These were nothing special, just a couple of sheepdogs, but they were clearly turned out of the house every night to guard it.

That third night, back in my motel room, I decided on something simpler: to follow them when they left the camp in their cars.

From the start, I'd observed them departing on a number of such expeditions. Most had an obvious purpose—carting their garbage to the dump, buying groceries—but others were less clear, and they were frequent enough to arouse my curiosity. For example, on the second day the red-haired man took off in the Scirocco just after nine and still hadn't returned when I came down from the knoll. Where had he gone? What had he done? Following them was the easiest way to find out, and I tackled the problem on the fourth morning, hunting for a spot on RFD 2 where I could keep the gate under observation. I found one, though it wasn't very good. Because of the way the road curved, I had to be almost on top of the gate to see it; and because there was virtually no shoulder here, my car wasn't even remotely hidden—which meant I had to stay very alert to avoid being seen. As soon as someone came down the camp road, I'd pull out, as if I was just passing by, and then watch in my mirror to see which way the car turned. I almost never timed this properly; I'd be around the first curve before the driver got out of the car, opened the gate, and emerged onto RFD 2. Because of this, I'd drive very slowly, waiting to see if he came into sight. If he did, I'd drive on normally and he'd usually pass me; if not—if he turned in the other direction—I'd have to make a fast U-turn and chase after him. All of this sounds clumsy, but it worked. Over the next three days, I followed them on seven separate trips away from the camp. On four occasions I broke away quickly—I was afraid they might spot me—but the other three times I was able to stay with them to their destination.

All of these excursions were completely mundane, and I only learned anything of significance from one of them.

They bought groceries, gas, stamps; they took their clothes in to the cleaner's; the Scirocco was repaired at Al's Garage, despite its enormous sign—WE SPECIALIZE IN JAP CARS—and they picked up a cord of wood from a farmer near Gorham, a little place about ten miles south of Berlin. None of this was very enlightening, though I was rather more comfortable than I'd been up on that knoll. But then, on the fifth day, the pickup took their trash to the dump and I decided to do a little garbage picking. No one saw me: the dump, up a short access road, was just an open spot in the bush. There was a wooden shack, presumably for an attendant, but that morning I only had two hopping crows for company. I could see where the truck had parked and three yellow garbage bags had been tossed nearby. Making like a real CIA man, I began poking through them, thereby discovering that garbage is garbage: orange rinds, eggshells, milk cartons, yuck. But the last of the bags contained newspapers and there I found something: in among the New York *Times*es and Boston *Globe*s were two old copies of a Russian-language paper, *Nasha Strana—Our Homeland*. I'd actually heard of it, though I'd never seen a copy before: it was published in Buenos Aires and served the large Russian émigré population there. Both issues were a couple of months old, the paper yellowed and cracked, and though I sat in the car and read them through from beginning to end, I couldn't see anything of particular interest. Nonetheless, it established something important: Travin's connection to the camp hadn't been casual.

An hour later, I made another discovery—also important, even if I couldn't say precisely what its significance was.

I was back in my regular position by the side of the road when a plumpish woman, in an old Toyota, pulled in by the gate and delivered the U.S. mail—one envelope, slipped into their box. As soon as she left, I did the obvious thing: the mailbox was an old one, and though it had a lock, this had long since been broken. The envelope, standard size, was fat, heavy, crinkly. I shoved it into my pocket and headed straight back to the motel.

When I opened it, I discovered three items: a wad of receipts, stapled together; twenty hundred-dollar bills; and a letter from a lawyer in Springfield, Massachusetts. This was addressed to "Mr. Howard Petersen c/o Gerry's White Mountain Camp." It itemized all the paid bills, noted that "your usual remittance is enclosed," and concluded: "After these transactions, your funds held in trust by this firm amount to $22,736.79." It was signed, as per the letterhead, by one Robert Evans.

Robert Evans—whose name was on the camp's deed. Interesting. I flipped through the receipts. They included everything from a county tax bill to an American Express account. The local items were all charged to the camp, the others to something called E. Arnott Travel Ltd. In the case of the Amex account this might even have been genuine—it certainly included plenty of trips: Boston–Montreal, Montreal–Toronto, Toronto–New York, Boston–London, Amsterdam–Frankfurt, Brussels–New York. . . . During the previous month, Mr. Petersen had been moving around and taking certain precautions to cover his tracks: he either hid behind his lawyer or paid up in cash—and indeed it occurred to me now that I'd never seen any of them make a trip to the bank.

It was three o'clock when I made this discovery. Given the sum of money involved, I assumed that Mr. Petersen was expecting his letter, so I drove straight to Springfield and put it back in the mail. It was late by then, so I stayed overnight and didn't head back to Berlin till the next morning.

That was a dreary drive. I had no idea where I stood. Something was going on, and Berlin was one of the centers; but Brightman, Dimitrov, and Travin revolved around it like unknown, mysterious planets. Above all, I couldn't see where Travin fitted in. Presumably, he'd been living at the camp. Did the people there know what had happened to him? Or had Travin been a renegade, whom they themselves had eliminated? This had to be admitted as a possibility, but if I accepted it I had to reject my previous theory—that the people who had dealt with Travin, and searched that hotel room, were "official." But they *had* been—I was sure of it. Which meant that I was dealing with two sets of Russians: the KGB—the men who'd killed Travin—and the people I was watching right now. But who could they be? A good question . . . which I couldn't answer. Yet, as I drove along, I wondered if I didn't have a few clues. They were Russian. They were apparently an organized group, and they might have émigré connections: witness the paper I'd pulled out of the garbage. What seemed to tie these facts together, albeit with a tenuous thread, were some of the remarks Travin had made on the phone in Detroit. At the time, I'd barely noticed them, but now they came back into my mind. "We can talk about the *byliny*," Travin had said, "or the *beguny* or the Black Hundreds." I'd taken him to mean: we can talk about anything under the sun—but perhaps he'd revealed more than he'd intended. The *byliny* are the great medieval folk epics of Russian literature, and their most famous hero—Ilya of Murom—has long been a symbol of Russian power, Russian unity, Russian Christianity, and the greatness of Russia's common man. The *beguny*—if I remembered correctly—were a crazy nineteenth-century religious sect (the word means "fugitive") who refused to have anything to do with authority (especially the census and passports) and took to the woods, like Robin Hood. And of course the Black Hundreds were a group of anti-Semitic thugs, with connections to the Czarist court, whose program was embodied in *The Protocols of the Elders of Zion*. At this point, you could even make a direct connection to myself. The *Protocols* were ostensibly the outline of a Jewish plot to conquer the world by subversion. In fact, they'd been concocted by the Russian secret police around 1900, and had continued to be important in anti-Semitic propaganda into the thirties—and even later. For, in September 1972, the Soviet Embassy in Paris had actually issued one version of them, *word for word*, as a document entitled "Israel: A School of Obscurantism." I'd been in Paris at the time, had written a piece on it, and, in consequence, hadn't been able to get a visa back to Moscow for the next year.

Could all that be connected? Was it possible that Travin, without meaning to, had hinted that these people were some sort of wild émigré sect—Russian and religious, anti-Semitic and anti-Soviet? There was no reason why this shouldn't be true; in fact, there are Russian émigré groups like this all over the world. But what was the connection to Brightman, to Dimitrov, to May—and why did the KGB take it so seriously that they were prepared to murder its members inside the United States?

When I arrived back in Berlin, I had no idea what the answers to these questions might be, and not much certainty that the questions themselves made any sense. In fact, I didn't have any ideas at all, and later that afternoon, when I returned to my customary position near the camp gate, I was really admitting that I couldn't think of anything better to do.

I got there about half past three and for the next couple of hours bored myself with the futility of my own thoughts. But finally, as dusk began to concentrate into full night, headlights swept over the gate. A man emerged, his shadow stretching over the road. The red-haired man—I could now tell them apart by their shape, bearing, stance. But there was someone else in the car with him, which made me curious, for I'd never known them to travel in pairs. It was the short, stocky one who usually drove the pickup. . . . But now I was well into my little trick, pulling out and heading up the road, and once again I hadn't timed it right. Forty seconds passed. There were still no lights in my mirror, so I U-turned and doubled back. The road was empty, but as I came through the curve I could see their taillights way up ahead. They were driving the Scirocco and traveling fast: away from Berlin, toward Route 26. This wasn't the usual pattern—most of the time they headed for town—but then I'd never before followed them this late in the day. We came up to the highway. Left turn. North. Which was also rare. As the road twisted into the hills, I fumbled along the dash for my map. North of here was a place called Colebrook, very small; then the Vermont border; then Canada.

The highway curved and climbed higher, then swooped down through the Dixville Notch. Hanging on to the wheel, I kept my mind on my driving; the Scirocco sprinted ahead—your glorified Rabbit—while my Ford drifted clumsily through the curves and grumbled up grades. Still, the further we went, the more content I was to hang back; on a road with so many hills and curves, it was unlikely that they'd spot me, but there was no sense taking chances, especially since there were so few places where they might turn off. Even so, I almost made a mistake. We passed through Colebrook, where I closed up a little, and the border, eight or ten miles beyond, came up quicker than I expected. The border post here is very small—Canaan on the U.S. side; a tiny Quebec village, whose name I never did learn, on the Canadian—so there's just one small hut and a single guard. I only realized what was happening at the very last minute—if I hadn't pulled over, I would have been sitting right behind their car as they went through. As it was, I gave them five minutes before coming up and they were just pulling away as I arrived. Once I was cleared, I took after them. The road here was gravel, twisting along the shore of a lake, and no matter what you were driving you couldn't go very fast. No one seemed to live in this district; there was an abandoned farm, a few scruffy cottages, "The Christian Frontier Camp." At last I bumped up onto asphalt and then I picked up their lights. They led me to a town called Coaticook, then further west along the same narrow road. There were hills in the distance, big lumps of darkness, but rolling countryside stretched away on either side of the double-barreled sweep of the headlights. Now there were more houses, and farms whose floodlit silos were painted with the blue fleur-de-lys. I hung back—there wasn't much traffic—and when the Scirocco turned down a still smaller road, I put out my lights. The night was like ink. Driving blind, I edged out to the center line, guessing the curves by the twitch of their taillights. Entering woods, we started to climb. I had to slow down, but every time they went round a curve, I flicked on my lights and shot ahead, before dousing them again. Finally, a mile further on, they swung right. I slowed right down, watching them across an open field. Their lights poked down this side road about two hundred yards and then stopped; and then backed up a bit before turning sharp left. That had to mean a house or farm. I waited till they were gone, and then followed, my wheels crunching over the gravel. Passing the spot where they'd turned, I could see a lane leading up through some trees, with a glimmer of light just beyond. Keeping straight on for a hundred yards or so, I backed around and pulled over.

With the motor idling, I rolled down my window. A soft, rustling night spread around me. The air was cool, full of the smell of grass and wet earth. After those miles in the dark, I needed a break and lit up a cigarette, but as soon as my nerves had knit back together I got out of the car. Silently, staying on the grass at the edge of the ditch, I walked up to the lane. There was a mailbox, of course—I wondered if the damn things wouldn't haunt my dreams in future years as banal symbols of hidden identity. This was an old one, with a name crudely painted in red: *N. Berri.*

I went up the drive a few steps, but all I could see was a vague pattern of lights beyond some maple trees. My nose quivered then. There was an odd, strange smell in the air. Presumably this place was a farm, but it wasn't manure. Chickens? Pigs? It was different, stronger. Something like skunk, but not that either. The breeze shifted, the smell wafted away. . . . I hesitated. I wanted to go further down the road, but I knew I couldn't. The two men in the Scirocco plus this N. Berri—that made it three against one, and if they caught me skulking around, what explanation could I possibly give?

I went back to the Ford.

An hour passed.

Then, around eight-thirty, a terrible howl cut through the night, ending with the most pitiful whimpering sound I'd ever heard in my life.

It was so sudden and startling that it froze me in my seat. Staring into the blackness, I leaned forward and switched off the engine, listening as silence hummed in my ears. Then a dog barked. Except—like that smell—it wasn't quite that; it was different, a quicker, sharper *yip.* And then another barking voice joined in, and then another and another, and for the next twenty-five minutes it didn't stop: the helpless, desperate baying of terrified animals pacing back and forth in their runs. It went on and on; cries of pain and fear and lamentation that made my skin crawl with horror. But what had happened? And what could I do?

Maybe I could have, should have, done something; but I didn't. I just sat there and waited.

Then headlights swept down the lane.

The Scirocco. As it paused at the end of the drive, I had a glimpse of two shadowy figures inside, one of whom was the red-haired man from the camp. Then the car turned and headed back toward the highway.

I watched till their lights finally winked out in the distance. Half of me, I admit, wanted to follow them, but I couldn't—I felt bad enough as it was and to have driven away from that pitiful howling would have left too much on my conscience. So I started the Ford and moved up the road. As I turned into the drive, stones popped under the tires and trees flashed silver in the glare of my headlights. For fifty yards the lane was black as a tunnel, but then it curved around in a crescent and a lawn gleamed like black ice. I could see the house then, and every light in the place seemed to be on. It was a small bungalow, not much more than a cottage, the roof slanting steeply over a small front porch. Bright fans of light spread out from two windows, but everything else was in shadow. As my headlights came around, I could see that the space between the porch and the ground was filled in with white-painted lattice. Shovels and rakes were leaning against this; a wheelbarrow, filled with dead leaves, stood just at the end of the drive.

I stopped the Ford but kept the engine running and then blew the horn a couple of times.

The crying and barking grew even louder, but no one came out of the house.

Very reluctantly, I stepped out of the car, then waited a moment, one hand on the top of the door and one foot inside. For a moment, I stared at the house over the roof of the car, reached in and blew the horn again, but still no one came. Beneath the grisly howling of the dogs—or whatever they were—night sounds whispered and cool air traced my cheek. The musky odor I'd smelled before was now very strong, but I still couldn't decide what it was. Closing the car door softly, I stepped around the hood, paused again, then went straight up to the porch. There was a metal storm door. I knocked and it shook with a rattle, but by now I was sure that no one was coming, so I eased it open, and then I saw that it was slightly ajar and I just pushed it ahead of me.

Standing on the threshold, I looked into a small, brightly lit room. A cottage room. It was crammed with the sort of old furniture that collects in such places, a clumsy sofa, a white wicker chair, a heavy square armchair from the fifties, floor lamps with tasseled shades.

But this wasn't what I looked at; not then.

Directly in front of me, on the other side of the room, was an arch leading into the kitchen beyond, and in the middle of this space, lashed into a straight-backed chair with a rope, was an old man—but pulled over his head, like a sack, was the head and shoulders of a fox: a white fox, whose lips were pulled back, grinning in death. The other half of its body was lying beside the chair, its guts bulging out of it in a bluish-pink mess, with the ax that had been used to sever the neck driven into the floor just beside it. Blood was everywhere. The room stank of it; it was matted like paint in the fox's fur, it glistened around the legs of the chair, great black stains had soaked into the carpet.

I sucked in a breath—but a breath whose stench made me choke it off in my windpipe. I wouldn't say that I'm squeamish, but God only knows why I didn't pass out at the sight of all this. Maybe, after Detroit, I was ready for anything. Or maybe the cruelty of the scene twisted the horror I felt into anger. In any case, my shoes skidding in gore, I crossed the room to the old man. He was alive. With a convulsive jerk, I flung the fox's head away, and for the first time he must have known I was there, for he started to struggle, almost overbalancing the chair. I caught him. He was shaking with fear, and as I reached around behind him to get at the ropes, he started to whimper, "They were going to kill them all, just like that. They said they'd kill them all one after the other . . ."

I coughed. If I coughed, I might not have to be sick. My hands, slick with blood, tugged at the ropes.

The old man kept whimpering; the foxes kept howling.

"It's okay," I finally said, getting him free. "It's okay. They're not going to kill anyone now, Mr. Berri. You're all right. Listen: I'm a friend. Do you understand that? I'm a friend."

I took him by the shoulder and eased him a little away from me.

"I was a friend of Harry's," I said. "Harry Brightman's."

At last something flickered into his eyes.

"Poor Harry," he whispered. "Things never end like you think."

12

As Berri later said, it wasn't as bad as it looked—but that made it quite bad enough.

They'd slapped him around, bloodied his nose, and the business with the fox's head had put him into shock; but he was more frightened than hurt. I laid him on his bed, covered him with a blanket, brought him water. He began to pull himself back together again pretty quickly, and then, I sensed, felt a little embarrassed. Unreasonable, but also understandable: he was a proud old man, as I soon discovered, and couldn't have relished being seen by a stranger in such a state. In any case, once I was sure he didn't need a doctor, I left him alone and went back into the kitchen. There, looking through the arch, I gawked at the horror of the living room.

The sight was nearly indescribable; the disgust it aroused almost beyond expression.

Once upon a time, it must have been a cozy room, and its odd, jumbled furniture—flea-market items, gifts from friends, "made that myself"—gave it a rough, homey quality. But now it was like the inside of an abattoir. Blood glistened on the shiny brocade of that heavy old armchair; it was sprayed on the walls; a bookcase made a dam for a red, thickening stream. The remains of the fox were lumps of meat in this grisly stew. The head was the worst. Raggedly hacked away at the neck, its face grimaced in agony, the enormous yellow eyes still bulging with the pain they had felt. They'd also cut open its belly, and the guts were spilled around the legs of the chair. It was hard not to gag; but this was, I knew, a horror I couldn't ask Berri to face, so I stepped as carefully as I could through the carnage and found a shovel outside on the porch.

With this, I pushed the gore into a bloody puddle in the middle of the carpet, then picked it up like a sling and dumped it into the wheelbarrow. Obscenity—there's nothing you can do except bury it. Trying not to look at what was directly under my nose, and cutting off each breath before it got to my windpipe, I grabbed up the handles and trundled the barrow around the side of the house. I was looking for a garbage can, an old carton, anything. But behind the house, stretching down one side of the yard, was a long strip of garden and so I humped my way across ruts and over old cucumber hills to the end of it. There, with the foxes' pitiful howling as a graveside lament—it had never ceased—I scooped out a hole and tipped everything in. Finally, having covered it all up, I flung the shovel into the night.

At last I could breathe again. Wandering a little away from the garden, I let the night cool me and looked around in the darkness. There was no moon, but it must have been shining somewhere, for the sky had a soft, pewter sheen. To my left, at the back of the house, was a muddy jumble of sawhorses, boards, a bale of old snow fence. Stretching in front of me, and away to my right, a dozen old apples trees twisted their shadows against the glow of the sky. The kennels—cages, pens, whatever you called them—lay just beyond this. They were made entirely of wire, and were lifted up off the ground on log pilings. Here was the source of that thick, musky odor I'd smelled, and the crying which, even now, still prickled the hairs on the back of my neck. Foxes: perhaps two dozen of them. I watched them as they paced back and forth, dim gray shadows, flitting like bats. With the blood of their own kind so thick on the air, they moved with the panic that only exhaustion can still. But all at once—I suppose a breeze brought them my scent—they fell silent and the emptiness of the night, like a crystal globe, dropped around me. I didn't move. And then I held my breath, almost in awe, as a dozen golden eyes glowed in the dark. For an instant, they froze me in my tracks. Then one voice began crying, a second joined in, and soon they were all howling again.

I went back to the house.

Despite my efforts, the living room remained, most literally, a bloody mess, so I tore a couple of flaps off a cardboard carton and tried to scrape up as much of the gore as I could. Then I spread a lot of newspapers around; after that, short of a mop and pail, there wasn't much more I could do. It was now after ten. While I'd been working, I'd heard the shower running, but now it was off and I tiptoed into the kitchen, assuming that Berri was trying to sleep. After a moment, though, I thought I heard him moving around in the back of the house and I called out to him.

A pause, long enough to be awkward, stretched out, before he called back, "I'll be there in a minute."

I looked around the kitchen. It was old and shabby, reminding me a little of Grainger's clinic: the lino was loose and wavy, the old cupboards bore innumerable coats of chipped white paint, and there was an ancient stove with big heavy knobs. I poked around in the cupboards, looking for coffee but finding tins of Campbell's soup, Chef Boyardee, Cordon Bleu Irish Stew, and a great deal of tea: Red Rose in bags, four small tins of Twining's—Irish Breakfast, Earl Grey, Russian Caravan, Darjeeling. Given this indication of his taste, I filled a kettle and put it on the old stove, then set cups and saucers on a table at the far end of the room. Here, pinned up in the corner, was the kitchen's sole decorative touch: a 1941 calendar, issued by the Hudson's Bay Company, which showed a brawny, ill-painted Indian carrying a canoe up a portage. While the kettle boiled, I sat down beneath it and tried to put together a picture of the man who lived in this place. He was lonely, I guessed, a solitary; a bachelor—certainly no woman had any claims in this kitchen; and there was a combination of clues (the homemade aspect to the house and its furnishings, the very location of the place, and the foxes themselves) that made me think of one of those self-educated, self-sufficient workingmen who take night courses, harbor pet obsessions and projects, but who are practical enough to bring them into cranky, quirky reality. As a guess, this turned out pretty well. When he stepped into the room a moment later, it was clear that Berri was a very definite character: a wiry old fellow with gray hair worn in a bristly brush cut and a trace of white stubble over hollow, leathery cheeks. He'd changed into a rough gray sweater and a pair of old wool trousers, but his feet were bare and this made him seem all the more vigorous. Inevitably, covered in vomit and blood, he'd looked rather pitiful, but now that feeling was entirely dispelled. An old sailor, you might have thought. Or a tough old jockey—except he was a bit bigger than that. He hesitated a second, as if embarrassed, then managed a brief, flickering smile. "I should thank you, I guess."

"That's okay, Mr. Berri."

"Nick," he said. "Nick Berri."

"Robert Thorne."

He nodded, tried out his smile again. "Guess it was just lucky you came passing by."

I poured out the tea, lifting the pot and trying to look cheerful. "I thought you could use some. . . ."

He nodded, crossing the room. I realized I was sitting in his regular place and began to get up, but he waved me down and pulled out a chair. He took a sip of his tea, a fussy, noisy, old man's sip, and as he did so, I was able to put my finger on something I'd missed before. Except for some mugs, all the china I'd found in the cupboard was of the same pattern: a heavy glazed pottery in an earthy yellow color. The cups were broad and very shallow, the saucers almost flat. They were rather elegant, in comparison to the rest of the place, and now I recognized them. They were "Russel Wright ware," a style that had been popular in the forties; my parents had had some, the last few pieces ending their days at the cottage.

As he set his cup down, I said, "Are you sure you're all right, Mr. Berri?"

"I'm all right."

"I've got a car. If you want, I could take you to a doctor."

"No." He shook his head. "Like I say, I'm all right."

The defensiveness in his voice was just this side of hostile. I tried to stay neutral. "That was quite an ordeal you went through. I guess what you really need is a good rest."

"I'm fine. I thank you again for all you did, but I'm fine now. Really I am."

I smiled. "And I guess you'd like me to get the hell out."

His mouth drew back in a deep, frowning crease up his cheeks. "Sorry it sounded like that. Like I say, I ought to be grateful and I truly am. But I'm okay now. It's late, and if you want to stay, you're welcome, but don't do it on my account. Those men got what they came for; they won't be back."

Got what? I wondered. But I asked, "Do you know who they were?"

He shook his head. "Never saw them before in my life."

"You mean they just came in—"

"Yes."

"What did they want?"

"I've no idea."

"But you said—"

"Listen, Mr. Thorne, what happened tonight . . . that would be hard to explain and I'm not sure there's much of a point. But it wasn't as bad as it looked."

I hesitated. A moment passed. The foxes were still barking out in the yard, and Berri's eyes moved to the window. His chair creaked as he shifted his weight. It was obvious that he had no wish to talk about what had happened to him, despite the gratitude he felt for his rescue; and certainly, if he'd wanted to wait till the morning, I wouldn't have blamed him. Indeed, I would have preferred it. But I also knew it was important for him to understand that he was going to have to talk, so, as easily as I could, I said, "I'm a friend of Harry's, Mr. Berri. I think I said that."

He nodded. "I guess you did."

"Do you know he's dead?"

"They said . . . they said he was."

"Yes. He died a couple of weeks ago in Detroit. The police think it's suicide, and maybe it was, but those men drove him to it. You're lucky to be alive, Mr. Berri."

He squinted at me. "How come you know all this?"

I shrugged. "I wasn't just passing by. I've been following those men for days. As you say, the reasons why would be hard to explain, and I'm not sure there's much point. I'm a friend. I'm on your side. That's what you have to remember."

"Harry had a lot of friends. But some things even his best friends didn't know."

"Listen, Mr. Berri. No matter what you say, no matter what anyone says, nothing can hurt Harry now. But other people can be hurt. *You* can be hurt—"

"*I don't give a damn!*" His voice was suddenly vehement. "Tonight, that's what I thought. Why should I? After all these years? Those sons of bitches deserve all they get." He smiled then, a quick, rueful grimace. "That's how come I'm alive, Mr. Thorne. No luck at all. No thanks to you. I just told those bastards what they wanted to know. Who the hell cares anymore?"

Unsure what he meant, I said nothing, but I watched his face. For a second, exhaustion flickered, a deep, inner emptiness into which his features collapsed; then he leaned forward, gulping his tea, though when my own hand touched my cup it felt cold. For a second, his eyes went to the window.

"Poor Harry," he murmured. "He called me a month or so back. He'd do that, every once in a while. Ask after the foxes—that was the excuse. He bought them for me, you see, when I quit working—six breeding pair, all registered. Harry liked to say it was a joint venture, just a hobby now but eventually the market was bound to come back. He always believed that. He loved foxes. 'They *are* cunning,' he'd say. He loved the mutations, like I've got, but he especially loved the natural reds. The most beautiful fur. Warm. Durable. Skins pretty easy to work. He was always saying we'd go in together in a big way—his money, what I knew. Harry always liked to have plans. That's what I noticed this last time he called. No plans. It was almost as if he was saying goodbye." He shrugged. "I guess maybe he was."

I took a moment, crushing my cigarette out in the saucer. He was talking now. Should I encourage him to continue, or put it all off till the morning? The trouble was, by the morning his defensiveness would probably harden to obstinacy—and Nick Berri, I suspected, could be a very obstinate old man. Making up my mind, I leaned forward a little and said, "Those men, Mr. Berri. Can you tell me about them?"

"They were Russians."

"How did you know?"

"They spoke it. They talked to each other."

"So you speak Russian?"

"Sure. My real name's Berzhin. My father was born in Kiev."

"But you're a Canadian?"

He nodded. "I was born in Montreal. Berri is French. My father, though, was Russian to the day he died. We always spoke it at home. That's how come I met Harry, you know. Because I could speak it."

"When was this, Mr. Berri?"

He shrugged. "Twenty-eight? Twenty-nine? I'm not sure."

"Around the time Brightman first traveled to Russia?"

"You know about that?"

"Yes. I didn't think it was much of a secret."

"No, no secret at all. Anyway, that's how it happened. I went with him. He wanted someone who spoke the language but also knew furs.

I was a grader by then—no one knew skins like Harry, but I knew enough."

"So you were his translator?"

"Sure, but I only went twice. After that, he'd picked up enough so he could go by himself." He coughed. "The Russians were really excited about furs back then, Canadian furs especially. Just a year or so before, Jack Caswell sold them sixty-five pair of silvers and that was the basis for their whole industry." He nodded, half to himself. "We got a real nice reception. The best hotels. Our own droshky to cart us around. Other people went to Russia and got the Black Bread Blues, but it was the caviar that did us in."

"This was when you met Zinoviev?"

"So you know that too?" He shrugged. "You're right, though. Kirov, then Zinoviev. The very first two the Bolshevik shot."

"Yes . . ." Then, on an impulse I added, "Didn't you meet a woman as well, Anna Kostina?"

"Bolshevik shot her too." He shrugged. "Poor Harry. He never had good luck with his ladies."

I remembered Grainger's words: *the best lies always contain some of the truth.* "Some people say he got her pregnant."

"That's crazy . . . though I suppose maybe not. You never know about women. She was interesting, though. A real Red—they say the women were even tougher than the men. Anna. The old lady, Breshkovsky. Anna knew everyone—Lenin, Trotsky, Kamenev . . . and the Bolshevik killed them all, every last one of them."

"What about Dimitrov, Mr. Berri? Wasn't that someone else Anna introduced Brightman to?"

He frowned. "Been a long time since I heard that name."

"But you know it, don't you?"

He shook his head. "Not then, I didn't."

"When did you learn about him?"

"Same time as everyone else. When the Reichstag burned down, the big trial. I remember I once asked Harry if he knew anything about him and he told me he'd met him back then. Great man, Harry said. Maybe he was. The Bolshevik never got *him.*"

"You must have been proud to meet him."

His eyes went shifty. "Did I? I guess you do know a lot—maybe more than I know myself."

"I wouldn't say that, Mr. Berri, but I think you did meet him. This would have been a little later, probably the spring of 1940. Dimitrov made a secret trip to Canada that year, for the Comintern. I'm not exactly sure why, but he probably wanted to tell North American Communists to forget about the Molotov-Ribbentrop Pact. He wanted them to ignore it. Stalin and Hitler were in bed together, but the workers were to back the war effort to the hilt. He came to Halifax to tell them that—maybe the Canadian and U.S. governments even helped him to get there—and I think that's when you met him."

"So what if I did?"

"But isn't that the point of all this, Mr. Berri? Dimitrov's *political* mission had a private side as well, and that's where Harry Brightman came in. Dimitrov was frightened. Kirov, Zinoviev, Kamenev, Radek, Tukhachevsky, Pyatakov, Béla Kun, Lenski, Warski, Copic, Eberlin . . . Stalin had already amassed a huge list of victims and Dimitrov was afraid he would be next. So he was trying to save what he could. He knew there was no hope for himself—even if he'd refused to go back they would have got him eventually—but he thought he could save the life of one little girl. Maybe the child was his, maybe not; that doesn't make any difference. In any event, with Brightman's help, he smuggled the child out of Russia and then Brightman adopted the child as his own. It was all done very slickly—but not slickly enough. Forty years later, someone got on to him."

I watched Berri's face. It concentrated in a frown of genuine puzzlement, then he shook his head slowly. "You've got it wrong. You still don't understand."

I shrugged. "Don't I?" But I was sure I did. "You tell me then, Mr. Berri."

He was silent. A moment passed. His eyes held mine for a second, then shifted to the dark window. The foxes were still whining, crying, and barking just as before. He listened; and I could see the pain which their pain brought into his face. Maybe I was pressing too hard, I thought, maybe I should hold off till tomorrow. I tried to keep my voice gentle. "If you like . . ." I began. But he was already shaking his head. Slowly, he pushed himself up from the table.

"No, no," he said, "that's all right. You don't understand—you don't understand nothing at all. But I'll tell you. Just give me a minute to settle them down."

———

A side door led out of the kitchen, and beside it, on an old newspaper, was a pair of muddy rubber boots, their tops turned down in a cuff, just like the boots I'd worn as a child. He put these on and opened the door. I made no move to stop him, and when the latch clicked shut, I stood up myself. Looking out, I peered through my reflection into the night. *You don't understand,* he'd said. Had I got it all wrong? I didn't think so; but I knew, of course, that the "all" still eluded me. I stepped outside. There was a cast-cement porch, tilted at a rather uncertain angle. From here the night seemed vast, stretching away, while high in the sky the clouds were like enormous shadows cast before some infinite, silvery light. Across the lawn, I could see the glistening tracks Berri's boots had made in the dew. I followed them across the wet grass, through the orchard, where the sharp, sour smell of fallen apples undercut the musk of the foxes, and then onto a stretch of packed dirt. Beyond this, the cages lifted out of the gloom.

I waited, standing a little away. Inside their cages, the foxes twisted and floated like puffs of mist, and as Berri moved past each pen, the fox inside would leap up and bark with excitement. I caught up to him as he reached the last of the cages. The wire was torn. As he pushed the mesh together, the edges sprang back with a twang. He murmured, "She was the mother of most of these. That's partly why they're so frightened."

"I'm sorry," I said. And then, remembering with guilt my long delay on the road, I added, "You understand, Mr. Berri, I thought you were one of them, with them. That's why I didn't come sooner."

He nodded; and then I saw his fingers tighten in the mesh of the torn cage. I looked away, toward the foxes. I could see why he loved them. They were beautiful, exquisitely so, their wild, golden eyes shining forth from dark, delicate faces. They moved like cats, with a slinky, elegant grace, and though I wouldn't have said they were tame, they looked friendly, pushing their muzzles up to the mesh for a sniff. They varied in color. Some, like the dead fox, were pure white; others, almost black, were overlaid with a sparkling silver sheen.

Beside me, Berri cleared his throat. "They were bastards, you know. Real sons of bitches. You can kill a fox so it doesn't feel anything. Grab them by their hind legs, and turn them over—they'll just lie there—and then step down lightly over their hearts. They don't feel a thing. Just go to sleep. . . . I think they even knew that. At least they knew how to handle her. But instead they . . ." He leaned back on the cage. A moment passed. "Sons of bitches," he murmured again. Then, as the animals began barking at the far end of the row, he shrugged himself off the mesh and began moving along. I fell into step.

"Let me tell you again, Mr. Berri. I have nothing to do with those men."

"I understand."

"I'm a friend of Harry's. I'm a friend of his daughter's, May Brightman."

"She has nothing to do with this. I told you, you've got it all wrong."

"There was a child. You know there was a child."

"Maybe. Maybe. I'm just saying it doesn't make any difference."

Stopping in front of a cage, he drew his hand up into the sleeve of his sweater, then pushed the loose end of wool through the mesh. The little fox inside was black as midnight. He ran over and tugged at the wool and started to suck. I waited. Up this close, the smell was very strong, though it was hard to be offended by anything produced by such beautiful creatures. They seemed calmer now, crying less, and even these cries were more like a bark. But most were still pacing up and down in their pens, and I could hear the quick *scratch-scratch* of their paws on the boards. After a moment, Berri pulled the sleeve back, then moved along to the next cage and did the same trick again. The fox chewed, licked, grunting softly all the time. And then, with his face pressed up to the mesh—as if addressing someone at the far end of the cage—Berri started to speak. Later, I sometimes wondered why he'd chosen that moment; maybe he was more comfortable out with his foxes; or maybe it was just because the choice was his. In any case, the words came out of him easily. I almost had the impression he wasn't speaking to me but was setting the record straight for himself.

"To understand," he began, "you've got to know something about Russia, Russia back then—1930, let's say, 1940. In those days, the Bolshevik had all sorts of problems, but his biggest was the one everyone's got. He was broke. But for him that had a special twist, because even the money he did have was worthless. All the rubles in the world didn't add up to a dollar. Actually, it was even worse, because when he did get a little together, he still couldn't go near a bank, on account of how

Lenin, when he took over, had refused to pay off on the old Czarist bonds. Banks all over the world were holding them, and every time the Bolshevik tried to open up an account or sell something, they'd like as not send the sheriff around. So, all in all, the Bolshevik was in a real fix, and he tried everything he knew to get out of it. He confiscated every bank safe in the country to get foreign currency, he tried to sell the Crown jewels—damn near worthless, he found—and in 1923 he took all the gold and silver out of the churches. Now, gold, of course . . . that was the one thing they did have. For egalitarian, proletarian, *Red Revolutionary* Communists you might say they took a keen interest in the stuff. In fact, first thing after the Great Revolution—first things first, you might say—they got the mines open again. But even that didn't do them much good. The Americans stopped them—in 1920, along with the Brits and the French, they passed a law making it illegal to bring Russian gold into their countries. You can see what that meant. No one would give the Bolshevik credit, he had no money—and what money he had wasn't worth anything—and people wouldn't even go for his gold. Just to get the most ordinary things, he had to pull all sorts of tricks. You follow me this far?"

I did. And I knew that everything he'd been saying was true. But I said, "I follow you, Mr. Berri. I'm just not too clear where you're going."

"That's okay. I'm almost there." But in fact he now paused, pulling the wet, ragged sleeve of his sweater back from the cage and moving along to the next one. The fox inside it ran over, and as it started to suck, Berri went on. "Just remember what I'm saying. It was almost impossible for the Bolshevik to get regular things, locomotives, machine tools, even food. Now think: what about those *other* things so dear to the Bolshevik's heart? Certain scientific supplies, for instance. Or military items. And what about the Red Revolution? They believed in it then, you remember—the World Revolution that would make the Bolshevik safe. These days, of course—when they don't give a damn—it's no problem. They want to support the French CP, they just slap some money into a bank account. They want to finance their friends over in Africa, they use the Swiss banks. Their gold's good enough now. So's their natural gas. Even the goddamned ruble's worth something."

"What are you trying to tell me? That Brightman smuggled gold out of Russia in the furs he was buying?"

"Think a minute. The furs *were* the gold. And year after year, Harry went over to Leningrad and brought it back."

"I don't understand. Those trips were no secret."

"That was the beauty of it. *Everything* was out in the open."

"And everyone knew he was doing it, Mr. Berri. There was no law against selling Russian furs."

"Well, time to time, place to place, that hasn't exactly been true. But it isn't the point."

"Mr. Berri, I'm asking. What *is* the point?"

"It's so simple, no one ever did see it. Year after year, Harry brought those furs back, and year after year he sold them, bale after bale. *But the Russians never sent him a bill.* That was his secret. They *gave* those furs to him. And though they made Harry rich, he had to use the money just like they told him." Berri chuckled then, an old man's laugh, deep in his throat. "You ever hear that expression, Mr. Thorne, 'Moscow gold'? Well, this was the real thing. That's what it was all about, you see. *The Bolshevik's gold.* Poor Harry's moneybags."

Overhead, the moon finally pressed a disk of silver light through a patch of clouds and beside me one of the foxes shoved its snout against the mesh.

"They are *cunning,"* he'd say . . . *he especially loved the natural reds.*

Harry Brightman: a red fox with golden eyes.

"I'll be damned," I whispered.

13

All.

Everything.

Now I knew it too, just like Travin. Yet, for a moment longer, I still couldn't take it in, let alone "believe" it.

As Berri reached through the cage to stroke the fox, he laughed again at my incredulity. "I always wanted to tell someone that story, just to see the look on their face . . . and, if you don't mind my saying, it's been worth it."

I smiled. "If it's true, Mr. Berri, it's damn neat."

"Oh, it's true. There's no doubt about that. I never knew what Harry did about his income tax, but I expect it wasn't even illegal."

"But why did he do it? Was he a Communist? Or was it just for the money?"

"No, no. Harry was a Red, all right. He *believed.* They did make him rich, but that's not why he did it. I know that because I saw how much it hurt when he *didn't* believe anymore. But I've never been sure about one thing. Was Harry a Red when he went over that first time, or did it all happen once the Bolshevik got him into his clutches?"

"You were a Communist, weren't you?"

"Red as a fire truck. I was even in a genuine cell—all garment workers, old Jews, smart girls with thick glasses. They sent me to him, that first time. Those were my orders: convince Harry Brightman to take me with him to Russia. But he might have been a Red even then. I never did ask him, and he probably wouldn't have told me. Later, we just assumed it between us."

I leaned back against the cage, the mesh sagging slightly under my weight. "Let me get this straight. You're saying he took these furs out of Russia—"

"All aboveboard. Right out in the open."

"And then he sold them, also out in the open. Which meant he turned those furs into hard currency—Canadian dollars, U.S. dollars . . . and I suppose he then passed this back to the Soviets?"

He was shaking his head. "Not quite like that. That wasn't the deal. He kept the money, built up his business. They wanted him to become a rich, respectable man. A banker. That was always his joke. 'I'm a banker, Nick. I run the Comintern Bank of America.' That's what he'd say."

"But if he didn't give the Soviets the money, what did he do with it?"

"That changed, I think, though you understand I never knew all the details. At first it was political—he just gave money to the fronts, trade unions, that sort of thing. Some of it was up here, but naturally it was really the States they were worried about. Later on, though, the Bolshevik wanted him to buy things, especially scientific equipment of various kinds. Harry told me he usually did that in Europe—and since he always traveled a lot, that wasn't too hard. Then the war came and . . ." Berri shrugged.

"So what happened then?"

"Figure it out. Harry bought what the Bolshevik needed, and what he needed then was . . . information, I guess you'd say."

"What are you talking about?"

"What the hell do you think I'm talking about? Spies cost money, Mr. Thorne, like everything else."

I was too stunned to speak. I just stood there, listening to the rustling wind and the foxes quietly settling down in their cages. Then Berri laid his hand on my arm. "They'll be all right," he murmured. "We can go back to the house."

It was his turn now to make the tea, and he did so with an obvious pleasure, relishing my discomfiture. He'd been right: I most certainly had not understood. And as the old man refilled my cup, and settled down in his chair, I wanted to make sure I understood now.

"Let's go back to the beginning," I said. "When exactly did you first go to Russia?"

He shook his head. "Exactly? I couldn't say. But I'd guess '29."

"Okay. And how many trips did you make altogether?"

"Two. I told you."

"I'm sorry. I meant Harry. How many times did he go?"

"Three, I think. Maybe four. He skipped a year here and there. But even if he didn't go, he still brought the furs in."

"A lot?"

"Sure. He sold a good deal of it to other dealers, you see. And he bought everything. Blues and kitts. Kolinsky—a Russian weasel, that is, something like mink. Not much karakul, at least not until later. Marmot. Seal. Suslik. Some lynx and a few muskrat, but their skins aren't up to ours." He shrugged. "Of course, the big item was sable. And that was partly how he worked out the fiddle. He'd bring in real prime Barguzin skins—'Crown sable,' as the Russians would say—but label them marten or even fisher. At customs, there was no way they could tell the difference."

"And how much were all these furs worth?"

"I never knew, but a lot. They were always big shipments and he kept it up till the start of the war."

"Tens of thousands? Hundreds of thousands? A million?"

"More than a million . . . but if I said more than that, I'd only be guessing."

"Okay, but whatever it was, you're saying that the money he made out of this arrangement was plowed back into his business?"

"Yes. But don't worry, the Bolshevik kept an account—the Bolshevik always knew to the penny how much Harry owed him. After a while, Harry even kept their share separate and turned it all into gold—real gold, I mean."

"It was like a trust fund, in a way."

"If you like."

"All right. Go back to what he did with the money. So far as you know, he mainly gave it to CP front groups—here in Canada, and in the U.S.?"

Berri made a face. "That's just how it started. But the Bolshevik didn't really give a damn about the CP, here or down there. Browder, those people, they were all idiots. Through Harry, the Bolshevik gave them what he had to, but not a cent more. What he wanted was patents, special castings, instruments, particular parts—"

"And Harry bought them all this?"

"Not directly. He put up the money. That was the point, don't you see—always the money. He worked through other people, but he set them up with his money. Companies, even."

"Except—according to you—this all changed with the war. He started out giving the money away—using it politically—then went on to supplying them technical goods, and ended up . . . as a spy."

Berri made a sour face. "That's your word. Who knows what it means?"

"You used it just a minute ago, Mr. Berri, and if we turned all this around, I don't think a *Russian* court would have any trouble deciding."

"Maybe. But Harry was way in the background. Always, he worked through other people . . . passed messages, collected them, but mainly he paid the bills."

"He didn't mind this? You said he 'believed.' You're sure about that? You're sure they weren't blackmailing him? Maybe that first time, in Leningrad, they trapped him by offering him a deal he couldn't refuse—those furs made *him* rich, after all—and then later forced him to help them."

But even before I finished, Berri was shaking his tough little head. "Nope. Don't kid yourself. He *believed,* just like I say. Just like the rest of us. I told you: the proof came when he *didn't* believe anymore."

"And when was that?"

Berri leaned back in his chair and crossed his arms over his chest—looking, as he frowned in thought, almost gnomelike. Then, with a little burst of energy, he rocked forward and tapped his index finger twice on the top of the table. "That's interesting, come to think of it. You mentioned Dimitrov and his coming here—which, you see, really had no importance in any of this—but that's when it started. Dimitrov told him the truth—about Stalin, the trials, everything. The Pact was the worst. I don't know what he told Buck—Tim Buck, he was head of the Canadian CP—and Browder and those other idiots they brought to Halifax, but he told Harry the truth. No excuses. Sometimes you hear people say it was the fault of the French or the British, that they wouldn't do a deal with the Bolshevik so he had to fall in with Hitler, but Dimitrov knew that was all so much shit. The British couldn't give him half of Poland, Latvia, Estonia, all the rest of it—but the Nazis could and *that* was the key. *That* was why he loved Hitler so dear, and turned over the German and Polish CPs to the Gestapo."

I waited a moment; a fierce, concentrated look had come into his eyes as he'd spoken, and two red spots had sprung up on his cheeks. All this had happened forty years ago, but for Berri that was yesterday. Finally I said, "What was Brightman's reaction to all of this?"

He shook his head slightly as if, in some obscure way, I was arguing with him.

"He took his cue from Dimitrov. You don't understand what a big man Dimitrov was in those days. To every Communist in the world, he was the model revolutionary and a man you could trust. He told Harry a struggle was going on inside the Bolshevik's guts. Smart people knew Stalin was a fool to trust Hitler, they all saw what was coming, and according to Dimitrov their day would come. So Harry hung on."

"But Dimitrov was wrong."

"So he was. But remember, the war was on, and once the Russians came into it, everything was forgiven for the duration."

"And after the war?"

He gave a bob of his head, and smiled. "He gritted his teeth—we all did—and waited. Of course, that got harder and harder—1948: the German workers; 1956: Hungary; 1968: Prague . . . I couldn't take any more after Budapest, but Harry stuck it out longer, till Czechoslovakia. Then he told them to go to hell."

"Wait a minute now. You're saying that up till the spring of 1968 Harry was still working for them?"

"So far as I know . . . which means yes, 'cause I know that far."

"And what was he doing?"

"What in hell *could* he be doing?"

"Jesus," I said. I leaned back in my chair.

"Actually, they almost got him when Gouzenko defected. He told me there was some sort of trail. But he cut it off and in the end the Mounties didn't get close."

I thought hard for a moment. There was no sense, absolutely no sense, in disputing any of this. It was either true or it wasn't, and there was no way I was going to be able to tell, one way or the other. And at least it *sounded* genuine enough. But what did it mean? Above all, what did it mean *now*, in the present? That was the trouble. The past was coming alive, but what was its connection to the present? After a moment, I thought I saw one possibility and leaned forward on the table. "You say he finally told them to go to hell, but I wonder if that can really be true. He was in too deep. And no one tells them to go to hell anyway."

He nodded. "You're no fool, Mr. Thorne. And you're right. He shouldn't have been able to do it—but he did. I don't know how. He had some kind of hold, some sort of threat . . . they were afraid of him for some reason. He never told me what it was, but it worked. They left him alone."

"Until a couple of months ago, you mean. Maybe it worked for a time, Mr. Berri, but not in the end."

He sucked in his cheeks. "Don't be so sure. Those men, tonight, weren't from the Bolshevik. They were something different. I'm not even sure the Bolshevik knows about this."

"The Bolshevik": I'd assumed he'd meant Stalin, but for him I suppose the word stood for some essence of Sovietism that went beyond any one man—and this was a spirit, a shade, that had haunted him for so long that he would know it better than his own shadow. If the men who'd attacked him tonight were *not* "from the Bolshevik," Berri would know it—but then who had they been and what had they wanted? I eyed the old man; he glanced away. We'd come full circle at last. Keeping my voice as gentle as I could, I said, "You know what I have to ask, Mr. Berri."

He nodded. "Guess I do."

"And I don't want to bully you, but . . . it's me or the police. You have to understand that."

The room was very quiet. The foxes were silent now, and there was no sound except the soft rush of the wind past the window. When Berri turned back to face me, his head seemed to hang, and there was a watery film in his eyes. He cleared his throat and swallowed. "It's like I told you, I don't know who they were. I'd just say this. They were Russian, but they weren't from the Bolshevik. And one of them—he was like a little weasel—was called Subotin. The other one called him that."

Subotin . . . a name for my ghost. But I didn't let this tidbit divert me. "Did they know what you've been telling me?"

"Maybe. Most of it."

"So what did they want?"

He shrugged. "The money, of course. Where to find it."

"What money?"

"I told you—the Bolshevik's. It wasn't all spent, you see, when

Harry got free. He told me he was damned if the Bolshevik would get any back, but he didn't want to spend it himself—it would only bring him bad luck. So he hid it away."

"This was still the money he'd made from the furs?"

"That's it. What was left."

"How much?"

A quick shrug. "He told me eight hundred thousand. But it wasn't in money, you understand. He always kept the Bolshevik's share in gold—gold certificates—because that made it easy to travel, and you could always cash them, no questions asked." Berri smiled. "He used to joke about that. 'J. Edgar's right,' he'd say, 'it really should be Moscow gold.'"

I hesitated now, thinking back. Gold certificates are issued by some of the big Swiss banks and a few other institutions. Each certificate represents a certain amount of gold, and as a way of owning the stuff, they're far more convenient than bars or wafers or coins; pretty pieces of paper that can be worth thousands. *And that's always what they'd been looking for,* something small, something like paper: in Travin's hotel in Detroit; at Grainger's clinic; in Brightman's house, where I'd first seen Petersen . . . whose real name was Subotin. And—was it possible?—even that first day, at my place in Charlottesville. Up to now, I'd assumed that whoever had broken into my place had been after the telegram from May—had wanted to make sure that I didn't help her—but perhaps they thought she might have sent the certificates to me for safekeeping.

I looked at Berri now, but even as I did so, he got to his feet and went over to the sink and splashed water over his face. As he dried himself with a towel, I said to his back, "Where did he hide it?"

"I don't know. That's what I told them."

I hesitated; I was only telling the truth when I'd said I had no desire to bully him. I kept my voice level: "Mr. Berri, you told me yourself that they got what they came for."

He was still facing away from me, leaning over the sink, but he nodded. "They knew I didn't have it, you see. They knew that already."

"They killed the fox, Mr. Berri. They killed one of your foxes and they threatened to kill all the others. Why? Because they were trying to get you to talk, to tell them something, or give them something you had . . ."

I listened. He took a funny, hoarse breath, but only when he spoke did I know he was crying. "They wanted a name . . ." He cleared his throat, but his voice kept breaking. "They wanted a name. . . . They knew I helped Harry. Somehow, they knew that . . . they knew I sometimes took messages to the people who helped him. They knew that Harry must have trusted those people, so they thought maybe . . . maybe he gave them the money to keep. I told them one name, someone who was already dead. But they knew that too, and so they killed the fox, and they said . . ."

All at once, with a groan, he leaned forward and was sick into the sink. I looked away. I heard him gasping, fighting for breath. Then he panted, "They said they'd kill all my foxes, just like the first one, and then they'd kill me. So I told them." He wheezed. Sucked in more air. "I don't give a damn. I swear to God I don't give a damn . . ."

After a moment, I whispered, "Who was it?"

"A man called Paul Hamilton."

"Who was he?"

"He worked in the State Department. I don't know more than that."

"Do you know where he lives?"

"Five years ago, Harry gave me a message. He was retired then—Hamilton, I mean. He was living in Paris."

I got to my feet. Now, at one level, I *did* know everything. Brightman had taken his final secret, the location of the gold, to his grave. Since his death, Subotin had been going from one of Brightman's old contacts to the other in the hopes of finding it. I suddenly felt very queasy: what had happened to Dr. Charlie? If tonight was anything to go by, his fate couldn't have been very pleasant. And neither would Hamilton's. He'd been a spy—why mince words?—and I owed him nothing, but simple humanity said I had to warn him. There was a phone in the bedroom. It was midnight when I started to dial, which made it five in the morning in Paris, but that was probably all for the best; and certainly there was no sense in waiting. It was unlikely that Subotin could have acted this quickly, but judging by his American Express account, he got around a good deal, and conceivably he had friends in France who were just a phone call away. In any event, I was forty minutes getting through. There was a bad line, and you'd be surprised how many Hamiltons there are in the Paris directory—I woke up two Peters and one Philippe before finding Paul. When I got him, he grumbled

French into the phone, but after I'd asked if he'd once worked for the State Department and then said the name Harry Brightman, he was fully awake. Even so, he was cautious.

"Maybe I knew someone like that. I'm not sure."

"If you've listened this far, Mr. Hamilton, you knew him. A Canadian. Wealthy. A fur—"

"All right, I knew him. Who are you?" His voice had the flat, neutral accent of Americans who've spoken French a long time, but he was from the East, probably Boston.

I ignored his question. I realized something: after speaking to this man for less than three minutes, I already disliked him. Heartily. Finally I said, "Brightman's dead, Mr. Hamilton. He killed himself—he was under great pressure."

"I know nothing about this. I'm not involved." An old man's voice now, a trace of whine. "This has nothing to do with me. It was all a long time—"

"Maybe so, Mr. Hamilton. But it *will* have something to do with you because the people who were applying the pressure to Brightman will soon apply it to you. They believe that Brightman left something with you, something valuable. Did he?"

"No. Absolutely not. I haven't seen him or heard from him in many years."

"All right. In a way that doesn't make any difference. The people who will be visiting you—who may be visiting you at any moment—won't take no for an answer. What—"

"Who are you? You still haven't answered my question."

"I'm a friend of Brightman's, if you like. I know he'd want me to give you this warning."

"And who are these people you keep talking about?"

"I'm not entirely sure. If you think about it, you might come to one obvious conclusion, but I believe that would be wrong. I do not believe these people are acting in an official capacity. On the other hand, I'm certain that they come from the same country as those people . . . . if you follow me."

A long pause.

"I see."

Another pause.

Then: "You're warning me . . . you're saying I'm in danger because of all this?"

"That's right, Mr. Hamilton. Grave danger. *Mortal* danger."

Now there was another pause, in which the word "danger" echoed back and forth under the ocean, or over it, or however they do these things now. For Hamilton, perhaps, the medium through which my words came was the past, a past he now feared and greatly resented. "Well," he finally said, "you're warning me. What do you propose I do?"

As if it was my responsibility; as if it was somehow my fault. I just said, "Whatever you like."

A pause. I thought I heard him clearing his throat. Then he said, "I'm sorry. I didn't mean to imply . . ."

I wondered who he was. What he had been. What he had done for them. And I wondered why. Was he a fool? A knave? Greedy? Homosexual? And then I wondered whether, at this late date, he could even have answered the question.

"Mr. Hamilton," I said, "just listen. You have to leave your home, and you have to leave now. Go to some place where you can't be traced. Not a hotel, I should think, or even a friend's—at least, if there's any obvious connection to you. But some place—"

"I could go—"

"Don't tell me. I don't want to know, at least not now. Just go there, at once. I mean that. Leave immediately. These people may have a Paris branch; they could be on their way now. So get out right away, even if you have to spend the next few hours wandering around in a park. You understand this?"

"Yes."

"All right. I'll come to Paris. I can't be sure when I'll get there, but within the next couple of days. When I arrive, I'll leave a message for you at American Express . . . the main office, near the Opéra . . . you know where it is. I'll tell you where I'm staying, and how to get in touch with me. Then you phone me as soon as you can."

A pause, while he absorbed this. But there was no nonsense now: he'd taken it in; he believed me. "All right, but I'll need your name."

"Thorne. Robert Thorne." There was a long, echoing pause, and then I realized something and said, "It's possible you knew my father, Mr. Hamilton. He also worked for the State Department."

"Yes. I think I do know the name . . ."

But in fact, from his voice, I wasn't sure that he did. I said, "Whether you do or you don't, just remember: leave *now.*"

"Yes. You're sure you can't—"

"Yes. Just get going. I'll tell you everything in a few days."

We hung up. I lit a cigarette. I was now absolutely exhausted. As I waved the match out, I looked around Berri's room. It was unfinished, the studs still exposed, and you could read the tar paper that had been laid over the walls: Ten-Test, Ten-Test, Ten-Test . . . Drawing my leg up, I leaned back on the bed and let a slow curl of smoke drift to the ceiling. The room was very small. A cell: Berri had belonged to one, and he still slept in one every night. I thought of Berri and Hamilton, putting them together in my mind. The two were very different, you could bet, but both were Communists and I could see the link that joined them together. It wasn't ideology, really; more a shading of character: a primness; a hint of puritanism; an effort of self-control—a set of inhibitions that kept their own authoritarianism under control. And when those inhibitions were taken away . . . I closed my eyes; I was very tired, and these dubious meditations, I knew, were just an excuse to keep me from going back to the room where the old man was waiting. His bloody clothes had been thrown over the end of the bed. Would he wash them, I wondered, put them back on again? Would he clean the furniture in the living room, scrub the blood off the walls? I supposed he would: it was his life, after all, and he'd have to pick up its pieces. Smoking quietly, I lay there and thought about that. His life, and what it was built on. The capacity to believe. Self-delusion. Paranoia. Who betrayed whom? Mendacity. Loyalty. Truth. . . . And in the end, what was the wish nearest his heart? *I don't give a damn. I swear to God I don't give a damn.*

There was no putting it off. I stubbed out my cigarette and walked down the hall. For the second time that night, Berri had cleaned himself up, and now he was sitting at the kitchen table, a bottle of whiskey before him. Canadian Club. I don't know where he got it: not from those cupboards. But perhaps, like the little tins of Twining's tea, it was secreted away, only brought out for special occasions. To his back, I said, "It's all right. I got to him first."

He tried to keep his voice level, but didn't quite make it. "Was he worth a fox, would you say?"

I shook my head. "Probably not, Mr. Berri. Or at least he wasn't worth your love for that fox."

Firmly, he lifted the teacup of whiskey to his lips and took a good sip, then set it back in the saucer, as prim and proper as at an old lady's tea party. "Like I told you, I don't give a damn."

I took a breath. "I'm just afraid of one thing. They may think you warned him. When they don't find him in Paris, they might come back here."

"Let them. I've got a shotgun. This time I'll be ready."

"You're sure?"

He shrugged. "I can't leave them anyway. Not for more than twenty-four hours."

I came into the room and sat down beside him; and then—the one gesture of sympathy I thought might be acceptable—I took a little whiskey myself. I sipped, and let its burning path wind down my throat. Then I murmured, "Just a couple of things. According to the police, Harry killed himself. And it does look that way. But does it make sense to you? If these people had been after him—the same ones that came here—would he have killed himself rather than give them the money?"

Berri shrugged. "Maybe. Or maybe they threatened his daughter like they threatened to kill all my foxes. He loved her—I know that. He'd have done anything for her."

"But that's arguing the other way. The simplest way to protect her would have been to hand over the money. Yet he didn't."

He shrugged again. "Harry could be a stubborn son of a bitch. . . . Or maybe it's the police. Why believe them? They could have been fooled. They could have made it look like he killed himself."

Which was what I was wondering about. Up to this point, not understanding its motive, the suicide had seemed convincing enough. But if Brightman could simply have given them the money—if there'd been such an easy way out—why would he have put himself *and May* through the horror? On the other hand, Subotin wouldn't have wanted Brightman dead—not before he'd told him where the gold was located. But maybe it didn't make that much difference. One way or the other, Harry Brightman was dead.

I said, "All right, forget about that. There's something else I still don't get. This hold Harry had on the Bolshevik . . . did it have anything to do with the child?"

He shrugged. Sipped. Then shook his head with impatience. "I don't know. Maybe. Who does know? You've got all that on the brain."

"But there was a child, Mr. Berri. There's no doubt about that. And I'm sure it came out of Russia at the same time Dimitrov made his trip here."

"Well, I'll tell you one thing. Don't kid yourself. Once upon a time, Dimitrov might have been your hero, but he ended up like the rest of them, a son of a bitch. By 1940, his hands were covered in blood. If he snatched a baby away from the Bolshevik, it was because he thought it might help save *him*, not the child."

I waited, but he turned back to his cup. I thought for a moment—his idea at least had the virtue of novelty. But was it really possible that a *child* had protected Dimitrov, and that this protection had then been passed on to Brightman? In 1940, everyone seemed to agree, Dimitrov had been living under a genuine threat: many of his friends were dead, and his policies had all been discredited. Yet, despite this threat, it was a simple historical fact that he had survived. So the question Leonard Forbes had asked now came back into my mind: *Who really knows why any of them were killed, or why any of them escaped? More than likely Dimitrov survived through blind luck.* But maybe he hadn't; maybe . . . I leaned back in my chair. It was all too vague; and maybe, in the end, Berri was right—he'd been right more than anyone else, after all—and the child really had no importance. Taking another sip of the old man's whiskey, I moved back to firmer ground. "One last point," I said, "about the money. You said he kept it in gold, in gold certificates. Do you know when he bought them? I don't mean exactly, but do you know if he bought them before 1970?"

He shrugged. "Long before that. What the hell difference does the year make?"

A great deal, I knew; but if he didn't understand, that was all right. Spilling a little more whiskey into his cup, I went into the living room.

I'd spread every paper I'd been able to find on the floor, and now they were stained with soft black blots of the dead fox's blood. But I found what I wanted, the print on the page glistening like a reflection on a black lacquer table: a Montreal *Gazette* from a week ago, the box on the stock-market page which showed the commodity prices.

I kneeled down, took out my pen, worked it all out in the margin.

It was simple enough. Before August 15, 1971, the U.S. Treasury had bought and sold gold at $35 an ounce. That was the price at which Harry Brightman must have bought his, and for $800,000 he would have received certificates equivalent to almost twenty-three thousand ounces. But after 1971, when the price of gold had been left to the free market, that value had soared. According to the *Gazette,* the price in London three days before had been around $500 an ounce—which meant that Brightman's certificates were now worth between eleven and twelve *million* dollars.

Kneeling in that living room, I stared at this figure for a long, long time. It explained a great deal. More than what I'd discovered about Dimitrov, far more than what I'd found out about May's adoption. Here was the past—Brightman's past—erupting into the present. Here were the motives for his disappearance, his suicide, and Travin's murder. But then I thought about May . . . had she known what was happening? If I could call her now, what would she say? Had she told Cadogan to stop me from going on precisely because she knew what I'd find? *But then why point me down this trail in the first place?*

Questions—to which I still didn't have answers. But then there was Berri's solution—that none of them made any difference, that they were merely an obsession, something I had on the brain. As I stared down at my figuring, he seemed to be right. May, Dimitrov, Grainger, Florence Raines—perhaps I was holding on to them like a scientist, in love with his theories, who's now been presented with fresh, contradictory evidence. I simply didn't like to admit that everything now pointed in a different direction. To Brightman as a spy, not a father; to Paris today, not Halifax long ago.

But what did this have to do with me? Here was the last, crucial question. I'd told Hamilton I'd go to France, and I felt I had no choice about that, even if it left me dead broke. Having come this far, there was no doubt that I'd go on to the end. But was there some inner, hidden logic driving me on? Paris . . . my mother's city. Paris: where my parents had met. It was truly uncanny. Each step I took into Brightman's past only seemed to carry me deeper into my own, and now, as I crouched in Berri's blood-spattered living room, Travin's words drifted back through my mind: *I'll tell you something personal, Mr. Thorne, something you wouldn't want a policeman to hear. . . .* Maybe, I thought,

I already knew what this was. The truth was there, at the tip of my tongue, in the corner of my eye—but I was too afraid to let myself say it or see it.

Maybe.

On the other hand, there was Berri's solution: all these vague questions were merely problems I had on the brain.

$12,000,000 . . .

For most people, that was reason enough to do anything. It was reason enough for Subotin, I thought, and it would do for me too. What did he want with that money? Why was he prepared to kill and maim for it? I had no idea, but I knew I didn't want him to have it. Whatever side he was on—or Berri, or Brightman, or even my father—my side was different.

But then, erasing these thoughts from my mind, the foxes once more took up their lament, a melancholy cry that sent a shiver up my spine. Stock-still, I listened. Their howls rose and fell in rough, pitiful harmony, like a banshee's cry that has come too late, or a ghost's agonized call to its own lost soul—the Red Fox was dead, but perhaps his shade, disturbed by this night, was restlessly moving through the forest nearby.

In the kitchen, Berri got to his feet; I heard him open the door. And then the scent that had troubled the foxes—whatever it was—must have passed on, for soon they fell silent again.

14

I arrived in Paris on the ninth of November.

If you're lucky, that can be one of the city's best months, but not this time. I flew Montreal–Mirabel to Paris–Charles de Gaulle, but only exchanged one rainstorm for another; and Paris was worse, the rain wind-driven and unremitting. On the bus from Roissy to Porte Maillot, the city swam mistily beyond the streaming window like a bad film director fading to somebody's memories. But maybe that was the best way to look at the place. Montmartre, Clichy, the *dix-septième*—as we moved around the *périphérique,* the beltway that runs around Paris, the rain softened the purple swirl of the diesel fumes and blunted the high-rise towers, transforming them with the gentle blur of an Impressionist's gaze. Inevitably, I thought of my mother, realizing that she'd never see the city again. But then she'd never looked at it with much illusion. "Paris is very beautiful," she used to say, "but if you live there, it only seems a city like all the others—a place where no one ever has enough money."

At the *aérogare,* I reserved a car with Hertz for later that afternoon, then went into the Métro. Getting off at Châtelet, I let the moving sidewalk whisk me under the river—past the usual gauntlet of beggars—to Place St.-Michel. Now I was on the Left Bank, the Latin Quarter, and despite the touristy resonance of its name, this has always been the part of the city where I've felt the most comfortable. This too goes back to my mother. Her family originally came from Lyons, and they'd only moved to Paris, fulfilling her own mother's dream, when she was fourteen. "It was all for *Maman,*" she used to complain, "the whole thing—moving, the big house near the Parc de Monceau, a new car.

For me it just meant I lost all my friends. I never really felt the city was mine till much later, at the Sorbonne." Only then, as a student on the Left Bank, had she been truly happy, and this was the Paris she always remembered and had taught me to love. It hadn't changed much; a hint of *doner* and souvlaki mingled with the traditional smells of bread and tobacco, but the student kids, even this early in the day, were still going into the cinemas. Head down, I stayed tight to the buildings and let my feet find their own way through the warren of streets around St.-Séverin until they brought me to the Pension Mull. Shaking myself off in the gloomy café underneath, I saw that it hadn't changed either, though a couple of video games were scattered among the pinball machines and there was a new color television over the bar. Totally lacking in atmosphere, it was a place tourists never came to, but that was all right with Madame: she catered to the poor immigrants and pensioners who lived behind the scenes of the tourist spectacle and who coveted, rather than sneered at, the new. I'd first used this place as a student, and now it was a habit, with the added virtue, this trip, of complete anonymity. After two glasses of *rouge* at the bar, I went up to my room. Stretching out, I could feel the wine begin to merge with the jet lag and in five minutes I was asleep.

I awoke at two-thirty, still tired and with a headache from the wine; but the frigid *douche* at the end of the hall woke me up, and a brisk walk up to the Opéra got my blood flowing again. American Express is right at the corner; outside, like so many mangy cats, the anxious, indigent young awaited money from home, while inside there was the smell of new carpet and a pretty Vietnamese girl to serve me. I cashed a check, paid my account, and left the café's number for Hamilton. It was four by the time I was finished. I decided to go on to Hertz and pick up my car, but I was back in the café, drinking Suze, by five.

For the next hour, I tried not to be nervous; but I was. I didn't think Subotin could have got here before me, but it was possible, and it was also possible that Hamilton, reconsidering, had decided to ignore my warning—or, panic-stricken, had taken a flit. But he hadn't. At twenty past six, the barman waved me round to the phone.

"Thorne?" His voice was low and tense, but he had himself under control. "I hope I haven't kept you waiting. I put off calling Amex till the very last moment to give you as much time as possible."

"That's all right. Where are you?"

There was a slight hesitation, but of course he had to tell me. "A café on the Quai des Grands-Augustins. The Café Raymond."

"All right. I assume you've kept away from your place."

"Don't worry, Mr. Thorne. I've been a good boy. I was out of there twenty minutes after you called, and I haven't been back."

I didn't like him; he didn't like me. Somehow, that was clear at once.

"Stay where you are," I said. "It'll only take me ten minutes or so."

"I'm the old man at the bar, drinking Stella."

The *quai* was just a five-minute walk. It was dark now, and the rain was a persistent, cold drizzle. Behind me, Notre-Dame lifted up through the mist like a poet's dream, and lights dimly glowed in the obscurity of the Palais de Justice. Traffic along the *quai* was heavy and irritable, and on the sidewalks the crowds jostled sullenly, full of that malice which the French use to preserve their egos against the mass.

The café, when I reached it, was nothing special: a big room crowded with after-work drinkers, tiny plastic tables and orange plastic chairs, a lot of smoke, and the harsh, staccato beat of rapid French. Hamilton was at the bar, and I recognized him at once, though I would hardly have described him as an old man drinking beer. He was a tall, handsome man with very shiny silver hair. This hair was a trifle long, and there were unruly little tufts of it behind his ears and at the nape of his neck, and as he looked up from his glass, he reached back, in an automatic gesture, to smooth them. I couldn't be sure of his age—in my parents' generation, but on the younger side of it, and he had that glow of comfortable, prosperous health that spelled "early retirement." He was dressed in a rough gray fisherman's sweater and gray wool pants, the effect casual but quietly stylish; a senior civil servant on his day off, you might have guessed—he probably sailed, and if he didn't, he rode or he climbed.

And I still didn't like him.

I wondered why. He was a "spy," of course; a "traitor." He was also a liar. He accepted trust, then betrayed it. Yet you could say the same of Berri and I'd felt sympathy for him. Maybe it was because Berri had paid . . . not just in the beating he'd suffered, but in the wider sense of having accepted responsibility for what he'd done. He'd dwelled on it, reflected upon it, paid a price in terms of his own self-esteem. But not this man. I watched him as he lit a cigarette. Blowing smoke down at the bar, he leaned back slightly and used his right hand to brush a flake of ash from the front of his sweater. Very cool; very self-satisfied; but then he cast a quick glance over his shoulder and I could see the anxiety in his pale, watery eyes. And for some reason those eyes offended me; their anxiety seemed insatiable, even greedy, glittering with selfishness. Only with reluctance did I now move toward him. All at once he was aware of me, but before he could get up or say anything, I began talking rapidly to him in French. There was, I thought, no reason why we should draw attention to ourselves unnecessarily. To give him credit, he played along nicely, and after a moment, quite casually, he got up from his stool and I followed him out.

Stepping outside, he paused in the face of the rain, and ground out his cigarette on the *terrasse*.

"You speak excellent French, Mr. Thorne. I'm fluent, but I've never quite managed to shake off my accent."

"My mother was French."

"Ah, yes. I was forgetting. But then that makes it definite: I did know your father." He gave me a smile. "He was senior to me, rather exalted in fact. But I can clearly remember being charmed by your mother."

This was interesting, but I wasn't that surprised—the State Department, especially before 1950, was a very small world. I merely nodded, and watched his smile fade as I didn't pick up on our family connection. I found myself wondering now if he was homosexual—perhaps some buried prejudice was making me react negatively to him—but I didn't really think that he was. He wasn't an old man who liked boys; rather, he was an old man who still echoed certain ancient fashions of boyishness: he made me think of private schools, of rich kids in blazers and gray flannel pants. Now, reinforcing precisely this image, he thrust both hands deeply into his pockets and darted confidently into the traffic, crossing to the Seine side of the *quai*. I followed as best I could, and caught up to him at the top of a broad stone stairway leading down to the water. We were now virtually in the shadow of the Pont-Neuf; but here, down a level, the sound of the traffic was just a low rumble and the brackish pungency of the river cut through the gasoline fumes. Boats were tied up all along here; beyond them, glittering slightly with the first lights of evening, the Seine branched blackly around the Ile de la Cité. Most of the boats were barges, moored three deep: perhaps thirty or forty altogether. Some had shiny metal hulls; others, more elegant, were wood. But all were about a hundred feet long and of much the same design: a wheelhouse in the stern, with a long, low cabin running up to the prow. People were living on them; silhouetted against the misty lights of the Cité was an intricate cobweb of clotheslines, awnings, and canopies. I smelled a charcoal fire; somebody laughed; a radio was playing Mozart.

Hamilton had run on a little ahead. Now he stopped and waited for me. The rain had beaded on the heavy wool of his sweater and lent an even glossier sheen to his hair. He smiled. His face was long, the excellent features marked with heavy creases in his darkly tanned skin. "You'll have to be a bit acrobatic," he said, then, quite gracefully, leapt across to the first of the barges. It was scruffy, steel-hulled, the deck streaked with rust. Clumsily, I thumped after him, then scrambled across the deck, avoiding pails and bits of rope. He stopped on the far side, more or less in the middle of the boat, where the gunwales of this barge were bumpered against the next further out. Deftly, he then hopped up and over. This second barge seemed deserted, its deck a dark minefield of obstructions, but finally I reached the far side and—a middle-aged pirate—once more stormed over the gunwales.

As I straightened up and tried to catch my breath, I saw he still had his hands in his pockets: which, I will confess, didn't exactly endear him to me. He smiled. "Welcome to *La Trompette,* Mr. Thorne."

I looked around. I was standing on the deck of an old wooden barge. Its freshly varnished decks and polished brass fittings glowed softly in the light that filtered down from the great mansions in the Place Dauphine and the cars streaming across the Pont-Neuf.

It was all very impressive, and I wondered how discreet it could be. "You're absolutely sure you can't be traced here?"

He shook his head. "I bought her in the spring, but they've been fitting her out at Janville. They only brought her up this last week."

That sounded safe enough, and better than a hotel or a friend. I nodded, then followed him into the high, square wheelhouse. Here, shadows leapt up from kerosene lanterns, and the sounds of the great city retreated, replaced by the gentle creak of the hull. Everything was hushed, and with the rain trickling mistily over the windows, I had that childhood sense of being in a separate, far-off world. But then Hamilton flicked on an overhead light and I could see all the new brass and mahogany, the chart table that folded into the wall, the brassbound lockers, the new gimbaled lamps. The wheel, though, was old, a spoked circle of rusted iron rod. Hamilton put his hand on it and said, "It was all they said they could save, but I damn well made them save that."

Paul Hamilton, man of taste . . . He flicked off the light. The golden glow of the lanterns, and the flickering shadows, returned. Edging through a doorway, he beckoned me, and I followed him down a short ladder to the main cabin. It was very large, a long, low mahogany chamber as cozy and plush as an Edwardian Club room. Toward the bow, one section was fitted up as the salon with built-in couches, a bookcase, even a television and stereo. Closer to us was a galley, a *décors modernes* assemblage of stainless-steel sinks, butcher-block counters, and cunning little gadget racks. He'd been working here; wrenches, bits of pipe, and a torch were laid out on a newspaper. By way of explanation, he slid open a door beneath one of the counters, revealing a large metal canister which he pinged with his fingernail.

"My great debate," he said. "Propane or NG, which was it to be? I just hooked it up this afternoon. I like propane better to cook with, but it's heavier than air, so if you get a leak it sinks into the bilges. Then poof . . . But NG goes straight out the window. Safe as houses."

"So I can smoke, you mean?"

"Please do. And have a seat. I'll even get you a drink, if you like."

The floor—sole?—was oiled teak. I walked through the galley and sat down on one of the couches. The dry, starched smell of new upholstery rose around me. On the other side of the room, Hamilton turned a brass catch on a neatly fitted locker, and a bar descended out of the bulkhead with various niches for bottles and implements. With his back to me, he splashed Johnnie Walker Red into crystal tumblers and murmured, "By the way, I trust you are being polite? No wires? Body recorders?"

I actually do own a Nagra, but that was back home in Charlottesville—which, right now, seemed a long way away. "Don't worry, Mr. Hamilton. This is just between us."

"Good. There wouldn't be much point talking at all if we couldn't speak frankly." He turned around, a glass in each hand. He smiled. And there was a condescending twist to this smile that acknowledged the hostility between us and suggested that I was being a bit of a bore . . . but he'd put up with me anyway. Then the smile faded and he handed me the glass. "So Brightman's dead?" he grunted.

I nodded.

"And bad men are chasing me?"

"Something like that."

"Because I'm supposed to have something that Brightman left with me?"

I sipped my whiskey. His wariness, overlaid with his facetiousness, only increased my dislike of him. But I tried to keep my voice even. "If you don't mind, I'd like to start with my questions."

He shrugged. He seemed very cool. But when he tilted his head back to drink, I could again see the anxiety in his eyes, and his lips worked greedily at the rim of his glass. The glass came back down. He'd swigged a good inch of whiskey. Sitting, he crossed his legs and began rubbing the glass in little circles on his knee. "All right," he finally said, "but what if I don't want to answer?"

"I don't think you have a choice, Mr. Hamilton."

"That wouldn't be true, not quite. You'd be wrong to think that. But . . ." He smiled. "Go ahead."

The small lamps on the bulkheads spilled pools of yellowish light into the cozy, leathery, masculine gloom. I said, "I'll start at the obvious place. When did you last see Brightman?"

He took a more gentlemanly sip at his whiskey and smiled. "As you say, that is obvious—but I'm not sure I want to answer. Could I reserve it? Just for a moment? I told you I want to be frank—I'd rather you let me be honestly reticent than force me into a lie."

"Have you seen him within the last six months?"

"All right. Yes."

"What did he want?"

"Help, I think. It was fairly evident he was in some sort of trouble."

"What kind of trouble?"

"Didn't say."

"What kind of help, then?"

"He was vague."

"Did he leave anything with you? Or did he want to?"

"I assume you mean a variation on the letter-to-be-opened-upon-my-decease theme?"

"Yes. But probably not that exactly. He had something that people wanted, wanted so much that possessing it made him a target. So I think he decided to pass it on. He was saying, in effect: I don't have it anymore, there's no point coming after me. When you saw him, did you have the impression that he felt himself in danger?"

"I'm not sure my impressions were that distinct."

"Then maybe you should have paid closer attention. He *was* in danger and was trying to cope with it—by passing on this particular item. It not only took him out of the direct line of fire but also worked as a kind of insurance. Since he was the only person who knew where it was, people interested in this item now had a vested interest in his well-being."

"I see. What you're saying is—"

"What I'm saying, Mr. Hamilton, is that he wasn't doing you any great favor. Anyone who possesses this item is in considerable danger. Don't make any mistake about that."

He got up, reaching toward my glass as he did so, but I shook my head. He went over to his fancy bar. As he poured himself some more whiskey, his back was to me. "This item . . . can you tell me what it is, more specifically?"

"If you have it, you know. If not . . . perhaps that's something you'll let me reserve."

He turned around. "All right. But what makes you think I do have it?"

"The choice of candidates isn't really that great. And you'll surely grant that Brightman and yourself had a unique sort of relationship."

He smiled. "Maybe. But I didn't know him well, you understand. Not as well as yourself, at a guess."

"If you're asking, I didn't know him at all. I'm just a friend of his daughter's."

"There you go. I didn't even know he *had* a daughter. Over the years, I think I met him precisely three times." He came over to the couch again and sat down in front of me. Leaning his head back and looking up at the ceiling, he made a show of remembering. "I guess the first time was somewhere in the early forties. I couldn't even say when exactly. Then '56. I remember that well enough. Then this last time . . . but that's it. I don't see why you, or anyone else, would assume that he'd come to me for a favor, especially a vital one. I scarcely knew him, and had never done anything for him in a personal way."

"So what *did* you do for him?"

I watched his face. For a moment he seemed undecided, but I wondered if this too wasn't show. After all, it was he who'd explicitly brought up the past, and I had the impression that he welcomed the excuse to start talking about it, that he'd already worked out precisely what he would say.

He shrugged and snatched a quick sip of his drink. "I took some science at school," he began. "Not much, certainly not worth boasting about, but in the U.S. Foreign Service, at least in my day, science was about as rare as straight talk. At the beginning of the war—people having worked out that science and warfare might have some connection—this meant that I gained a number of important assignments virtually by default. Some of these involved various advisory panels on the export of scientific equipment. To the combatants, during the period the U.S. was neutral, to our allies afterwards."

"Including the Soviet Union?"

He hesitated. "So far as I was concerned, Mr. Thorne, I was helping a nation that had been beleaguered since its very conception and was now fighting for its life against the same enemy we were fighting—the greatest enemy humanity has ever known."

I couldn't help smiling at the hypocrisy of these noble sentiments—as the barge was worked gently in the swell and the lamps pushed golden tongues of light through its luxurious interior. "I'm not sure that speech fits your style."

"It was my style back then. Believe me, it was."

"You were a Communist?"

"Don't be idiotic. I was trying to be a decent man, I was trying to do the right thing." His voice, to my surprise, suddenly trembled a little. "I was surrounded by fools, that was the trouble. Fools, who couldn't see the menace Hitler represented—and fools, once they had seen it, who let their own ideological prejudices prevent full cooperation with Russia."

I watched his face, trying to decide if he believed this now, as he spoke, or whether he was only recollecting a passion long since suppressed. Conceivably, too, it was even more subtle: those former beliefs, however briefly held, may nonetheless have been the only beliefs he'd ever had in his life. Today, even if he thought them ridiculous, he might have nothing else to fall back on. Except Hitler, of course. I wondered if that wasn't the most enduring legacy of the Nazis: their horrors had become a virtually limitless excuse for the lesser horrors of others. But, despite the annoyance I was feeling, I had no desire to argue with him. I said, "In effect, you had a fundamental disagreement with U.S. foreign policy?"

"If you like."

"And you used Brightman to . . . circumvent it."

He gave a little smile. "What a nice way to put it. . . . But you needn't be so polite. I was, undoubtedly, a spy. And I knew precisely what I was doing."

I'd underestimated his ego; he had earned his title, "spy," and bore it proudly. "All right," I said. "You spied. What on? What did you tell him?"

He smiled. "You think I'm putting on airs, Mr. Thorne, and I mustn't. It was all minor league. As I said, most of it revolved around scientific equipment. There were certain requests the Soviets were particularly anxious about, and I tried to make sure they were seen in a favorable light. As well, it was useful for them to know what other countries were asking for. . . . I suppose it gave them a kind of index of their own efforts."

"What other countries?"

"Britain, of course . . . but Canada, Australia . . . any Allied center of war and scientific production. After the war, France, the Scandinavian countries—"

"So you kept on after the war?"

"To a degree."

"We're talking about atomic materials now?"

"No. Not materials. I told you—equipment, apparatus."

"And all of this," I said, "went through Harry Brightman?"

He shook his head. "I couldn't say. That didn't concern me, you see. There were arrangements . . . I expect quite usual under such circumstances. But I was never precisely sure who received the information I transmitted."

"Then why did you meet with Brightman at all?"

He shrugged. "Well, the first time was in the middle of the war. I was told to meet him in New York. It turned out that he wanted to obtain a particular piece of equipment—something electronic, I think, but I scarcely remember. He had money; any amount. I told him that what he wanted wasn't commercially procurable—it existed, but it had been custom-made in one of the university labs—and so we worked out a plan to get hold of it in a different fashion."

"Which was?"

He leaned back comfortably and took a quick sip. "It was his idea, and quite ingenious. I was to go back to my little committee full of pious anxieties: Wouldn't it be possible for someone to put together this piece of apparatus by combining items that were more readily available? Wasn't our security lax in that way? This set off a great flurry, and the researchers involved were asked to break the whole thing down and give us all the bits and pieces . . . most of which—confirming my conscientious worries and Brightman's suspicions—*were* available. I passed this list on to my contact, and I assume Brightman went off and got them." He shrugged. "It wouldn't have given them a hundred percent of it, but damn close."

I wondered what that piece of equipment had been, but at this late date it could scarcely make any difference—outside a law court. What was clear, however, was that Hamilton was telling at least part of the truth: according to Berri, this was precisely the sort of thing that Brightman had done.

I said, "You claim you met him a second time . . . in 1956."

"Yes. Hungary, you'll remember. That was special again. By this time—not that anyone ever told me—I think I was under Brightman's control. A number of people must have been, and one of them was having pangs of conscience. Apparently he believed all that talk about Freedom Fighters and was threatening to do something foolish. He must have been an idiot. The Hungarians positively *welcomed* the Germans; men *lined up* in the streets of Budapest to fight on the Russian front. So far as I was concerned, they deserved everything they got. . . . In any case, this person worked in the State Department and Brightman wanted me to calm him down."

"Who was it?"

"I've no idea. I told Brightman to forget it—I wasn't going to expose myself to somebody who was already getting cold feet. That was his problem. I just wanted him to keep me out of it."

"Did he understand that?"

"Yes."

"Was he angry?"

"No. . . . He pushed me hard to speak to this person but I think he understood my position well enough."

Interesting. Brightman *had* asked him for a favor, then. But Hamilton hadn't come through. I said, "These were face-to-face meetings . . ."

"Yes."

"But there must have been other forms of communication with him as well. Messages. And—at least once—a messenger."

"You know about that? He was a funny little fellow. A French-Canadian. He told me his name but I forget it. I was living here then, just nicely retired. Brightman wanted me to set up a meeting for him, through the embassy . . . the Soviet Embassy, of course. I told him no."

"Why?"

"Why should I? Why should I take a risk for him?"

"All right . . . but why do you think Brightman asked you to? By all accounts, he was higher up in the hierarchy—closer to the embassy, if you like—than you ever were."

He shrugged. "It's a good question, and at the time I asked it. But you understand I wasn't dealing with him, just his messenger, and he clearly knew nothing. I assumed that Brightman had his own procedures for getting in touch with them but this time, for some reason, preferred to use an outside party. Or perhaps he'd had unsatisfactory results using his normal channels and wanted to try another. In any case, I didn't see what business it was of mine, so I said no."

"You have to admit it's a little strange. Brightman was never close to you . . . personally or professionally . . ."

"That's right."

"Yet under these circumstances—which we can assume were exceptional—he again picked on you for a favor. Why?"

"I don't know, Mr. Thorne. Using me might have been safer. More effective. Quicker. Who knows? Perhaps it was something entirely mundane. All these events happened a fair time ago. I was young when I started out—if I may put it like that—but quite probably the other people Brightman knew were much older. By the time we're talking about—this was just a few years back—there probably weren't many of us left."

That, at least, could be true. Of Brightman's original "ring," few could still be alive. This was all ancient history. 1939: the Molotov-Ribbentrop Pact—more important to these people, strangely enough, than the outbreak of the war itself. 1941: Germany invades the Soviet Union. Communists, no longer embarrassed by their alliance with the Nazis, can come out of the closet and "help" the Russians under the guise of aiding the common effort against Hitler. 1945: the Cold War begins. A man like Hamilton—like the Rosenbergs, like Alger Hiss—is now in great peril. Worse: by 1956, and the Hungarian Uprising, disillusion has begun to set in; the risks no longer seem worth it. And by 1968, with the invasion of Czechoslovakia, even diehards like Brightman were beginning to search for a way out. But even the most recent of these dates was a dozen years ago now. Few people who had started out with Brightman would have been left, and even they would have been old men—like Philby or Anthony Blunt. Thus, Brightman could have been forced to come to Hamilton, whether he liked it or not. But he couldn't have liked it; given what I knew about Brightman and could guess about Hamilton, the two men had nothing in common. Yet he had trusted him . . . asked him for favors. Why?

As I thought about this, Hamilton went to the bar and poured himself another finger of whiskey. "So we're back to the present," he said. "The present, and Harry Brightman. Except Harry isn't part of it, is he?" I said nothing. I watched him drink. Again there was a nervous sucking of his lips at the rim of the glass. He looked back at me. "He *is* dead? You're sure of it?"

Since it was obviously so important to him, I said, definitely, "Yes. I saw his body myself. Harry Brightman is dead."

He gave me a look, then simply shrugged. "He never betrayed me, Mr. Thorne, and I have no wish to betray him. But there's not much point worrying if he's dead. . . ." Coming from him, such a testament of loyalty had to be ludicrous . . . and it was a mistake, for now he'd drawn my attention again to that one crucial point: for Hamilton, Brightman's death mattered more than anything else. I watched him now as he set his glass back on the bar, then turned around, leaning against it and facing me.

"In any case," he continued, "I might as well tell you . . . about the last time I saw him, I mean." He picked up the glass again . . . a nice, casual gesture not quite perfectly acted. I knew, even before he opened his mouth, that he was going to tell me a lie. "It was in the second week of September. I had no idea he was coming. In fact, he just appeared at my elbow one day in the market—he was obviously taking the strictest precautions. We had a drink and talked. As I said, it was clear he was in trouble and wanted my help. I'd turned him down before, of course—and I don't make any apologies for that—but this time, I admit, it seemed something special. I tried to get out of him what it was. He refused to say, not until I committed myself. I just couldn't do that. Surely you understand? The only reason I've survived this long is because I've been very cautious."

I shook my head. Because I'd worked it out now. "I don't believe you, Mr. Hamilton. Not a word."

He turned away. "Believe what you like."

But I shook my head again; the most important thing about any lie is its motivation, and now I knew his. "He came to you that first time and you turned him down—but he kept coming back, time and time again. How come? Why bother? If you were so cautious, you'd *always* refuse to stick out your neck . . . but he kept coming back. In fact, he kept coming back to you because you always did *exactly as you were told.* He was blackmailing you, Mr. Hamilton—that's what I believe. He had a nice bundle of documents stashed away in some vault and so you had to do just what he wanted."

"Don't be ridiculous. If he could blackmail me, think of what I had on him."

"Nothing. Certainly nothing on paper. Besides, he didn't give a damn. Threaten him and he might call your bluff—he was a disillusioned old man, sick with himself and sick with the world. But you? Oh no . . . you've got something to lose. You want to enjoy a cozy retirement on your beautiful barge. So you did just as he told you."

He couldn't keep it out of his eyes; I was right. He looked away. "That's ridiculous. Listen—"

"No. You listen. Don't kid yourself, Hamilton. He left that package with you because it was too dangerous to leave with his daughter or anyone else he cared for. And it's no less dangerous now. If you've still got it in forty-eight hours, believe me, you're as good as dead."

He tried to light a cigarette, get back his composure, but now his anxiety was coming out like sweat.

"I don't believe you," he stammered. "Why should I? If your theory's right, why was Brightman killed *after* he gave me his package? *You're* telling the lies."

Again I shook my head. "That's something else you'd better get straight. You've got that package, so you probably know what's inside it. A key? A combination? Some sort of document that gets you into a vault? Whatever it is, it leads to a great deal of money—but don't be tempted. It's part of the money the Soviets originally gave Brightman to buy that equipment you were putting him on to. A lot was left over. Certain people, certain Russians, are trying to get hold of it, and your former employers are trying to stop them; they want to cover the whole thing up. So whatever you do, don't go to *them* for help. I think that's the mistake Brightman made."

I'd been working much of this out as I went along, but as soon as I started to speak, I knew it was true. Subotin on one side, the KGB on the other: there'd be more complications, but that was the heart of it. Brightman had probably gone to his old masters to get Subotin off his back, but they'd eliminated him instead, and then done likewise with Travin. I was suddenly convinced of this—and my conviction must have got through to Hamilton. When I was finished, he poured out more whiskey but then thrust it away. "I don't believe that," he said. "None of it. I was loyal . . . perfectly. I've kept up my contacts—it's been a long time, but there are still a few people left who'll remember my name, who'll be grateful. And everyone knows that the Soviet Service takes care of its own."

I looked at him, amazed. It was incredible if he actually believed this. "Mr. Hamilton," I said, "you are a forty-year-old skeleton in the closet. They just want to make sure you don't rattle."

An expression of shock spread over his face; strangely enough, I think it was my contempt that got through to him. He realized I considered him a fool and was embarrassed—he didn't like to be thought of that way. He suddenly strode out of the salon, through the galley, and opened a door into a cabin under the wheelhouse. A light went on, and I could hear him rummaging in a desk. I had a moment's panic then, thinking of a gun. But he pulled out a bottle of pills and popped a few down his throat. He looked back at me; then his eyes faltered. As he started to speak, I could barely hear him. "All right," he said. "You've made your point . . . and I'll admit I haven't told the whole truth. But listen, you've got to help me."

"Just give me the package, the envelope . . . whatever it is. I'll get rid of it for you and I'll make sure they understand that you don't have it anymore. Then you're home free."

He shook his head. "No . . . listen, I can't. Not just like that—it's not that simple. You have to believe me. I need time to think." He looked up at me now and made a quick gesture with his hand, to take in the barge. "How safe am I here?"

"As safe as a man on the edge of a cliff. They have your address, your apartment. Is there anything there that will lead them here?"

He put his hand up to his head. "I don't think so . . . at least not immediately."

I shrugged. "Then they won't find you—immediately. But they'll find you eventually."

"Twenty-four hours . . . that's all I need. I must have that long. Could you do that? Wait till tomorrow? Come back tomorrow evening, Thorne. We'll work out something then."

I looked at him, down the length of the boat. An old man: tarted up. If old men can be tarted up. . . . The pleading tone that had come into his voice should have increased my contempt, but, despite myself, I felt a little sympathy. I shrugged. "You understand, Hamilton, I'm not your problem."

He nodded. "Of course . . . of course." He even tried a smile. "I realize you're trying to help. I thank you for that. But don't do anything now. Just give me a little more time. Till tomorrow. . . . Come back then, Thorne. Same time. We'll work something out."

I said nothing. In truth, I felt more than a little sick, and half of me wanted to send this nasty little man straight off to prison. Except he wouldn't go there. What he'd done was too long ago; and the CIA, never having let the British live down Philby, weren't going to expose themselves to the embarrassment of revealing Hamilton's existence. No, they'd make his life difficult—tax audits, passport restrictions, bureaucratic harassment—but these discomforts would be marginal. And he knew this. Which meant I couldn't even threaten him with the police. Yet I also knew he was going to do something stupid. He had Brightman's "package," whatever that was, and he wanted some time—he was going to do something stupid, all right.

But I got up and shrugged myself into my raincoat. Then I said, "Hamilton, do you have any idea who these people are?"

He made a little gesture with his hand. "Brightman mentioned something. . . . I think he said they were a faction of the Service—the KGB—with connections into the military. . . . Not very nice."

"You're not thinking that you can convince them that you're on their side?"

"No," he said. "Of course not. Nothing like that."

"And don't try convincing the embassy, either."

His face suddenly twisted in anger. "I'm not on anyone's side—I don't care—"

"Don't give me that. You've been on the same side from the very beginning. Your own."

He sneered then. But not very convincingly. "What do you know? You didn't have to live through the times we lived through."

"No, I didn't. But people like you didn't make it any easier for those who did."

As a rebuke, it wasn't much, but it was the best I could do. And it shut him up as I walked past him, through the galley, and climbed the stairs into the wheelhouse. Stepping outside, I looked at my watch. It was after eight; we'd talked a long time. The rain had stopped, but a cold wind was blowing down the river. It snatched traffic sounds from the Pont-Neuf and made lights from the Ile de la Cité dance in the water. I made my way over the barges; someone had boiled chicken for dinner, and I could hear the splash of water and a clatter of pans. Nearby, a man coughed and murmured, *"Bon soir,"* and I waved vaguely into the darkness.

I climbed up to the *quai.* On the sidewalk, lighting a cigarette, I felt very uneasy. I knew he was up to something, and whatever he did would be on my head. Partly. But then I told myself, no, I was damned if I was going to take responsibility for people like Hamilton. But I still didn't want to let him out of my sight, so I crossed the road to a café and found a table that let me keep watch on the stairway up from the river. Sure enough, twenty minutes later, Hamilton appeared—but not very dramatically: he just went into a phone booth, made a call, came out again. Half an hour went by. And then a car drew up, the sort of American car that always seems ridiculous on a European street: a huge Dodge Charger that was painted bright yellow and festooned with spoilers and window slats. It stopped, hazard lights flashing. Someone got out . . . and I smiled at myself and swore for the thousandth time never again to speculate about other people's sex lives, for Hamilton's friend was a young, pretty boy. They talked for a minute, then the boy drove away. But Hamilton stayed where he was, smoking a cigarette and running his fingers back through his long silver hair. A few minutes later, the young man returned, this time on foot. Together, they went down to the river. After an hour, when they still hadn't come back, I was sure they were settled in for the night. But I was taking no chances. Making a quick tour of the streets near the *quai,* I found the boy's Dodge squeezed into an alley, and then fetched my own little machine from the *pension* and parked up the road.

Ten twenty-two . . . Eleven-sixteen . . . The rain stopped, then started again. Slowly, one by one, the hours passed by. I dozed intermittently. The front seat of a Renault Cinq doesn't make much of a bed, but it will do.

15

I passed a busy night.

There were four drunks, a couple of cat fights, a whore who found it hard to take no for an answer, and even a *flic* who shined his light in the window and asked for my papers. All in all, I didn't get much sleep . . . though no one came near the big yellow car. Around four o'clock the city seemed to drift off, lulled into drowsiness by the distant hum of trucks on the *autoroutes* and the *périphérique,* but an hour later deliveries started to the cafés, and soon afterward the working people of the *quartier* emerged. In Paris, as everywhere else, the poor are always up before the rest of us. Early-shift workers cycled through the rain, old women, bundled up in heavy coats and with kerchiefs on their heads, trudged off to their jobs as domestics in the big hotels, and an old man in a blue serge jacket took up his position at the kiosk on the corner. By six, the sidewalks were crowded. By six, even exhausted, unshaved, out-of-cigarettes men who'd slept all night in their cars had got up and stretched. I walked over to the *quai* and the stairway that led down to the water. A gray haze of drizzle hung over the Seine. On some of the barges, life was stirring—a smudge of smoke, the thump of a pump—but *La Trompette* seemed to be slumbering on. For the time being, that was fine by me. I crossed the street, found a café, and began drinking coffee.

By seven, I felt halfway human, except for the beard, and began wondering what I was going to do, since Hamilton didn't strike me as an early riser and probably wouldn't show for hours. But almost at once, I got a surprise: the boyfriend appeared. He even seemed fairly perky, popping up from the stairway and then darting briskly through traffic.

I wondered if I should follow him; but then that question became moot, because he came straight over to the café where I was sitting. For a second, I was worried that Hamilton might be tagging along behind, but he ordered right away and settled down to eat alone. It was easy to watch him—he was only half a dozen tables away, but he opened a paper and began reading it closely. I put his age at nineteen or twenty. Tall. Slim. A lean, elegant face but with a rather boyish lick of hair that kept falling into his eyes. He was wearing a brown leather jacket and jeans and a pair of Nocona boots, and he was very tanned: Mr. Franco-California, you might have called him. But, as so often happens with European imitations of American styles, the very sincerity of his efforts produced something quite different from the original. In this case, it was a rather appealing innocence. Five years ago, he'd been full of rock 'n' roll and movie stars; now, after his night with his older American lover, he was trying hard not to be too shocked by himself. Lighting a cigarette, he shook out his paper, and when the waiter brought his coffee and croissants, he deigned to acknowledge them with only the slightest of nods. Deftly, he stubbed out the cigarette, then began eating slowly, looking about the room as he did so . . . for an instant, his glance touched mine, but then passed on, quite normally. He seemed perfectly calm: if Hamilton had communicated any of his problems to him, he wasn't showing it.

As the boy ate, I pondered. Hamilton was up to something, I was sure of that, so I was reluctant to give up my watch on the *quai*. On the other hand, the boy might be important too. Hamilton had called him immediately after seeing me, and there was also the question of the car. Presumably Hamilton had enough sense to understand that his own was too dangerous to drive, and last night I'd been half expecting him to use the Dodge for a midnight flit; and he might still do that. Or he could send the boy off on errands. It was this that created the potential dilemma . . . and in point of fact it arrived just after eight. Folding his paper, the boy pressed a button on his watch. Informed of the time to the millisecond, he then rose and headed out of the café. I hesitated . . . and if, in the end, I decided to follow him, I was very tentative. Only back to the barge. To the car—he might meet Hamilton there. Or . . .

He stepped onto the *quai*.

The sidewalks were crowded, and out on the street Paris was "accommodating itself to the automobile"—to use President Pompidou's immortal expression—just like Newark, New Jersey: with a traffic jam that jostled and banged and grumbled for miles. Heading up the Quai des Grands-Augustins, the boy continued onto the Quai St.-Michel, then turned up the Rue St.-Jacques. He was going to his car; I took a shortcut and beat him to it. Hamilton wasn't there, but I hadn't really expected that—he was probably still in bed. I decided to string along a bit more and started the Renault, so its engine was already warm as the big Dodge coughed in the damp. Backing out of the alley, he squealed his tires—another California touch—and sped away. Doubling back onto St.-Germain, he crossed the river by the Pont de Sully and continued onto the Boulevard Henri IV. . . . In the traffic, there was no trouble following him; and even when we got out of it, you would have been hard-pressed to lose that huge splash of yellow. Forty minutes later, I pulled up to the curb of the Avenue Foch in St.-Mandé, an eastern suburb just outside the city proper.

I didn't know the place, but I knew lots like it: streets of old, solid stone apartments behind black wrought-iron fences; very quiet; the curb jammed with cars, including some Peugeots and Citroëns and one carefully maintained MG. The yellow Dodge was out of place, but as I watched the boy go into one of the buildings, I had the feeling that this was where his parents lived.

I never found out if that was true, but he was back inside of twenty minutes, carrying two soft suitcases. Throwing them into the trunk of the Dodge, he now led us onto the *périphérique*. He went east as far as Gentilly and then turned into the Boulevard Jourdan, a big street that runs through one of those areas that all cities have to put up with: a bare, barren expanse that was dotted with big hospitals and other institutional structures. The principal example here was the Cité Universitaire, a huge educational complex where the French put a lot of their foreign students, housing them in *maisons* built in the appropriate national style—the Thai house, for example, is like a little pagoda. Turning onto one of its access roads, California Jacques headed for a parking lot.

I almost didn't follow—I assumed he was going to a class or was visiting someone. But why the bags? The question intrigued me just enough to wait a moment, engine running, by a loading bay in behind one of the buildings. Sure enough, he appeared about three minutes later. And he didn't go into the school. Striding quickly, he crossed a stretch of dead lawn and headed out to the street. Getting out of my car, I followed him across. There was a Métro station here, but he didn't go into it, instead cutting across the corner of a park, finally coming out at the entrance of a small side street. Only when I saw the name of this street did I finally understand. It was Hamilton's street. I almost couldn't believe it. I'd already formed a low opinion of the man, but this was incredible. Despite what I'd told him, he'd let the boy come here—must have *asked* him to . . . and clearly hadn't told him there was any danger, for now, with no attempt at deception, he turned into a doorway. I had a sudden spasm of guilt, but then told myself that it was still unlikely that Subotin had made it to Paris, and I crossed over the street to a *café-tabac.* Five minutes, I thought; I'll give him that long. But even five minutes is a long time for your conscience, and when that five minutes was up, I gave him five minutes more . . . and two minutes and twenty-six seconds later, he appeared.

And seemed quite unconcerned.

The drizzle was turning to rain. Slipping his hands into the front pockets of his jeans, and hunching his shoulders, he ran in a funny, stiff-legged lope up to the corner, just across from me. He paused; squinted both ways; then dashed across the road, into the park. From inside the café, I watched his back, but if anyone was following him, I didn't see them . . . though in the next ninety seconds or so, one car turned into, another out of, that street. Still, it seemed that he'd gotten away with it—Subotin probably *hadn't* arrived in Paris yet—and so I took after him. The rain began to come down hard, trickling under my collar. I could see the boy up ahead; he was hustling along, but that was clearly because of the rain: whatever he'd done in Hamilton's apartment hadn't worried him. And if he'd taken something out of it, it was small enough to fit into his pocket. So it was probably nothing exciting: money, a checkbook, credit cards—the sort of thing Hamilton might have forgotten in his rush to get out of the place after I'd phoned. Head down, I ran through the park, catching up to him as we arrived back at the Boulevard Jourdan. Sparing his fancy boots, California picked his way across, neatly avoiding puddles, but by the time I came up to the curb, the traffic was heavy and I had to wait. I could see him plainly, though. And this time he went into one of the buildings. He was long gone before I was across the street, so I went straight back to the parking lot.

I had a twelve-minute wait, but then he emerged and walked slowly across to the Dodge. Again, he displayed no signs of anxiety or suspicion. He got in, started the engine, and nosed past me, leaning forward over the wheel to rub a clear spot on the windshield. He turned onto the boulevard; then, returning to the *périphérique,* he led us back the way we'd come: through St.-Mandé, then onto the A4. This was done, I might say, rather cautiously; he'd put his foot down if the traffic really opened up, but only for a few seconds, and I had the impression that he wasn't quite familiar with the car, and was even a little afraid of it. I didn't complain; I was having a hard enough time as it was. The rain was fairly heavy now, and in the little Renault I was constantly drowned in muddy spray from the big trucks. With relief, just before Villiers, I followed him off the *autoroute* onto a smaller highway running through the smaller towns and villages near the banks of the Marne. I hung back cautiously—on the *autoroute* I'd been one Renault among a thousand, but here I was much more exposed—though he showed no signs of being wary at all. Keeping a pleasant, sedate pace, we wiggled along behind the river—like a map illustrating the front line in September 1914—until he turned off the highway and then, almost immediately, turned again, down a small side road. We were now about twenty-five or thirty miles from Paris, not far from Meaux. Here, all the land sloped down toward the river, whose course was marked by a gray, fuzzy line of trees in the distance. Slowly, bouncing over potholes, we made our way toward it, passing a few farms, huddled houses, and orchards and woodlots where the bare branches of the trees shook stiffly in the wind. After a couple of miles, a biggish, barnlike structure appeared on the right. The boy flashed his turn signal; I took my foot off the gas. The place was a roadside restaurant of the sort commercial travelers go for: big, fast service, decent, cheap food. Judging by the number of cars out front, they were doing good business. The boy headed in. Though there hadn't been the slightest sign that he suspected anyone was following him, I was cautious and drove past the entrance, then doubled back. As I parked, I was just in time to see him disappear inside.

I thought a moment. He hadn't seemed suspicious: but he had seen me in the café on the *quai.* Still, it was a little early for lunch, which made me curious, and there was a possibility—though I didn't see how—that he might be meeting Hamilton here. Deciding to chance it, I followed him in. And in fact there was no risk at all: in front of the main dining room (very large) was a gloomy bar. I was able to sit there, pretty well hidden, and catch a glimpse of the boy every time someone opened the big swinging doors and went in to eat. He was alone and, I judged, had no expectations of meeting anyone.

I ordered a vermouth, then found I could get a sandwich and ate two ravenously. After that, I enjoyed an hour of French sociology. The bar was used by the locals, Meldois as they are called in this region; there was a fair traffic, but it kept moving, so the place was never crowded. Some of these people were farmers, taciturn but friendly, while others were men who'd retired to the country—comfortably off, but not rich, a sort of subgentry. They talked to each other about the weather and the roads and fishing, and made Paris seem a thousand miles away. After half an hour, I bought myself a second vermouth, and was just starting a third when the boy finally emerged. Once more, nothing seemed out of the ordinary. He stood for a moment in the foyer, buttoning his jacket carefully and making people step around him, then pushed through the doorway. Still bearing in mind that he'd seen me in Paris, I stayed where I was until I heard the Dodge's big engine start burbling. Then I got up, watching from the doorway as he drove across the parking lot. But now I got a surprise: instead of turning *left,* toward the highway, he headed right, down toward the river. But even as I sprinted back to the Renault, I understood. Indeed, it was obvious. I was within ten kilometers of the Marne, which flows into the Seine near Paris. The boy *was* meeting Hamilton—but *Hamilton would be arriving by barge.* So following the boy had been a terrific stroke of good luck . . . or so I thought until I turned the key in the Renault's ignition.

Nothing happened.

After three tries—and a slow count to fifty—I got out and propped up the hood. The engine was still warm after the morning's drive, and raindrops hissed on the block . . . but no matter how warm it was, or how well tuned, there was no way it was going to start when two of the ignition cables were missing.

I sat in the car.

The rain drummed on the roof and sheeted over the windshield, turning people leaving the restaurant into wavy, aqueous ghosts. Lighting a cigarette, I watched my warm breath turn to mist on the glass and told myself there were two possibilities, one frightening, the other merely annoying, but why be alarmist? I was certain that Subotin hadn't been in Hamilton's apartment; if he had been, he'd never have let the boy come out again. And I was *almost* sure that no one had followed us away from the place. . . . But the lack of certainty made me shiver. There was no sense getting into a panic, however; more than likely, I'd just been too confident, too careless, and the boy hadn't been as innocent as he looked. He'd got on to me. And then he'd led me into this place—thereby getting me out of the car—and skillfully beached me: he'd been out of my sight just long enough to do it. Very neat, I thought; except it didn't make any difference. That is, it didn't make any difference if I was right about Hamilton coming by barge. I was too close to the river; I could walk there in an hour. I stubbed out my cigarette. I was fairly sure about all this—but not so sure that I wanted to waste any time. I ran back to the restaurant. The barman gave me plenty of sympathy, and offered to call a garage further down the N3, but I knew that would end up taking hours.

"It's nothing, you see. If I had the part, I could do it myself."

"A taxi would have to come out from Meaux."

"A bicycle? If it's not too far . . ."

"In this? You're sure?"

One of the girls in the kitchen had one. She thought I was crazy, because of the rain, but wouldn't take any money. Her machine, not exactly a *vélo,* was padlocked to a drainpipe in behind the restaurant: a lady's bicycle, old and squeaky, with a red plastic basket on the front handlebars. I got onto it and wobbled off, and found that people are right, you never forget: it's not your memory, just thirty years of food and booze and cigarettes that keep you from being a kid again. But at least the road was downhill, carrying me down to the Marne. I rattled on; fell into a rhythm: push, push, and pant, and every third time around, a quick squint into the rain. The wheels juddered through potholes, the saddle delivered unladylike prods, my pants were soaked so completely that they molded to my thighs. I passed a farm and a couple of cottages, but in this weather no one was out, and I didn't see a single car. For twenty minutes or so, I struggled ahead. Then the road narrowed and the surface changed to hard-packed gravel, and I entered a dark lane of huge oaks, so dense that even without their leaves they kept the rain off. The grade steepened; I sat back, coasting. It was very dark, and a sort of hush fell, or at least a peculiar kind of resonance: close to, filling my ears, were the sounds of my panted breaths and the constant soft

crunch of the wheels over the gravel, but beyond these sounds was a
vast zone of silence, enclosed in turn by the patter of the rain in the
branches high overhead. The light here was soft, dim, silvery; as if everything was reflected in a misted mirror. Leaves were thickly matted in
the ditches; on both sides, the woods seemed dense. I started pedaling
again, then coasted some more as the road grew even steeper. I glided
round a curve, and it was just at this point, as the road straightened out,
that I saw the yellow Dodge.

It was in the ditch: tilted sharply over on the right, with its big snout
crumpled against one of the oaks.

I braked, hard. The bike slewed round. I got my feet down and
straddled it, and stared down the dark, wet road.

Nothing was moving. The Dodge just lay there, like a huge piece
of road junk. It was hard to be certain, but I didn't think anyone was
still inside. The driver's door was ajar, the passenger's wide open—like
an arm that was trying to brace the car and keep it from flipping over
completely. I listened. All I could hear was the rain. With the doors open
like that, there should have been a warning buzzer if the keys were still
in the ignition.

So . . .

The boy had driven his car off the road. Unhurt, he'd taken the
keys out and was walking for help. . . . Yes, that was possible; but I didn't
like it. There was nothing tricky about this road, unless you took it too
fast; and despite his tight jeans and fancy boots, I would have said the
kid was a cautious driver. Besides, I hadn't passed him, and the restaurant was the first place he'd think of for help. No; I didn't like this at
all, and felt a queasiness that was becoming all too familiar. But could
Subotin be here? I just wasn't sure. Coming out of Paris, on the *périphérique,* I'd been working too hard to see out the front window without
worrying about the back, and once we were on the N3 it would have
been easy for someone to follow us without being spotted.

Reluctantly, I got back on the bicycle.

Jiggling and rattling, I came up to the car. There was nobody in
it. And there was no blood, which was the next thing I looked for. I
walked around to the front. The right side was jammed hard against the
oak, having gouged a white, gleaming wound out of the trunk. As an
accident, it was more than a fender bender, but nothing spectacular; although the fancy grille resembled a crushed beer can and there was a

drip from the radiator, I doubted that he'd been going fast enough to hurt himself.

But that was assuming it *had* been an accident.

And when I stepped back, and saw the scraped patch above the right front wheel well, I wondered again.

A crow squawked in the woods. Its call drew my eyes there. These woods were very dense, for between the huge, ancient oaks, many smaller trees—birches and little pines—were growing. The rain had beaten the leaves from their branches and they lay in great piles around the trunks . . . except for the wavy path where something had been dragged through them, pushing them to one side and turning up the leaves underneath in wet, matted patches.

I stared at that path the way you look at a door you don't want to open. And just as I'd felt in that garage in Detroit, I now had an urge to call out, to see if anyone was there. But I kept my mouth shut and stood very still, listening to the slow, steady drip of coolant out of the radiator.

A minute passed. There was no getting away from what I had to do. I stepped around the car and over the ditch. The wet leaves were spongy underfoot, and each step released a pungent smell of mold. Everywhere, there was the drip and trickle of water over vegetation, and a gust of wind spattered down more rain from the branches above. You couldn't move without making a hell of a lot of noise. Every few yards, I stopped and listened. Birds clucked and rustled around me, and high up, somewhere in the gray lattice of sky beyond the trees, a single-engine plane was droning along. I pushed past a wet pine bough. Everything I touched was wet; soaking already, I was soaked again. My feet began to itch inside my wet socks and my crotch was chafing . . . sensations I now concentrated on just the way, as a child, I'd concentrated on the cracks in the sidewalk as I ran down a dark, frightening street.

I was thankful that I didn't have to go far; they'd simply wanted to get him out of sight from the road. He was sitting in a little hollow, at the base of a birch tree. His legs were stuck out in front of him, his fancy snakeskin boots buried in dirty leaves, while his arms were tied behind him, lashed around the trunk. His head too was tied back to the tree. They'd used his belt; they'd looped it around his neck and the tree trunk, and then they'd jammed a stick through the loop, twisting it tight, as if they were winding up the rubber band on a kid's model airplane.

His face was very bloody. He didn't move, and a sick, guilty feeling began to spread through the pit of my stomach. There was no way to duck it. It *was* partly my fault. I could have stopped him—at the *quai,* at Hamilton's apartment, in the restaurant . . . but then—thank God, thank God—his eyes opened, glittering, and his whole body strained toward me. With a tremendous sense of relief, I skidded down a slope of mud and leaves and reached him.

He was groaning. The belt had dug a red furrow into his throat and was tight enough to stop him from speaking. When I got it off, he gave a hoarse gasp, and then I undid his hands. With a single quick look, a child's imploring look of helplessness and shame—like a child who can't stop soiling himself—he toppled onto on his side and just breathed . . . huge, deep breaths, sucked in, released, over and over. . . .

I waited, kneeling in the muddy leaves. Despite the blood, I thought—as with Berri—that he was more frightened than hurt. Lying there, he drew his knees up to his belly, his breaths came in long, trembling gasps, and the tears made glistening tracks through the blood on his cheeks. Giving him a chance to recover, I looked away. And only then realized that the ground all around the boy's feet was littered with money, fresh, bright leaves among the old—French and Swiss francs, Swedish crowns, British pounds. . . .

He got his breath back. He gave me one quick look—almost furtive—but then looked away. His voice was soft and trembling as he said, "I thank you. I thought no one would come. I thank you very much."

"If you like, I can go for a doctor."

He shook his head. "I'll be all right in a minute. . . . But a handkerchief . . . if you happen to have one . . ."

I gave him a Kleenex. It was sodden; as he scraped it over his face, bits of it stuck in the blood. Then he said, "Excuse me," and pushed it up his nose, which was still bleeding, and leaned his head back. "I'm very sorry . . . I don't know what to say, how to explain. . . . I was attacked by some men . . ."

His voice petered away. He was bewildered. He seemed very young and frightened, his adolescence more evident now than his sexual style. He could have been a kid out joyriding—he'd had too many beers, rolled the car. Now he was injured and his best friend was dead. But he didn't know that yet.

I said, "You don't have to explain. I know Hamilton . . . I know who those men are. They must have followed you from his apartment. . . . I did as well, but I didn't see them."

His head came upright again, his left hand still holding the Kleenex up to his nose. But before he could speak, I added, "It's all right. I'm not with them—I'm on your side. Tell me, at the restaurant, did you touch my car?"

"No . . . I had no idea. . . . You followed me? I don't understand. Who are you? Who are those men?"

"My name is Robert Thorne. I'm an American. You can ask Paul about me. He knows who I am. But you must tell me . . . when you went to his apartment, what did you get?"

He took the Kleenex away from his nose. A little blood trickled from his left nostril; reaching the line of his lip, it flowed around it, like a pencil mustache or a trace of chocolate ice cream around the mouth of a kid.

"You know Paul?"

"Yes. I'm a friend of his from America."

"He said he was in trouble. He wanted me to do something for him. I asked him what the trouble was but he said it was too complicated to explain. People were watching his apartment, that was the point—he couldn't go there, but I could because they wouldn't know who I was."

"Except they did."

"But that can't be possible. Paul said so. . . . It was safe, because they wouldn't know me."

"Maybe that's what he thought, but he didn't think hard enough. Does he have any pictures of you? There, I mean . . . in the apartment."

There was a flicker behind his eyes. Then he looked away. "Yes . . . perhaps. I'm not sure."

But of course Hamilton had pictures of him—lovingly posed, beautifully taken; and when Subotin had broken in, and seen them, he'd known a way of getting to Hamilton anytime he cared to. "It doesn't make any difference," I said. "Somehow they recognized you. They followed you from the apartment to the Cité and then here. . . . They wanted to know what you were doing for Paul."

"Yes."

"And what *were* you doing?"

"I'm not sure that I should tell you."

"You must. . . . It's very important—not for you now, but for Paul."

He looked straight at me, absolutely directly, like a child searching for trust. "You swear? You are Paul's friend?"

"I swear."

He believed me. He wanted to: because this was one secret he wanted to tell. The words tumbled out. "Paul had a locker in the Cité, in the library. I had to get the key from the apartment to open it. There were three envelopes inside. I was to mail one of them—I did that right there, in the Cité—and bring him the others."

I looked around us, at the bills scattered among the leaves. "This money was in one of them?"

He nodded. "Yes."

"And the others . . . you mailed one, but you had the second with you?"

"Yes. Paul said not to mail it; he wanted to look at it first. But they took it away from me. It had an address in Canada—I don't think it was important because they opened it and then crumpled it up."

"This Canadian address—did it include a name?"

"Yes. It was supposed to go to a man named Cadogan, in Toronto."

"All right. Think of the one you did mail—who was that to?"

He looked at me and swallowed. "That's what they wanted to know. They said they'd choke it out of me . . ." But now his voice faltered and his face twisted with anguish; anguish, God knows, that he was under no obligation to feel, not for a man like Hamilton.

"Don't blame yourself," I said, "not for anything. Because that's exactly what they would have done—they'd have choked you to death."

"Yes . . . I know. But I tried not to tell them anyway. And I didn't tell them everything."

"All right. Again, I promise you . . . it won't harm Paul to tell me."

He brought his head back, tossing the bit of Kleenex away, into the leaves. His voice was very soft, almost a mutter. "It was to Russia . . . and it was in an envelope from the Russian Embassy in Paris—it had a big label in the corner, printed with their address. Of course, I was surprised and I looked at it carefully. The address it was being sent to was written in French and also in Russian—the names were harder to read, but I'm quite sure it said Yuri Shastov in a place called Povonets. But I didn't tell them that, you see . . . only that it was going to Russia."

He looked at me, as though for approval, and I nodded. "Did you have any idea from the envelopes what might have been inside them?"

He shook his head. "Not really. The one they took, the one to Canada, was in an ordinary envelope, like a letter. The other was bigger, padded. But not heavy. Even to Russia, it was just a few francs." As he finished speaking, he reached back, bracing himself against the trunk of the tree, and tried to stand up. He made it, but his face went pale as the blood rushed out of his head. He bent over, resting his hands on his knees.

"Take it easy," I said. With his head down, more blood began to drip from his nose, patting dark red splashes on the dead leaves. I was silent a moment, trying to understand what he'd said. At best, I thought I could understand half of it. I'd been right about one thing: Brightman had been holding something over Hamilton's head. But Hamilton had done a deal; in a funny way, you could even say that he'd honored it. Hamilton's payoff, for hanging on to Brightman's envelope, had presumably been the return of the incriminating material, whatever it had been. And he'd even made sure that he'd get it if Brightman disappeared—the letter to Cadogan, probably written by Brightman, would have contained instructions about this; or at least that's what Hamilton assumed it contained. But there was more—and it was even more interesting. Brightman must also have left Hamilton with orders about what to do with the other envelope, the one to Russia, and Hamilton had obeyed them. He was probably too afraid not to—afraid, if he didn't, that his own reward would be withheld. But what sense did it make from Brightman's point of view? If the second envelope contained the key to all this—if it was the buried treasure Subotin was looking for—why in hell would Brightman have instructed Hamilton to send it to the Soviet Union?

No answer.

I looked up at the boy. "I don't know your name."

He tried to sniff back the blood and coughed, spitting some out. "Alain," he said.

"Alain . . . it's important that all this is true . . . what you've told me . . ."

"I understand."

"That's all you remember about the envelopes?"

He looked straight at me, but I could tell nothing from his eyes. "It's all I remember. I swear it."

"And it's true?"

"Yes."

"All right. What else did these men ask you about?"

Carefully, he straightened up, taking a breath. "They wanted to know where Paul was."

"He's coming here, isn't he? On the barge?" Now I got to my feet as well. Without noticing, I'd been feeling through the leaves, picking up the money. It amounted to several thousand dollars: Hamilton's emergency hoard.

Alain drew his hand back across his nose. "You knew he was leaving?"

I shook my head. "I guessed. I knew about the barge. I was there with him yesterday, just before he called you."

He nodded, as if this explained something to him. "They didn't know, you see. But I didn't understand that soon enough. I told them we were going to meet tonight, in Meaux, at the end of the canal."

"The Marne, you mean?"

"Yes. But between Chalifert and Meaux, it's a canal."

"But that's something else you were trying to keep from them?"

"Yes. We really intended to meet at the end of this road. There's a place where you can tie up, and I could leave the car. Paul left early—he could get to Meaux in one day—but he didn't want to be in a city, where it would be simple to find him."

Two lies, two bits of information held back—the boy had far more guts than Hamilton deserved. I said, "Do you think they believed you?"

"I'm not sure. I thought they'd go toward Meaux . . . to wait . . . but by the sounds of their car . . . I don't know. It's possible they turned back to Paris."

Which made sense. They wouldn't want to wait. They'd drive back, staying on the highway, cutting down to the water every few kilometers on the side road. Eventually, they were bound to run into him. I wondered if he was dead already, but I said, "All right, Alain, where do you think he is now? How far could he have come?"

"A long way. He must be close to here now . . . I'm not sure. Already he's been sailing for hours."

"And when did they leave you? The men . . . the man with red hair?"

He shrugged. "Half an hour . . . even forty minutes, perhaps."

A good start; probably time enough to find him if he was close. And Subotin had a car. On the other hand, they might overshoot their mark—underestimating his progress, they could have passed him, gone too far back toward Paris. Or perhaps they'd taken the easy way out and waited at Meaux . . . though I doubted it.

"We must warn him."

I nodded. "Yes, but I'm going to do that. You've done enough. In fact, you've got to get the hell out of here." I shoved the money toward him, and when he tried to protest, shut him up with a wave of my hand. "This is dangerous, very dangerous, and you're in no shape for it now. Just listen to me. Go back to your car. There's a bicycle there. Ride it back to the place where you had lunch, then call a garage and get them to fix the red Renault in the parking lot—here are the keys. Take the car back to Paris. Take it to Hertz and leave it there, and then get on a plane—just listen to me—get on a plane and go anywhere outside of France. At least for a couple of weeks."

He looked down at my hand. I'd pushed the money into his, and he was holding it, but he didn't reach for the key. He was dripping more blood, but he didn't bother to wipe it. He said, "What is happening? . . . What is Paul doing? Who is he really, and what do these men want from him?"

I hesitated, gave a shrug. "I'm sorry. That's something you'll have to ask him."

"Why?" he said. "Why can't you tell me?"

"Because there's no time. Because it's not my story to tell . . . and if you knew what it was, maybe you wouldn't want me to tell it."

His head lifted a little; I saw a flicker of feeling behind his brown eyes . . . suspicion . . . resentment. His ego was coming back to him, and this was the form that it took. It assumed hostility; searched for someone to blame. He reached out, plucking the keys from my hands. His voice was sullen. "If I do what you want," he said, "how will Paul know where I am?"

I hesitated. "You're sure you want him to know?"

It was something I couldn't help asking, but it brought a small, defiant smile to his lips. "You're not a friend of Paul's, are you? That was a lie."

"Maybe . . . you could say he was more a friend of my father's."

The smile changed; he was taking satisfaction from catching me out, in confirming old expectations. "I know what you think of me," he said. "Don't think I don't."

"Don't be too sure of that."

"You think I'm a fool. You think I'm a dirty little queer. But maybe, you know—about some things—you should mind your own business."

I said nothing.

His hands tightened over the keys. "I will do what you say, my friend, but make sure you tell Paul . . . tell Paul I will write him in a week at my uncle's."

I nodded. He gave me a last, angry look. Then, turning away, he climbed out of that hollow. It wasn't very deep, but he was still wobbly and he had to stop at the top. It was a weakness he didn't like to admit, and he brushed at his jacket, as if this was the real reason he'd halted, and then lifted up each foot and swept the wet leaves from his boots. When he was finished, he seemed about to turn back and say something more; but he didn't. Straightening his shoulders, he walked off toward the road.

I waited, letting him go.

The wind stirred, sifting down a little more rain from the trees. But I could not have been wetter. Even pinched between my fingernails, every cigarette turned into a sodden mess after three puffs, and I flung this one away. I listened. In the distance, the trunk of the Dodge slammed shut. Alain: probably changing his clothes. That would help restore his dignity, but wouldn't change the fact that the horrors and humiliations he'd suffered meant nothing. The more I thought about it, the more sure I was that Hamilton was dead. Worse. Alain's courage, rather than protecting his friend, had only made his death inevitable: with the importance of the envelope established, Subotin's pursuit would be nothing short of relentless.

Still, I had to try and warn him. For myself, for the boy, and even a little for Hamilton himself. So I walked down to the Marne. Alain had been right: at this point the river was really a canal, a trench about thirty feet wide. And I could even see the spot he'd been talking about, where he was due to meet up with the barge: huge iron rings, all rusted, had been driven into the trunks of two massive oaks, making a place to tie up at. But no one was there, and there was nothing to do but slog along the towpath beside the canal. I had no clear idea where I was: west of

Meaux, north of Villiers, was the best I could do. To my left, as I started out, there were fields and small farms, and to my right—quick glimmers through the screen of trees—I realized that the Marne itself was flowing, so that the houses I saw in that direction were actually on its farther bank. Finally, after a couple of soggy kilometers, I hit a built-up area, with roads, and then the canal turned into an aqueduct, crossing a valley, before entering Esbly. There I waited, watching a man on a railway bridge; but it wasn't Subotin and so I kept on—exhausted now, soaked to the skin—until I'd reached the other side of Coupvray. Then I saw it: even before I could read the fancy gold letters that spelled out *La Trompette,* the gloss of the hull gave it away. The canal curved here, through some trees, with the fields of a small, muddy farm just ahead. This curve must have created a current; the barge was tied up at the bow to an iron picket driven into the bank, but its stern had tugged out a bit into the channel. I edged closer; but then I told myself that Hamilton wasn't worth taking any kind of a risk for, and ducked off the path and watched the boat from behind a thick hedge of lilac. Five minutes passed. On the barge, everything seemed quiet, peaceful, quite normal. Her black hull, slick with rain, gleamed like plastic, and the pristine, varnished superstructure almost made the vessel look like a toy. I was about to step forward—but then I peered intently ahead as the rope from the barge to the bank suddenly tensed and a figure stepped from the wheelhouse onto the deck.

It was a woman, a navy blue rain cape over her shoulders, a kerchief tied on her head.

She looked away from me, down the canal, but then turned her head so I could see her in profile. I couldn't believe it—she looked just like May.

16

The rain streaked down. It splashed against the dark leaves of the lilacs, stirring up a lingering trace of the summer's scent, and washed the image of the canal, the barge, and May—was it May?—in the silvery, monochrome tints of an old silent film. For an instant, in fact, she seemed to hang in the air like an unreal, ghostly projection. Was she there? Could it be true? But then, as a gust of wind parted the rain, I was sure.

At once a dizzying rush of feeling swept over me. What I was looking at was surely impossible—May *couldn't* be here. But she was. And then, as the full implications of her presence sank in—as all my old doubts and suspicions returned—my astonishment leapt far beyond this moment or these particular circumstances. Everything changed; even the past. Peering through the leaves, I watched her unobserved as on that first day in Toronto, but the distance I'd felt from her then was now compounded a thousand times over. What was she doing here? Had she betrayed me? Then, too, I'd wondered who she really was, but on the assumption that I had some special claim on the answer. Now that assumption died in my heart. We were strangers. She wasn't a woman I'd loved or a woman I'd intended to marry, but a woman I still hadn't met. I felt a quick jab of pain, a final twitch from that ancient wound, and the last bonds that had joined us were cut—indeed, the dizziness I felt might even have been a sensation of freedom. And yet . . . This was so odd: it was precisely now that I felt drawn to her, *called* to her, more powerfully and urgently than at any time since all this had begun. Shrouded in her kerchief and cape, the hissing rain scratching the air all around her, she seemed so alone and forlorn, so remote. If she was cut off from me, did she have ties with anyone else? I didn't know who she was, but—whoever she was—something in her called out to me, and called out so strongly that I was pulled from my hiding place onto the path.

She turned then and saw me. "Robert!"

I stood transfixed. I didn't know what to say; I scarcely knew how to address her. And now I was astonished again. Taking a step across the deck to the gunwale, she came closer and I could see her more clearly. My last memory of her was that day in Detroit, in the waiting room, when she'd looked so drawn and tired. But now she was completely transformed. All the old, contradictory elements were there, and she still seemed to exist in some earlier time, but now she was beautiful. With her navy blue cape spreading over her shoulders and her hair tied up under her kerchief, she might have been a sturdy French peasant girl walking through a Pissarro, or a young nurse trudging back to her aid station in the days of the Somme: but, either way, she was beautiful. The rain had washed away years, her face shone with life, glowed with it, as if this was indeed an old film and I'd stepped into it with her, going back in time to the first time we'd met—perhaps *that* was the time where she truly belonged. And her voice was strong; she was again in charge of her life. "Robert, what are you doing here? You have to leave. I told you—"

"Are you all right?"

"Yes, of course. Where did you—?"

"Is Hamilton there?"

"No. But I don't—listen to me—"

"In a second, but get back inside."

She hesitated an instant: but now there was an edge to my voice, for I was back to myself, this place, what was happening, and the urgency that had drawn me forward was now dissolved in another—Subotin might be watching. "Hurry," I said.

May disappeared. I looked down the path, into the distance; but there was no sign of anyone. Dashing to the boat, I pulled myself over the railing, then ran across the deck to the wheelhouse. May was waiting inside, her face turned up anxiously. "Robert, I don't want you to do this. I told Stewart Cadogan—"

"I got the message."

My tone made her hesitate and her glance shifted away. "I'm sorry about that."

"Forget it."

"It was the money, wasn't it?"

"Partly—"

"I only meant . . . I just wanted you to know how grateful I was and I couldn't tell you myself. There just wasn't time."

"All right. It's not very important. You're in danger now—great danger."

"I don't think so. I just have to be careful."

"Subotin—do you know that name?"

"No."

"Travin—Petersen—do you know those?"

"No. But I don't see—"

"Then you don't know the danger you're in. When did you get here?"

"About twenty minutes ago."

"Where was Hamilton?"

"He wasn't here. Nobody was. I called out, but no one came. At first I couldn't get on the boat, but then a big barge went by on the canal and the waves pushed it in toward the shore. I climbed on. There's nobody here."

But somebody had been; a book and a chart were open on a table, with an empty coffee mug beside them.

"Did you look inside?"

"No, I didn't want to. I just waited here. But I called. There's nobody there. Robert—"

"Wait." I went down into the cabin, May hesitating a second but then following after me. Lights glowed dimly down the length of the barge. In the kitchen, the butter was out, along with a crock of Dundee marmalade. Bread crumbs were scattered on the cutting board . . . a bit of tomato. . . . I looked all around, and discovered nothing more suspicious than this—certainly no signs of a struggle. But where was Hamilton—and why leave the barge here? Where would you go? And when I found the bright yellow oilskins neatly stowed in their wardrobe, a chill ran up my spine. Given the rain, he wouldn't have gone out without them. Peering into the dark interior of the salon, I listened as waves gently lapped at the hull. And the emptiness I felt had a cold, final quality.

May felt it too. "What is it?" she whispered.

I turned to face her. "I don't know . . . but he's clearly not here."

Fringed by her long golden lashes, her eyes seemed huge; and now, for an instant, they were touched by fear. She took a step closer; instinctively, seeking protection. Then stopped. Did she also feel the new distance between us? Since I'd joined her on the barge, we'd made no move to touch, let alone embrace. Maybe she was thinking this too, for she now took another step closer and reached out for my arm. "Robert," she whispered, "I wish you hadn't come. I wish I hadn't. . . . My God this is terrible."

"I know."

"I don't want you to feel—"

"It's all right." Now I was whispering too. I squeezed her hand. "But you have to tell me everything, and you have to tell me the truth."

Her face turned up toward me; I could smell the wet wool of her skirt, feel the warmth of her breath. For a moment, her gaze held mine and then she said, "I've tried to, I swear. In the beginning, when I first called you—do you know why I was afraid? It wasn't only my father—I was frightened when I couldn't get through to you, when you weren't at your house. Because I knew you were the only person on earth I could tell the truth to."

"Then why did you want me to stop?"

"I had to. I was afraid for you. I was afraid that . . ."

Her voice trailed away—because this was a lie that she couldn't bring off? But I wasn't sure—now, here, in her presence, I wasn't sure of anything. Why hadn't she remembered about her father's car? Had she been manipulating me from the very beginning? Had she ever told me the truth? All these questions and doubts flooded into my mind; and yet, somehow, I wanted to believe even more than before. I said, "What are you doing here? How did you learn about Hamilton?"

Her body shifted and her eyes looked away; and I thought she might turn away altogether. But then she looked up at me once again. "I was supposed to meet him here. When I got back from Detroit—the next day—or the day after, I can't remember—a letter came in the mail from my father. He'd sent it from Detroit. He said that if I got this letter it would mean he was dead and he wanted me to do certain things."

"What things?"

"Robert, please—I beg you—"

"You *must* tell me."

She hesitated. "He said . . . he told me to go to a post office box—he sent the key with the letter. He said I'd find an envelope inside. It was addressed to Paul Hamilton, here—in Paris—and I was to take it there and give it to him in return for . . . another envelope, one that would be addressed to Stewart Cadogan—I was supposed to destroy it—and something else, some sort of slip. . . . There was a second envelope, you see. Hamilton was to mail it but give me a receipt—a registration form, something from the post office—to prove that he had."

"But not the envelope itself?"

"No . . . not if I could help it. It was dangerous. If there was no choice, my father said, I should take it, but then mail it immediately."

"And in return for this . . . ?"

She stepped back. She was wearing a heavy, cable-knit sweater under the cape; reaching beneath it, she pulled out an oversized envelope, fairly thick. I took it from her and squeezed it, feeling a wad of papers inside. I didn't open it. I didn't need to. I was certain now that my speculations had been close to the mark. This envelope contained the material that Brightman had held over Hamilton, which ultimately would have been redeemed by the letter to Cadogan—which Subotin had taken from Alain. Now, this ring-around-the-rosy scarcely made any difference . . . but something else did.

"The second envelope," I said, "the one you were supposed to get the slip for . . . what did your father tell you about it? If all you had was the slip, how would you know Hamilton had mailed it at all?"

She looked at me. Doubt passed through her eyes. To lie or not to lie—now, without doubt, she was trying to decide. But then she made up her mind. "He gave me the address, the address that had to be on the receipt."

"And it was an address in the Soviet Union?"

"My God, yes. How did you know?"

"Please—let me see it."

She took a piece of paper from the pocket of her skirt and handed it to me. The address was printed in firm block letters: *Yuri Shastov, Povonets, Karelia, U.S.S.R.*

"Do you know who this person is?"

"No. I've never heard of him. In my father's letter, that's all there was. Just the name and that address."

"What was in the envelope?"

"I have no idea—I swear it."

I believed her; I almost believed all of it now. And I realized something else too: Subotin must know all about this. Because Alain had lied; he'd told me he'd mailed the letter, but not that he'd obtained a receipt—and why else would he do that unless he wanted to cover up the fact that Subotin had taken it from him? Not that I blamed him; giving up that receipt had undoubtedly saved his life. And it might even have another good result: if Subotin already had the Russian address, he'd have no use for Hamilton, and that meant we were now safe. But could I be sure? If Subotin hadn't come here, where had Hamilton gone? There were so many questions, I thought, so many doubts. . . . Even the precise nature of Brightman's demise was problematic again. I'd been assuming he'd been murdered, but if Harry had actually sent May a letter from Detroit, then it implied that he'd killed himself, after all. He just hadn't trusted Hamilton to follow his instructions, and had used May, in effect, as a posthumous bully. This seemed out of character, since it exposed her to danger, but then he'd told her not to handle the envelope itself; and presumably, in other ways, he'd weighed the risks and decided that her safety required the absolute certainty that Hamilton did as he'd promised.

I looked back at May. "You spoke to Hamilton?"

"Yes."

"But not from Toronto?"

"No . . . In the letter, my father told me how I should reach him. I wasn't to phone, they had a special way. . . . I flew to Paris, but then I went straight to my place—I still have it, outside Sancerre—and then I came back. I spoke to him yesterday—"

"When?"

"In the morning first, then later—late last night. That's when he agreed . . . and he told me how to get here."

I thought it through and it worked out. She hadn't phoned Hamilton from Toronto, I was certain of that; my call from Nick Berri's had taken him completely by surprise. But yesterday, when I'd seen him on the barge, he'd already spoken to her: which was why he'd had so many questions for me—and why, above all, he wanted reassurance that Brightman really was dead. I'd given him that; maybe, in the end, that's why he'd agreed to see her. Then he'd called Alain, and later—while I was dozing away in my car—he and May had worked out the details.

Yes, I thought, all of this fitted together, and once you accepted it, you could—*must*—accept everything else. All my suspicions about May came to nothing . . . and the only reason left for suspicions was the very strength of my desire to give them up.

Because, indeed, I so much wanted to believe her. I watched her now as she stepped across the salon, peeled off her kerchief, and shook out her hair; a few strands stuck to her damp cheeks and she pushed them away. How extraordinary she looked. Peasant . . . hippie lady . . . but in that cape and her thick wool skirt—and wearing olive-drab gum boots—she also looked like a perfect aristocrat, a country lady who'd just returned from a fine muddy tramp across her estate. And how alive she was. Her father was dead, she ought to be grieving, and yet she was radiant. More suspicions? But then I wondered if her new vitality wasn't a clue. Did she already know the truth about Harry? Was she feeling relief that his long struggle was over? Had that struggle been hers as well?

She may have sensed these questions forming in my mind, for now she broke in: "You think he's dead, don't you?"

"I'm not sure. He could be."

"Robert—if he is—you should go. I'll be all right. If he doesn't come back in an hour, I'll leave."

"That's crazy. *You* should go. There's no reason for you to stay. The first letter—the one to Cadogan—will never be mailed, and the second one, to Russia, already has."

An anxious look crossed her face. "You can't be sure—you don't know."

"Don't worry, I'm sure. I can't explain how, but I am."

She took this in and considered; for the first time, perhaps, she was now wondering if she could believe me. But then decision, and relief, settled into her face. "All right, then, we should go together. If he's dead . . . if there's no reason to stay . . ." She came toward me; she stood so close to me that I could feel the warmth of her breath, taste its fresh, flowery scent on my lips, and then she leaned forward further and kissed me, a soft press of her lips on my cheek. My response to this—the desire I felt—was a shock: as pure and unexpected a sensation as the astonishment I'd felt on first seeing her. Was that her purpose? Was she trying to tempt me? Something had happened that had wiped the slate clean . . . whatever had kept us apart in the past was now gone—it was, in truth, as if I'd never met her before, and therefore I could be attracted to her all over again. And if that had only been true, there was no doubt that I would have gone with her. But it wasn't. Gently, I kissed her. "I have to stay," I said. "He may have hidden something, something that might connect him and your father."

She stepped back. "I don't want you to. I don't want you to do anything more."

"I have to."

"*No*—I beg you. You'll hurt yourself. You'll hurt me."

"May, you're not afraid for me," I said, "or for yourself, you're still protecting *him*. But Harry's dead—he can't be hurt anymore. And what I find out from now on doesn't make any difference—I know all his secrets."

"Robert . . . you may think you do, but you don't. Nobody does—I'm not even sure that I do."

"You're wrong. I know everything. Russia. The gold and the furs. Who he was, what he did. What Hamilton did . . ."

"Dear God . . ."

"There's only one secret I don't know—I don't know how much *you* know, or when you found out."

She turned away and a long moment passed. In the silence, I could hear the waves working at the hull and the rain streaming down on the deck. Then she turned slowly around. "Can't you guess? Don't you remember? After you asked me to marry you, I went up to see him—you remember what I said, that if you wouldn't ask for my hand, I was going to ask for you—and that's when he told me. That's why I couldn't . . . go through with it."

Silence. The rain. The whole world suspended. Had I seen this much of the truth? If so, it didn't soften the blow. I couldn't move; I couldn't feel. Or not directly. I could only watch my feelings mirrored in May's face—in her anguished expectation of my pain, in the consolation she longed to offer but knew was much too late. It was extraordinary, that moment. I've always known a secret that most of you never learn—tragedy doesn't happen to other people, it happens to yourself. My father's death had taught me that . . . but here it was again. Yet, in another sense, this was, quite precisely, tragedy at one remove: it had all been so long ago. And when I began to breathe again I felt a spasm of grief, of sympathy—as if for someone else—and then a terrible regret. What a fate to suffer. To lose love like that. To give up half your life.

To withdraw. To hide. To live so emptily. . . . But then it hit me. I was not the understanding friend; I was the victim. And I could have cried, I wanted to—but part of the price I'd paid was the loss of all my tears. So May wept for me; it was her consolation, and final testament to what we'd almost had. I held her against me. She whispered, "What a time to tell you."

I tried to smile. "I always was a little curious. And I never did believe that nonsense . . . whatever it was you told me."

"But I couldn't tell the truth. When I saw him, he said he couldn't let me marry you without knowing because he was afraid that the police were on to him. Our lives might be ruined—he couldn't help it—but he didn't want to ruin yours." She stepped back and looked at me. "I almost did tell you later on. I thought we might get back together. But it was too late then. And everything had changed with Harry; I couldn't leave him. We'd always been very close—everything I said about the adoption, all that was true—but once I knew . . . somehow that meant . . ."

Yes, I knew just what it meant, for I'd already seen that much: our lives, though separate, had been on a curious parallel, both of us living in the shadow of our fathers. But Harry was dead and she was free; that had to be the reason for the transformation she'd undergone. Now, looking at her, phrases began going through my mind. It's never too late. We can get together now. Start again. Pretend it never happened. . . . But that's where those phrases stayed—in my mind. Something held me back, though she stood there, all open, and I think—

But then she tensed against me: a quick, dull knocking sound echoed through the hull.

I held up my hand.

It came again, on the far side—a boat rubbing or . . .

"Wait here," I whispered.

But she followed me up the steps, and as I entered the wheelhouse, I had to hold her back. "Keep your head down. If something happens, run—get off the barge and run."

In a crouch, so I couldn't be seen through the window, I scuttled over to the door. After listening a moment, I stepped out on deck. The rain drowned every sound in the splash and hiss of falling water. But there didn't seem to be anything alarming, and when I looked around I was almost reassured: on the bank, just beyond the barge, an old man was trudging along the path, a fishing pole over his shoulder. But then I heard another thump against the hull and edged across the deck; when I reached the rail, I leaned out and took a quick look down.

Behind me, May called softly, "What is it?"

I turned around. "It's all right. But look, you have to go—staying here is dangerous. And pointless."

"Come with me, Robert."

I shook my head. "I can't. I told you. I have to stay and search the boat."

"But when you've finished . . . come then."

I shook my head. "I can't stop yet. I'm not sure how it's happened, but this is my story now as much as yours."

She thought a second—and maybe she was thinking a step ahead of me. "Robert, please—don't go to Russia."

"Don't worry. I'll be all right."

She faced me and I think was going to argue; but then she touched my hand and said, "You're sure?"

"I'm sure."

She gave a little smile. "A moment ago, I knew just what you were thinking . . ."

"What?"

That it's too late. But she only smiled again and so I said, "You should go. You have a car?"

She looked away. "Hamilton told me to leave it on a side road."

"All right. I think you'll be safe enough, but don't go back to Sancerre just yet—drive around, stay in a few hotels. Then, if you want, go back to Canada."

"You'll call?"

"Of course."

"But if I'm not there . . . you mustn't worry." Again, she tried to smile. "Who knows? This is all over now. I might go traveling."

"Somehow we always find each other."

She nodded, and almost spoke again, but then, quickly, she turned away, stepped across the deck, and jumped down to the bank. Stumbling, she landed on one knee.

"All right?"

A smile. "I'm fine." She pulled herself up; then, knotting her kerchief on her head, she gave a little wave, and turned along the path.

I watched her go. She caught up to the old man, the one with the fishing pole, and then turned to give me one last look. The rain came slanting down, a misty window . . . but behind it her face seemed bright again, as bright as the first moment when I'd seen her on the barge. I waved back, and a moment later she disappeared around a bend.

Turning away, I took three steps across the deck and leaned over the rail. My eyes searched the muddy water. It was still there. A twist of tattered cloth . . . a lump that bobbed up, then rolled under again . . . bumping its way along the hull, all shrouded in a cloud of greasy red.

Paul Hamilton: wrapped in the flag of his own choosing.

Paul Hamilton: the "decent" man who'd tried to do the "decent" thing.

I stepped back and buttoned up my coat. A thousand thoughts began swirling through my mind, what-ifs, and might-have-beens. But surely she was right—and I was right—it *was* too late. And too late, perhaps, in other ways. Subotin had a good head start, and Russia—as Brightman surely knew—is a long, long way from anywhere.

There was no time to waste. I clambered off the barge, hurried down the path. Behind me—one last look back—*La Trompette* was glistening in the rain.

PART THREE

ALEKSANDR SUBOTIN

It has been necessary to turn attention to the fact that there are influential circles in the U.S.S.R. which have, as their ideology, chosen an open racism, taken *in toto* from the propaganda arsenal of Nazi Germany. This ideology is essentially a tactical weapon for these circles in their internal political struggle for power. They wish to unite about themselves broad circles of the ruling apparatus and the population with the aid of racist slogans. . . . Although, evidently, these circles do not yet have a predominant influence on the nation's political course, they have enough influence to achieve . . .

—Mikhail Agurski, *Novyi Zhurnal,* 1974

17

After Vienna, the plane headed north, over Czechoslovakia, and then east, across Poland.

There was no stop at Warsaw.

Soon it became hard to know where we were—hence the peculiar agony of Polish history—but as the the miles drifted by, the landscape grew whiter, and the rust-red blotches of the winter-plowed fields showed up like the patches of a piebald pony. With the snow, my Russian memories began: whispering, like the breeze through a birch forest; eddying, like the smoke from some poor peasant's *izba;* and then flowing, as hypnotic and remorseless as the spring thaw. Russia . . . Closing my eyes, I could see the sun set over Lake Baikal and flash from the bright domes of Suzdal, and when I listened hard even the roar of the Kuznetsov turbofans was drowned out by the deep-throated music of the language itself. Memories and images mingling, I drifted away into sleep and then a dream came, very simple and clear. *A ship is arriving in Leningrad. A figure appears on the gangway, enormous inside a bulky fur coat* . . . It must be Brightman; even in my dream, I'm conscious of this. Slowly, he shuffles down to the dock, joining an immense line that tortuously winds through a shed, past a desk. On the desk is a sign: *Old Russian Custom—to Wait. Are You from the States?* As the man steps forward, passport in hand, he turns slightly, smiling to himself at this attempt at a joke. But the man isn't Brightman; it's me. And as the official looks up, I see the face of . . .

I awoke with a jerk. But I'm not sure I had a right to be startled. This was an Aeroflot flight, we were on a Tu-154 (the peculiar smell of their cabins), and our destination was mysterious Leningrad—for most of my fellow travelers, it was precisely the strangeness of this that excited or disturbed them. But with me it was the reverse. As if suffering from some variation of déjà vu, it was the familiar that distressed me—I'd been here so often before, but what was I doing here now? Following a total stranger, I'd ended up on my own doorstep. How could it have happened? Charlottesville, Halifax, Paris . . . Leningrad had to be the end of the trail, yet I kept feeling I'd been moving in a circle—unless I had it all wrong, and the circle had been moving around me.

But all of these questions, even if I should have known the answers to them, were secondary; I had more concrete problems ahead of me. Who was Yuri Shastov? Why had Brightman's package ended up in Povonets, a dot on the map four hundred miles northeast of Leningrad? And even more difficult than these questions was the consequent one of how I was going to answer them, for no matter how you define "totalitarian," the bottom line is "police state," and I was now proposing to enter the greatest police state in history and operate in a fashion that would be both clandestine and illegal. To make matters worse, I was a Westerner; worse still, an American; worst of all, a journalist. This meant automatic suspicion and possibly surveillance . . . which was precisely what I had to avoid. Somehow, in the most tightly controlled society on earth, I had to "disappear," find a way to gain a free hand.

I had a plan—a variation of a stunt I'd pulled once before—and its first step was simple: be as normal as possible.

Pudvolko, Leningrad's airport, is south of the city. There's a perfectly good airport bus that takes you right down the Nevsky, but I've always preferred a cab—and so that's what I took now. It was a cold, gray day; the first snowbanks were heaped up at the side of the road, and in the windblown fields the frozen earth was the color of steel. Rolling down the window, I sucked in a breath. The air was thick with the smell of all the big Russian cities, a compound of cement dust and diesel fumes from the huge Belaz transport trucks, which people will proudly (and truthfully) tell you are the largest trucks in the world. Following my usual, roundabout route, I had the driver take me past the old Putilov ironworks, with its huge statue of Kirov—arms outstretched, he points toward the factory in a gesture, supposedly dramatic and revolutionary, which the local inhabitants interpret more rudely—then under the Neva Arch, toward the gray, bleak expanse of the port. It would be closing up soon, except for the lanes they keep open with the nuclear icebreak-

a skin of ice on the canals. We bumped across ndred bridges and headed downtown.

ie Astoria. People used to say that it has an air it's just faded. I like it all the same. The beds akes about an hour to fill up your bath, but the be comfortable and the staff always strikes me as being more sophisticated than in other Russian hotels. Ordinary room service requests, often met by puzzlement elsewhere, are here handled routinely, though that afternoon I didn't want anything except the routine: one bottle of vodka. After a couple of welcoming slugs, I unpacked, then left the hotel and walked across St. Isaac's Square. Kitty-corner to the Cathedral is a massive stone building that was once the German Embassy and which now houses the main office of Intourist. After a long argument and several loudly dropped names, I got what I wanted: an approved travel itinerary and a dark blue Zhiguli—Fiat to you—which I picked up at the Aeroflot Terminal on the Nevsky Prospekt. From there, I returned to the Astoria.

It was around three o'clock in the afternoon; I lay down on the bed and waited for the phone to ring.

Because I knew it would.

Presumably Subotin had ways of getting into the U.S.S.R. without attracting attention, but for me that was impossible. Having lived and worked here as a journalist, I was simply listed in too many files. Besides, in Paris I'd pulled some strings to get a visa inside twenty-four hours rather than the usual three days or a week. Each of those strings had had a bell at the end; inevitably, they'd start to ring here. The first call was from a man I knew in Tass's translation section, just to say hello. Then there was someone at UPI who said he'd been tipped off by Aeroflot. (Reasonable: my fixer in Paris, so far as the visa was concerned, had been an old acquaintance in Aeroflot's PR department—it was his *blat*, in addition, that had got me the car.) And lastly, at quarter to five, I was welcomed to Leningrad by an official greeter from the Soviet Union of Journalists. I'd met him before. Viktor Glubin he was called, but in fact he was a typical Ivan Ivanov, the sort of idiot bureaucrat who reassures the people "upstairs"—the *nachalstvo*—that their will is being done, while actually ensuring that nothing very much is being done at all. Just this once, I was glad to see him: in fact, he, or someone like him, was almost essential to my plans. Before picking up Subotin's trail,

I had to cover my own. Even if the KGB were not aware of what doing, my arrival would have been noted, and would have piqued the curiosity. To reassure them—the second step of my plan—I'd carefully prepared a soothing little explanation, and now I needed someone to deliver it. For that, Viktor Glubin was perfect: when it comes to the *Komitet,* he was as "amateur" as a Russian athlete. I happily accepted his invitation to dinner, then began running a bath. After that, I lay down and dozed.

Glubin arrived around seven.

He was a chubby, rumpled man, with a sour, puckered mouth and a forehead that was as greasy as the back of a spoon. I bought him a drink in the Astoria bar. Trading gossip about various journalistic acquaintances, we tested the waters between us. With Russians, this is always a tricky business, and maybe it's especially true of Russian newspapermen. They want it assumed that they're part of the same world as you—that "journalist" means the same thing in Leningrad as in New York—but as soon as you apply the standards of that world to them, they are prone, like little children, to pick up their marbles and go home. Tonight, I was very careful to be the perfect diplomat, and was too worried about my own performance to notice any equivocations in his.

Perhaps they weren't there; everything, indeed, proceeded quite normally. He took me to the Byka, an Azerbaijani restaurant. It was fairly small by Soviet standards, perhaps thirty tables, and the otherwise gloomy atmosphere was enlivened by some bright rugs on the walls and a band. In Russia, there's always a band—Russians consider dancing a necessary part of a night out, like certain Midwesterners. As we came in, this one was playing a mournful version of "Memories Are Made of This," and the room was hooting, considering the tune much too old-fashioned. Our meal was superior to the entertainment. Azerbaijan is a Soviet Socialist Republic wedged between northern Iran and the Caspian Sea. The people are Shiite Muslims, the cuisine something like Turkish. I started with a sort of *tolma* (stuffed vine leaves), went on to *dovta* (sour milk soup) and then *shashlik kebab*—each of these dishes being accompanied, not very authentically, by Starka vodka, which Glubin poured out remorselessly, glass after glass. With my tongue thus loosened, I blurted out all my secrets, including my true reasons for being in Leningrad. I was writing a book, it seemed, a *personal* book—no politics—that would contain anecdotes and reflections based on my years of living in Russia. The idea behind the trip was to revisit all the parts of the country where I'd lived or traveled before . . . as anyone could confirm by checking my "Travel Memo" at Intourist.

Viktor, listening dutifully, gave an understanding nod. "It sounds very interesting, Robert. It will be a book full of feeling."

By now the band was playing "A Hard Day's Night"—apparently more acceptable to the audience—and men were going among the tables, asking the women to dance.

"You're right," I said. "It has to have feeling. But I don't want it to be too sentimental . . . too *Russian,* if you know what I mean."

Viktor smiled. Russians are proud of being sentimental and don't mind being teased about it . . . though they wouldn't like you to point out that the obverse of the sentimental is brutality.

He raised his glass. "To Russian tears. Let us drown them."

We drank. Then, showing he'd read my file, he remarked that I would have a long trip, for I'd lived in so many places—Kiev, Kharkov, Moscow, even Semipalatinsk—and we drank to each of these spots in turn. He grinned happily, and somehow there was nothing objectionable, or even hypocritical, about all this. We were in Russia. He knew, and I knew, that the purpose of our dinner was to enable him to make a report to the police. But this wasn't its "real" purpose, any more than the real purpose of taking a breath was to avoid suffocation; you simply did it, without thinking. Indeed, two weeks from now, with complete sincerity, he'd be telling his pals about his nice evening with "my American friend Robert Thorne." But, one way or another, my story seemed to have convinced him, and after a time I set down my glass and looked around the room. The band had started up again, some tune I didn't recognize. Opposite our table, a pretty Hungarian blonde adjusted the straps of her dress to cover the straps of her bra, then gave her hand to a soldier wearing the blue beret of a Soviet paratrooper. Everyone started to move; I think they might have been doing the frug. After a time, even Viktor got up, though only to announce a trip to the john. I took another sip of vodka, then a forkful of baklava. As my eyes moved over the tables, I remembered the time when I could have made a feature story from any of them: the old waiter whose grandmother had marched in the Peace and Bread demonstrations that had brought the

Bolsheviks to power; an East German engineer who'd last been in Leningrad in 1942, when the German siege of the city had come within a
few hundred yards of the Putilov works that I'd passed this morning;
and a Rumanian poet, disciple of Barbu, who was being shown around
town by a cultural commissar. As the second city of a great empire, Leningrad has always had plenty of stories to tell . . . though my eyes, I admit,
kept coming back to the Hungarian blonde. She was a real stunner; and
there was the irony of the paratrooper. But then, as I watched her, I
began to catch the quick, wary looks she'd dart to the far corner of the
room as the movements of the dance turned her that way. I followed
those looks . . . and that's when I saw him. Short, chunky, but wearing
a well-tailored dark blue suit that slimmed him down. I should have spotted him before, I realized, because he was the only person in the place
with a table to himself.

I set down my fork.

I should say that I wasn't afraid, though, right away, I had no doubt
that he was there because of me. But KGB officers come in all shapes
and sizes. Many are thugs; quite a number are young CP careerists taking
a fast route to the top; and most are merely the petty bureaucrats of
oppression, the *fonctionaires* that all totalitarian states need to carry on
business: the censors; the people who manage the internal "passport"
system which, like South Africa's, controls people's movements through
the country; or the *upravdom* in Soviet apartment buildings whose task
is to report on all the occupants' comings and goings. These men exist,
as the mandate of their organization candidly puts it, to be the "shield
of the Party"—that is, to defend the Party against any possible threat
from the people. Thus, very few of them have much involvement with
espionage or even foreigners, and those that do are relatively sophisticated, well educated, even well traveled. Like this man. And I took that
as a good sign. If they'd intended anything nasty—even a quick-step out
to the airport—they would have sent someone else.

I watched him, and when the music stopped, he got up from his
table and crossed the room.

"Mr. Thorne?"

There was a polite, even formal, expression of inquiry on his face.

I have a rule: be polite but don't be obsequious. So I just nodded
and said, "That's right."

"My name is Valentin Loginov, Mr. Thorne. Viktor mentioned

that he'd be bringing you here tonight and asked me to drop by. He thought it might be useful if we talked."

The Hungarian girl, returning to her table, looked away; a waiter, hurrying past, averted his eyes.

"May I?" he said.

I nodded.

"It's a good band?"

"Not bad."

"For rock and roll, however, a band doesn't work. There are too many players. All those instruments just get in the way."

"Yes, I suppose that's true."

He nodded. "That's why they don't like rock and roll. The professionals, I mean. The musicians. There are not enough jobs. They prefer Tommy Dorsey and Benny Goodman, but the people no longer like them."

I expect he was right. As they began "Serenade in Blue," only a few people got up and danced. The Hungarian and her paratrooper had now shifted positions—so the girl had her back to my table.

"Of course," Loginov said, "Benny Goodman began with a trio—him and Gene Krupa and Teddy Wilson. And then Lionel Hampton."

"I don't know much about music . . . about swing."

He smiled. "It only shows I am much older than you."

No; it showed that he was "friendly," and that he wasn't a hick. He was about fifty years old, with a barrel chest and a fair belly, though the suit made him look sleek. He wore a small pin in his lapel: a cross made by a flyer's wings and a propeller. This is the insignia of the Soviet Air Force, but KGB officers frequently hold commissions in other branches of service and wear their uniforms—the Air Force being favored because theirs are the best-looking. Since our conversation about music seemed to be over, I said, "I'm afraid Viktor didn't mention you'd be joining us, Mr. Loginov."

"That is because I wasn't sure I'd be able to. Happily, however . . ." He smiled pleasantly and turned his hands palms up, as if to say, "Here I am and isn't it fun?" Then the waiter came hurrying up, setting down an extra glass; and naturally it was Loginov who poured out the vodka—a straightforward demonstration of who was in charge. We drank a simple *vashezdorovye*. When I put my glass down, I said,

"You have the advantage, Mr. Loginov. I think you must know more about me than I do about you."

He brought out a package of John Player's Special, and extended one to me. "I suppose that is true. To begin with, I think I have read everything you have written."

"I doubt that."

He shrugged, lighting our cigarettes. "Well, not all . . . but a great deal. And I have read careful digests of the rest. And estimates of you."

"That's a file I'd like to see."

"I can tell you, Mr. Thorne, that its conclusions are all very positive. You've taken the trouble to learn our language, you've done your best to understand our country, and you are a fair man. That doesn't make you less critical, but at least your criticisms are not stupid. And intelligent criticism is as rare . . . is the same as . . . good advice." He lifted his glass then. "Let us drink to that—to good advice."

I drank, or rather sipped; though, as usual in this life, it was too late to worry about how much I'd drunk. As he put his glass down, Loginov added, "Perhaps I can return the favor, Mr. Thorne. Not with advice, exactly, but information."

"Really? Your organization isn't famous for passing it out."

His voice sank a little; he looked very levelly at me. "Look, Mr. Thorne . . . I have mentioned no organizations, and though I naturally have an employer, why don't we forget it. For now. Put it out of your mind . . ."

"That's easier said than done."

"I won't disagree. But—you understand?—there is nothing official about this conversation. Tell me to leave, and I will. And there will be no repercussions. You are very welcome in the Soviet Union. That *is* official." He paused, then added, "I would simply like to help make your stay more profitable."

"By giving me information?"

"Exactly."

I could hear the band again. They were still flipping around through the musical eras, and now everyone chuckled at "How Much Is That Doggie in the Window?"

I said, "As you know, Mr. Loginov, I'm a journalist. Information is one thing I never have enough of."

"Good . . . and, as it happens, I am especially well informed about the subject of your current project . . . which Mr. Glubin mentioned to me."

I said, "I see," though of course Viktor Glubin had supposedly known nothing about my current "project" till twenty minutes ago.

Loginov nodded. "Yes," he said. "The dissidents. Naturally, they are a subject of great fascination in the West. But they are much misunderstood. I'm sure it would be very worthwhile for a man of your knowledge and sensitivity to tackle the subject."

I leaned forward, knocking ash from my cigarette. "Mr. Loginov, I wouldn't want you to think me ungrateful, but just for the record, my current project—as you call it—has nothing to do with the dissident movement."

"No?" He looked skeptical. "I will note that—for the record, as you put it. But I'm not sure that you're right. Possibly it is a confusion of terminology; we may be speaking of the same thing, but with different words. You see what I mean?" He added, "It may become clearer as I go on."

He was a KGB officer and this was Leningrad; if he wanted to go on, I had no intention of trying to stop him. I leaned back in my chair. "I don't suppose you're a dissident, Mr. Loginov?"

He smiled. "Not quite. But I know many of them. . . . Or does that surprise you?"

I shrugged.

"Of course, personal knowledge is not the same as friendship, though everyone knows Yevtushenko was very friendly with Khrushchev. You see, what people in the West don't understand is that the liberal dissidents are very few in number and are almost all drawn from the elite elements of Soviet society . . . our intellectuals, scientists. They are a closely knit group, and if you know one, you know all the others. They are like a family. Or the characters in our great novels—there is always a chart on the flyleaf that shows you how they are related." He reached for the vodka, pouring us each another glass. "Perhaps it's even hereditary," he added, "or at least a tradition—like the painting of icons—that is passed down from generation to generation. Think of Yuli Daniel. He was a student of Sinyavsky, the famous 'Abram Tertz.' And Sinyavsky, of course, was a great friend of Pasternak's—he was a pallbearer at Pasternak's funeral—and Pasternak, in his turn, came from a family who were friends of Tolstoy, and *he* was enough of a dissident in his day to be excommunicated by the Orthodox Church. So you see, in the veins of Yuli Daniel, you might say there is running the blood of a tradition of resistance that goes all the way back to the Czars."

"That's a fascinating theory, Mr. Loginov. Maybe this is a book *you* should be writing."

He shook his head. "I wouldn't be interested. And neither should you—if you don't mind my saying so. Why? Because the dissidents I have been talking about—the democratic, liberal dissidents you so admire in the West—can have little importance here. I don't say *no* importance, you understand; but only a little. It's interesting. The reason they have a *little* importance is the same reason why they can never have very much: it is because, as I've said, they come from the elite. Any regime must pay some attention to what its top people say, men like Sakharov, but in the final analysis they don't count, for they have no popular power."

"You mean, they are separated from the masses."

"Sneer at the words, Mr. Thorne, but not the idea. Ask Johnson and Nixon why they couldn't win their ugly little war in Vietnam—it was because, in the end, they didn't have the people behind them. That is the same problem the liberal dissidents have. You understand, this isn't because the people support the regime, or that they love Communism. In Russia, Mr. Thorne, Communism is not even a bad joke anymore, just an old one. It simply doesn't work, and even when it does, it works to no purpose. It's like that old story about Gorky, you know. He was supposed to have visited a wonderful, modern, efficient factory—everything humming along at top speed—but when he asked them what they made, they told him, 'We make signs that say "Elevator Out of Order." ' That's Communism for you—that's the best it can do—and everybody knows it. But this 'everybody,' you see, is Russian. That's the trouble. And 'democracy' is not Russian, 'freedom' is not Russian, 'human rights' are not Russian. These ideas come from the West, where Napoleon came from, and Guderian's tanks. That is why the liberal dissidents have always been doomed."

I said nothing; in Russia, "sophistication" can often be expressed by this sort of talk, but it might also be a trap. After a second, Loginov smiled. "You are surprised, Mr. Thorne?"

"I don't want to bring up organizations again, but there's one, you know, that's supposed to be the 'shield of the Party.' "

"Ah. The Party. Have I said a word that's critical of it? I would hate to think so, Mr. Thorne—I would hate myself for saying it. But the Party is over eighty years old, and only a foolish old man believes in the dreams of his youth." He shook his head. "When you speak of the Party, you speak of Soviet power—legitimate Soviet power . . . and that has less and less to do with Communism."

"All right. I won't even quibble about 'legitimate.' But what does any of this have to do with me?"

"Yes. For that, I return to the dissidents. I told you why the liberal dissidents couldn't succeed—they're too identified with the West, with foreign ideas. Ordinary Russians, even if they're unhappy with the state of affairs, can find nothing there—so they look elsewhere. They look to themselves, to Russia, to their past. In its own way, of course, that is rebellion . . . to find anything good before 1917 is a criticism of what has come after, whether you like it or not. At the same time, how can anyone disapprove? What is wrong with loving your country, its being, its history?"

I shrugged. "Nothing. What you're describing sounds very much like patriotism, Mr. Loginov . . . as in the Great Patriotic War."

"Perhaps it is. But let us reserve that word 'patriotic' for something undoubtedly honorable. We should use another one . . . something different, maybe just a neutral word like 'nationalism.' But it doesn't make any difference—the important thing is to understand what it means."

"And what does it mean?"

"Listen a moment. What I'm talking about began in the sixties, with students. But our students in those years were different from your own. Their rebellion was expressed by looking *back*, searching for old ways rather than new ones. They became fascinated by the Russian past, and took little trips to Vladimir and Suzdal to look at the old buildings and monuments. It was all very innocent. But soon, you see, they attracted quite a following—respectable people like Antonov, the airplane designer—and then the Party decided to play along, and something was formed called the All-Russian Society for the Protection of Historical Monuments. By '67, according to Tass, they had three million members . . . which was just the tip of the iceberg. Aboveground, nationalist themes began getting played up in the press—even the Party press—and underground, in samizdat, you began seeing ultranationalists like the Veche group take over. . . . I think you must have heard of them."

"Yes," I said. "Vladimir Osipov. A Slavic nationalist: Russia for the Russians as opposed to the Uzbeks, the Tatars, the Jews, the Kazakhs, the Yakuts, and all the other minorities. Who now make up more than fifty percent of your population."

"I think you are too polite. 'Slavic nationalist' . . ." He made a face. "People like Osipov are anti-Semites, racists, and chauvinists. And if you don't want to say it about them, then what about VSKhSON?" He spat out the name: "The All-Russian Social-Christian Union for the Liberation of the People. . . . They speak of 'spiritual rebirth,' the 'revival of Orthodoxy,' 'freedom of conscience,' but for them these words mean nothing more than they did to the Nazis."

"Mr. Loginov, VSKhSON never had more than forty members and was crushed . . . by an organization we've agreed not to talk about."

"True. Officially, that is true."

An interesting qualification. But I hesitated now for another reason. I was making connections: I was hearing Travin's voice on the phone —*We can talk about the* byliny *or the* beguny *or the Black Hundreds* . . . and there was that émigré paper I'd found in the dump.

Carefully, I said, "You understand that I do not support such people?"

"Yes. I know that."

"And you surely don't expect me to believe that you're really afraid of them? Even the CIA has given up its fantasies about the Soviet people rising up to throw out the Bolsheviks and bring back the Czar."

He shook his head. "That is not the point, Mr. Thorne. Of course you are right. No one—from 'below'—will overthrow this regime. With us, all change starts 'upstairs,' in the Party. But think of the Party for just a minute. Do you imagine it is composed of fools? Of idiots? Do you think our good Party people do not see the grave problems that now face the Soviet Union? Naturally they do. Let me give you even a single example. Everyone knows that Soviet agriculture is a disaster—this Western talk about our attacking America is crazy, Mr. Thorne, because if we bombed Kansas or Manitoba, we Russians would all starve the next year. But why? Our land is huge and rich. Our farmers have enough tractors—that can no longer be the excuse. The reason is the system itself. Do you know that the private plots of our collective farmers—the 'capitalist plots,' we like to say—occupy less than three percent of our agricultural land but produce about thirty percent of what we eat? If you are in the Party, what does that tell you? That the system has failed, Mr. Thorne, that's what it tells you."

"So change systems."

"Yes, but how do you do that and keep the Party in power? How do you do that and ensure that Russia doesn't fall into pieces? Ideology, belief, faith, myth—this is the glue that holds a nation together. If you take the system apart, and try to put it together in a different way, you must have a new glue. Do you see?"

I saw. But I wanted to make sure I saw right. "You're saying that elements in the Party are thinking that an extreme right-wing form of nationalism—"

"Might create in the country the sort of spirit that saw us through the war with the Germans."

I looked at him, then sat back in my chair. I should say that I wasn't shocked or startled by any of this; in fact, he really had told me nothing I didn't know already. But hearing it from him . . . somehow, that seemed to make a great difference.

I said, "You talk about 'elements in the Party'—who exactly do you mean?"

He shrugged. Smiled. "They are all politicians, of course. Some are Stalinists: for them it is just a chance to return to the hard line of the past. Others truly believe what they say; they talk about a 'new vision of Russia.' There are also some of the young technocrats—technocrats, you might say, who see the limits of their technocracy. They understand that 'management' can't do everything; at some level, there must be belief. And of course—you understand—there are also followers of this tendency outside the Party, in other Soviet institutions."

"Such as?"

"Surely you can guess. Where does this sort of ideology traditionally flourish?"

"The military, you mean?"

He nodded. And there was something in the abruptness of this nod that denied the sophistication of his clothes and his manner—that labeled him KGB in a different way altogether.

I said, "This must be a great worry."

He pursed his lips, wiggled his hand in an equivocal gesture. "A cloud on the horizon." Then his fingers fished a cigarette out of the pack on the table. He frowned as he lit it. "I don't wish to exaggerate," he said. "Nothing will happen about this today or tomorrow, or even next month . . . but five years from now? Who knows? . . . In any event, there is one aspect of all this that you might find especially of interest. It concerns the West, you see. A clandestine group—representatives of this tendency—are trying to establish themselves outside of Russia. . . . They are, if you like, putting the resources together."

"Why would they bother?"

"Don't fool yourself, Mr. Thorne. What happens outside of Russia—the attitudes of foreign governments—has great effect on what goes on here. Besides, there are many practical advantages. Safe havens. Lures. Certain allies. . . . Mundane considerations: for example, if you wished to speak with the captain of a Soviet destroyer, to influence him, it would probably be easier to do it in Djakarta than here in Leningrad."

I nodded. Of course he was right. Such a "tendency," to use his word, would need a Western base, even if it was only Switzerland again, to wait out one more Russian exile. And establishing this would require resources . . . such as some old gold certificates worth a cool twelve million dollars. Yet how had they discovered the map that told them where to dig for such treasure?

I turned back to Loginov. "You say the military might be one center for this kind of tendency. . . . Might there not be another as well, closer to home—to your home, I mean?"

"Perhaps."

"In fact, there might even be a certain loss of control?"

He leaned forward, resting his elbows on the table and his chin on his clasped hands. "Mr. Thorne, I don't know about that. But I can tell you one thing. The men I've been describing to you are very dangerous. Very, very dangerous. They are serious men. They have abandoned everything for what they believe. You said, at the beginning, that you had no interest in the dissidents I proposed telling you of—your current project had nothing to do with them. You said it yourself. If so, nothing is lost: you simply have the basis for an interesting article quoting unnamed, but reliable, Soviet sources. On the other hand, if you do have an interest in this and wish to pursue it, be warned. Be wary. Be cautious. Above all, Mr. Thorne, understand that if you ever meet *this* man, you are meeting a killer."

And then, reaching into his jacket, he drew out a small white envelope and handed it across to me. Inside, there was a crudely lit photograph, of the kind that is used for official identity purposes. It was a full-face, head-and-shoulders shot of a young man in a Russian Army uniform, and must have been taken before 1970, because he was still wearing the old, high-collared *gymnasterka* of the Soviet Army. Dark eyes, slightly bugged, perhaps because of the flash . . . the face almost squeezed, or compressed, with the teeth shoved forward into the mouth . . . and though the photograph was in black and white, I knew the crew-cut hair had to be red.

I said, "Can you tell me, Mr. Loginov . . . did this man ever work for your employer?"

He hesitated; then shrugged. "Let us not be coy, Mr. Thorne. Aleksandr Subotin worked for the GRU. It is even possible that he still does. He was a specialist in certain security problems in connection with the Soviet Navy." The GRU: Soviet military intelligence. Once, this organization had been a genuine rival to the KGB, but now it was a sort of subsidiary. "But I can tell you no more than that," Loginov added. He started to rise. "From this point, you are on your own."

"But I've been warned?"

He smiled. "Informed."

I nodded. For a second longer, he stood by the table. I wondered if he was thinking of shaking my hand, but in the end he didn't offer and neither did I. I watched him go out the door, then waved at the waiter; but Glubin, whatever his other deficiencies as host, had taken care of the bill. As I got up to go, the band began playing again—"You Light Up My Life"—and everyone was dancing, cheek to cheek. The Hungarian blonde was back with the paratrooper, but as she looked over his shoulder, her eyes wouldn't meet mine.

Waiting till the end, I clapped with the others, and then went into the street.

18

It was snowing as I left the Byka, large, soft flakes that floated down so lazily you could follow each one individually. I walked to the Nevsky. The snow, falling faster, caught on my eyelids, turning the globes of the streetlights into stars which sparkled magically in the darkness above Leningrad's great main street. Traffic was quiet and the snow hissed softly in the stillness. Then, two blocks away, a trolley clattered through an intersection, the row of colored lights on the cab—visible even in the worst blizzard—proclaiming its route. On the sidewalk, a thin stream of people passed by. These were bureaucrats hurrying home from No. 41, the Leningrad Party headquarters, or clerks from the Gostinyy Dvor department store, which had just closed up, or students, wrapped in scarves, leaving the old Imperial Library. Heads bowed before the prospect of the coming winter, and thickly clothed in the resolute silence of Russians in the mass, they trickled into the Metro stops.

Standing there, watching them, I thought over what Loginov had told me. Did I believe him? Was there really a *Russian* dissent within the "Soviet Union"—a dissent that might truly matter? In a way, I thought, this street proved his words. The Bolsheviks had tried to re-name the Nevsky "Avenue of the 25th of October," but it just hadn't stuck. And a lot else hadn't stuck either. Since 1917 Russia had come a great distance, but so had the rest of the world; relatively little had changed. She was the *real* "sick man" of Europe, with a vast, rebellious empire, a desperately backward economy, and a cruelly repressive government. I lifted my eyes. In the distance, framed by the long perspective of the trefoil streetlamps, the sharp golden spike of the Admiralty Tower was brilliantly lit up by spotlights. It had been the city's symbol

It was now eleven twenty-five.

I washed my face and spruced myself up—a fresh shirt, a different tie, a navy blazer I'd bought in Montreal. The total effect was nothing fancy but at least respectable. Now I laid my coat out on the bed. It was an Aquascutum raincoat, not very warm, but it had a zip-in lining that now proved handy. Opening it up, I packed away a couple of shirts, a sweater, and a pair of socks, then stuffed it into a pillowcase and put my boots in on top. Knotted up, this made a fancy version of a hobo's satchel. Next I got a towel from the bathroom. Doubling it around my hand, I gave the window a couple of hard raps, cracking the glass. It was a sealed, double-glazed unit; with my penknife, I opened up the cracks, then wiggled the pieces of glass away from the plastic. I was able to manage all this very quietly; even if my room had looked onto a main street, I don't think anyone would have noticed. As it was, I was at the back, facing another building. When the hole was big enough, I pushed my bundle out. It disappeared in the darkness and I didn't even hear it land.

Midnight.

I stepped into the hall, walked along to the elevators. The night clerk saw me, but that was okay. She also saw that I wasn't dressed to go out, and she already knew I was off to the bar. And that's where I went. It was old, rather gloomy; a fuzzy imitation of a British club. The room was already pretty full, and more people began to come in as I did, for Leningrad closes up around midnight, only the Western hotels, like the Astoria, staying open late—and even they were only open till two.

I sat at a table with a Danish designer of injection molds and two German patent attorneys. They were drinking "No. 1," a decent Russian white wine. I followed suit, and bought us a bottle, and after a couple of glasses it was Sven, Dieter, and Bob—I never did catch the second German's name. They all knew Leningrad well. We traded stories, compared notes. Around one o'clock, two more Germans joined us—also attorneys; there was some sort of international conference—and a few minutes later one them asked us all back to his room for a nightcap. I declined, saying I was too tired, but went with them as far as the elevators. Then I headed straight for the lobby, and two minutes later was out on the street.

No one had noticed my departure; the clerk on my floor would assume she'd just missed my return, and that I was back in my room. With luck, I wouldn't be missed till the next day.

Outside, the snow was still falling, but now, wind-driven, it fell in sharp, slanting streaks. And of course it took me a good ten minutes to find that damned alley—somehow, the world looked very different down here than it had from my window. But finally, shaking with cold, I blundered into it and found the pillowcase. Shivering, hopping about on one foot, I got into my boots, then put on the raincoat; it worked all right, though I had to cinch the belt tight to stop all the stuff I'd packed inside from slipping down to the hem.

The alley appeared to serve no purpose; there weren't even trash cans. At the far end, a spill of light glistened on the street, but there was no sign that anyone had followed me. I made my way out. Now I walked directly to my car, which was parked about two blocks away: for although this was "downtown" Leningrad, one of the great virtues of Soviet cities is that you can park virtually anywhere, anytime. Indeed, I could see only one other vehicle parked on that block. I got into mine. The cold engine coughed, pushing at the heavy weight of the oil in the crankcase, then kicked over, falling into a ragged, faltering idle. Letting it warm, and trying to warm myself, I lit a cigarette and looked down the street. At the far end there was a glow from St. Isaac's, and a block beyond this a taxi passed by, probably on its way to the Leningradskaya, another hotel just behind the Astoria. But nothing else moved; just the snow, slicing down through the glow of the streetlights. So if I was being watched, it was being done very well; and in fact I doubted that I was. Except in Moscow, there is so little traffic in Russian cities that you can't possibly follow another car without giving yourself away, and though that might be a useful intimidation tactic, Loginov had already passed on the chance to intimidate me much more directly. All the same, I knew the car was the weak link. It was too easy to trace. For the time being, I'd disappeared into thin air—but now I had to pull the same trick with it.

I turned on the headlights. The Zhiguli, a Russian Fiat, is no better than the original; with a grind and a clunk it finally agreed to go into gear. Slowly, I rolled down the street, inspecting that other car, but it was empty, the wind building a ramp of snow up its windshield. Hitting the gas, I made for the Nevsky, reached it, but quickly turned off, cutting in behind the Gostinyy Dvor. I know Leningrad like the back of my hand, and now that was no small advantage; above all, no one watching me drive—the *militsia,* for example—would ever have guessed that I was a foreigner. Following Kirovsky Prospekt, I crossed the islands that the Neva carves out as it flows into the Gulf of Finland, and then turned into Novaya Derevnya, the old country-house district on the far side. Here, without incident, I pulled into Service Station No. 3.

A combination garage and filling station, it was fairly large, like one of those interstate truck stops you see in the West. But it was the standard Soviet type: several islands dispensing various grades of *benzin,* and a cinder-block building with an old woman behind a slot in the window. Snow swirled like moths in the cones of light over the pumps, and a service vehicle was hectically clearing an area at the back of the lot. Since there are only a few gas stations in Leningrad, and fewer still are open all night, they were doing good business. Cars, trucks, transports, and a couple of snowplows jockeyed for position, their engines chugging with the fat, bubbly sound that comes from low-octane gas. I got into line behind an ancient Skoda and walked up to the booth with its driver when our turn came.

"Not a good night," he said.

"If it gets any worse, I will stop in Novgorod," I replied. "At my cousin's."

"Your car is new, though. Very nice."

"Yes. But it would feel better in Italy."

He laughed and we went inside. I paid for twenty liters, then trotted briskly back to the car: in Russian gas stations, you pay the attendant for the gas, then she (usually) dials it up on a sort of telephone gadget, which turns the hose on—the sudden jolt of pressure frequently spraying your purchase all over the place. But in this case my run was purely for form; Intourist had given me a full tank, so most of what I'd bought was spilled anyway.

When I was finished, I put the hose back and pulled over to one side of the lot. I was still in the light here, but at the very edge of its arc, and as cars and trucks moved in and out of the service area they hid me from anyone inside the booth.

I went around and opened the hood. The oily warmth of the engine swelled up at my face and the snow hissed on the block. I checked the dipstick; it was fine. I wiggled the battery connections; terrific. But then, apparently discovering something wrong, I returned to the car and came out with the tool kit. Taking out a screwdriver and a pair of pliers, I fussed for a couple of minutes, adjusting the idle until it was absolutely the same as I'd found it. Then, leaving the hood up, I got back in the car, sitting in the front seat but leaving the door open and keeping both feet outside, on the ground.

I lit a cigarette.

Five minutes passed.

Traffic, mainly trucks, kept pulling into the station. As they came up to the pumps, their powerful headlamps shone right at my little car, stretching a long wedge of shadow behind it. When I ground out my cigarette, and stepped into this darkened patch, I must have been almost invisible. I worked around to the service area. The snow had been cleared here, but the bays were dark and locked. Beyond them, extending out from the back of the building, was a metal fence; I probably could have got over this easily, but I didn't have to. There was a gate, and the padlock was broken; I just pushed hard to shift the snow behind it and stepped quickly through.

I looked around. I was on a small asphalt lot, where they kept the cars that were waiting to go in for repairs. Parked in two rows, they were now being buried under a blanket of snow. Behind them, bringing back a faint echo of that day in Detroit, was a junkyard: piles of tires (but chained together); a lot of twisted scrap, one old door jutting up like a broken wing; and a tangled heap of exhaust pipes sticking up through the snow like old bones. If there was a guard, I couldn't see him. I made my way to the cars. The one I wanted was in the back row. A Zhiguli. It was dark green, but at night it would be hard to tell from the one I was driving. Its owner must have tried to drive it through a brick wall. The front end was a twisted mess, the grille ripped right away, and a piece of cardboard was taped over the windshield. But, bending down, I saw that the front license plate was intact and hanging by only a single bolt. Rather than try to unscrew it, I just levered hard with the screwdriver—one ugly screech—until it popped free. I went around to the back. Here the damage wasn't so bad, though the trunk lid was off its hinges and jammed inside. I set to work with the screwdriver. One of the bolts was a little rusted, but in ninety seconds I had it off, and with both plates shoved under my coat I headed back to the gate. No one had seen me; in twenty minutes, the snow would have covered my tracks. And it might be days before anyone noticed the missing plates; even then, the assumption would be that someone had taken them off and put them away for safekeeping.

I returned to my car.

Sitting there, with its hood up and the door still open, it seemed part of the landscape; already the windshield was covered with snow. I slipped inside, shoving the plates under the seat. Then I lit a cigarette and started the engine . . . though my door remained open and the pantomime still wasn't over. I let the engine warm. Finished my cigarette. Turned on the wipers, waited as they carved two perfect arcs in the night. At last, getting out, I slapped the hood back into place; and this time, getting back in, I pulled the door shut behind me. But both my coming and going had been so slow and gradual that I felt sure neither would have been noticed.

I edged into the road.

A mile away, turning into a side street, I pulled up at the curb, and ten minutes later, despite the cold and my clumsy fingers, one Zhiguli had vanished and another had taken its place.

I had disappeared. The car had disappeared. For one night at least, I could enjoy the greatest freedom—or horror—conceivable in a totalitarian country: I had no official identity.

But I knew this freedom would be very brief; I had to make quick use of it. I sped south through the city. In an odd way now, my plans depended on my being seen at least a couple of times by the police, so I kept to main roads: back to the Nevsky, past Alexander's Palace onto Oborony Prospekt, then on toward Route 22. Here, at the junction, was a GAI post, the yellow light of its interior floating high over the road; I dutifully slowed. The GAI are a Soviet equivalent to the highway patrol; they cruise around in yellow cars and man observation posts along the highways. Some of these are small, but others, like the one I passed now, are high towers. Inside, they would take down my license, and conceivably transmit it to the next post in line. And I wanted them to: tomorrow, when my car was posted missing, these records would be checked, and as long as its license—or the entry *unidentified Zhiguli*—didn't appear, everyone would assume I was still somewhere in Leningrad.

As I accelerated away from the post, the road opened up. On either side was the blackness of the subarctic night, but in front of me, trapped in the headlights, was a blizzard of gold. The wind rocked the little car, and after half an hour my arms ached from the task of holding it steady. But the road was level and reasonably straight. I kept the speedometer at ninety kilometers per hour, and the miles unwound. There was little to see in the blackness, just the snow heaped up on empty fields or around the rim of the forest, but I knew I was traveling along the southern edge of Lake Ladoga, the largest lake in all Europe, and occasionally the void beyond the car took on a limitless sheen. There were one or two towns—Novya Ladoga, Perevoz, Lodeynoye Pole—but at Olonets the road swung north and east, across country. Five A.M. . . . Now I was into Karelia, a stubby finger of rock and bush that sticks up between the Finnish border and the arctic seas. It's a desolate land of rocks, trees, lakes, tumbling rivers and waterfalls whose towns are depots for pitheads and lumber camps. A lot of it was once part of Finland, and though almost half a million Finns left when the Russians invaded, East Finnish is still spoken here and I saw it printed on the occasional sign. I was tired by now; my shoulders ached and my eyes burned a little. But then, at Pryazha, where a smaller road joined the one I was on, I fell in behind a couple of lumber trucks and gave them the task of finding the way. There were three of them, empty, traveling in convoy. Huge black chains, used to strap the logs on, jostled and jounced on their long, flat beds, and I followed their thumping music through the wind, the night, and the snow into Petrozavodsk.

Sitting on the edge of Lake Onega—the *second*-largest lake in all of Europe—this is the capital of the Karelian Autonomous Soviet Socialist Republic (K.A.S.S.R.); about 200,000 people live there. In Imperial times, it was called "the near Siberia" because people from Petersburg convicted of minor offenses were often exiled here, but now it's an administrative center, has the regulation tractor factory, and boasts something of a tourist industry based on a hydrofoil service that runs to Kizhi Island, with its ancient wooden church, out in the lake. But there'd be no boat trips today. As a gray, bleary dawn streaked the horizon, I could see that the low, snow-covered shore merged with the ice on the lake in an unbroken white plain, and only far, far out was there a dark sparkle from open water.

Sticking close to the trucks, I cut through the western edge of the city. Soon we rejoined the highway. There was more traffic now, and although the snow was letting up, enough had fallen for some drifting to start. I cut back my speed; the next fifty kilometers, to Kondopoga, took almost an hour. Shortly afterward, around nine-thirty, the trucks turned away, down a side road. But now I had no need of a guide; the road led only one way, due north. It was the single track through an almost trackless waste. To my right was the pure-white desolation of the lake; on my left, endless fir and pine forest, the thick purple boughs of the trees pressed low by the fresh white snow. With only an occasional glimpse of a railway line for company, I kept on, beating the miles into submission. Finally I won total victory. Medvezhegorsk, with twenty thousand people or so, was the last sizable spot on the line, and then came Pindushi, a small village perched on a long, icy bay jutting in from the lake. After that, the road swung inland through bush, scrub, cut-over land. I rumbled over a bridge. Two or three kilometers went by, then the road narrowed, snowbanks pinching in, and finally I could see a scattering of dark buildings along the rocky shore of the white, limitless lake. There was no sign—like myself, the place was anonymous—but I knew this was Povonets, home of the man who'd inherited Harry Brightman's strange fortune.

I eased back on the gas. All at once, I felt very tired. I'd come a long way; I only hoped that this was the end of the line.

19

A few streets of rutted ice and mud . . . gray log buildings and metal shacks . . . black smoke oozing out of stovepipe chimneys. . . . This was Povonets. And a million other Russian villages.

If there were any cars at all in this place, people would know them by sight and a strange one would attract immediate attention; so I took the first turnoff I came to. It was a cul-de-sac. The gray, spiky trunks of dead pine trees pressed tight to both sides of the road, and at the end of it stood the burned-out shell of a cinder-block building. The roof had fallen in, and the top edges of the walls were blackened with soot. There was obviously no one there now, and it might have been abandoned for years.

When the snow deepened, I stopped the car and got out, the sound of the door closing behind me hanging in the cold air. I didn't move. The trees and the snow seemed to go on forever, stretching out under the endless gray sky. It was very quiet. The wind worked softly, smoothing out the fresh snow, and the stiff dead branches of the pines shook in the woods; but the only man-made sound was the faint drone of a plane, a brown speck, over the lake. It made me think of Halifax; there'd been a plane overhead as I made my way up Grainger's lane. And sometimes, crouched on that knoll in New Hampshire, I'd hear a plane droning by.

I waited till it disappeared before I headed back toward the main road. I walked in the ruts the car had made, my body leaning forward with the effort and my pant legs chafing together. It was irrational, but inside the car I'd felt a certain sense of security. Now that was gone, and I was feeling nervous as hell. At the road, I glanced behind me. The car was hidden by a little bend, though its tracks were obvious enough. In front of me, the road sloped sharply downhill, hedged in on both sides by these same mournful pines. To my right, partially screened by the trees, I could see the lake and the village away in the distance. The lake was a pristine white tablecloth; the village, dribbles from coffee cups: three or four thousand people, a few hundred dwellings. Squinting against the glare of the hazy sky, I could see that some of the dribbles were sufficiently regular to make up a street, and in front of one of them—metaphor breaking down—an idling bus was sending up a purplish plume of exhaust.

I took a breath and started ahead, walking in the deep, hard tracks the bus must have made on its way in.

The road wound down the side of the hill, and after a moment the village disappeared from my view. I walked along, still nervous. But I knew if I tried to be "cautious," or play it too safe, I'd just seem more suspicious. And I had to show myself sometime. There was no other choice. To find Shastov, I would have to speak with someone; in fact, I'd have to pass as a Russian. I knew I could manage this up to a point— but only up to a point. For all practical purposes, I speak the language flawlessly; in Moscow, I'm sometimes taken as a Leningrader, and in Leningrad as a Muscovite, but no one ever thinks I'm not a Russian. But I had no papers—one inquisitive *militsia* and I was finished—and my clothes were all wrong. That's what worried me most. The boots might just make it (though Russians spend a lot of time studying boots), but the coat was hopeless; it was too light, and too snazzy. Only its peculiar bulky shape, the result of the other clothes still packed into the lining, was even vaguely Russian. But that wasn't much camouflage. I was a stranger, I wasn't properly dressed, and I was surrounded by some of the more suspicious people on this earth—Russian peasants—so I was going to be noticed. All I could do was reach Shastov as fast as I could, then get out before people began asking serious questions.

Now, at the foot of the hill, the road leveled out; for three-quarters of a mile, it ran through a low, humped landscape of black rocks, bluish-gray snow, the streaky shadows of trees. A few huts crouched among the boulders, a boy watched me pass from a hillside, but the only adult I saw was an old woman, with a huge black apron wrapped around her middle, who studied me from her front yard. Then, quite suddenly, the ground flattened out entirely, and I found myself at the end of the town's "main" street.

It was short and dark, like a mouth of bad teeth: low, shabby buildings pressing together, then a gap. Some of the buildings were log *izbas*, but there were also frame structures and one large, boxlike dormitory coated with peeling stucco. Bare wooden stairways zigzagged up the sides of these structures, and stretching from behind one of them I could see a clothesline, with four gray sheets, frozen stiff as sections of plywood, creaking in the wind. The snow was deep, piled up against the foundations of these buildings, and was smudged gray with cinders and ash. There were no sidewalks, but narrow, slushy trails, like chicken tracks, crisscrossed the street. It could have been an old refugee camp; all the buildings had been erected as temporary structures, but people had been living in them as long as anyone could remember. Or perhaps it had now been evacuated, for there was an air of total abandonment, and the only sound I could hear—the whine of a saw—seemed to enhance this. I sniffed the air. There was a smell of vinegar. After a moment, the saw, with a diminishing, wobbling sound, came to a stop.

I lit a cigarette. I was unsure what to do. But at last, almost reassuring, a woman emerged from a door and set off, away from me, down one of the tracks: dressed all in black, she was carrying an *avoshka* string bag that gave her an odd, canted progression. She disappeared between two of the houses. But almost immediately a man emerged from the flat-roofed, cement-block building further down the street—probably the liquor store—and gave me a look. Yes, I'd definitely caught his eye; I was now officially the stranger in town. . . . I stood for a time, undecided. Beyond the liquor store was a two-story brick building with a corrugated-iron roof—a splendid structure for Povonets, so presumably a government office. I could ask for Shastov there, but that entailed obvious risks. I decided not to chance it. Instead, following in the path of the old woman, I walked up the street and then turned. Up ahead, the bus I'd seen from the car was still chugging away, its exhaust spreading a sooty fan over the snow. It was parked in front of a dark, squat structure, probably the village store. Almost certainly, they'd know where Shastov lived, though asking would also create its own risks. But I had to start somewhere. Tossing my cigarette aside, I followed the track I was on till it merged with another, then crossed the street.

In the bus, a wool glove cleaned a wedge in the frost and two eyes peered out: probably the old lady with the string bag. Stepping around the back of it, I stayed out of the driver's sight. There was a porch on the front of the store, snow piled up on it, which was supported by heavy logs still covered with bark. A nail had been driven into one of these to hang a hurricane lamp, and the skis, snowshoes, and burlap sacks piled up around the door made me think of old steel engravings of "Life in the North."

I pushed the door open. At once, I was swallowed up in a cloud of tobacco smoke, dust, and coal-oil fumes, a fog so thick that I needed a moment to adjust my eyes to the murk. When I could see again, I realized I was in a low room—I almost felt I had to crouch—that was divided by a wooden counter. Behind this counter was a window, but one of its panes had been replaced by a square of cardboard, and the rest of it was so completely obstructed by various pots, pans, and other goods hanging from hooks along the back wall that it admitted almost no light. I stepped deeper into the room. There was a plank floor, spread with sawdust to stop the cold from seeping up, and the walls were bare boards. After I'd taken a couple of steps, a voice grunted, "It is after one now. The electricity has been turned off. So I regret that the store is now closed. Tonight, at six, we will open again. When they turn it back on."

Tracking down her voice, I was able to see her: a middle-aged woman, behind the counter and at the far end of it. In this dark corner of the room, she was lost in the shadow of a stovepipe, which stretched from an immense black space heater to a hole in the ceiling. Behind her were a series of shelves, empty except for a single bolt of dark cloth and a small pyramid of tins. She was a big woman, tall and stout, her bulk being further increased by layers of sweaters and shawls. As she stood, regarding me, she hugged herself with her arms, though in fact the place seemed warm enough.

"Perhaps you could help me anyway," I said. "And . . . would you have any cigarettes?"

"Only *papirosi*. Today, he didn't bring any more."

Perhaps "he" was the bus driver, for now I could hear the engine revving outside.

I said, *"Papirosi* will be all right."

She reached under the counter. *Papirosi* are cardboard tubes with a little loose tobacco inside. Inhale too deeply and you get a mouthful; puff hard and you're likely to spray ash all over the room. Pinching off the end, I lit up. The woman eyed me—and despite the meagerness of her stock, she had a shopkeeper's eyes: they added me up and made change. "You are from Moscow," she said.

This was, in fact, a fair guess. The truth of my origins was so incredible that not even the keenest intuition would grasp it immediately. But she knew I wasn't from here, and she knew that something about me made her suspicious—and people from Moscow, tentatively, fitted that bill. I didn't argue. "That's right."

She smiled. "If you don't mind, I'll have a good look. We don't see many from there."

I smiled back. "You should see the back of my head. I have eyes there as well." Then I shrugged. "I'm from Moscow, but I was born in Pestovo . . . which you've never heard of, just as people there don't know Povonets. Still, it's a real place to be from."

A little shift in her posture indicated some sort of acceptance. She smiled. "So what do you want, Moscow Pestovo?"

"I'm looking for a man name Yuri Shastov. I want to know where he lives."

Her mouth tightened. She didn't like that; friends know where their friends live—and so anyone who asks isn't a friend. Russia is the country that invented "the knock on the door," and so even today the doors in older apartment buildings often don't have any numbers. I tried to seem casual. "I could ask up the street, but why make it official?"

"Why not? If it is . . ."

"No, no. It's not necessary. I have a message, from an old friend. He told me where to go—the road, near the burned-out factory. I walked up there, but no one had heard of him."

She hesitated, then made up her mind. She shrugged. "He's never lived there. Everyone knows. . . . I suppose there's no harm . . . he rarely comes here anymore. He lives on the second road to the canal. You can recognize his house. There's a fancy roof over the well."

"He lives by himself? I understood . . ."

"An old woman looks after him."

"Ah, I see, then. Thank you."

She smiled. "It's no trouble . . . helping a man from Pestovo."

"But you've saved me a great deal of trouble—and in Pestovo I will tell everyone that they must help you when you come there."

She laughed then, and, indeed, the chances of her ever leaving this village were purely humorous. "The second road," she said as I turned away. "You'll have to walk to the end of the street."

I retreated through the gloom. Outside, the chill air misted my breath as I heaved a sigh of relief. But I'd done all right; my strangeness had been defined for me, "the man from Moscow/Pestovo," and despite the awkwardness I'd felt, she'd found me convincing; at least she wouldn't run to the police. But this just bought time. At six, when the store opened again, the questions would start—she now had choice gossip to sell to her customers. Who would want to see Yuri Shastov, and come all the way here from Moscow to do it? Of course, I thought, there was one simple solution to that: get out of here before six o'clock rolled around.

I turned up the street. The sun was now trying to come out, and it had grown a bit warmer; the snow was turning sticky as cake. Following the storekeeper's directions, I kept straight on. As the houses petered out, the road swung inland, away from the lake. For a time there were tracks I could follow, but then these ran out, and I trudged on, the snow coming to the top of my boots. It was tough going; soon I was huffing hard and walking with my head down, and my nose began streaming. After a mile or so, the road ascended a little hill and I paused to rest at the top. I could see a fair distance. Behind me was the white plain of the lake. In front, a thin, sickly woods enclosed both sides of the road—small birches and pines that grew up from the stumps of old cuttings—but farther away the forest grew thicker. Still farther on, I could see that the woods thinned again, and I guessed that I was seeing the line of the canal. It was only when the storekeeper had mentioned this word that I'd remembered the peculiar significance of Povonets. From 1931 to 1933, more than 100,000 people had starved, frozen, or otherwise perished while constructing the Belomor Canal, linking the White Sea, between Murmansk and Archangel, to Lake Onega. This was its southern end. I was now walking parallel to the "Povonets staircase" of locks—in effect, an immense graveyard, and if the trees here grew poorly, it was because they were feeding on the bitterest bile. For an odd reason, this is one of Stalin's crimes that could never be covered up or forgotten. At the time the canal was built, a tremendous amount of propaganda was generated around the "great socialist triumph"—books by Gorky, celebratory cruises up the canal by Stalin and Kirov—and one aspect of this involved the creation of a brand of cigarettes called Belomorkanals, whose package features a picture of it. Russians are devoted to tobacco—it's one of the things I have in common with them. You can tell them any number of lies, and rewrite their history . . . but tamper with their cigarettes? No regime would take such a chance. So even though the canal isn't used much anymore—it's too shallow for all but the smallest barges—the cigarettes persist, and might even be a bit less repellent than most Russian brands. I wondered if they were sold in the woman's shop, and, if they were, if anyone bought them.

I walked on. Ten minutes later, a road crossed the one I was on: the "first" canal road, I assumed. A truck had turned off it, giving me fresh tracks to follow, and now I moved faster. By one-thirty I reached the second road, and then minutes after that I arrived at Shastov's house.

I stood there, panting, very hot under my coat. Through a thin screen of birches and pines, I could see a cabin of squared logs, chinked with cement. A footpath, partially obliterated by the snow, led up to it, and a crib of split logs reached to the edge of its steep, slanting roof. This was an *izba:* if Yuri Shastov lived here today, he was following a pattern of life Russians have known for centuries.

I looked across the bare, frozen landscape. It seemed incredible that I should be here, and as my frosted breath prickled on my unshaved stubble, I wondered again if this wasn't some bizarre trick on Brightman's part—perhaps he'd pulled Yuri Shastov's name out of a hat, sending his fortune off into the blue and returning it, at random, from whence it had come. . . . But that possibility didn't bear thinking about, so I felt through my pockets for a Kleenex, blew my nose, and headed up the path. It lay, like a shadow, beneath the recent snow, ascending a gentle slope through the birch trees. No one—Subotin, for example—had passed here in hours, and snow had drifted in an even line against the door. I knocked. And at once, as if he'd been waiting for me, a voice softly called, "Come in, come in."

There was no lock or door handle; just an iron latch which I lifted and pushed, releasing a little avalanche of snow before me.

Stepping ahead, I found myself in a darkened, smoky room. It was more like the inside of a shed, or a small farm building, than a house.

The log walls were blackened with soot, the plank floor was strewn with straw, and a fire smoldered on an open hearth. Two black electric wires dangled down from the roof, but it still wasn't six, so the only light came from the fire and two kerosene lanterns; these were sitting on a stool which, in turn, was drawn up beside a wing chair of enormous proportions: curved legs that ended in eagle's claws gripping brass balls; "wings" like a nun's cowl; a seat as large as a bed. In such a place, a chair like that was an incredible sight; but even odder was the fact that it somehow "belonged." In fact, it was the natural center of the room. Ancient, very worn, it was covered in a faded paisley brocade, but this still had a sheen, as if it had been lovingly polished for years. Reflected by that brocade, the flickering flames of the fire took on a misty, coppery gleam and the light from the lamps spread through the shadows with a silky glow, transforming everything it touched; indeed, whatever that light touched—a simple jug on the table; the color photo, cut from a newspaper, that hung on the wall—was set apart from its surroundings and drawn back again to the chair itself. The chair was like a jewel box, with a diamond nestled inside. And, appropriate to this, the chair's contents were enclosed in layer upon layer of blankets and rugs, the whole being covered with a sheet as white as tissue paper. The diamond, however, took the form of a little old man. Very wizened, he had bright dark eyes and a flowing mustache—and those eyes were the real points of light in the room. He was reading and, clearly expecting somebody else at my knock, had gone back to his book. When he finally noticed me, he stared for a second before letting the book settle gently into his lap. Then he said, "Who are you?"

"Are you Yuri Shastov?"

"Naturally. And I ask you again: who are *you?*"

This was a crucial moment, though I didn't know it at the time. How was I going to account for myself? I'd been so concerned about getting here that I hadn't considered the question. Now my consternation was obviously genuine—and therefore convincing. Finally, with those eyes staring into my face, I just told the truth. "My name is Robert Thorne, Mr. Shastov. I'm an American."

He took this in. "An American?"

"Yes."

A log cracked on the hearth. A spark spat onto the floor. I looked around. Accustomed now to the gloom, my eyes made out a length of black stovepipe, suspended from the roof, over the fire. A curl of smoke rose toward it, but most of this eddied back into the room.

Glancing down, and frowning, Shastov closed the book on his finger. "I apologize, but I must ask you to confirm what you've said. You are an American?"

"Yes."

"That is hard to believe."

"I've come a very long way to see you, Mr. Shastov. I just hope you'll understand . . . this isn't going to be easy to explain."

As I looked at his face, it was clear he didn't believe me. I could hardly blame him. It was almost certain that I was the only American—perhaps the only foreigner—he had ever seen; and, for all I knew, no American had been in Povonets in this century. Or ever. After a moment, he glanced away—but then, as if afraid to take his eyes off me, glanced quickly back. "You say you are . . . from the United States of America?"

"Yes. That's right."

He nodded; then his mouth went very firm. Hitching himself up a bit in the chair, he said, "All right, then, tell me this. What is the capital of the American state South Dakota?"

Now it was my turn to gawk—not only because of the question he'd asked but because he'd asked it in passable English. I hesitated; with those eyes staring at me, I felt very much as if I was in the third grade. And I couldn't have done very well in the third grade. I shook my head. "I have no idea."

"No? Guess . . ."

"I couldn't. I don't know."

"That surprises me, since you are an American. The answer is Pierre. The state capital of South Dakota is Pierre."

"Really? And what is the capital of *North* Dakota?"

Those eyes flashed even brighter. "Bismarck. I don't know, but I suppose a lot of Germans must live there. Bismarck . . . am I right?"

I smiled. "Honestly, Mr. Shastov, I don't know that one either. But I *am* an American."

He shook his head. "Your English is very good for a Chekist, but your Russian is much too good for any foreigner, let alone an American. I don't understand, however. Why did you come here? Why are you playing with me? If you have something to ask, why not just ask?"

"I'm not a Chekist, Mr. Shastov. Believe me."

A moment passed. He looked at me, straight on, without fear. And I think he was going to say something—some equivalent of "Go to hell"—and I didn't want that, I didn't want him painted into a corner, and so I said, "Your English is excellent. May I ask where you learned how to speak it?"

He eyed me. "Perm," he said. "In a school."

"Are you from Perm?"

"A long time ago. It's all in my papers. You have the authority to look at them . . . as you well know."

"No, Mr. Shastov. I assure you—I have no authority at all."

He shrugged; and now, if he didn't believe me, I could sense that he was at least confused. "In any case, I have been a resident of Povonets for many years. By order of the state, you understand. I was deported here to work on the canal."

"Why . . . were you deported?"

A little smile flickered over his lips. But maybe my foolishness helped, for he said, "Perhaps you *are* a foreigner. Who knows why they are deported? Maybe they needed deportees here, and so I was sent. Or perhaps, deportees being available, they decided to use them on the canal."

I hesitated. I couldn't tell whether he was angry or amused. "You worked on the canal?"

He laughed softly. "No, no. If I worked on the canal, my bones would be out there someplace. I was deported here later. They called me a kulak, you understand. In my case, this meant that I was teaching in a little village not far from Perm. But I could read and write, so the Bolsheviks decided I must be a threat and Stalin sent me and my wife to this place. I was to help run it. The locks, maintenance, keeping records as hundreds of ships began sailing through . . . not that they did. But we were ready. No one can ever deny it. I have been here ever since. I even stayed when the Germans were here."

All the time he'd been talking, his eyes had never left my face, and I had the feeling that now curiosity was beginning to overcome his suspicion. And my confusion was genuine, God knows. Perhaps, too, he was working it out by process of elimination. I was completely incredible; Chekists, most definitely, weren't: therefore . . . I felt through my pockets and came up with some real cigarettes. I moved across the room and extended the pack. He took one; examined it. Then, from beneath the rugs covering his lap, he extracted a smoothly polished black pipe. Carefully, he unwrapped the paper from around the cigarette and stuffed the tobacco into the pipe bowl. It wasn't very full, so I gave him another. He smiled, and nodded. "You are generous."

"Chekists aren't generous."

"Perhaps not. I expect, however, that many smoke American cigarettes."

I thought of Loginov. "Or English ones."

He had tamped the tobacco with the first two fingers of his right hand; now he worked his palm against the bowl as if to polish it even more brightly, or perhaps, through friction, to set alight the tobacco within. I lit my own cigarette more conventionally, tossing the match into the fire . . . and as I did this, he made a quick little gesture with his pipe hand to indicate that I should sit.

There was a table against the right-hand wall of the room. I pulled one of the chairs away from it and drew it near his. He nodded his satisfaction at this arrangement. Then, rummaging beneath his blankets, he found matches of his own and set his pipe going. I was close enough now to see the book he'd been reading; it was Turgenev's *A Sportsman's Sketches.*

I said, "Mr. Shastov, I am not a Chekist. I hope now you believe me."

"Yes, I'm beginning to." He puffed his pipe and smiled. "But, since you are an American, it is only fair if I tell you a secret about Russians."

"What is that?"

"They always lie."

I smiled. "Do they?"

He nodded. "Yes. Do you know why?"

I shook my head.

"Being an American, you will understand the reason. It is a question of profit. Think . . . if you tell the truth, what do you get? Nothing. But if you know the truth and lie about it, you make a secret. The truth *becomes* a secret. That can be very valuable."

"You mean, like the secret you've just been telling me?"

"Exactly."

"So you *don't* believe me?"

"Oh no. I do. That is the truth." Then he grinned.

I took a breath. "Mr. Shastov, let me tell *you* a secret—a truth, but one you must always lie about. You understand?"

"Of course."

"It is the reason I've come to Povonets. To see you . . ."

"Yes."

"Someone has sent you, or will send you, something very valuable from the West. It will be bigger than a letter, but it will come to you in the mail."

He peered through the smoke curling from his pipe. "A letter from the West . . . the Chekists would know about that. And wouldn't like it very much."

"No. But I'm not a Chekist. And I don't think the Chekists do know about it, because the man who sent this letter was very clever. It will come from Paris, in an envelope from the Soviet Embassy there."

"I have not had such a letter. I have never known any Frenchmen. And I can think of no one who would send such a letter to me. Or to anyone."

"His name is Brightman. Harry Brightman."

I was three feet away, watching his eyes. But Brightman's name didn't register . . . so far as I could tell. But then his life had probably taught him a better poker face than I was ever going to master. He shook his head. "I don't know him. You are the only American I have ever met. . . . Once, in a newspaper, I saw Nixon's face."

"Well, Brightman wasn't American. He was Canadian."

He shrugged. "I still don't know him." He adjusted himself inside the chair, leaning against the arm and sitting a bit more upright. "What is in this letter?"

"A great secret . . . and a valuable one, just as you've said."

"Valuable in what way?"

"Valuable the way gold is valuable."

He smiled, gesturing around his little room with his pipe stem. "Now you have proof that this letter hasn't arrived."

"You have no idea what I'm talking about? None of this makes any sense?"

"Exactly. You have said it very well."

I paused. I believed him; and in the back of my mind I'd been afraid this might happen. Day one: Alain puts the envelope into the mail at the Cité Universitaire. The next day, I'm back in Paris seeing my friend at Aeroflot. Two days later, the visa arrives. Another day, arranging the flight. Then yesterday. Six days altogether—not very long for a letter to move between Paris and here . . . especially considering a detour through the censor. Even assuming that Brightman's ploy—the embassy stationery—would hurry things up, I really couldn't be very surprised.

I said, "Have you ever had communications, mail or anything like that, from someone in the West?"

"If you were a Chekist, you would know."

"But I'm not."

He smiled. "All right, I admit it, then. When I was a boy, in Perm—before the Revolution, even before the Great Imperialist War—I collected stamps. Twice, I received packages from Berlin."

I wondered again if he thought I was mad; if he believed any of what I'd told him. I said, "You have to understand that this is serious, Mr. Shastov. Several people have already been hurt and even killed because of this letter. I know someone who will kill *you* to get it."

"But you would not?"

"No."

"Why not?"

"That doesn't make any difference. You must believe me, however. That *does* make a difference."

The fire spat and hissed again; a sharp rattling sound emerged from the chimney. Then there was silence, enclosed only by the soft rush of the wind around the hut. I tried to think of how I might convince him. In a way, when the letter arrived, it would be easier. On the other hand, that could well be too late.

But then, looking at me quite calmly, Yuri Shastov broke the silence. "Mr. Thorne, I am trying to believe you. Yet there is one thing I don't understand."

"What is that?"

"Why would anyone in the world send me this letter? Why me? Why Yuri Fedorovich Shastov?"

I shook my head firmly, and this time I was the one who looked him in the eye. "You know the answer to that, Mr. Shastov—you know it better than anyone else in the world. It's your great secret, I think . . . a secret you've spent your whole life lying about."

He smiled. "Despite what I said, Mr. Thorne, I'm just an old man. Too old to have secrets."

"But I know you have three. Three at least."

His eyebrows raised slightly. "Maybe you are a Chekist, after all—for they always do that, invent secrets for other people to have. They don't even trust you to lie on your own."

"I'm not a Chekist, as I've told you, but your first secret is the one you won't tell me because you're still afraid I might be . . ."

"I will say nothing . . . since I've already told you that Russians only tell lies."

"Then there's the secret of how you've survived to such a great age—"

"But that is no secret, my friend. Yuri Shastov, as everyone will tell you, has led a good and virtuous life."

"And finally there's the secret—and it must be a great secret—of the chair that you're sitting in and how it ever came to be here."

He chuckled softly. "Ah, well, that is not my secret at all. It was my wife's doing. This chair was always my father's chair at our home in Perm. When he died, it became mine. I took it with me everywhere. Then we were sent here, and I thought I'd lost it forever, but somehow—and she never told me how—my wife found a way to get it. All the way from Perm! Can you imagine? We were deportees! Two winters in a row, it was almost turned into firewood, but it always survived. Like me. When I go, I swear it will die too . . . only my weight, pushing down, gives it a reason to go on."

He was lying to me, of course. In the past five minutes, he'd probably told me five hundred lies: lies knitted together in his mind like the intricate steps of a peasant dance. And I couldn't blame him. Why should he trust me? Why would he trust anyone, but especially a foreigner who arrived out of the blue with the story I'd told? To get over his suspicion would be equivalent to climbing Mount Everest. And now, after that drive, having gone thirty-six hours without any sleep, I wasn't sure I still had the energy. But perhaps that was the key . . . perhaps the secret I searched for, like a forgotten dream or memory, would only come to me when I'd ceased trying to recall it. In any case, when I began speaking again, I had no particular purpose; my remark was purely conventional, uttered only to keep the ball rolling. I said, "Your wife sounds like a very remarkable woman."

"She was. Of course, she has been dead many years. She died the year before the Great Patriotic War—and you mustn't say you are sorry, for it was a blessing to miss so much that was horrible. Only now I regret that she's not here, just to talk." He smiled then, and his right hand dove under his blankets, bringing forth a small framed photograph, which he then held out to me. "She was very beautiful, as you can see."

In fact, what he gave me wasn't a photograph, but something earlier; a tintype, even a daguerreotype. The frame was heavy, conceivably silver, and the picture itself was sealed behind a sheet of thick glass and an oval matte. The picture was a portrait, the subject being a darkly beautiful woman in three-quarters profile. The antiquity of the image itself and shifts in fashion—she wore a black, high-necked dress and her dark hair formed a single thick wave on one side of her face—made it impossible to feel certain about her age, but I would have put her in her thirties. Her beauty was striking, and very Russian; if you needed someone to play Tolstoy's Natasha, this sharply featured woman with enormous dark eyes might be a good choice. And yet it was not her beauty in itself that now made my hand tremble. Rather it was a strange, ethereal quality, part aristocratic aloofness, part shyness, which, once seen, was quite unmistakable. Placing the photograph carefully on the old man's lap, I reached into my coat and brought out my wallet. I'd carried two of Travin's photographs with me: one of Georgi Dimitrov picnicking with the good North American comrades, the second of May Brightman emerging from her home in Toronto. This was the photograph I smoothed out, and laid by the first.

"If this is your wife," I told the old man, "then this must be your daughter."

20

If I'd known the message I was carrying, I might have delivered it more carefully; or I would have tried to. But I'm not sure, in fact, if that was possible. In those strange circumstances—in the glow of two kerosene lanterns, enclosed by the aura of this old man in his chair, dancing back and forth between past and present, truth and falsehood, and with the photographs of the two women lying between us: in such circumstances, my announcement was nothing short of a miracle. And miracles aren't led up to; they simply happen.

Strangely, I think the effect was the same on both of us. Transported beyond bewilderment, disarmed beyond confusion, we were equally amazed. Shastov's face moved through a dozen expressions, settling on none, and when he finally tried to speak, he couldn't; I suppose forty years of the unutterable was lodged in his throat. So, in the end, I did the talking. I told him everything; about Brightman, about May, about what had happened. At a certain point, I mentioned her name and it was then, for the first time, that he cried: May, virtually the same word in both English and Russian, had been the name he and his wife had given their child. Brightman had kept it. The tears began trickling down his cheeks; and, as he wept, it seemed to me that his tears were as much for his wife as for anything else—she had suddenly been brought back to life by that photograph, only to die once again; and, once again, without knowing that her daughter was safe. In the midst of hope, hopelessness. After that, there didn't seem to be much more to say. So I waited. But then I reminded myself that this was a Russian house, and Russian homes always have one solution for grief. In the back wall of the place, beyond the light from the lamps (we still awaited the witching hour of six), there was a door that led into a kitchen. It was a small, bare room, the floor strewn with sawdust. A Dutch door, opening over a table and sink—for preparing the animals' feed—gave onto a lean-to shelter with a wooden trough that was filled with black, rotted straw. An iron stove with a fire burning stood on the far side of the room. To give the old man more time to recover, I added a log and stoked it up, then found vodka and glasses in a small cupboard and returned to the front room. He'd got himself back together. When I gave him the vodka he drank it straight back, then held his glass out for more. I poured, and this time he sipped.

"Dear God. You will think us so wicked."

"No. I don't think that, Mr. Shastov."

He shook his head. "You will think she was wicked to do it and that I was even more wicked—the husband—to let her."

"Why did she want to?"

One of the lamps sent an oily curl of soot into the air. Bending forward, he turned down the wick. Then, taking another sip of the vodka, he wiped at his eyes with the edge of the sheet.

"You must understand," he said, "we had a baby in Perm, when we were first married. A baby boy. But he died almost at once. My wife was grief-stricken and swore never to have any more. And she didn't. People here in the village used to say that I must treat her like a saint, or the very devil, but in truth it was her doing—she was always so careful. But then she thought that was all finished, that she couldn't have any more, and shortly after, she became pregnant. I was glad. Honestly, I was glad. Even here—even as we were living here then—I wanted a child. But she was very upset; I think, once, she tried to end it. There was a woman in the village . . . yet it didn't work, for the child came. It almost killed my wife, however. She was too old. The child was all right, but my wife knew that she was going to die, and if she died, how could the child live? There was no milk here . . . there is almost none now . . . you see? That's why she wanted to."

I could see it. In that hut—in that light—so near the canal and its graveyard of anonymous bones—I could believe desperation without any limits. "Yes . . . so she thought—"

"She asked me to let her save the child's life. She said she knew people who would take her, look after her. If she lived through the winter, then fine, our little girl would come back, but if she died, or if I died, the child would go on. I was frightened. Because she didn't tell me who these people were—she wrote a letter that she wouldn't let me read. But she grew weaker and weaker . . . it was clear what was happening. . . . To have refused her would have killed her last hope. So I let them come and they took the baby away. Not long after, she died and then the war came—I always thought that my wife had seen the war coming, and I told myself she'd been right. She was dead, and whatever might happen to me, at least our daughter was safe."

"Who were the men?"

He looked me straight in the eye; and now, without doubt, I was getting the truth. "I don't know."

"Why did *they* want the child?"

"I don't know . . . I'm not sure they did. I thought then they were only taking her to somebody else."

"What did they look like?"

"Ordinary men, but from the city. From Leningrad, I expect. Two of them. One did all the talking. He had bushy hair, very curly, like Trotsky's. The other was bigger and said nothing. A big man with a big chest, a dignified face."

Harry Brightman, taken by May Brightman with her own Brownie. . . . I could see it then. I could see the dark interior of some smoky hovel, or their corner of a barrack. I could smell the sweat and the filth, hear the wind moan through the cracks in the walls. A baby cries. The woman's voice is desperate and weak. And Brightman waits calmly, off to one side, with Dr. Charlie's passport in his pocket. *But why? Why Yuri Shastov's little girl?*

I said, "You say that the first man looked like Trotsky—but he wasn't? You're sure of that?"

"No, no. I'm sure. By then, I think poor Trotsky was dead."

In fact, he hadn't been killed till that summer, but the chances of his being in Russia at that point were nil. I nodded. "The second man . . . that was Brightman."

"So I have met him?"

"Yes."

"And now he's sent me this letter?"

I nodded. "And now you know why."

"No, Mr. Thorne . . . I still don't understand that."

I wondered if I did. Had Harry sent the money to Shastov as a final, despairing gesture? Had he simply wanted to put everyone off the trail? Or had he decided that Shastov might be the only person on earth who had any moral claim to the gold? But then, thinking this through, I decided that the answer was probably simpler.

"He loved his daughter, Mr. Shastov—*your* daughter. At the end of his life, I think he loved her more than anything else in the world, even more than life itself. He felt he owed you a great deal, and he was trying to repay the debt."

A moment passed. Shastov picked up the photograph of May, held it up to his face. He said, "You know, what you say is wrong, Mr. Thorne. I owe him more than he owed me—and I owe you as well. It is I who have the debts to repay." He set the photograph down. "And now I shall pay them. I have the letter Brightman has sent me. Olga brought it this morning—she is a woman who helps me—and it was just as you said, from the Soviet Embassy in Paris."

I sat back, startled; then smiled. "You're very good at keeping secrets, Yuri Fedorovich."

"As I warned you, I think."

"What did the letter say?"

"See for yourself."

Hitching himself to one side, he now reached under his blankets and drew out a heavy, padded envelope, just as Alain had described: a large printed label bore the address of the new embassy on the Boulevard Lannes. The envelope was already torn open. Taking it from him, I extracted the contents. There were two items. The first was a letter, typed in Cyrillic on very genuine-looking embassy letterhead. It read: *Your letter more properly should have been addressed to the appropriate Ministry in Moscow, or directly to the Government of the Republic of France. However, on this one occasion only, we have fulfilled your request.* It was signed by a second assistant consular officer. The "request," apparently, had concerned horticulture, for the only other item in the envelope was a publication from the French Department of Agriculture on apple orchards. It was a thick, soft-cover book—not unlike a museum catalogue—and was printed on glossy stock, with numerous black-and-white photographs and drawings.

"This was all?"

"Everything. You understand, I had no idea what to make of it."

It was obvious what Brightman must have done. Carefully, I began cutting up the envelope with my pocketknife, scattering fluff every-where. There was nothing inside, however, so I turned to the book—and it held the treasure. Stripping the spine away from the binding revealed a length of carefully fitted plastic wrap, which protected the following:

—one flat metal key;

—one birth certificate (Province of Ontario, Canada) for Harold Charles Brightman;

—one Ontario driver's license in the same name;

—and a receipt to Brightman from a branch of the Dauphin Deposit Bank, Harrisburg, Pennsylvania.

The old man eyed me. "Have you found what you expected?"

It was a good question. *Was* this what I'd expected? But then I nodded. "Yes. The papers let you use the key . . . and the key is the key to a great fortune."

I passed the papers across to him. Turning them over in his lap, he picked up the bank receipt and squinted at it. "Harrisburg," he said. "That is the capital of Pennsylvania. The *Commonwealth* of Pennsylvania."

I smiled. "That one I know, Mr. Shastov."

"You have been there?"

"Many times. My father was from that part of the country and we spent our summers there."

Harrisburg . . . Should I have expected that too? But even as my mind had registered the coincidence, I realized, deep in my heart, that I'd known all along.

Shastov, leaning forward, handed back the papers. "They were sent to me, Mr. Thorne, so please accept them as my gift."

I said, "It's hard to know whom they truly belong to."

"You must have heard that famous expression, 'Possession is nine-tenths of the law.' "

"It creates something of a problem in this case."

"I don't understand."

"I told you, other men have been searching for this. I possess it now—but they think you do. When they come here, you'll be in danger."

"Why should I be? I'll tell them you have the envelope. I'll tell them it came, what was in it—no lies, you see, no secrets—and that I gave it to you. Or I could say I sold it to you. They'd believe that. I had no use for this foolish pamphlet, but you wanted to give me money, so I took it."

I looked at the old man; his notion was logical, but I didn't like it. On the other hand, time was moving on; I wanted to get out of here fast, not only to avoid Subotin but also to reach Leningrad before I was missed. And his idea *might* work. Might . . . If it didn't? Not a pretty thought. Not something I wanted to have on my conscience.

I shook my head. "Listen, Yuri Fedorovich. What you suggest could work, but it frightens me. These men are going to be very, very angry to learn that I've beaten them to this. So they could hurt you, even if it doesn't make sense."

"No. For them, that would just make more trouble."

"Maybe. But I'm not sure—and I have another idea. Remember, you have a daughter again. She's well off. Rich. I'm sure she would be happy to see you. Why not go to her? . . . Wait now—I'm not crazy. I know certain things about these other men that the Chekists would *like* to know. In return for what I could tell them, I'm sure they'd let you out of the country."

He picked up May's photograph, stared at it a moment, and then his gaze wandered away. He looked around the room. My eyes followed his: sculpted by the flickering flames, it was like the inside of a cave, but a cave where men had lived for centuries, like the catacombs of the old Russian Church Fathers. Finally, with a little smile, he shook his head. "I don't think so," he said. "I am glad to have this"—he held up the photograph of May—"but would she really want to see me?" He shrugged. "Who can tell? . . . Besides, this is my home, Mr. Thorne. It may not seem much to you, but I don't think I could live anywhere else. I'm like the old man in the story of the wolf. You must know it. He is an old man who lived with his wife, five sheep, a colt, and a calf, and one day a wolf came and sang them a song. At once, the man's wife said, 'What a wonderful song! Give him a sheep.' The old man did so and the wolf ate it, but soon he returned, singing again. And he kept singing that song until he'd eaten them all, all the sheep, the colt, the calf, even the woman. Then the old man was alone. Again the wolf came. But this time the old man grabbed up a stick and beat him. So the wolf went away, never to return, leaving the old man alone with his misery. . . . You see, Mr. Thorne? This place, Russia, may be as mean as a wolf, but it is all I have left. If I leave it, or drive it away, what would I do?"

Again, he shook his head. "No," he said, "I will stay here. But I don't want you to worry—"

"I will."

"No. Tell me—do you have any American money?"

"Yes."

"A lot? One hundred dollars?"

"More."

"That is enough. Give it to me. If these men come, I'll show it to them. Have no fear, they'll believe me then. And you know what they'll do? They'll threaten me . . . for it's illegal to take foreign money. All I have to do after that is act frightened and tell them everything. You came here in a car—"

"A dark Zhiguli."

"Good. And you told me you were going from here . . . ?"

"Back to Leningrad."

"So, they'll believe it. And leave me alone."

It was shrewd; and he could bring it off if anyone could. "All right," I said. "I agree. But do one more thing for me. Go and stay with someone, or have someone stay here . . ."

He was making a face. "No . . ."

"What about this woman, Olga . . . ?"

His expression turned even more sour. "She wishes to marry me. On the day before I die, I may let her—but not one minute sooner." He flapped his hand. "However, I will do it for you. . . . I'll tell her to come here. That is more natural." Then, rather to my surprise, he began to get up from the chair: not spryly, perhaps, but with somewhat more locomotive power than I'd assumed he could muster. He was dressed in a flannel nightshirt, long underwear, many pairs of socks, and a pair of knitted slippers—Olga's handiwork?—that came up to his knees.

"We should go now," he said. "She'll go down to the village when the store opens again."

Passing through a curtained doorway, he emerged a few minutes later as heavily bundled up in sweaters and coats as he'd been in his chair. We stepped outside. He took my arm, and I led him down to the road.

It was late afternoon now, the sky was darkening, and the gray shadows of the birches and pines stretched over the snow. But it was warmer, and only a few flakes drifted reluctantly down. As we walked in the tracks of a truck, separated by the space of its body, I had to slow my pace to Shastov's, but it was nonetheless clear that he could manage; stiffly, and a little anxiously, but carefully, staying within himself . . . which, I concluded, was a good sign, and I began to worry less about him and Subotin. After ten minutes, we reached the "first" canal road; it was here that Olga lived.

"I'll fetch her," the old man said, "but don't come with me. It isn't far, and it would be best that she not see you."

I nodded. We shook hands. And then, with a little spasm of embarrassment, he reached into the folds of his clothing and drew forth a small, black, leather-covered box. "For her," he said. "For my daughter. It was her mother's. It's all I have to give to her . . . if you would."

"Yes. Of course."

I took the box from him, though in fact it wasn't really a box but a small traveling icon: the sides and top were flaps, which could be folded open and propped up as a little altar. It is a traditional Russian present to honor a child's "name day"—that is, the feast day of the saint whose name forms part of the child's own. As was usually the case, an image of the saint was embossed on a small gold disk on the top flap—I didn't recognize which one it was—and this, in turn, was superimposed over a coat of arms. The Russian nobility usually employed their own arms here, but ordinary Russians, not entitled to such dignity, borrowed the national crest, the Imperial eagles of the Romanovs; and this was what Yuri's wife had done. Beautifully enameled, outlined in gilt—a little worn—they glared up at me in all their ancient glory.

"It's very lovely," I said. "I'll see May gets it."

He smiled, and his dark eyes, peering out from under a huge wool cap that came down to his eyebrows, brightened. "And you'll also remember Pierre—"

"South Dakota—"

"And Bismarck—"

"Yes, I'll remember."

"Very good." Then, with a wave, he turned away. I watched him go. Further on, he waved again, and then I turned, toward the village.

It was dark now; the road was empty. I trudged along in the tracks of the truck, but then, approaching the village, swung off to my right. I waded across a rocky field toward some trees. They were the same dying pines, their ash-gray bark peeling off in long strips, but the black shadows they cast reached out and swallowed me up. I struggled on. The wind was coming up, snow sifted down from the branches over my head, and there were sudden hollows where I plunged in to my thighs; but I knew this was safer than the road. And then, just as I began to sense the lake up ahead, there was a sudden spatter of lights to my left: I knew it was six. Turning back, I looked through the misting plume of my breath and had my last glimpse of Povonets, glimmering through the trees.

Twenty minutes later, I arrived at the car. It was as I'd left it. Saying a prayer, I turned the key. . . . It chugged a couple of times, but the battery was strong and it kicked over. As the engine warmed, I thought about this incredible day. I couldn't complain; I'd found more than I'd come for. Yet, even as I squeezed Brightman's key in my palm, I thought again that each aspect of this "case" which I seemed to "solve" only opened up another mystery. Unfolding the little icon, I set it up on the dash. I stroked the leather; it was soft as silk and I realized that it must have been in Shastov's family, or his wife's, for generations. May was the last of her line. But who was she? And what connection was there between her real identity and Brightman's disappearance? The very questions I'd begun with had returned. Shastov had given me most of her story, but in truth I had no idea what that story meant. . . . *I assume that some of what Brightman told me was true,* Grainger had written. *He did go to Russia, after all . . . and I'm sure he did get to know many men in the senior Communist leadership. So I suspect that Brightman's daughter is the child of one of those men—someone who believed he would soon fall victim to Stalin's Terror.* At the time, it had seemed a good guess, but now I was sure it couldn't be true: neither Shastov nor his wife had been a prominent Communist. And Berri's notion wasn't much better: *Don't kid yourself. Once upon a time, Dimitrov might have been your hero, but he ended up like the rest of them, a son of bitch. By 1940, his hands were covered in blood. If he snatched a baby away from the Bolshevik, it was because he thought it might help save* him, *not the child.* No doubt he was right about Dimitrov—but how could Yuri Shastov's child save anyone? And who would wish to save her?

These were the questions that occupied my mind as I headed back to Leningrad, but they seemed unanswerable, and for the time being I had other problems. Most urgently, I was exhausted, and after winding back along the lake for thirty miles—to thoroughly warm the engine—I found a side road and plowed up it. There I slept for three blissful hours, and when the cold awoke me I was almost myself again. I started off.

Now the miles and hours passed—and the tension built. What would happen back in Leningrad? I'd escaped Subotin—but if Loginov really wanted me, there wasn't much to stop him, for Russia is as hard to leave as it is to enter. But perhaps he didn't want me; for him, I was the lure to draw Subotin out. In any case, when I got back to the hotel, no one seemed to notice, and when I returned the car—the original license plates once again in place—there was no comment. Gradually, my worries shifted. Where was Subotin? If I really was a lure, then I had to expect a strike, but I had no proof that he was even close. He must have come to Russia, but he would have his own means of moving here and might be miles ahead of me—or just behind. That last night, as I lay exhausted in the Astoria, my conscience would have given anything for the power to make a simple call to Povonets. Had Subotin been there? Was the old man all right? I guessed he was—when it came to survival, I would have bet on him no matter what the odds—but there was no way of telling. So, the next morning, I crossed my fingers, filled out all the forms, and headed for my plane, and as I felt the big engines thrust us up, I turned my thoughts to my destination—Harrisburg, Pennsylvania. Once again Brightman had shown a fox's cunning, and once again his secret trail circled back upon me. What did it mean? I had no idea; but as the Polish darkness drifted by below us, I fell asleep and dreamed, or rather I rejoined the dream I'd dreamt as I was flying in. It was just the same. I could see a ship drawn up beside the pier at Leningrad: an ancient steamer, with belching funnels and swiveling cranes. I could see Brightman, bundled up in his fur coat, as he made his way through the customs shed. And finally I could see the desk where he turned in his passport. He looked up then, showing his face: and it was *my* face. And as the passport official stamped the documents and handed them back, *his* face was revealed as well; darkened, the features obscured by the shadow of his cap, but clear enough: my father.

21

Everywhere I looked, as I came into Harrisburg, there was a disturbing sense of *déjà vu:* a feeling of strangeness, of alienation, which utterly failed to disguise the fact that what I was seeing was all too familiar.

Paris: where my parents had met.

Leningrad: my own Russian city.

Now this place, a town where every turning led back to my past. . . .

I was like an amnesiac who builds up a new life only to find it repeating the first. Market Street was still there, but looking seedy and grim: Pomeroy's held on, but the old Capitol Theatre had finally expired, drowned in a miasma of kung-fu movies and stale popcorn smells. Yet, despite the decay, despite Three Mile Island, it was still the same place. In the years when we'd had that cabin in the Tuscaroras, it had represented something special to me, a sort of benchmark for American normalcy. Having been brought up either outside the country or in Washington, I think I took Harrisburg as representative of the places where "ordinary people" lived. The broad, lazy Susquehanna with the early-morning mist rising around its islands, and the long run of solid, middle-class homes out on Second Street, united in my mind the America of the pioneers and the America of Ike. How could such a place be the scene of the crime? Yet it must be—since I was returning to it. And if it was, what had the crime been, and who had committed it?

But I put those questions on hold. For one thing, I was still tired after the flight back from Paris; it was ten in the morning as I drove into town, but God only knows what time my body thought it was—some hour, in any case, when my eyes ought to have been decently closed rather than blinking back a cold drizzle on Market Street. And there were other considerations as well. Brightman's safe-deposit box held an immense fortune, a fortune that rightly belonged to May; or so I supposed. But I also hoped that it might contain the answers to a few of my questions, and for that reason I wanted to be the first one into it—which meant, in turn, that I was going to commit fraud. But impersonating Brightman might not be so easy. A Canadian driver's license and a foreign birth certificate weren't the best identification in the world, so I was keeping my fingers crossed.

The bank, when I reached it, didn't do much for my nerves. Guarded by fluted Greek columns, it had the air, inside, of a proud, prosperous Victorian railway station: huge fans turned slowly beneath the domes of its high vaulted ceilings, and aisles of red velvet ropes led you up to the tellers. All of this communicated probity so powerfully that I had a mild urge, as I went up to the counter, to confess my larcenous intentions—though by this time, even if I didn't know it, such a confession would have been impossible, for there was no longer a crime to commit. My request to get into Brightman's box, accepted routinely, quickly produced a Frown, Looks, and Whispers, then Professional Concern, and finally Profuse Apologies—delivered by a civil young man named Mr. Corey.

"I'm sorry for the delay, Mr. Brightman, but there seems to be some sort of mix-up. According to our records, this box was canceled and all outstanding charges cleared as of yesterday afternoon."

I took it well, on the whole. No staggers; no fainting spells. Merely the sort of frown which anyone, having been informed that their safe-deposit box has been canceled by someone else, surely has the right to assume. And I was cool enough to play the Affronted Customer reasonably well.

"I don't know about your records, Mr. Corey, but most of yesterday I was either thirty thousand feet over the Atlantic or in a taxi trapped inside the Holland Tunnel. I certainly wasn't in Harrisburg, and I certainly didn't cancel my box." Taking the key from my pocket, I held it up in front of his nose. "When you cancel a box, don't you get the key back?"

He looked unhappy. I'm not sure what I felt, though my anger was only partly an act—I'd come a long, long way to get to this point. On the other hand, I probably didn't have much right to be surprised. Why should the last act of this drama be any simpler than the earlier ones? In any case, after a certain amount of backing and filling a lady was fetched: one of those older, professional women whose eyes, never quite focusing on anyone, radiate hostility everywhere. But with a prim nod she solved our little mystery.

"This was yesterday afternoon, Mr. Corey. Mr. Simmons was really the one who handled it. A lady appeared with legal papers giving her title to the box as executor of her father's will. She was Canadian, I think—she had Canadian papers and Commonwealth papers. And she had a lawyer. Mr. Simmons spoke with him."

"Do you remember her name?"

"Mr. Simmons has it in his file, Mr. Corey. If I remember correctly, the lady's name was also Brightman."

I was very smooth, the Truth Dawning on my face with fair conviction. "This begins to make sense, Mr. Corey. Miss Brightman is my sister . . . in fact, she *is* the executor of my father's estate—she's been living with him up in Toronto—and I suppose some of my papers must have got mixed up with his. It's not impossible, you see. We're both Harold; I just never use the 'junior.' "

This was a touch too elaborate. Mr. Corey looked dubious. But his ultimate concern was the bank, so he took advantage of this opening to say, "I take it, then, that no harm's been done?"

"No. And certainly nothing that the bank's responsible for." I looked at the woman. "Could you tell me when my sister was here? You said yesterday . . ."

The lady too now had her doubts and solicited Mr. Corey's nod before speaking—and managed to do so without actually addressing me. "She came in around one and left her papers with Mr. Simmons. She returned much later, around half past four. I'm not sure when she left."

I nodded. "Maybe she's still in town, then. Or I'll contact her in Toronto. In any case, thank you for your trouble . . . and here, you'd better keep this."

I then pushed Brightman's key over the counter and, before Corey could speak, extended my hand. By then, I think, suspicions had definitely formed in his mind, but the civilities were his sharpest reflex. We shook, said goodbye, and a moment later I was out on the street.

I took a breath. I was very tired, but now I thought hard and fast—what was May doing? For a second, my old suspicions flickered, but after what had happened on Hamilton's barge, I couldn't believe them. But what were the alternatives? Had Brightman made a terrible blunder and allowed some record of the safe-deposit box to stay in his will? It seemed incredible. Wills are too public . . . but then if she hadn't learned about it from the will, how else could she have?

In confusion, I made my way back to my car, and by the time I reached it, I was beginning to feel fairly anxious as well. I'd shaken off Subotin in Russia, but there was no reason to think he'd disappeared for good. And did May even know he existed? Had she any idea of the danger she was now in? I had to find her. Which meant another airplane and a trip to Toronto—hardly a thrilling prospect after the past forty-eight hours. But then I thought again. She'd been here yesterday. Conceivably, she'd gone back right away; on the other hand—if she was driving—she might only have left this morning, or might actually still be here now. It wasn't impossible. She was never one to hurry, and it wasn't eleven yet—checkout time, but still worth a try. What I needed was a phone, so I walked along Market to Second Avenue—past the Senator, with skin flicks beginning at ten forty-five; past the hotels with rooms by the day, week, or month—and went into a greasy spoon called the Olympia.

Therein, I wasted five quarters.

She wasn't in the Sheraton, Marriott, Holiday Inn, or any of the other big places, but then it occurred to me that she never stayed in places like that. Tourist homes . . . guest houses . . . funny little residential hotels that no one else knew about—they're what she liked. A number of candidates came to mind, but they were the kind of places you do better to visit in person, so I went back to my car, drove past Brightman's bank again, and then straight through to the old railway station, where passengers now catch the Trailways bus. I parked, then walked back to Blackberry Street. On the corner of Fourth stood the Alva.

I couldn't think when I'd last been there; years ago. It was a big old place, three stories high and half the block wide, and the ground floor was taken up with one of those old family restaurants the fast-food chains are killing: American food, plenty of "regulars," the cops stopping by for their "coffee and . . ." The hotel, over the restaurant, had its "permanents"—mainly pensioners—and was used by people up at the Capitol when they couldn't get home during the session. Stepping inside brought back a flood of memories, for it had changed very little since my childhood: the same booths (but no jukeboxes); the same photograph of the prize steer they'd bought at the State Farm Show; the same middle-aged waitresses, spiced up with a few pretty college kids.

I asked after May—and it seemed that my logic had been right but my timing wrong.

"This is a lady with long hair, sort of red?"

"That's right."

"I know the one you mean, then. She was here for a couple of days. Just left this morning, around ten. She had one of those old Volkswagens, the kind you don't see so much anymore."

So that was that.

As consolation, I decided to get something to eat and slid into a booth. Given that I was in a place like the Alva, I ordered coffee and the *spécialité de la maison*, peanut-butter cream pie. Waiting to see what this could possibly be, I lit a cigarette and looked around the room. There were booths along the outside walls, tables elsewhere. Coming right into the center of the room was a staircase from the second floor, the hotel. *Washrooms* said a sign, and pointed up. After a time, my pie arrived. It was astonishing, but also delicious. As I ate it, I listened to the pretty Chinese waitress flirting with a man in a Caterpillar Tractor cap a few tables over. "Oh, you!" she exclaimed, dissolving in giggles. "You just behave!" Another girl, behind the counter, was having trouble fitting a filter of coffee into the machine. Then a man came down the stairs from the second floor. He was zipping up his windbreaker and stopped halfway when the zipper got stuck. He worked it free and came down the last steps, into the room. I could see him well now. It was Subotin. Short, red-haired, that hard, narrow face—it was definitely him. With his hands thrust deeply into the windbreaker's pockets, he shouldered open the front door of the restaurant and passed into the street . . . while I, hand trembling slightly, set a forkful of peanut-butter cream pie back on my plate.

Chance, as someone once said, is merely a nickname for Providence: in which case this particular encounter was providential in many respects—such as the million-to-one shot that I'd been sitting there, and the billion-to-one shot that he hadn't seen me. It was enough to take your breath away—but not so completely that I didn't have the presence of mind to get up and dash out the door.

I was in time to see him crossing the road, heading for a large concrete parking garage on Fourth.

Relying on luck for another ninety seconds, I ran back to the station and fetched my car. Then I waited, breath held—because there might be a second exit from the garage which I couldn't see. But the gods were still on my side, and after a couple of minutes, Subotin emerged and pointed a Chevrolet down toward the river. There he slowed; in front of us stretched the Susquehanna, broad and placid, the reflections of its bridges mingling on the surface like a pioneers' Avignon. Front Street was quiet; a few joggers puffed along the bank, but almost no one lives in the fine old houses now, for they're all taken up with lawyers, PR men, and lobbyists specializing in "issues management." At the corner—a bit clumsily—Subotin turned left; but then he had to, for Front is one-way. And evidently he wanted to head in the other direction, because he immediately switchbacked onto Second. Now, straightened around, he became more confident and picked up speed, heading north toward Interstate 81. I stayed right behind him, and my brain started working. What was Subotin doing here? What had led him to the Alva? . . . Had he simply been using the washroom? Looking for May? Had he missed her, just as I had—or was he *with* her? It seemed a preposterous notion, but then I realized something: I had absolutely no proof that he'd been to Russia at all. Maybe he'd come here straight from France.

As my logic ran into these complications, we also hit the interchange and I concentrated on my driving. Following the Marysville signs, Subotin got onto 81 South . . . a highway I know as well as any in the world, for, if you stay on it, you'll end up in Washington. But Subotin didn't stay on it. Beyond Marysville, he swung north, onto a side road—and, if anything, this was a road I knew even better. It carried you through the Blue Mountains, across the Mahanoy Ridge, into the higher, rougher Tuscaroras beyond.

In tandem, we wound our way across the peaceful, dun-colored slopes. At first, the settlements were almost suburban—expensive bungalows built along the ridges of the hills so they could enjoy the views of the valleys below—but soon we left the city behind. The woods thickened. The leaves had turned, and many trees were already bare, so that on the exposed faces of the higher hills, veins of silver-gray wiggled through the rust and the gold. After a time, we slid into a valley. Here there were farms, the swaths cut by the combines neatly marking the contours of the fields, and marshaled around the crossroads were all-American villages, with their steeples, picket fences, and shiny coats of white paint. I knew all these places; one by one, their names came back to me. And every time I lifted my eyes, patches of landscape jumped out of the past: the way the road, darkly overhung by tall oaks, doubled back through this curve; a valley, opening up to display every shade of Thanksgiving brown and gold; a scar of rock on a hill. I did not need to summon memories, they were simply there, and as we entered the Tuscaroras themselves, I could hear my father, explaining—explaining that the Tuscaroras were Indians, that they'd been driven from their own confederacy in North Carolina to join with the Iroquois as the last of the famous Six Nations, that they were among the most advanced of the woodland tribes. Did they take scalps? I'd wondered. Maybe, he replied: but if they did, it was only because the white man—specifically the French—taught them how, just the way your mother took mine. At which we all laughed, and indeed it became a family joke: that my mother, born in Lyons, was a Tuscarora princess at heart.

There were more memories where that one came from, and for a time, in fact, I had the uncanny feeling that Subotin might actually lead me back to our old cabin. But then he turned into a side road which climbed up a ridge of these hills and then dove down into a narrow valley on the far side. There were no houses here, and few cabins, and on these steep slopes the maples and oaks gave way to spruce and pine. I remembered that a stream flowed along the floor of this valley, and soon I could see it flashing beyond the cold dark trees. The road, fighting to keep its grip on the sharp grade of the ravine, writhed like a snake. I didn't mind: because of the curves, I could stay right on Subotin's tail yet remain out of sight. He kept his speed down, which also made things easier, and it was clear he was unfamiliar with the road, for he had a map open on his dash, and he slowed at each sign. We kept on like this for seven or eight miles. The rain had stopped, but the wind blew quick spattering showers from the trees, and leaves, spinning down, stuck to the car's hood and jammed under the wipers. At length, as I knew it was going to, the road swung sharp right and passed over the stream. *One Truck on Bridge* read a sign, and, perhaps a little timorously, Subotin slowed right down as he crossed. I let him get clear, then followed. I knew it would be hard to lose him now, there were so few turnoffs.

For another two miles, the road would keep the stream on its left, then climb the slope of the ridge and continue on the far side. If I remembered correctly (for us, on the way to the cabin, it had always been the wrong way around), it would eventually reach Evansville and actually pass by the steps of Father Delaney's little frame church . . . though that, needless to say, wasn't where Subotin was going. Just as the road began climbing, he slowed, and a hundred yards on turned down a narrow dirt side road. I didn't follow. Continuing past the intersection, I pulled over and stopped.

I twisted back in my seat and looked over my shoulder.

He'd probably made a wrong turn: I was almost sure the side road was a dead end.

I waited, rain dripping from the oaks overhead with a slow *plop-plop* on the roof of the car. Five minutes passed. When there was still no sign of him, I began to get nervous and put the car back into gear. But then I stopped myself. If I was right, if the road was a dead end, that meant his destination must lie along it; a car would only give me away.

I decided to walk.

Killing the engine produced an edgy, unnatural silence which made me ease the door shut, and as I walked back to the intersection, the quick squawk of a jay in the woods made me jump. The air, even at this slight elevation, was already cooler than it had been in Harrisburg; my breath misted, and I thrust my hands into my pockets. I came up to the side road. Narrow, unpaved, it split off from the main road in a "Y"; Subotin might well have turned down it while thinking he was going straight on. I hesitated. But there was no sign of him. For a hundred yards, the road ran straight downhill and I had an unobstructed view. Reluctantly, I started ahead. After the first straight stretch, there was a slight curve; then another, much sharper. Now the woods closed in on all sides and the air took on a gray, misty gloom. A mourning dove, crouched in the ditch, lifted away with a soft whirring of wings; jays and chickadees, flushed ahead of me, chirped and complained. I walked slowly, stopping to listen every few yards. Ten minutes passed and I still didn't see him. I began to worry now that I'd made a real blunder—he might be miles away—but there was nothing to do except go on. Then, a moment later, I saw my first sign of man—a tattered *No Hunting* poster matted on a tree trunk—and shortly thereafter, another: a crudely hand-painted sign erected at the side of the road. *No Exit* it read. . . . So I'd been right. It made me even more cautious, but I kept going, and finally, a quarter mile on, I saw the car. It had been run up a narrow track leading into the woods, on the right-hand side of the road.

For thirty seconds, I stood stock-still; the car, masked by the trees, almost seemed like a predator waiting to pounce. But Subotin couldn't have seen me; if he had, I'd probably be dead. Cautiously, I walked up to the track. Which is all it was: two tire ruts leading into the woods. If he'd run the car up just another few yards, he could have hidden it completely from the road, but no doubt he'd been afraid of getting stuck in the wet, spongy ground. Moving forward, I peered in the car's windows . . . and saw, on the back seat, one of those canvas rifle holders. Empty . . .

I didn't like this at all. Where was he? What in hell was he doing here? I looked up the track, and the dark, wet trunks of the pines stared impassively back, giving nothing away. I waited. I knew I was going ahead, but I needed a moment to let the idea sink in. Then—without comment, as it were—I simply started forward. I walked briskly; in that soft ground, my steps were silent, but there was little point to concealment. The track was very narrow; if he was hiding along it, he'd certainly see me. Still, every twenty yards or so I stopped and listened; it was just possible, if I had any warning at all, that I could throw myself into the bush and get away—it was so thick and dark. But I heard nothing. Just the occasional chirp of a bird, the trickling of water, the soft tread of my steps. I kept on. Conceivably, I thought, the track was the remains of an old logging road, or might lead to a hunting camp. It was probably five miles to my family's old place. If you imagined the side road continuing, you'd end up—

I stopped dead.

Ahead, the track widened and the gloom lightened.

After six paces, I could see that the track opened out into a clearing fringed with birches. Something gleamed there, in the shadows. I knelt down. Looking beneath the spreading branches of the pines, I could see the front bumper, and about half the hood, of a pickup truck. In the half-light, I couldn't be sure of the color; maybe dark green or dark blue.

I stood up. I knew it would be suicidal to go on. Subotin had to be there. Waiting. With a rifle . . . I turned and hurriedly retraced my steps. Then, when the track had curved enough to take me out of sight of the clearing, I paused to consider. What was happening? Was I doing the right thing? But I knew I was. I'm not a coward; but then I'm not an idiot either. It was possible that Subotin had merely come here to meet with someone, or perhaps to join them, but the more likely explanation was far more menacing: he was lying in ambush. He was, no doubt, expecting someone to come into the clearing from the opposite direction; but as soon as I did so, I'd be a dead man.

What should I do?

I couldn't just leave. I remembered all too clearly how Berri had paid for my dithering. Worse, some of my previous speculations now reversed. Could May be in there? Probably Subotin *had* been looking for her at the Alva. Had he come here because this was where he thought she would be?

But questions like that were unanswerable, and I let intuition take over. Backpedaling another fifty yards, I found a gap in the trees and stepped into it; then, at right angles to the track, I began working my way into the woods. Within a minute, I was soaked. Every step brought a shower down from above, and the ferns and bushes on the forest floor tugged at my legs like seaweed. I blundered on. Then, when I judged I was two or three hundred yards into the woods, I changed direction, striking out parallel to the track. My intention, of course, was to skirt the clearing and cut in behind it; and the problem lay in judging when I'd gone far enough. Now I got a break. Pausing to catch my breath, I heard the rush of a stream—a constant whispering behind the steady drip of the leaves—and a few minutes later, working away to my right, I came to its bank. It was a tributary of the creek that the highway had crossed. In the spring, during the runoff, it would have been impressive, deep and swift, but now there was just a thin trickle of black water to meander along the bottom of its bed. But it was precisely this that I now took advantage of, for the streambed, exposed, was as good as a path. And it ran the right way. I scrambled down from the bank. The bed was gravel and hard-packed mud; I could stride along. Only when it curved sharply, and the banks constricted, did I have to leave it. In twenty minutes or so, I must have gone the better part of a mile. Then, on the bank above me, I saw a path.

It was, as paths go, nothing unusual—merely a line of least resistance through the pines. It ran up to the bank of the stream, then veered away again, like the arms in the letter "K." The upper arm, I was sure, would lead back to the clearing; the lower would continue into the woods, probably to a cabin. In fact, the general layout, from beginning to end, wasn't much different from the one I remembered as a child. The track let you get your car off the road, but you had to carry your stuff the rest of the way . . . like the *voyageurs,* my mother had complained.

I stood a moment, catching my breath, then started down the lower arm of the path.

It was shoulder wide, edged by pines and small oaks. Tramped down by the years, dead pine needles formed a smooth, springy turf and, in spots where the path descended, the roots of trees had wedged the earth into neat little steps. I was hurrying now as fast as I could, and my panting sucked in the pungent smells of wet leaves and forest rot and my flushed face began stinging with pine resin and sweat. Detouring around a huge, rotting stump, ascending a rugged range of boulders—a rhythm of crevices worked out by the years for your feet—the path twisted on for about two hundred yards. Then, again, a pale patch appeared up ahead. I slowed my pace. A moment later, I could smell woodsmoke, and a moment after that the cabin appeared. Through the trees, outlined against the gauzy, purplish gloom, it had an unreal appearance, like a painted flat in a play: the home of a woodcutter . . . an exiled fairy-tale prince. . . . But then, as I crept forward and crouched at the end of the path, it jumped into focus and turned real.

Pressed down among some ferns, I peered into a small, rocky clearing.

The cabin stood in the middle of this. It was merely a frame shack, dignified with cedar-shake siding and a stovepipe chimney. Set up off the ground on concrete blocks, it had a tottering, precarious air—a distinct list to port—but was nonetheless clearly inhabited. A cozy plume of smoke curled out of the chimney; fresh kindling was stacked by the door. Catching my breath, I calmed myself. For I now realized that I could have this all wrong. I was assuming that Subotin had stopped in the clearing, but why shouldn't he have continued straight along the path and come here? No reason at all. He could be inside now. Someone was, without doubt. The cabin possessed one small window and a dark shape moved past it . . . and then I held my breath as the door began to swing open.

Who, in truth, did I expect to come through that door?

My fears said Subotin. My mind, such as it was, would have guessed May. But my heart—what I *felt*—told me my father.

Which was crazy, of course. But, in a funny way, I wasn't far wrong, for what I saw with my eyes was just as miraculous.

He was a big man, heavyset, with a broad chest sloping into a heavy belly. His face was broad and genial, his hair thick. . . .

Yes, he looked like a bear—but he had a fox's cunning.

I rose and stepped into the open.

He stared at me, a piece of kindling in hand.

"Who are you?" he said.

"My name is Robert Thorne . . . Mr. Brightman."

I was shocked, stunned, flabbergasted . . . but perhaps I should have known. I closed my eyes, and could see May, standing on that barge in France. How beautiful she'd looked. And what else could have transformed her so? What other life could have let her live again?

Yet whatever I'd expected to find in that cabin, it had not been Harry Brightman. Harry Brightman had disappeared; Harry Brightman had killed himself; Harry Brightman had been murdered. This progression into oblivion was even more fundamental than an assumption, because at least you think about assumptions every once in a while. But this was one possibility that hadn't crossed my mind for an instant. So long had he been the object of my curiosity, and the subject of a thousand speculations, that his real presence—his occupation of any space outside my thoughts—was almost an affront. Harry Brightman was alive. How dare he be?

But he was—the Red Fox had been run to earth.

Seeing him in the flesh, in that cabin—and hearing his voice—demanded modifications of all my previous impressions. Yet they hadn't been completely wrong. The photograph of May's, *taken with her own Brownie,* and my own fantasies—the figure of a man bundled up inside an enormous fur coat; the figure coming off that ship in my dream—had caught his presence, his solidity. You describe many old men as "spry," or "lively," but not Harry Brightman. He communicated the physical force of a man half his age. On the other hand, my imaginings had all possessed an antiquated quality that his appearance denied. He had seemed trapped in the past of the newsreels, the past of Zinoviev, Trotsky, the Second World War: yet clearly he had a contemporary existence—he knew what an automatic transmission was, and he knew how to check in at an airport. And allied to this was another shifting of emphasis: in the past few weeks I had discovered the major course of his life, but it flowed in other directions as well and was fed by tributaries I'd scarcely bothered to notice. You could hear that in his voice, which was easy, rugged, and gentle: the voice of a man of the world, and of several worlds.

I must have stared at him for a long time before I finally said, "I'm not sure how to talk to the dead."

"In Greek, isn't it . . . alpha and omega? Or perhaps you're supposed to blow a trumpet. Come inside, please."

I looked around the dark cabin. It was a large, low, square room. A bunk bed stood in the far corner, the upper mattress bare, but the lower neatly made up with a dark brown blanket and a neatly plumped pillow. Just inside the door was a counter and sink, and directly in front of me stood an immense black wood stove. A sooty pipe emerged from the back of it. Suspended from the ceiling by loops of rusty wire, it ran along to the far end of the room, where it disappeared through the roof. Reaching up, Brightman leaned against it. The wire loops creaked. His hands were big and strong . . . he was certainly the most substantial ghost I'd ever laid eyes on.

I turned back to him. "I don't feel that angelic," I said.

He smiled. "Perhaps more judgmental, Mr. Thorne."

He was very cool; but he had to be feeling a certain amount of surprise himself. I said, "You *do* know who I am?"

"Yes. May's told me what a great help you were."

My smile, inevitably, was a trifle ironic. "I'm sure."

"Please, don't feel resentful. Or not at her. I know how upset she was at deceiving you. And you should understand that when she first called you, everything she said was quite true. She didn't know then that I was alive. It was only later, after what happened in Detroit, that I told her."

"Because you had to. You knew the police would want her to identify . . . whoever it was in the morgue."

"Yes."

"Except I did the dirty work for her."

"As I said, Mr. Thorne, I understand your resentment—but direct it at me. In fact, it was I who insisted that she bring you to Detroit.

I realized then that her original impulse had been sensible. She needed a friend, someone she could trust and rely on. I thank you for being that person—though I hardly expect you to thank me."

Was resentment what I felt now? I wasn't sure. I watched him silently as he drew a small black cheroot from the breast pocket of his shirt—a checkered lumberjack shirt, virtually identical to the one in May's picture. Now that I knew he was alive, a good many things began to make sense. But I still wasn't sure about May. To what extent had she manipulated me—despite her reluctance? Or had she too been duped by her father? It scarcely made any difference; not now. And he'd certainly duped everyone else. While we'd been chasing all over the world, he'd had his feet up, relaxing in his woodsy lair. It was even comfortable. The wood stove was primitive, but its heat would be abundant; the kitchen table was a nice piece of pine; and the Coleman pressure lamps would provide enough light for a pleasant read in the evening. There was even one engraving, beautifully framed: palms, waving gently on the beach of some Pacific isle. Perhaps Robert Gibbings . . .

Struggling to take everything in, I stepped to the cabin's single window and parted the curtain. It was late afternoon now, growing darker each minute; already the clearing held an opaque, silvery light, like the back of a mirror: crouched in the dark margin of the woods, Subotin would be completely invisible. If he was there. . . . I turned back to the room. Brightman lit his cheroot; behind the cloud of black smoke it produced, his eyes regarded me impassively. It was my move, he seemed to be saying—but he was planning his too. He was not only alive, I realized, he was still very formidable. God knows what I felt about him; his existence, in itself, was still too disorienting. And yet this turn of events, however unsettling, also gave me a certain sense of satisfaction. For on some level my intuition had proved right. He'd been alive all along, and as I tracked into his past, he'd been waiting ahead of me, around the next corner.

I said, "Where is May now?"

"In Toronto, I assume."

"Did she come here first, on her way?"

"I haven't seen her for weeks, Mr. Thorne."

A lie, and it stole a little of his dignity. I shook my head. "We don't have time, Mr. Brightman. There's no point trying to hide things. I saw Grainger. I know all about Florence Raines. And Dimitrov. I saw Berri, and he told me the truth. Hamilton . . . your embassy package . . . Yuri Shastov . . . I know all that. I know May was in Harrisburg, and I know what she was doing. I know . . ." But then I stopped. I'd asked the question because I was trying to work out how Subotin had found him—presumably he'd been following May—but this too really didn't make very much difference. So I just added, "The pickup in the clearing at the end of the track . . . I assume it's yours?"

Brightman looked at me, his eyes level with mine. I'd told him that I'd unraveled all the secrets of his life, but he only gave a slight nod—an acknowledgment, but hardly of defeat. "You've been very enterprising." He shrugged. "And yes, the truck is mine. I was about to walk up there. You can't drink from the stream anymore, so every other day I go into the village for water."

On the table, a length of rope was looped through the handles of three plastic milk jugs.

"I wouldn't advise it," I said. "You'll find a man waiting there. His name is Subotin, or at least that's how I know him. In any case, he's Russian, he has a gun, and he's planning to kill you—or worse."

The effect of this was immediate, though I wouldn't call it devastating: you just don't "devastate" men like Brightman. But the news hit him hard. The skin tightened over his skull; for an instant, he was very much his age. Steadying himself, he drew on the cheroot.

"You're sure, Mr. Thorne?"

"Yes."

"If you know as much as you say you do, you know how important this is. Tell me—"

"I saw him at the Alva, the place where May was staying. I followed him here. He's in the clearing with the truck. I went around him, following the stream, then picked up the path." I added, "I assume he followed May when she came here."

He shook his head. "May was never here."

"You must have met her."

"Yes, but in Harrisburg."

"Then he must have followed you from that meeting."

"No." He walked over to the window and looked out. "Remember, Mr. Thorne, I've been covering my tracks longer than you've been alive. No one followed me here. But you say he found Hamilton—"

"He killed Hamilton, Mr. Brightman. I suspect he also killed Grainger, and he very nearly killed Berri."

He turned to me. "Years ago, Hamilton was here. It's possible—"

"Does it make any difference?"

"Oh yes. He only wants the money—but May's got it now. If he found out about this place from Hamilton—if he *doesn't* know about her—then she's safe. *That's* the difference."

And now his eyes met mine. At once his expression changed utterly. His sophistication vanished; calculation, cunning, duplicity—even his strong sense of himself—dropped away and were replaced by a look of total frankness and vulnerability. This was his heart; this was all that he cared about; everything else was pretense. This look lasted only a moment, but it was almost frightening. . . . Relief spread through him; but in its wake came resignation, acceptance, surrender. All at once, in retrospect, everything May had done—her fears in the beginning—seemed much more reasonable; she had understood how completely he was devoted to her. Feeling an echo of this now, I said quickly, "Don't be too sure."

I was right; even this one hint of doubt as to her safety flashed life back into his eyes.

"Yes," he said, "you can *never* be too sure with him. Do you know who he is, Mr. Thorne? Who he represents?"

"People in the Soviet military. With friends in high places."

"You have been thorough. He was in the GRU, military intelligence—though it's really just a subset of the KGB. His 'friends' are in the Navy."

"And they want to make the U.S.S.R. safe for the Russians?"

"They want power, Mr. Thorne, for themselves and their country—and they know that Communism merely gets in the way. They want an efficient economy, national loyalty, rational political structures . . . so they can have even bigger guns and more submarines. They'll try to get this power through the military and the secret police—they're going to try and bring them together, end their infighting. Once they've done that, they'll turn Russia from a Communist dictatorship into a military one."

"And you want to stop this?"

He turned away from the window, and smiled. "No, Mr. Thorne.

I just want to be left alone. That's why—I was in despair—I sent the
key back there. Let them deal with it—let them deal with their own
damn problems in their own damnable country."

I looked at him carefully; he was lying, or partly—but then he didn't
know that I knew who Shastov really was, only that I knew his name.
But maybe it wasn't entirely a lie . . . he'd been in despair and by returning the key to the gold to Shastov he'd been making a final, despairing
gesture. But perhaps, too, he'd hoped to send everyone on a wild-goose
chase through the Soviet Union while he and May sneaked away quietly—this might have been his last, despairing hope. I said, "You say May's
got the money . . . do you truly still want it?"

The look he gave me was compounded of pity and anger. "Don't
be a fool, Mr. Thorne. I suppose I'll destroy it, burn it. . . . They're only
paper, you know, those certificates—the real gold's in a Swiss bank vault
and it can stay there till eternity for all I care. I only want to make sure
. . . I only want to live out my life with no more shame than I already
feel."

But I knew what he wanted to make sure of: that the gold no longer
served as a prize that drew everyone on . . . toward May. I said, "Maybe
that's what you want, but from what I've seen of Subotin, it's not the
kind of sentiment he'll find terribly compelling. He'll kill you, Mr.
Brightman. Or he'll hold you as a way of getting the money from May.
So I suggest we get the hell out of here. If we move fast—before he
gets too impatient—we should be able to go back the same way I came."

"That sounds like an excellent idea—for you. But not me. Even
if I got away, it wouldn't do any good. Now that he knows I'm alive,
he'll only track me down somewhere else."

"Not if we call the police."

He smiled. "I can hardly do that."

I flipped my hand. "It was a long time ago, Mr. Brightman. I suppose the FBI would want to talk to you, but I doubt—"

He shook his head. Once more he was completely self-possessed.
"I doubt if you're so naïve as to believe that the FBI would be so forgiv-
ing, but that's not the real problem. You forget: I'm dead. Buried. If
I reappear . . ."

I hesitated. I'd forgotten that little detail—and I suddenly realized
what a nasty little detail it was. But when I looked him in the eye, his
gaze didn't flinch. He smiled again. "You see?"

"Whose body was it?"

"Does it make any difference?"

"As a practical matter it might. Was it a bum, some drunk you found in an alley?"

His face twisted sardonically. "No, Mr. Thorne. He was a friend—a 'comrade' if you like. I was attempting, through him, to make contact with our former employers."

"Another Hamilton?"

"A more substantial fool. He still believed."

"And what happened?"

"I'm not sure. He had never severed his connections, or at least not as completely as myself—which is what made him useful. It is possible he transmitted my requests and received certain orders in return. Or possibly he decided to kill me on his own because he was afraid that I might expose him. I threatened to do so—I admit that. But I had to bully him. In any case, he did try to kill me . . . and failed. I killed him instead . . . and though I've lived a life that I regret almost totally, that's one detail that will never grate on my conscience. No. The worst of it was the next half hour, when I had to sit in the motel room with his body beside me. But that's when it came to me. Preston was smaller than me, but more or less the right age. It seemed worth a try. If I failed, after all, I could simply stick with my original plan and kill myself. So I bought a shotgun, dressed him in my clothes, set him in my car, and blew his head off. It worked—worked too well for me to undo it now." He walked over to the stove, opened the lid, and tossed his cheroot into the orange glow of the fire. Turning back, he added, "The point is: I'm now dead. And I'm going to stay that way. Everything hinges on it. With me dead, everyone else is much better off."

"I'm not sure May would agree."

But he was two jumps ahead of me. "Yes, in the short run. But I'm going to die soon enough anyway. I'd already worked that out, you see, when I first went away. I knew it would hurt her—but she'd get over it, and still have a long life ahead of her. All that hasn't changed."

Once again, I sensed the despair and resignation beneath the surface of this man. In truth, it was more than that: it was a kind of self-contempt.

Perhaps he was reading my mind, for now, turning away from the stove and lighting another cheroot, he said, "Do you know what a Communist is, Mr. Thorne? How you can spot one? Pick him out of a crowd? Let me tell you. It's very simple: a Communist is that person who can most skillfully justify the greatest number of the murdered dead. Which makes me a *failed* Communist. Undoubtedly, I can still murder and maim, but I could no longer *justify* it—I've lost the greatest skill I could once claim to possess."

I nodded my head toward the window. "Very interesting . . . but a bit theoretical. We have a practical problem."

"You're wrong. I'm being very practical. The solution to our problem is that I stay right here. As you say, Subotin will eventually grow impatient and come and find me—and either I'll kill him or he'll kill me. Ultimately, one more dead body won't make much difference, not to my conscience. What I want you to do—no, please, hear me out—is to make sure that you're safe. God knows, you've done enough. Please don't argue. Just . . . just believe me, Mr. Thorne. For reasons you may be able to guess—but for others I'm sure you can't—your safety is important to me. May and I have asked far, far too much of you already, and when I said that everyone is better off with me dead . . . well, that includes you as well."

For a second, this remark hung in the air. And of course I knew then—and knew that I'd known all along. My father had spied for this man. My father had been the other man in the State Department, whom Hamilton had refused to reveal himself to. Here, at long last, right out in the open, was the "something personal" that Travin had hinted at. As a revelation, I suppose it was obvious enough, and it hardly struck like a blow—God knows, I'd let myself come to see it so gradually—but for one instant I closed my eyes and winced in pain. I think Brightman saw this, but, between us, there was a collusive failure of nerve and neither of us said anything. Which was probably all for the best. Turning my head, I again glanced out the window. It was raining again, streaking the glass, hissing down on the roof . . . and hissing down on Subotin, a professional killer. For the time being, we'd have to let the dead bury the dead—or we'd be joining them. I turned back.

"Do you have a gun?" I asked.

"Yes. A couple of old shotguns, and I think there might be a rifle. Don't worry, Mr. Thorne. I won't have much of a chance, but I will have a chance. If he makes a mistake . . ."

"That's not what I'm thinking. There might be a better way."

"I'm not interested, Mr. Thorne. Just get out. I beg you."

"Do you really expect me to simply walk away, leaving you here?"

"Of course. Why not? Conscience doesn't require anyone to be a fool, Mr. Thorne. If you truly want to do me a favor, save yourself and continue being a friend to my daughter. Isn't that why you began this—to help her?"

"Just listen for a moment. Subotin doesn't know I'm here—and he doesn't know that *you* know *he's* here. That gives us the advantage. In that clearing, he's out in the open. If I go back by the stream—the way I came—and you go straight down the path, we could take him from either side."

He began to protest, but then stopped himself. Because he knew it might work.

I said, "And when I say 'take him,' I mean take him alive. If possible. We can knock him out, tie him up, get him back here. Then give me a couple of hours on a telephone. I used to be a journalist, Mr. Brightman—I suppose you know that. I have certain contacts—CIA contacts. I can guarantee that they'd happily take Subotin off our hands. You could stick around and justify yourself or clear out, that would be entirely up to you. Either way, I don't think you'd have to worry about him ever again."

Brightman took the cheroot from his mouth, and gave a little smile. "If this fails, I'd be no worse off anyway."

"Exactly. Nor would I."

"You're sure?"

"Just get me a gun."

He crossed the room. Pushed into the corner between the bunk and the wall was a hardboard closet. The guns were in there: though he had to go around, opening drawers, before he discovered some shells. I looked out the window and saw that it was growing much darker. Not good; Subotin would be growing restive, waiting for Brightman to show. For a moment, I wondered if this whole scheme wasn't crazy, but it was the best I could think of. And I wasn't being naïve; capturing Subotin was a long shot, but keeping Brightman from killing him might even be harder. I knew something else: Brightman killing me wasn't entirely out of the question.

Now, though, he brought me the gun. It was a venerable double-barreled Stevens, from the era of exposed hammers and twin triggers;

the sort of gun I'd learned to shoot with. I opened it and loaded both barrels, then put two more shells into my pocket. I tried to look him in the eye then; but he couldn't meet my glance. Yet instead of confirming my suspicions, this suggested another: that, rather than killing Subotin, he'd contrive events so that Subotin killed him. It was a paradox. Brightman had been resurrected in front of my eyes, but so far as he was concerned, he was dead—and better off for it, just as he'd said.

But I'd have to cross that bridge when I came to it. I looked at my watch. "It's almost four. The quicker, the better. Give me till half past to get into position, then wait for my signal. Do you speak any Russian?"

"Yes."

"Okay. I'll shout *'Stoy!'*—'Stay where you are'—when I'm ready. Wait and see what happens then before you reveal yourself."

He nodded. "All right." And then he stuck out his hand—though whether this was a sign of alliance or a farewell, I couldn't be sure.

I went to the door and stepped out. The air was cold and raw, the day darkening swiftly. The sky held all the shades of a bruise; with the drizzle, the trees in the little clearing had lost definition while the surrounding forest blurred to a dark, indefinite smudge. Slipping the gun into the crook of my arm, I stepped down from the cabin.

Then it happened.

Three hard *cracks*—a flurry of splinters flying into my hair.

Throwing myself to the ground, I scrambled desperately under the cabin.

23

Everything happened so quickly now that there was no time for thought. My breath was knocked out of me as I hit the ground, and as I rolled and twisted under the cabin a stone slashed my knee and something reached down from above to gouge at my cheek. Yet I felt nothing—not even terror: I just kept rolling until I banged up against one of the pilings that held up the cabin. Wedged against this, I sprawled flat on my belly. I was in a low, dark crawl space. Six inches above my head were the floorboards of the cabin; on either side were assorted bits of junk and debris—old boards, a rake, a screen, a splintered scrap of plywood that cut at my hand; and all I could see in front of me was a maze of pilings and the narrow strip of light where the foundation ended. And then another shot rang out and I pressed my face into a puddle of mud and dead leaves. Somewhere over my head, the shot smashed through the cabin, the sound feeding back with a nasty whine. I began wiggling back even farther, till my head hit a joist. That stopped me and then I listened for a moment. Subotin was calling something, but I couldn't hear what it was. And as I peered at that gray strip of light all I could see were the stalks of dead grass around the foundation. Now came two more shots, quick, one on top of the other, and I wormed back some more. Sensing light behind me, I began slewing around. A cobweb stickily matted over my mouth, I pushed an old bucket out of my way, but then I scrambled ahead, elbows working madly, and rolled into the open. I pulled myself up—and just then a voice hissed, "Thorne? Is it you?"

I spun around—almost more startled by this than by the shots. But then I realized it was Brightman, on the other side of the wall; there was no window, but he was whispering, his lips pressed to a crack.

"Listen! He thinks you are me. He must. *Run!* Get into the trees. There's a path that takes you down to the stream—*stay in the stream!* Hurry!"

I could scarcely understand this—I was too confused—but even as my brain fought to get control of my tongue, I heard Brightman rolling away and sensed Subotin, on the far side of the cabin, making his dash through the clearing. I looked up. The dark, oysterish light swam and pulsed in front of my eyes. Here, behind the cabin, the clearing continued for perhaps fifty yards, the black massed shadows of the trees beckoning beyond. There was no time to think, to "decide"; I just started to run, running for my very life, head down, lungs gasping, one step fleeing another. Leaping over rocks, blundering through bushes, I barely knew where I was going, for in the dying light the world had lost all definition. Everything floated in murk, space itself had discovered new rules. Before me, the safe shadow of the forest seemed to retreat forever, like a mirage; but vague, remote forms suddenly came into focus an inch away from my face: the bare bones of a birch, the bright beaded pattern of a spider's web, a withered seed pod hanging from a bush. And in the same way, even as I began to feel I was running through a hopeless dream, the dark trees suddenly reached out and grabbed me.

Only then did I allow myself a single look back—the clearing was empty. At once, taking a breath, I began running again. Then, a moment later, I stumbled onto a path. *The path to the stream:* for the first time I realized I was doing just what Brightman had told me. And why did that raise a doubt? But my desperation was still too intense to consider this question and I merely followed the path until, just as he'd said, it joined up with the streambed. Jumping down over the edge of the bank—which gave me the protection of a parapet—I finally stopped and turned around.

Struggling to catch my breath, my face pressed to the scurf of dead grass along the top of the bank, I looked into the dark whorls of shadow that spread back, into the forest. But there was nothing to see, and all I could hear was the rush of my breath in my throat and the whispering wind in the trees. I was safe—for the moment. But where was Subotin? What had happened to Brightman? What should I do?

He thinks you're me. . . . Run. . . . Stay in the stream. . . .

Now Brightman's words came back to me . . . and with them, cold as the shadows around me, a swirling mist of doubt: the same small doubt

I'd felt in the cabin, but now a thousand times magnified. Had I walked into a trap? All at once, every hint and fear and suspicion I'd felt these past weeks seemed to become crystal clear. I cursed—swore aloud: right there, staring back into the woods, my lips against the mud of the bank—for I was sure I understood now. Admitting the truth about my father let other truths in as well. Why had *I* been chosen to play May's protector? Because Brightman knew he could always control me—my father's guilt gave him an even greater hold over me than he'd had over Hamilton. But I'd gone too far; found out too much. That's why Brightman might have been forced to do a deal with Subotin—two wily foxes joining their cunning—a deal whose final clause was my elimination. So Subotin had let me see him in Harrisburg; I'd been *intended* to follow him here. Yes: the ambush in the clearing had been designed for me to walk into, and now that I'd escaped, Brightman was trying to set up another. *Stay in the stream. . . .*

But almost as soon as I thought this, my mind jerked away. It couldn't be true. . . . Brightman, coming out of his cabin when I'd first seen him, had not been a man expecting to hear a murderous shot. And May—could she do this? After what had passed between us on Hamilton's barge, I simply wasn't prepared to believe it. Besides, *Brightman was probably right.* Subotin didn't know who I was; he could have had no idea that I was in the cabin at all. *Subotin thought I was Brightman.* It was probably the only reason why I was still alive. Knowing Subotin's background, it was hard to believe that he could have missed me as I came out of the cabin door; despite the bad light, it was just too easy a shot. But he'd not been meaning to kill, only to frighten: *because his main interest remained the money, and for that he needed Brightman alive.*

But why the stream, why stay here? I looked around; curving through the trees, the streambed was dark as a tunnel except for the faint glitter from the trickle of water that still flowed along it. Yet the darkness made very thin cover; if he knew I was there, if he was watching, any man up on the bank would have a clear shot. . . .

My mind leapt back and forth, circuits of paranoia arcing through exhaustion and fear—and then, almost as if these mental currents had set it off, the detonating sound of a shot boomed through the darkness. Instinctively, I pressed myself flat, hugging the bank. Yet, even as the shot faded, I realized it was nowhere near here . . . and I found myself

staring down the streambed, *back* toward the cottage—*back* toward the
road, if you went far enough. Logically, this should have increased my
confusion, but in fact it decided me, and rolling onto my back, I skidded
down the bank to the base of the streambed. At this point, I don't know
what I was thinking, or even if I was thinking at all, for as I headed along
the stream, I was going in the direction of danger, toward the spot where
the shot had come from. Perhaps I felt I had no choice—at least, in
that direction, I had the chance of reaching the road and my car, while
going the other way would only carry me deeper into the bush. Or possibly I already suspected the injustice I might have done to Brightman,
at least in my mind. And then, with a terrible sick feeling in the pit of
my stomach, I was almost certain of this. The deep boom of a second
shot rolled up the streambed toward me—and I knew this was the sound
of a shotgun, not the rifle Subotin was carrying. Rather than setting a
trap for me, Brightman was trying to draw him away from my trail. With
a wrench of guilty desperation, I rushed on. It wasn't too hard—right
down at the water, the streambed was gravel and hard-packed mud, and
there was still just enough light to see by: a wedge of dusky light pressed
down through the darkness of the forest around the stream and, high
up, there was the first opalescent glimmer of a moon. In a few minutes,
I'd reached a spot that must have been level with the cabin, though the
building was in fact out of sight. I rested there, listening; but after a
moment, hearing nothing, I moved forward again. Soon I had no idea
where I was; there were too many switchbacks and curves, and the dark,
hulking mass of the woods up on the bank made a featureless backdrop.
Then, in succession, I ran into two obstacles. An enormous pine, under-
mined by the encroaching bank of the stream, had toppled across it; its
dead, brittle branches were as bad as barbed wire. And, just beyond this,
the stream narrowed sharply: which, compressing the water, created a
deep enough flow to force me up on the bank. Now, for a good ten minutes I had to fight through brush, in the pitch darkness, which inevitably
made a hell of a racket; but then the stream broadened, its flow fell back
to the same meager trickle, and I was able to walk along the bed once
again.

Five minutes later, I stopped, knowing I must be close to the spot
where the shots had come from. Thus, if Brightman had been giving
me a chance to escape, I'd defeated his intention—but if that *had* been
his intention, why had he told me to stay in the stream? Probably I

should have been able to figure out the old man's plan at this point, but a moment later I didn't need to. Moving forward cautiously, I heard a slipping, sliding, scrabbling sound up ahead.

I stopped dead in my tracks.

For a second, I thought it might be an animal, but it came again and I knew that it wasn't. Someone had skidded down the bank of the stream. Subotin . . . or Brightman. . . .

I held my breath; in front of me, the streambed stretched ahead into a black, dizzying void. Then stone knocked against stone . . . rattled away . . .

Silence: the trickling stream: the wind rustling past.

"Brightman? I know you are there. And your old blunderbuss doesn't frighten me at all."

It was Subotin—it had to be. Standing just where I was, I slowly looked around. I was virtually in the middle of the stream; and the stream here was at its widest point. I couldn't reach either bank before he—

"You see? There is no point. Don't try to hide. Come here. I won't hurt you, Brightman. You know that. For me, that makes no sense."

More silence . . . the crunch of a footstep . . . then the glare of a flashlight.

For a second, I was dazzled, like a jacklighted deer. But in fact the beam wasn't pointed toward me; it probed along the top edge of the opposite bank. Shadows leapt up and danced, and for an instant, as in an old photograph, the vague outlines of the bushes and trees were tipped with silver. Then the beam started moving. Wet stones and mud glistened and gleamed. . . . The arc swept closer. . . . I lifted the shotgun—

A shot boomed through the darkness. At once the light died.

But my finger still hadn't touched the trigger. The shot, a great red flash, had been fired from high up on the far bank. Brightman . . . it had to be. . . . And then he fired again, a red flashing strobe that etched my shadow into the darkness. But he'd missed, for a quick burst of rifle fire exploded in front of me and sent me scrambling for cover.

I lay, pressed down behind a small pile of rocks. More shots, coming so fast they seemed to stumble over each other, whined up the streambed. I could hear them slash through the bush, thump into the bank . . . but all on the far side of the stream from myself. And now I understood . . . *stay with the stream* . . . and a feeling passed through me that

I'd never felt before in my life. I had to kill a man now—there was no other choice. Brightman and I were both foxes now, and he was deliberately drawing the hound close to my teeth. What I needed was cover. These rocks weren't enough; if I missed with my first shot, he'd have me. The bank . . . but I'd make noise getting up there and, for an instant, going over the top, I'd be caught in silhouette from below.

Then, as I listened to the stream, the simplest idea of all slipped into my mind.

Quietly, running in a low crouch, I retraced my steps down the streambed—hearing two more shots crackling behind me—until I'd reached the spot where the banks constricted. Here, after a bare slope of gravel, there was only the water itself. It was about two feet deep, flowing swiftly, bubbling over the stones.

Silently, I stepped to the edge.

The first touch was like ice. With the next, a steel band gripped my ankle. My foot skidded . . . I splashed . . . but the rush of the water covered it and I kept going. In the middle, where the water reached up to my knees, I looked around. A few feet away, three bigger rocks formed a dam, a curve as neat as the back of a chair. Wading quietly toward them, I sat myself down.

The shock of the cold was a kind of compression, a fierce grip on my chest. Yet I had what I wanted—cover: even if he'd been expecting me, he'd never look here. Scooping up mud from the bottom, I blackened my face. Now I was just another rock, a lump of dark in the lumpy black darkness—even the fiercest hound wouldn't catch my scent here. I didn't move. I don't think I breathed. The cold, something concrete to struggle against, was almost a blessing. . . . And then I thought that I saw him, working along, in a crouch, on the far side . . . or maybe I didn't, for nothing happened. I waited. *Don't think. Hold your breath. Be the water. The stones. Your reflection like syrup . . . your shadow a mist . . .*

And then he was there, and so close I almost jumped—a bulge in the darkness I might have reached out and touched. I think he must have crawled the last yards flat on his belly. But now, slowly, he rose. His shape disengaged itself from the shadows. He came up to the water. At the edge, he stepped out, onto a stone. . . . Twelve feet. No more. One step. Only one single step more . . . The barrel of my gun was actually under the surface, the action and butt resting on my flexed knee. . . . One motion. Don't think. Do it, do it. Up and point and squeeze the front trigger. . . .

Did Brightman know I was there? Had he seen me? Or did he just sense me, or perhaps Subotin himself—the old fox now turning the tables and scenting the hound? I never found out, afterward there was no time to ask, but even as my own finger tensed on the trigger, a shot erupted high on the bank. I think he must have fired into the air, certainly he didn't come close to Subotin, but if he'd been trying to draw the other man out, he couldn't have done any better. Because Subotin now flashed on his light. Its beam traced a brilliant path through the darkness, sparkling on the water, glistening lustrously across the wet stones, and turning his face into a smooth, silver mask. And that's when I fired. Once. Then again. For a split second, an image was burned into my retina: the banks of the stream, the water rushing up to my chest, the man tumbling back, his arms outflung. . . . Then there was only the echo, a vague red pulse before my eyes, and I was staggering up, stumbling and splashing in horror.

"Thorne, is that you? Are you all right?"

"Yes . . . for Christ's sake don't shoot."

My voice, that strangled sound—it had to belong to somebody else. I was dazed and I was freezing; freezing and trembling all over. Brightman came down the bank, clattering over the stones. "I only hoped you understood what I meant. He didn't know there were two of us, I was certain. . . ." But I didn't hear anything more. I was staring down at this bloody shape in the water. The current bubbled around him, eddying against the curve of his shoulders; bobbed his hand on the surface, splayed out his arms. And this time I could not look away; could not retch, could not even spit the foul taste from my mouth. For the shot whose echo had now faded in the night air could only summon another, and the sight in front of my eyes was merely a memory made real.

Coming up, seeing me, Brightman must have understood this. For I'm sure his words were meant only to comfort—they could hardly be revenge for the dark thoughts I'd had about him—but their kindness delivered the only blow I wasn't expecting.

"Thorne, I did all I could. I swear. That afternoon, we tried everything, your mother and I, but nothing we said, nothing we did, could—"

I looked at him in horror. " 'We'—what do you mean?"

"What I say. We . . ." But then his face turned aghast. "Dear God,

I assumed you knew that. They were in it together, your mother and father. Both of them. From the very beginning."

All I could say about the next hour was that it passed: like certain hours in the depth of an illness, it took all I had to get through it.

I was stunned, physically, spiritually—if, in fact, any spirit was left to me. Half of me was already dead; the other half wanted to die. And indeed, I probably came very close to getting my wish. I'd never felt so cold in my life; pneumonia was a foregone conclusion, death by hypothermia a very near thing.

Yet there was almost no time to worry about dying. We had to move fast. This was Pennsylvania, we were into the hunting season, but it was possible that our shooting had attracted attention. There wasn't even time to feel the horror of the irony: we were now acting out the same scenario that Brightman and my mother had acted out long ago. A bloody corpse . . . a death that had to be turned into an accident . . . what else could we do? Since I was already wet, I went through Subotin's pockets for his keys and spare clips of ammunition, and checked to make sure that nothing in his wallet tied him to either of us. His gun—a Valmet semiautomatic—had fallen into the stream, but I was able to find it and threw Brightman's shotgun down in its place. After that, there wasn't much we could do. If the body was found right away, there'd be lots of questions, but this was a deserted spot and he might lie here all winter; by spring, no one would be able to say what had happened.

We returned to the cabin. It was vital that I get into dry clothes, and though Brightman was certain that no one in the area had recognized him, we had to make the place look as if no one had been here for weeks. He began cleaning up while I changed into a pair of his pants and then huddled close to the fire. Slowly, I began to thaw, and since the fire was going anyway, I made us some coffee, the first swallow sending a marvelous spill of heat through my chest. When I had that down, Brightman went to a cupboard and got me some whiskey; I stirred in a splash and its burning sweetness began washing away the bitterness that now filled my mouth. I came back to myself; rose through the fever; focused my eyes. And that's when I said, "Tell me what you know . . . what you know of my mother."

He was rolling a sleeping bag. He paused, just for an instant, then went on, stuffing it into a blue nylon bag. "I don't know very much."

"Maybe. But about some things, you know more than me."

There was another instant of hesitation; then, abruptly, he said, "I didn't meet her till 1942, Mr. Thorne, when she came to America. I think she was at the Sorbonne and became involved with the PCF in the ordinary way. Communism, idealism, the Popular Front—in those days, it was all part of being young and alive."

"Except with her it went further."

"Perhaps. Or perhaps that was just chance. I don't know how it happened. . . . I think—but this is only a guess—that she mixed herself up with some of the expatriate leftists who were in Paris then. I know she met Melinda Marling, for example—the American woman who married Donald Maclean. There were a lot of Americans. That's probably how she met your father."

"Had she been recruited by then?"

"Yes, I think so."

"So their marriage—"

"No. No, you shouldn't think that. She always knew, you see, that he wasn't a Communist, not really. She once told me that: 'But I love him anyway,' she said."

"So what he did . . . what he did for you—that all came through her?"

"No. That would be unfair to both of them. He wasn't seduced, Mr. Thorne, at least not in that sense. They each acted from slightly different motives, but both were completely sincere." He paused then, and looked back at me, lighting one of his cheroots and throwing a tin box of them toward me. "He was a decent man, a diplomat who knew what the Nazis were doing and was appalled at his own country's lack of response. He once told me that the most horrible and shameful period of his life was the years when America stayed out of the war. That showed what America *really* was, he said."

I thought of Hamilton then—the "decent" man; I couldn't help it. And to place my father on the same level made my stomach turn over. But I steadied myself. "At that time, though, the Russians weren't in the war either."

"No, but he excused them. They signed the Molotov-Ribbentrop

Pact to buy time, not because they wanted one quarter of Poland. That was true, in a way: they in fact wanted both."

"Then that's when he started working for them?"

"Yes."

"But that couldn't have been through my mother. He sent her away—before Paris fell."

"Françoise—your mother, I mean—was an amateur. By then the professionals had taken over."

"Like you?"

"I'm not sure I deserve the title, but yes—like me. Though I wasn't the first. I only assumed control over him after the war."

I'd been sitting wrapped in a blanket; now I tossed it over to him and he used it to bundle up some of his food. Watching him work, I thought: I discovered his secrets but he's telling me mine.

Then I said, "After the war, when you knew him, what did he do?"

"At first he kept on. But he became more and more uneasy. McCarthy, the witch-hunts—that sort of thing kept him going. But he wasn't a Communist and he certainly wasn't a Stalinist. He'd supported the Russians because that seemed the best way to strike at the Germans, but as time went on, thinking like that became more and more difficult."

"He was hooked, though."

"Yes."

"By you."

"He was on the same hook I was on, Mr. Thorne. But I expect your mother was much more important. She *believed.* I was prepared to let him wiggle away, and in fact I did—he began shifting his career, taking himself out of the path of the more important material. But your mother would never have let him stop altogether."

"Except he did. With that gun."

"That week was terrible for him—it was the week of the Hungarian Uprising, you remember—"

"I was only a boy."

"Well, it was a terrible week for a lot of people. Your mother became very frightened and phoned me—she was afraid he'd turn himself in. I panicked, I'll admit . . . partly because that's just what I wanted to do myself. You met Hamilton. I called him, and asked him to do something—since they were both in the State Department—but he refused. That made me even more frightened. I knew, if he *did* turn himself in, that I was finished. He was an honorable man—he wouldn't have wanted to betray me. But he would have."

"So what happened?"

"We came here and talked. I'd had this place for years, you see; it made a discreet, convenient meeting place between Toronto and Washington—your father had helped me find it. . . . He was terribly upset. The Russians hadn't sent in the tanks yet but he knew they were going to—he had access to all the State Department estimates and that's what they were saying. I told him he couldn't be sure and calmed him down. But of course he knew he was right. Still, I always wondered if that's why he did it *when* he did—*before* the Russians made their move. That way, at the end, he could still have a little doubt, a doubt which was equivalent to a last faint hope that things might have turned out differently. In any case, he became very despondent and your mother got a message to me, but I didn't feel safe coming here so we agreed to meet in the woods. I remember wondering later whether he'd brought that gun intending to shoot us all, but in fact he'd killed himself before I arrived. I remember, just as I was leaving, that there was someone—I always wondered . . ."

"Yes. That was me."

"I'm very sorry."

"What happened after that? What was my mother's reaction?"

"In what way?"

"Toward you."

"It . . . steeled her, I suppose you might say. She went on. I didn't really want her to, but she did. She passed me gossip, little items. . . . It was useless but it made her feel she was important and let me . . . keep an eye on her."

"You mean, in case she ever took it into her head to betray you."

"That wasn't a worry. I just felt responsible . . . even for you, if you don't mind my saying so. When we met, she'd usually mention you. One year I realized you were in New York at the same time as May, so I arranged that you meet . . . and I suppose that's one more thing I should apologize for."

Should he have apologized for anything? Then, I didn't care; later, I wasn't sure. But what he said after this, even if he meant it as an apology, was a hundred times better, for it seemed to explain. And though he was attempting to describe my father, to give me some guide as to how I should feel toward what he'd done, his words ended by giving me a clearer picture of Brightman himself.

"I just want you to know something," he said, "about your father and who he was. Above all, I don't want you to think he was that much different from the person you remember—don't overestimate the impor-. tance of any of this. You knew him, as his son, better than I ever did. Who you are is a truer indication of his qualities than any of his 'secrets' reveal. And I'm not trying to comfort you—in fact, I'm trying to warn you about the dangers of romanticizing him. That's what's happened to those times, you see; they've become part of the movies. Even the Depression—even treason—has been given the golden glow of nostalgia. I hear it all the time. People were wrong—but committed. What they did was mistaken—but daring. You see? Philby, Blunt, Burgess, Maclean . . . they can all be turned into heroes. I can even do that to myself, and you may be tempted to think of your father that way. Don't. You'll do him a disservice. It's easy, looking back, to forget the distinctions between people, but I lived through those times and, believe me, they were there. Some people were attracted to Communism because capitalism was collapsing—people were starving—and the liberal democracies were turning Fascist. In principle, there was nothing shameful in that; under the circumstances, it only made sense to consider alternatives, and Communism—at first glance—was no worse than the others. But only at first glance. Closer inspection revealed to a good number of people enough of the truth to turn them away. There's distinction number one . . . because, of course, a good many stayed. And of course each purge, murder, or massacre eliminated some of them . . . and these, if you like, are sub-categories of diminishing gullibility. Some could swallow what they said about Trotsky, but not about Bukharin, and that should honorably distinguish them—say—from people who were still justifying Andropov when he was murdering Imre Nagy in Budapest. Compare the two extremes, if you like. At one end of the spectrum is the loyal, dedicated Communist who left the Party over the Molotov-Ribbentrop Pact—and at the other are the loyal, dedicated Communists of today who still try to pretend that the Gulag only existed because Stalin was mad. Of course, I'm condemning myself. I've been dedicated and loyal and committed to barbarism . . . though in fact that's probably too generous, too grandiose. In the end, I haven't even served an ideology, but rather a second-rate country that can't even feed itself. And if, toward the end of my life, I've come to realize this—realize the obvious—it's been the result of pure accident. . . . May, as you know, was an accident. That chance—having her—loving her . . . a freak of sentimentality . . . is the only reason I can speak this much sense. But now compare me to your father. Draw *that* distinction. You see? You can't claim him as a hero, but give credit where credit is due. He saw the truth; not immediately, but before many others. And where others permitted themselves to be black-mailed—literally, or through their own guilt, or simply by circum-stance—he refused. This far, but no farther . . . and the ultimate price for his mistake was paid by himself." He paused then and shrugged. "For me, his death wasn't even entirely wasted, because when I saw him lying there in the woods, I understood in a way I hadn't before. *This is what it comes down to. This is what it all means. One more dead body . . .*"

What could I say?

Not much, I suppose: it was his speech, he spoke it well, and I had neither the experience nor the wisdom required to comment. Besides, there was no time. We'd done as much as we could to the hut, and Subo-tin's gun, disassembled, was stowed in my bag—we couldn't take a chance on the police tracing a high-powered rifle to a man who'd tripped over his shotgun. Staggering beneath cartons and satchels, we made our way down the path and up to the road. Last problems: inching the pickup around Subotin's parked car. Last details: getting the scabbard from the back seat, remembering to shove his keys over the visor. Then, headlights off, we drove up the side road to the road where I'd parked. My car was still there; no one had touched it. No one, we both felt cer-tain, had seen us. So, still clad in the old man's sweater and pants, I got down from the pickup; and then, for a last instant, I leaned on the door. Now, much too late, my mind was filling with questions, questions that only he could give answers to. If May was the key to his life, how had he found her? What was the truth about Dimitrov . . . and Grainger . . . and what did he know about Travin? . . . Perhaps he saw all this running through my mind, and I think he relished keeping these mysteries. But then, at the end, I gave him one: or at least we exchanged them. For just as he extended his hand, I told him to wait, went to my car, and fetched him that little traveling icon that Yuri Shastov had given me.

"For May," I said, "from all her fathers, real and imagined."

He took it from me, opened it. And then his eyes seemed to beseech me. "Do you know?" he asked. "Have you found out?"

"Whatever I've found, Mr. Brightman, you knew it already."

"Then I beg you—don't look any further."

And even as I formed the words to ask what he meant, I knew I'd waited too long. Letting go of my hand, he backed the truck around. And finally, two headlights running over a hill—a last image of golden eyes—Harry Brightman passed out of my life.

But not quite.

24

A year passed.

As years go, I've known better.

But I survived; I suppose you always do. There was my work, the blessed necessity of earning a living, even a lady. . . . Life went on and, despite what I felt, refused to leave me behind. It's even possible that Brightman's little speech played its part. What I'd learned about my parents—the tale my father's headstone had finally told—changed a great deal, but not everything, and perhaps the most important things stayed just the same.

In any event, by the spring, I was halfway back to myself, and with the mystery of my father's death finally resolved, and accepted, all those other mysteries began to come back into my mind. There were enough of them, God knows. Would Subotin's body ever be found? Did Loginov know he was dead? Who was Travin? What role had he played? And what had happened to Grainger?—though, in fact, a couple of discreet phone calls to Halifax answered that one: it seemed that the old man had survived, and was soldiering on at his clinic. Indeed, as I worried away at these questions, I was able to come up with quite a few answers, for, in a general way, I was now reasonably certain about what had happened.

Subotin—it seemed obvious—had wanted money to finance the activities of his group, and through his contacts in Soviet intelligence had learned about Brightman; a unique find, to say the least. Immensely wealthy and immensely vulnerable, he would have been well worth pursuing even without the remains of his "gold for furs" fortune. And Subotin had pursued him—but then, I speculated, had pushed too hard. I was thinking of May. So far as I knew, Subotin had left her alone, and indeed she would have been too obvious a person for Brightman to pass the gold to. But this wouldn't have precluded Subotin from threatening her in order to put pressure on Brightman; in fact, it was the most powerful threat he could have possibly used. *Too* powerful, however: as soon as he made it, Brightman had bolted. For Brightman, May's safety had been everything, and the only time he'd exposed her to danger—in France, when she'd gone alone to the barge—had been unavoidable; for he had to make sure that Hamilton did as he'd promised while, at the same time, not revealing that he was still alive. Yes, Brightman, quite literally, had been prepared to die for his daughter, and as far as Subotin was concerned, that's just what he'd done. But this hadn't stopped Subotin at all—for, with Brightman's KGB file in his hand, he'd simply gone from one member of Brightman's old group to another: Grainger, Berri, Hamilton. . . . Brightman would have had to leave the gold somewhere and these were the best candidates. Once you understood this, it even suggested another explanation to the hoary old riddle of why Subotin had broken into my house. Most likely, as I'd originally guessed, he'd been trying to keep me away from May by taking the telegram—but since he knew about Brightman's group, he must also have known about my parents, and so I *might* have been one of the names on his list. Even if this was true, however, I wouldn't have had much importance, not at that stage: only later, after my abortive contact with Travin, had my role become potentially dangerous—hence their surveillance of my mother's old place in Georgetown.

But that brought back another question: who was Travin? There was no way to be sure. It was always possible, of course, that he was KGB, but, the more I thought about him, the more he seemed to be a man with his own, independent agenda. He'd had the photograph of Dimitrov, all those shots of May, and he'd attempted to set up a contact with me all on his own. Had he wanted the money for himself? Did he have other political goals to rival Subotin's? Even if I couldn't answer these questions with certainty, I began to put together a theory, based on what he'd said on the phone and on that paper I'd discovered in the Berlin dump. Travin was an émigré, part of that wave of Russian immigration that has swept into the United States since the early 1970s; since that time, tens of thousands of former Soviet citizens have settled in New York, Los Angeles, San Francisco, and other large cities—thirty thousand in the Brighton Beach section of Brooklyn alone. Most of these people are Jews; few have any sympathy with the political goals Subotin was working for. But the extreme Russian nationalism that Loginov had talked about also has its adherents within this community, and Subotin and his group might have used such people for assistance and cover. Travin—if my theory was right—might have been someone like this; someone who'd been used by Subotin but then had broken away. His attempt to contact me would have doomed him, though he knew far too much in any event; he'd known about Dimitrov, somehow he'd known about my father (*something personal you wouldn't want a policeman to hear*), and he'd suspected something of the truth about May: why else had he taken all those photographs of her?

But, again, there it was, the real mystery—May herself. Who was she? Why, indeed, had Travin taken those photographs? And why, if he so wished to protect her, hadn't Brightman just given Subotin the gold right away? I knew the answer, or thought I did: in the end, the gold had counted for nothing, and Brightman had protected it only to prevent a far deeper secret from being revealed. But what was that secret? After all I'd found out, and all of my theories, I was back where I started, faced with the very first question of all: who was May Brightman, and why had she been so important?

It was a question I never expected to answer; in fact, I never expected to hear from her again. Through mutual friends, I tried to find out where she'd gone, but no one knew; and a letter to Cadogan—the lawyer in Toronto—only revealed that he didn't know either. Yet I couldn't let it alone. At a certain point, I remembered, I'd felt that her secret was becoming my secret, and mine was merging with hers; and I still felt that way. What I'd learned about my father was half of the truth, but I wanted it all. So, as the summer went on, I kept worrying at it.

And now, at least, I knew one or two things.

Shastov—not Brightman, not Georgi Dimitrov—was her natural father; I was certain of that. And the mother, of course, was not Florence Raines—she was a Russian woman who, in 1940, had tried to save her child from the desolation around her and the carnage she could see ahead. That was something to think about. Indeed, she must have been a remarkable woman (would Yuri Shastov have married anything less?), for even if many women had wished to do what she had done, few would have been able to: she possessed some sort of influence, some power which—ultimately—had enabled her to summon Harry Brightman all the way from Canada to the Soviet Union. What was that power? Why had he responded? In frustration, I remember, I got out Travin's photographs, the ones I'd found in New Hampshire, and stared at them for hours, hoping to discover the answer. Who are you? I asked. And who was your mother, and why did they all care so desperately?

But I got nowhere. Indeed, for a time, I resolved to drop the whole subject. But I couldn't; I kept coming back to it—or it came back to me. In September, a magazine sent me a book to review, a history of the Stalinist Comintern, and it was full of stuff on Dimitrov; so I went over that angle again. And kept coming up against the same old blank wall. The child wasn't Dimitrov's, and why should he have cared about Yuri Shastov's daughter? In 1940, especially, he'd had other things on his mind. Berri must have been right: if he'd saved that baby, it was only because it might have saved him . . . which meant that May must have been a truly miraculous child.

Still, I didn't give up, and, in the end, I decided that Dimitrov must be involved in some way. In 1940, Harry Brightman had been in Povonets, in 1940 both men and the child had turned up in Halifax—the coincidence was too great to be without meaning. Night after night, I thought about what Leonard Forbes had told me and read over the letter Dr. Charlie had written, the one Subotin had been trying to steal. Was it true, any of it? Some of it had to be. Travin's photograph confirmed that Dimitrov was there, and Brightman would hardly have gone through the Florence Raines business without having a reason. But what was that reason, and why had he gone to Russia in the first place? Grainger, of course, claimed that he didn't know; and I believed him. That whole story about Brightman and the woman on Zinoviev's staff—Anna Kostina—that all rang true: rang true, that is, as the sort of lie Brightman would have told him. But perhaps, I considered, it might even be more substantial than that. Hadn't Cadogan mentioned, right at the very beginning, that Brightman had worried aloud about someone named Anna? And as Grainger himself had pointed out, the best lies contain a germ of the truth. So one might reasonably ask: did Anna Kostina truly exist? Leonard Forbes hadn't heard of her, but then he doesn't know everything—quite—so I spent a day trying to find her; and, to my surprise, came across her name almost at once. *Khostina, A. P. . . .* It was right there, in the index of one of the standard histories; and then, having found her the first time, I began seeing her everywhere.

Just as Grainger had said, she'd been part of Zinoviev's entourage, and had been sentenced to a term in the Gulag during the first wave of the purges—I could find nothing about her after 1935.

Earlier, however, she'd been a genuine political actor, albeit with a small part. Close enough to Zinoviev to be considered a confidante—though probably not his mistress—she carried out several sensitive missions on his behalf. Of these, the most interesting had been in 1917, for it was she who'd actually received, and transmitted, the order to murder the Czar. Fearful that the local soviet might take matters into its own hands, Lenin and Zinoviev had dispatched her to Ekaterinburg, where the Czar and his family were being held prisoners, with strict orders on their treatment and a new set of telegraph codes. Everything that had happened afterward had passed through her hands. . . .

What could I think when I made this connection? The possibility which it raised was so improbable, so unrespectable—if you call yourself a professional in this field—that I dismissed it immediately. Or I tried to. But it kept coming back. Was it possible that Yuri Shastov's wife had a personal claim to the arms on the little icon he'd given me? Was it possible that Travin had taken all those photographs of May because he wished to compare her face to another? Was it possible—even for a second—to imagine a survival, an escape, a moment of pity?

If one could, then it became almost certain that Anna Khostina, alone, had known what had happened.

If any of the family had survived the original massacre, they must have done so because of her; and if any of them had ultimately escaped or been allowed to go free, that moment of pity must have come from her heart. And later, either fearful over her failure or regretting her moment of weakness, she might have followed the fate of her own private hostage, realizing later, as her own pitiless fate was revealed, what a weapon she had. Except she couldn't possibly use it—*as long as the child, or the child of the child, was still inside Russia.* The child of the child . . . But if she'd told someone, and that person had managed to get the child out—away from Stalin's long grasp—then they would have possessed a talisman, a surety, of almost magical potency.

The child of the child . . .

Did I believe it?

Could anyone?

Russia, as Peter the Great once said, "is the land where things that don't happen, happen." God knows, he was right about that. As the weeks passed, and Indian summer came and went, I found myself wondering if this was one of those "unhappening" things. I would never know—obviously. But now it became a question of what I believed in my heart, and beliefs, notoriously, are much harder than facts, so I swung back and forth . . . until late in October I received the only sign, the only help, that I ever would get: a message from May.

Except it was hardly a message.

Only a photograph, May smiling into the sun, with a scrawl on the back: "All our love, M."

Postmarked in Schiphol, the Netherlands—the great airport for Amsterdam—it merely proved that they were alive, and might be living, or traveling, any place in the world. And the photo wasn't any more helpful. It reminded me of that picture which had been so much in my mind, *taken by May, with her own Brownie,* for it had precisely that stolid, amateur competence of a generation brought up on box cameras: Harry Brightman was positioned with the sun right over his shoulder and his shadow filled up the foreground while his daughter's eyes squinted into the glare. She was standing on a pier. Tied up to it, grand yachts jostled together, filing away in magnificent perspective, and a blue sea glittered beyond—it could have been Cannes, Rio, Palm Beach, any place where the rich spend their time; it could have been that same scene, years ago, when May had first learned that she'd been adopted. I studied her face—for hours, I studied her face. She was the woman I'd loved. Was she happy? If she was who I thought she might be, did she know? There was no way to tell. The breeze pressed her dress around her legs, she had to hold her hat on with her hand, but it was hard to make out her expression. In fact, her face wasn't even in focus: it wasn't in focus because the focus of that picture was behind her, halfway down the pier.

And about the tenth time I looked at it, that fact caught my eye. No; May wasn't in focus—because the focus was on one of the yachts, a good piece behind her. It was a fine, old vessel; not a sailboat, but one of those old diesel yachts from the twenties, all bright varnish and shiny brass trim.

One afternoon, I took a glass and studied it carefully.

Huge, upright, very old-fashioned, she bore the proud lines of an era when the rich were not afraid to look rich: her deckhouse was high, the teak lovingly polished, and her name was spelled out in gilt. In itself, the style of this reminded me of both Brightman and May—reminded me of that anachronistic quality she always seemed to possess—but in truth there was nothing to connect them to it, or even—I repeat—to tie them down to this place: they might have been just passing through, spending their money, enjoying the sights, their presence here pure coincidence. Still, for whatever it's worth, the name of that yacht leapt up through my glass, bright as gold and clear as life: a hint, a hope, or a last message from Brightman . . . believe what you will. In any case, I can only say what I saw, tell what I know; and I know she was called *Anastasia*.

A NOTE ON THE TYPE

The text of this book was set in a digitized version of Electra, a
type face designed by W(illiam) A(ddison) Dwiggins (1880–1956)
for the Mergenthaler Linotype Company and first made available
in 1935. Electra cannot be classified as either "modern" or "old
style." It is not based on any historical model, and hence does not
echo any particular period or style of type design. It avoids the extreme contrast between thick and thin elements that marks most
modern faces, and it is without eccentricities that catch the eye
and interfere with reading. In general, Electra is a simple, readable
type face that attempts to give a feeling of fluidity, power, and
speed.

    W. A. Dwiggins began an association with the Mergenthaler
Linotype Company in 1929 and over the next twenty-seven years
designed a number of book types, including Metro, Electra, Cale-
donia, Eldorado, and Falcon.

Composed, printed, and bound by
The Haddon Craftsmen, Inc., Scranton, Pennsylvania

Typography and binding design by Tasha Hall